NORTHARGYLE *Abbie*

NORTHARGYLE
Abbie

A ROYALLY AUSTEN NOVEL

JANELLE LEONARD

WhiteCream
PUBLISHING

NORTHARGYLE ABBIE
Copyright © 2025, Janelle Leonard

WhiteCrown Publishing,
a division of WhiteFire Publishing
13607 Bedford Rd NE
Cumberland, MD 21502

ISBNs: 979-8-88709-072-6 (paperback)
979-8-88709-073-3 (digital)

To Hannah
Because of you,
Abigail's story has a heartbeat.

WESTONIA, PENNSYLVANIA

In 1814, Captain George Weston and his Grecian goddess wife, Elizabeth, were lured from "no elbow room" Long Island in search of rocks and valleys and mountains. The natural beauty, breathtaking scenery, and fewer people succeeded in trapping them in this siren of the Endless Mountains. Fortunately for the Westonians, the founding family arrived during the newness of spring. If they'd stumbled upon this oasis in booger-freezing winter, they would've named it We-leavin-a before inventing the first rocket ship and pointing it south.

At the heart of Westonia, resides the Westonia Historical Society & Museum. This fine establishment exists in the former mansion built by George Weston and sons. After 150 years, the Weston offspring decided they wanted a McMansion, double the size and distance from the hubbub of the steadily growing town. The Westonia is a beautiful two-story, twenty-five room building filled with wonders and a rather creepy basement. Not only do they keep town history, artifacts, and collections, but the Westonia ballroom—which was added a mere ten years before the Westons skedaddled—is the "must-have" place for large events. Our gorgeous ballroom was created for magical weddings, baptismal celebrations, and the occasional cheese exhibition.

—Abigail's Notebook of Silly Placards

Chapter One

M y life's trajectory of scraped knees, shower aversions, and sports scholarships came to a screeching halt when Grandma Brown moved in next door on my fifteenth birthday. Gran, so elegant and poised, took me under her wing like a canvas slated for restoration. I traded my bare feet for dancing shoes and my ripped, mud-caked jeans and food-stained shirts for polished ensembles. My tangled, dirty (literally) blonde hair was introduced to a hairbrush, fishtail braids, and elaborate updos. But, most importantly, summer sports were replaced with hours of time spent wandering museums and antique stores.

Some girls might have complained and wrestled with the change. I fell in love. With vintage postcards, priceless tea sets, handsewn books, and weapons aged by time. Every piece, from the smallest button to the grandest tapestry, had a story. And I was captivated by the hunt.

Who'd made it?

Who'd used it?

Where had it been?

When Gran passed away six months ago, she'd left a hole in my life larger than the Colosseum. I'd thrown myself into my volunteer job at the Westonia Historical Society. The work kept me connected to Gran, as if through my "storytelling" I was keeping her legacy alive.

With a fortifying breath, I adjust my museum-approved gloves and unclasp the handles on the rubber bin in front of me, grinning like I'm about to discover one of the lost Fabergé eggs. The sticker on the side of the bin labels it as one of the lot donated by the Weston family. It's anyone's guess what the founding family of Westonia, Pennsylvania, might consider worthy of showcasing at the two hundredth celebration on May 10.

The first item is encased in protective wrapping. I resist the urge to pop all the bubbles as I unwrap the layers to find an urn. A Grecian funerary urn, to be exact, with painted warriors atop horses, their swords raised for an epic battle. An odd choice for the founding mother—who I've been tasked with researching the most—but Elizabeth Weston was originally from Greece. I hope there aren't ashes inside.

I set the urn on the table, the scene coming alive on the theater of my mind.

A magic awakened. Defense of the kingdom needed. Swords clanging. Horses snorting and strong. Sweat and blood. True love hanging in the balance. A handsome warrior sacrificing all to save those he loves. A princess with fine hazel eyes waiting for him to return and whisk her away from her mundane life in the research room of the Westonia.

I savor the moment, inhaling history and my story for a beat before grabbing the camera to capture the visual documentation. I snap pictures from every angle, zooming in on the detail. I'll choose the best to upload on the website and other places the information will be stored.

Gran used to say, "Remember, Abigail, every piece of art wants its story to be heard." Our favorite game to play on our antiquing and museum trips was "What's your story?" For a few stolen minutes, we'd ignore the placards or tags with the truth and create our own epic tales.

A severe pang of nostalgia hits at the memory. Gran's stories were always closer to the truth. Mine veered more toward the fairy tales. Forbidden love tokens forged by secret societies. Portals to another world passed through generations until they found "the one." Magic talismans which granted the wielder supernatural powers and abilities.

"So?" Libby, the Westonia's research assistant, breezes into the room, a pile of documents in her arms. She heads to the vertical files and tugs out the drawer marked "Deeds," slipping papers into a labeled folder before turning to face me. "What's its story?"

"I haven't had a chance to ask it yet," I confess.

Libby laughs, her dark eyes sparkling. "Someday, I hope I'm here when something answers back."

"Considering everything I ask was created way before modern tech, that's highly unlikely." Besides, I don't want the ending to be spoiled before I've had a chance to imagine. Where's the fun in that? "There are cookies on my desk. Help yourself."

"Girl, you are way too good to us. I'm going to need to buy a bigger size."

Libby would be stunning in a burlap sack. With her ever-changing braids—some of which are works of art—the depth of her soulful eyes, and flawless dark skin, she'd win the Miss Westonia contest with ease if she entered.

While Libby retrieves a cookie, I jot down the urn's description on the official WESTONIA ITEM FORM, leaving off my story enhancements. Those belong in my *Notebook of Silly Placards*. Also known as my brain on paper. For better or worse.

The door opens again and the Westonia's events coordinator enters the research room. *Kasey. Wonderful. Just what I need today.*

"Abigail, more boxes arrived for the Founders' Day exhibit. They're in the ballroom. The weaver for the Threading through History event needs to set up her loom so I need the boxes out ASAP."

I look around, but there's not even one box. Far be it for the blonde-haired, self-proclaimed social media goddess to actually be helpful.

My stomach loops like a roller coaster as the herbal scent of her tea wafts around the room. As much as I love a delicately painted vintage tea-cup, I can't stand tea. I catch my disgusted face. God forbid Kasey thinks it was directed at her. I haven't quite figured out why she openly dislikes me but the awkwardness whenever we're in the same room abounds.

Kasey sips from her Smithsonian mug, the sparkles on her manicured nails catching the light. The fact that the vile liquid rests in an American History Museum mug is an extra slap in the face. Like when Jo March learns her sister is going to Europe. "My Europe." That mug is "My job."

Kasey eyes the bin on the table. "You still aren't done with that?"

"She has to have her moment," Libby adds. Her quiet fear of Kasey is the only thing that causes her infectious smile to slip behind a wall.

"Didn't the Westons send papers with the vase?"

"Funerary urn," I correct. "I like to make my own notes before I read what they've sent."

As Ronald Reagan said, "Trust, but verify." The notes donors send with their items are usually extensive, but if we believed every word of their research without verifying, we'd have to promote ourselves as fairyland. Family history has a way of twisting over time.

Then there's the fact that I'm a Morgan. We pour one hundred and ten percent into everything we do.

"Whatever. Good thing you're just a volunteer and aren't paid to daydream." Kasey's lip curls as she rolls her eyes. "While you're at it, maybe you should clean up. Giovanni is giving a private tour today."

"Mr. Romano doesn't bring tours back here." If I could, I'd set up an ornate fence around the research room, a hedge of protection from the sneering and uninformed. Authentic research is the backbone of museums and historical societies. It's what makes them tick.

"This tour is with an author." She huffs then shakes her head. "Not your aunt. This author's never been published. I guess the main character works at a historical society."

I try to eye the research room from an author's perspective. Dim lighting. Metal filing cabinets. Shelves stuffed with acid-free boxes. Paintings in disrepair. Stacks of papers. Journals, leather-bound books, and photo albums. Tables covered in projects in varying stages. Research logs. Various forms. A motivational quote poster that reads: ONLY A GENEALOGIST REGARDS A STEP BACKWARD AS PROGRESS. My desk topped with a bouquet of purple tulips and sunflowers shoved in the corner as an afterthought.

"If the author wants to be authentic, then we should leave it. The Westonia is a working place." I twist my verse ring, a habit I've formed since working with Kasey, and remind myself of the words from Psalm 19 etched in its silver.

May the words of my mouth and the meditation of my heart be acceptable in your sight, Lord, my rock and my Redeemer.

"Maybe the author will use me as inspiration since Abigail's already been used," Libby says, daring to wiggle her eyebrows.

I return Libby's smile. Yep, ladies and gentlemen, Violet Morgan used her only niece as the inspiration for Detective Faith Mackenzie. I'd always known, of course, but my aunt informed the rest of the world in a televised interview last year. The eyes on me tripled in response to that tidbit. As if I didn't have enough of them judging me already.

Geoff, the maintenance man, joins the ranks in the research room. "Where would you like this?"

"On the table is fine." I lead him to a cleanish spot.

He sets down a cardboard box, wiping dust from his INSTANT PIRATE, JUST ADD WATER T-shirt and ripped jeans. His maintenance uniform always entertains me. Yesterday's read, HOUSTON, I HAVE SO MANY PROBLEMS.

After thanking Geoff, I study the box. Margaret Weston is written on the top in black Sharpie. Margaret married George Weston III, adding her name to the founding family tree in 1962. She passed away in January, two months before Gran.

"Abigail was going to get that," Kasey says.

"I don't mind." Geoff crosses the room, the container on my desk locked in his sights. "Especially when I heard there were chocolate chip cookies."

I chuckle. "Make sure you take some for all your friends."

"I have three today." It's our running joke. Geoff will take three cookies all for himself. "There are two more boxes, but it may be a bit. The first graders misunderstood that the gift shop wasn't a playroom. I have to go untangle Slinkies." He eats a cookie in two bites, starts on the second, and salutes me with the third on his way out of the room.

Kasey's black stiletto heels tap out a cadence until she's inhabiting Geoff's recently vacated space. Her lip curls as she eyes the cheerful bouquet, ignoring the container of cookies beside it. "You send yourself flowers? Or did you finally get a boyfriend?"

While Kasey shuffles guys like Uno cards, I retain the status of "never had a boyfriend." An unsolicited comment that "Dating Abigail Morgan would be like dating the whole church" branded itself on my life résumé when I was a teenager. Much like a princess or an American First Daughter, the title "Pastor's Daughter" comes with much responsibility. I'm in the spotlight, my every action, or inaction, critiqued.

What guy would willingly subject himself to the pressures and obligations and the proverbial microscope?

God, I know your timing is perfect, but I'd love to be married. To have someone choose and love me for me and not for who my family is.

Kasey clears her throat and narrows her eyes.

I haven't answered her question. "They're from my brother." I leave off why he sent them. I don't want the attention.

"Which one?"

"Asher." She's justified in asking given I have five. Although my oldest brother's name was the only one on the card, I'm pretty sure my sister-in-law, Rachel, did the actual ordering and sending.

"That was sweet of Mayor Morgan," Kasey gushes. "Your brothers are all so accomplished. Didn't your youngest brother win the Winter in Westonia logo contest? He's only sixteen, right?"

I nod and try to smile.

Mayor. Pediatrician. Soldier. Harvard-bound aspiring lawyer. Teenage da Vinci. Yes, you could say they're accomplished. Then there's me, lone daughter, ex-sports star, and underachieving dreamer. Volunteering at the Westonia and working part-time as Dad's church secretary. Waiting until God opens the door to a real job that pays me to use my museum studies degree.

"We still on for dinner? I've been craving truffle mac and cheese."

I catch my reply of "having cake with my family" seconds before making a fool of myself. Kasey isn't talking to me. She wants to make sure I hear her ask Libby. A pointed dig at how lame I am.

Some days, I wish I'd said yes to that first invitation a year-and-a-half ago, or even the second or third. They stopped asking after that, giving up on me ever accepting. Kasey has this idea that I think I'm better than her. I'm not. And I don't. Yet another "curse" of the pastor's daughter life. Everyone assumes they know the real me. And that I'm holier-than-thou. None of them see I'm just trying to find a way to fit in.

Gran never treated me like a pariah. Aunt Vi doesn't either.

My cell phone blasts "Inmates (We're All Crazy)."

"Sorry, sorry." I rip off my gloves and make a dash for my desk.

"I thought your kind wasn't allowed to listen to Alice Cooper," Kasey says as she takes a cookie from the container.

"My aunt likes to mess with my ringtones," I mutter as I dig through my tote. Pens, sticky notes, empty straw wrappers, scrunchies, a spork, notebook, and a well-loved copy of *Howl's Moving Castle* make their way onto my desk. Guess it's time to clean out this tote.

I finally locate the blaring phone. It's Mom, of course. Aunt Vi gave her that Alice Cooper ringtone. Kasey would probably faint if I told her I'd been in the third row at Alice's concert last year alongside my aunt. All in the name of research, of course.

"Hey, Mom," I answer, cutting off the song before the chorus. I move away from my desk, turning so I have some semblance of privacy.

"Abigail Rosiah."

I wince. While I love my names, having Mom use both is a prelude to unpleasantness.

"I have an emergency I have to deal with—"

"Is everyone okay?" Has something happened to Dad? The brothers? Did Rachel have her baby early? Do I have another niece or a nephew?

"Felicity needs help finding basketball sneakers," Mom says.

Ah, Felicity. One of the teens on Mom's "mentoring the female sports community" radar. One of my replacements. There's been a long line of them throughout the years. From church and the community. They always need help. And always take precedence over me since I turned my back on sports and "abandoned" my mother for antiques.

"What do you need me to do?"

"I forgot to grab coffee ice cream and won't have time to stop." Mom sighs dramatically, even for her. "You're the only one who likes it anyway."

"I can pick some up on my way home. Anything else—"

Mom hangs up without another word.

My cell phone vibrates as I'm about to toss it into my tote. The sibling group chat has been extra active today. All the brothers, even Jaxon, who's stationed in Japan, have wished me a happy birthday. The next text thread bursts my excitement bubble.

LUKE: *Not going to make it tonight. Emergency surgery.*

PHILIP: *Yee-yee! More cake for me since the mayor's having date night*

ASHER: *Can't help that my wife and baby #3 are craving Romano's.*

LUKE: *Any contractions yet?*

PHILIP: *EWWW! NO CONTRACTIONS TALK!!*

CALEB: *There's a party tonight at the country club. I'll try to make it after.*

PHILIP: *Have fun schmoozing the lawyer snore-yers*

ASHER: *Philip Morgan, get off your phone and pay attention in class.*

PHILIP: *I already finished my sculpture*

JAXON: *I still plan on eating half the cake.*

I wish you could be here, Jax. That would be the best birthday present ever.

"Ew! That's not going anywhere near my Threading through History exhibit," Kasey says. "It belongs in a dumpster."

I slip my phone in my tote before turning. My breath catches. It can't be. The vibrant, neon-like colors. The flowers and birds. The spread of dots. The purple fringe along the bottom.

"W-w-where did you get that?" The question scrapes along my throat as I reach for my desk, my knuckles losing color.

Kasey points to the donation box as Libby flips the shawl around her shoulders. Just like that, I'm sixteen and standing in Gran's attic, draped in the shawl, posing in front of a full-length mirror that I'd dusted off to use. I'd been playing hide-and-seek with Jaxon, Caleb, and Philip, and in true Abbie fashion, I got distracted. My imagination took off when I'd spotted the steamer trunk. I'd hoped for a secret, but the shawl was the only thing inside. No hidden compartments. No letters or journals. No treasure map. Not even a scrap of paper with a shopping list.

Lightning struck close to the house, sending the attic into darkness moments after I'd put on the shawl. My screams gave away my hiding place. Then Gran was there, flashlight in hand. Her eyes filled when she saw me—part tears, part horror. She took the shawl off my shoulders and lovingly refolded it.

Her words resonate in my heart and imagination as they had that day. "Oh, darling girl. One day you'll grow into this story, just as you'll grow into this shawl, but not today. Today, it must keep its secrets. Some stories are too dangerous to tell."

I never saw the shawl again. It became a thing of mystery and intrigue, the only story I'd never been able to explore with Gran. I'd brought it up a couple times, asking if I was grown enough to know the truth. Gran had changed the subject by berating me for not paying attention and using the dessert fork instead of the salad fork, or straightening my posture, or editing how I wrote a cursive Q.

"Abigail?" Kasey snaps her fingers in front of my face, startling me from the memory, summoning me from hypnosis.

"Sorry." I reach for a tissue, dabbing at the tears that slipped from my eyes.

"This bird is a kiwi, right?" Libby says. "And these colors and dot patterns look like Aboriginal art. Maybe Australian?"

"New Zealand," I choke out. "Kiwis are native to New Zealand." I'd learned that detail while helping Aunt Vi do research for her latest novel.

"Cool." Libby takes off the shawl and places it on the table. I cross the room, beating my speed for silencing Alice Cooper, and grab the shawl before Kasey can make good on her threat to throw it away.

"This is my gran's shawl," I blurt out, deciding that's the best way to share the info. Fast and all at once.

Kasey quirks a shapely brow. "What's it doing in a box labeled Margaret Weston?"

The question burns a hole through my brain. Had the shawl been with Margaret ever since Gran took it from my shoulders? Why in the world would Gran trust a stranger over me? Even though they were around the same age, Margaret was a recluse, rarely seen by anyone in town, and Gran wasn't born in Westonia. Had the two of them been secretly meeting at the senior center?

I clutch the shawl to my chest like a life preserver. Musty. Hints of cardboard and the hyacinth perfume Gran had worn. I release a deep breath, squeezing my eyes shut, willing the tears to stay hidden.

"You know you can't take that. There's a process," Kasey reminds me.

"I know," I whisper, my heart dying a little. I don't want to let Gran's shawl go, to wait for forms and permissions. But where am I going to find proof that this belonged to Gran since she'd kept it hidden?

"Seriously?" Kasey scoffs. "People should take their own trash to the landfill."

When I open my eyes, Libby is lifting a painting from the box. I recognize the tropical scene right away. Gran loved to show off her finds, but this one never made an appearance. I remember it had a SOLD tag on it when she'd spotted it at Timeless Treasures, but that hadn't stopped Gran from haggling. As much as she fought for it, and won, she'd never displayed it.

Libby sets the painting on the table and begins rummaging through the box, pulling out jewelry and knickknacks. Keeping the shawl in one hand, I flip the painting over. My fingers run over Gran's handwriting, the words swimming through my tears.

Margaret, this view reminded me of our home.
Oh, how I long to return.

I study the painting, imagining its placard.

8x8 watercolor on canvas. Breathtaking beauty of the seacoast, showcasing the raw majesty of the vast ocean meeting rugged shoreline. Vibrant turquoise hues of blue in the sea. Bright green botanicals. Magenta abstract florals adding pops of color. There's a sense of depth and movement in the textures and brushstrokes. You can almost feel the gentle sea breeze and hear the rhythmic crashing of the waves upon the shore. Warmth. Calm. Rest. Home...

Home? This painting looks nothing like Ohio.

Chapter Two

⊶⊷⊶⊷⊶⊷⊶

What do a shawl, a painting, an eight-by-ten discounted picture frame, a handful of plastic necklaces, a Westonia golf tournament hat, a fully functional turbo engine key chain, and a Cabbage Patch Kid have in common? Nothing! That's what.

Gran's shawl wrapped around my shoulders lends a hug and support as I eye the contents of the boxes in front of me. I'm missing the connection. Missing the importance of this hodgepodge of items to the founding family. It's reminiscent of the time Philip showed me a painting by his favorite artist, Salvador Dalí. What am I actually looking at?

Fortunately, the second and third boxes—also marked Margaret Weston—hold exhibit-worthy items: a gilded hand mirror, a christening gown, a hand-painted tea set, carved bowls, and a rather creepy porcelain doll. I'd retrieved the boxes from the ballroom myself, too impatient for Geoff to finish untangling Slinkies.

Samantha Weston, Margaret's granddaughter, dropped the boxes off at the Westonia but hasn't returned my call. Maybe Kasey is right in saying the first box is junk. But then why were the shawl and painting included? Maybe I want the other contents to be junk, so I can take the shawl without all the red tape.

So many questions beg to be answered. What is Gran's shawl doing in the box? Did Gran know Margaret Weston? Was Gran not from Hopalong, Ohio? Will digging into the painting and shawl produce a story

I don't like? And what about Gran's warning that some stories are too dangerous to tell? Are the dangers still there, or did they only exist in Gran's mind?

I almost growl with frustration as I tug the end of my fishtail braid. Deep breaths. Focus. I can solve this puzzle. Research is my jam. I even have an award for helping Aunt Vi do novel research. I'd saved my favorite review that said, "Violet Morgan's research gives readers the whole five senses experience, sucking them in with the vividness and evoking emotion from every scene."

Shaking myself out of this propensity for despair, I take off the shawl, so I can study it. I am going to treat this like every other donated box that's missing its paperwork. The hunt is afoot.

Gran didn't grow up in Westonia, so there'd be nothing in the historical files, and the extent of my family tree on Mom's side starts with her parents and ends with me and my brothers.

There was a time I imagined my grandparents were in witness protection, that they were secret agents on the run. I'd pretend I had epic ninja skills and would be able to save them no matter who came. But that was ridiculous. Grandpa was a janitor, and Gran was a home healthcare nurse.

I run my fingers over the shawl, examining every inch. The memory is dull in comparison to the reality. Having helped with the Threading through History exhibit Kasey organized, I've grown familiar with fabrics, gleaning more knowledge than I'll ever need.

Hand-painted. Silk. Vibrant neon greens, pinks, yellows, oranges. Jagged-edged diamond shapes. Dotted lines in swirls. Pink flowers. Kiwis. Short purple fringe stitched to the bottom of the shawl. A purple silk patch has been added—not part of the original. Green and blue silk with roses on the seam. A single hyacinth embroidered as if hidden in the corner.

Wrapping the shawl around my shoulders once more, I grab a pen and scrap of paper, jotting down what I do know about Gran.

- Christine Rose Henry was born in Hopalong, Ohio, on April 16, 1938.
- Christine married Josiah Brown in 1959 when she was 21.
- Christine and Josiah had one daughter, Heather Rosiah Brown (married Felix Morgan in 1993).
- Christine moved to Westonia, PA, in 2015, a year after Josiah passed away.

- Christine passed away March 5, 2024.

A tear hits the paper as I write that last one, my handwriting shaky and barely legible. I brush the next tear before it can drop, open a tab on my phone, and type Christine Rose Brown, Westonia, Pennsylvania, into the search engine. Her obituary is the first entry to appear. Though I've read it so many times I've memorized it, I click it open. The stab of grief blurs my ability to see Gran's picture. Even at eighty-five, she was stunning. So vibrant and full of life, like the antiques she favored.

An article about Gran winning the over-seventies dance competition hosted by the community center pops up. Gran loved to dance, and I soon shared that love. It combined my athletic skills with my flare for the dramatics. We'd spend at least one night a week learning everything from ballroom to salsa. I haven't been back to the dance studio since the night before she passed.

There has to be more information. I try a search for *Christine Rose Henry, Australia*, and am directed to a handful of social media links. Gran believed in being present, not living online. Perhaps New Zealand?

Twenty minutes and several rabbit holes later, I've found lots of Christine Browns and Henrys, but none who were Gran. I consider the Brick Wall—the Westonia's version of a murder board. A place where we post when we've hit a dead end in research and want others to take a look, maybe see an angle we've missed. Five "cases" currently occupy the board, but are mine. I've always been able to produce results for the projects I'm assigned.

Maybe Margaret's story will be more telling.

I move to my desk, log into the Westonia database, and bring up the Weston file, clicking on Margaret's name. What pops up on the screen adds more questions to my list. Margaret Weston, née Collins, was born in Colorado Springs, Colorado, on April 16, 1938. The same day and year as Gran. Colorado is even more landlocked than Ohio. Neither place looks like that tropical painting.

"Where were you really from?" I zoom into a picture of Margaret from her wedding, immediately throwing out the thought she was Gran's twin. I mean, it could be possible, but Margaret was a redhead with blue eyes and a short, stocky build.

I find the Weston Collection inventory and search for Margaret. Only two items are cataloged under her name in the collection. A brooch and a journal. Score! A note says the journal is on display even though it hasn't been transcribed, which means there's no digital copy easily available for me to do a search for Gran's name.

That leaves me only one option. I have to read the journal.

I take off Gran's shawl and slide it into my tote beside *Howl's Moving Castle*. The proper procedure is to verify that the shawl was Gran's, but I don't know how to prove it. What I wouldn't give for a picture of Gran wearing it.

There aren't many pictures of Gran, and those that do exist—few and far between because Gran hated being photographed—are no older than nine years old. Gran's childhood home burned down when she was in her teens and all her pictures were lost. I've longed to see pictures of when she was little or even in her twenties. I imagine Gran looked a lot like Mom—tall, blue-gray eyes, dark hair.

I weave my way from the research room and through the foyer. A group of fourth graders from Westonia Elementary are finishing a tour of the second-floor museum exhibits with a visiting archeologist. Perfect timing. The museum will be empty. Smiling, but not making eye contact, I rush past their excited chatter to the stairs, praying no one asks for help.

"It's fine, I'm just off researching," I mutter. "I am invisible."

The Westonia Museum isn't huge but is filled with some amazing pieces of our county's history: furniture, paintings, photographs, tools, toys, hints of the Underground Railroad, hair memorials, and a hat with a bullet hole from the Civil War.

The founding family exhibit has already taken over most of the west wing. I've enjoyed getting to know Elizabeth Weston. She was a feisty pioneer who makes me long to leave everything I know and head to the wilds. Having never left Westonia, even for college—which I did on-line—I don't know how adventurous I'd be. But as Elizabeth said often throughout her journals, "God gave me the strength to do the next right thing."

Margaret Weston's leatherbound journal sits beside the brooch in the display case. The brooch catches the light, like it's winking at me. I allow myself a moment to admire the small bird among the silver and gold flower spray. After scanning the room to make sure no one snuck up here, I open the case.

"I need to know your story," I tell the journal once it's in my hands. "No worries. I'll bring you right back."

Guilt makes my breath quicken as I tuck the book safely within my crossed arms and head for the stairs. I'm one step down when a man wearing a gray sweater enters the stairwell. My hold tightens around the journal.

Caught.

He looks up, sees me, and steps to the side, motioning for me to pass.

I register in the back of my mind that he's clean shaven and handsome as I continue my trek to the safety of the research room, the scent of eucalyptus following me. Trying not to run, I make my way down the hallway.

Mr. Romano steps out of his office as I'm rounding the corner, and I smack right into him. Margaret's journal flies from my arms.

"Abigail Morgan." Mr. Romano always uses my full name, as if he wants to remind me whose family I belong to. "Just the woman I wanted to see. Step into my office."

I retrieve the journal, heart pounding as an explanation pours out. "I'm researching Margaret Weston, and this was on display, but it hasn't been transcribed. I thought I could transcribe it. I know I'm just a volunteer, but transcribing this won't take away from my work on Elizabeth Weston, I promise." It comes out in a nervous, breathless rush. Curse my ability to overshare and confess whenever I'm nervous. This is why I could never be a successful spy.

Or could I? No one would ever suspect a clueless babbler.

"Excellent. Such initiative. Exactly what we like around here," my boss says with a nod. "Let me know if you find anything interesting."

Oh. That was…underwhelming.

He enters his office and instructs me to take a seat. I haven't been in here since my interview a year ago. Not much has changed. Masculine, minimal furniture, air straight from Mr. Romano's family-owned restaurant—garlic, parmesan, and marinara sauce. A Lotario brass chess set imported from Italy is displayed in the corner.

I sit in one of the leather wingbacks. On the table beside the chair is today's *Westonia Gazette.* A picture of my aunt, holding her latest Faith Mackenzie release, *Inside the Oath,* smiles at me from the front page. I set Margaret's journal on top of the paper.

During my interview, all Mr. Romano wanted to talk about was my famous author aunt. I'd say Mr. Romano is her biggest fan, but hundreds claim the title "President of the Violet Morgan fan club." He'd fired questions at me like I was at a speed dating table instead of applying for the volunteer position. *Is Violet single? How does she feel about Italian men? Would she care that I'm fifteen years older?*

I often wonder if he would have let me volunteer if she weren't my aunt. If my last name was anything but Morgan.

"Bet you're wondering why you're in my office, Abigail Morgan." He settles in his chair, steepling his fingers under his chin like he's about to take over the world.

Am I supposed to answer?

Before I can decide how to respond, he shifts position, pulls out a folded piece of notebook paper, and starts reading.

With every word, my breath catches and my body heats. I am so getting fired. I should have shredded that page I'd ripped from my notebook instead of playing garbage-can basketball.

"Mr. Romano, I'm—"

"Interesting take on the founding family. I especially like the 'If they'd stumbled upon this oasis in booger-freezing winter, they would've named it We-leavin-a before inventing the first rocket ship and pointing it south,'" he says, eyeing me. "I'm told you're the author."

"I didn't expect anyone would read that. It's silly nonsense. I like to write placards for things—" I stop rambling because Mr. Romano is smiling. An excited smile. Like a proud uncle.

"What an imagination. You must get it from your aunt."

My dad actually, but I don't correct him.

"Have you ever thought about writing placards?"

Ever since I'd learned that writing placards for museums was an actual job, I've dreamed of the day I'd be given license to do it. Me sequestered behind the scenes. My words on display. Guiding people to fall in love with history.

"Here's the deal," Mr. Romano says, leaning forward, elbows on the desk. "The Westonia could use a good refresher. The board is looking for someone with your wit and sass. We'd like to offer you a full-time position researching and rewriting the display placards."

He's not firing me. Quite the opposite.

My voice catches as I try to make the realization stick. "Full-time?"

"What say you, Abigail Morgan? Ready to become a full-timer?"

"I—" The instant yes is stolen by my inner panic.

What about my job at church? I can't let Dad down. Yes, this is a step toward my dream job, but can I do it? Am I ready for a full-time position and the possibility of making enough money to move out of my parents' house?

What if I mess up all the placards and no one comes to the historical society or museum? What if they close because of me?

"Why don't you think about it, maybe talk to your aunt"—he winks—"and let me know by the end of the week."

"Thank you, and I will let you know."

He stands and offers his hand for me to shake.

I jump to my feet, knocking a business card from his desk as I fling out my hand. Red-faced, I crouch to retrieve it, taking note of a colorful coat of arms with a contact number beneath it. If my mind weren't still reeling with everything happening today, I might have wondered why there's no name listed. Instead, I drop the card on the desk, shake Mr. Romano's hand, and walk toward the door.

"Don't forget Margaret's journal," Mr. Romano says, laughter in his words. "Have fun transcribing."

I grab the journal and book it out of there.

My body shakes, high on adrenaline, as I sit at my desk with Margaret Weston's journal. I reach for my coffee, taking a sip from the extra-large tumbler that Dad handed me this morning on my way to the Westonia. He was excited because it was the first coffee he'd ever ordered from the posh new café all by himself. Thankfully, the tumbler he poured it into is insulated so it's still hot even hours later.

Why couldn't I say yes to Mr. Romano?

He'd practically handed me my dream job on a Wedgwood serving platter. What if I can't give him an answer by the end of the week and he offers it to someone else? What if I say yes and regret it? What if I say no...?

Focus on the next right thing.

With Elizabeth Weston's motto brought to the forefront, I take three deep breaths before focusing on Margaret's leather-bound journal. I know the next step in this process: read and transcribe.

When I first started at the Westonia and saw the shelves full of diaries and journals, I was curious and horrified. Curious to read another's secret musings and maybe discover something about history that no one ever had. Horrified that my private thoughts could one day be on a shelf in a historical society for anyone to read and dissect. Now that a page from my *NOSP* has been read and resulted in a job offer...well, I'm still processing.

"Hopefully you like to overshare, Margaret Weston," I say to the journal. "And hopefully you'll tell me all about Gran. That'd be wonderful."

This journal begins in 1962. The day written before the month, the handwriting a tight cursive.

5 January 1962
I never thought I would have the chance to love, not after
I travelled all the way to America. George is a good man,
nothing like the men back home. I love Westonia. This town
is quaint and quiet, the perfect place to raise a family. The
perfect place for a fresh start.

Margaret used the British spelling of traveled. Gran did that occasionally but would correct herself before anyone pointed it out.

I smile as I continue reading. Margaret paints a lovely picture of her wedding in May of that same year and setting up house, of taking care of one person as opposed to many. Was Margaret a nurse like Gran?

The last entry, even though half the journal is empty, is dated 22 May 1993. That's the day my parents married.

God, is it true? She's in Westonia? She's alive and has a
daughter? I never thought I'd see her again, see anyone from
home. Thank you for the blessing.

I catch myself gripping the back cover and uncurl my fingers. Mortified that I damaged something, I turn to investigate. The top corner of the blue fabric has peeled away from the leather. Something white peeks out. A piece of paper?

Instead of the repair glue, I pull open my drawer and find a knife and tweezers. With practiced precision, I slice the fabric then ease the paper out with the tweezers. The thick vellum is like the paper from Gran's stationary set. For the second time today, I'm greeted with Gran's familiar cursive.

I knew it was only a matter of time before they found us
all. It was unrealistic, as much as I dreamed it so, of me to be-
lieve I would never be found, that they would never learn the
truth. That they'd give up the search. Maybe you're right, and
it's time for the world to know our story. Take her the shawl.
It's time for it to return home. I long to go with you, but I still
fear the consequences for my actions.

Chapter Three

I check my rearview mirror one more time before turning onto our mile-long driveway. There's still no one behind me. The sense that someone's been following me since I left the grocery store is giving me paranoia with a capital P. I used evasive maneuvers, calmly turning left instead of right. Frequently changing lanes. Stopping to buy mozzarella sticks and an iced coffee. Researching for Aunt Vi comes in handy more than it probably should. Although, I pray I'm never given a test on getting out of a chokehold.

Given the day I've had, I'd love nothing more than to soak in a bubble bath, sip sparkling grape juice, and finish *Howl's Moving Castle*. I'm such a party animal. But Philip and my parents are waiting on me to celebrate my twenty-fourth birthday.

My deep exhale catches, morphing into a scream when Aunt Vi, dressed in jeans and an oversized neon pink sweatshirt perfectly matched to her Converse and suitcase, appears in the tree line, thumb up in hitchhiker pose. I slam on the brakes, barely catching the empty box of mozzarella sticks before it slides to the floor. Shifting into PARK and throwing the e-brake, I unfasten my seat belt and vault out of my Jetta. Aunt Vi tackles me in a hug, her fanny pack digging into my stomach. She isn't much taller than me, so our faces smoosh together. People always assume we're sisters, which thrills my forty-year-old aunt. We have the same dimpled smile, hazel eyes, and light brown hair. Although mine is closer to blonde on the color wheel. At the moment, Aunt Vi's is a deep auburn with red and gold highlights. Fall imitation hair.

"I didn't think I'd see you until Thanksgiving." It's been a month since I received a vintage postcard from Lake Placid, New York, letting me know she'd arrived at her rented cottage. Lack of contact from anyone else would have had me imagining all sorts of horrid accidents. But it's Aunt Vi, and it's September. She hates this month even though I love it.

"I couldn't miss my favorite niece's golden birthday." As she hugs me, I don't point out that I'm her only niece. We both know the drill. "You're twenty-four on the twenty-fourth in the year twenty-four. Only happens once in a lifetime."

"Hadn't thought of that." That is pretty cool.

"Also, I was kinda sorta hoping to talk you into going on the book tour with me." She wiggles her brow. "After all, you did do a lot of research on Australia and New Zealand for *Inside the Oath*. We could have a Faith Mackenzie experience—without all the murder, preferably. And maybe a Legolas sighting?"

Instant sweat builds on the nape of my neck, panic tingling down my back and arms all the way to my toes. "U-uh, I'm good. I'm still recovering from the last time I tried to fly overseas."

"It's been, what, seven years?"

Seven years ago. Junior year of high school. Missions trip to Honduras. I was all gung ho about going with our church group to build a school and shine the light of Jesus, but I had to bow out two days before. I got so sick with the fear of flying that I couldn't even climb out of bed. That was the first time I had a panic attack. The second one happened when the team returned, alive in a way I envied. I'd missed the chance to build strong friendship bonds and experience God's life-altering work.

"No, I—"

"I'll stop. Just know the offer is there." She lifts her suitcase. "Give a girl a ride? I planned on walking since I sat on a bus for three hours, but O.L.D. is kicking in. I knew you'd be heading this way soon, thus my lounging in the trees."

"Forty isn't *that* old," I say with a smile.

"I still feel eighteen most days."

I eye her suitcase and have a slight panic moment unrelated to planes. "Just put the suitcase in the back seat. The trunk's full."

The shawl and painting are in the trunk along with Gran's note and the turbo key chain because I couldn't resist. Samantha Weston had stopped by the Westonia embarrassed by her box mix-up. She'd delivered the right box—full of more exhibit-worthy items—taking the hodge-podge box to its intended home: Goodwill. She gave me full permission to keep Gran's things without the red tape.

I may have permission to possess the shawl and painting, but I'm not ready to talk about them yet. Aunt Vi would want to dissect it all, pondering the whys and hows and what-in-the-worlds like they were a shiny new novel idea.

There was nothing about Gran in Margaret Weston's journal. Well, nothing with her name. I'm pretty sure Margaret was talking about Gran, considering the date of my parents' wedding and other hints about long-ing for home. I'd finished transcribing and, after I'd repaired the back cover, returned it to the display case.

I clear my throat as I shift to second, driving toward home, "Was your trip successful?"

Aunt Vi groans, banging the back of her head against the headrest. Her tiny suitcase earrings swing dangerously. "The place was magical, but I wrote nothing. Absolute rubbish." The purpose of her trip to the "wilds of Upstate New York" was to become one with nature in the hopes of being inspired and plotting her next novel. I'm suspecting her time was spent soaking in the hot tub and rewatching *Castle* for the tenth time or maybe the newest version of *Little Women*, depending on her mood.

"You'd think I was plotting my first novel instead of number nine. Nine. Wow, can you believe it? My first novel was published when you were fifteen. A lifetime ago."

Fifteen was a year to remember. Violet Morgan made the bestseller lists the same month Gran moved next door.

"You'll get there. You always do." I then repeat words I've heard her mutter a time or ten. "It doesn't have to be perfect. It just needs to be written. Your editor will work his magic."

"I know, but I wish it was already done, at least the mess draft."

It's always a bit like a beloved movie script—one where you quote all the lines—until Aunt Vi finishes that first draft, this roller coaster of "I can't author. I'm worthless. I should take up knitting." Once draft one is done, she switches back to her spunky, I-could-rule-the-world-but-choose-not-to outlook. I'm glad the writing stuck because the blanket she made for me returned to its natural ball state in less than an hour.

When people learn Aunt Vi is an author, they assume she writes rom-coms or even young adult novels because of her quirky attire and personality. But my aunt is the queen of crime fiction with a supernatural twist. She doesn't do romance—on or off the page. Mystery. Murder. Mayhem. Give her a web-twisty plot that messes with her readers' heads, and she's happier than a kid in an inflatable T. rex costume jumping on a trampoline.

"Thanks for the information on coffin quilts. It was a nice break from banging my head against the table." She winces at the memory. "I have a few ideas brewing on how to use the info."

"If you have time before you leave, you'll have to stop by the Westonia to see the one on display," I say. "It's elaborate, complete with entry gate and picket fences. There are fifteen coffins with names embroidered in red."

The discovery of coffin quilts came from a side trail I'd taken while researching for the Threading through History exhibit. Before cemeteries became popular, most family members were buried in clusters of graves on family property. The quilts served as important family records. Small coffin shapes were appliqued into the borders, with each coffin representing a family member. When a family member died, the quilter moved the coffin from the border to the center of the quilt and added the death date.

I park in front of the white farmhouse Dad's grandparents built in the mid-1940s. It's sprawling and spacious and has always been home. No extra vehicles claim places on the driveway. Guess everyone really is too busy for cake. With a sigh, I gather my tote and the ice cream, closing the trunk before Aunt Vi notices that it definitely was not full.

It's way too quiet in the house, and the fancy ice cream cone-shaped bowls we use for every birthday aren't on the table. While Aunt Vi takes her suitcase to the guest room, I put the ice cream in the freezer. A small coffee for me and a gallon of vanilla for everyone else. If I'd known my aunt would be here, I would've grabbed three tubs of coffee ice cream.

I close the door, just catching the flyer for Winter in Westonia before it escapes from the bedazzled magnet my oldest niece made at VBS. The winning logo Philip designed features the historical society as the center of a Westonia skyline.

December 13–15. Come celebrate close-knit, neighbor-help-ing-neighbor values. Pictures with Santa, hot chocolate, cookie decorating, horse-drawn carriage rides through our beautiful downtown. Visit the chocolate shop, farmers market, historical society, and museum. Enjoy a Christmas concert by the wor-ship team from Westonia Baptist Church on Sunday morning.

Not only will I be playing piano and singing for the concert on Sun-day, I'll be running in the annual 5K race Saturday morning. My brothers signed up as well. Long live our TEAM MORGAN shirts.

Speaking of Team Morgan.

"Mom? Dad? Philip?"

"Maybe they're out back? I smell barbecue." Aunt Vi licks her lips.

My stomach growls when I catch the scent of Dad's Morgan-famous burgers. "I'm gonna go change." I love this dress, especially because it has pockets, but there's nothing like the comfort of sweatpants.

"You look beautiful. That color makes your eyes pop."

"It's black." I quirk an eyebrow, eyeing her ensemble. "I'm way over-dressed."

Her hair is still piled on top of her head. But the neon has been replaced by a more subdued purple plaid flannel and matching bright purple Converse. The red eyes of her loon earrings are beady and mis-chievous. I can't decide how the birds feel about swaying from my aunt's lobes.

"Whatever." Aunt Vi takes my tote and sets it on the dining room ta-ble, ushering me toward the backyard. Before I make it through the door and onto the wooden deck, an air horn blasts, colorful confetti raining down on me.

"Surprise! Happy birthday!"

If Aunt Vi hadn't been behind me, I would've bolted. My worst night-mare is before me. Don't get me wrong, I love people. But being sur-rounded or the center of attention? Nope. Don't like that, not one bit. I require mental prep time to enter a crowded room. There's a reason I don't lead tours at the Westonia.

I bite my lip, hoping to keep my tear ducts lethargic. The mozzarella sticks and iced coffee I'd inhaled on the ride home threaten to make an appearance. How did I miss the signs? House too quiet. Aunt Vi being shifty, not allowing me to change into sweats. The smell of burgers when we were only having cake and ice cream.

I didn't buy enough ice cream for a crowd.

"What did you do?" I twist around to glare at Aunt Vi.

"Everything." She grins unapologetically. I swear her loon earrings smirk. Definitely her evil minions.

"I'm not giving a speech."

"We wouldn't want you to anyway."

With a deep breath, I face the crazy gathered in the yard. I spot friends from church—the majority older than fifty. Neighbors. Several people I don't recognize. One is male and suspiciously close to my age. When I find Dad in the crowd, he shrugs, offering a sheepish smile. He knows exactly what he did. And is not sorry at all.

Surprise successful, everyone disperses, congratulating themselves on how well they did in not giving it away. I wonder how long they've been planning this. I'm impressed none of the brothers revealed the secret.

"There's my girl," Dad says as he joins us on the deck. I settle into his embrace, inhaling the comfort of his Irish Spring and burger spice scent. "How's it feel to be twenty-four?"

"It's been an interesting day," I get out as Mom takes her turn.

Asher rips me from Mom, wraps me in a crushing bear hug, and lifts me off the ground.

"Happy birthday, old woman."

When he puts me back on my feet, I narrow my eyes, giving the brothers—all of them minus Jaxon—a look. Standing in a line, they resemble varying shades of brown-haired, hazel-eyed, Russian dolls. Except Asher is the shortest and it goes up in height to sixteen-year-old Philip, still in his scrawny and awkward era.

"I thought you all said you couldn't make it." I eye them each in turn. "Emergency surgery? Golf event with lawyers? A pregnant, hungry wife?"

"We've confessed our lies," Luke says. "It was for a good cause."

"My wife is still pregnant and hungry, but Dad made burgers." Asher's grin is the widest.

"Was Jax lying?" I search, spotting Jax's face on the iPad in Philip's hands.

"Happy birthday, Abbie."

My tears begin to flow as I take in Jax's words. "It's so good to see your face, to hear your voice."

"You never cry when you see me," Philip says with a huff.

"Maybe you should go away for a month," Asher suggests.

"Nah, she still wouldn't cry. Unless it was tears of anger because I came back."

I ignore their razzing as I take the iPad and grin at my favorite brother. Barely a year older than me, we've gotten into lots of scrapes together and always chose each other first when picking teams. He's my rock even though he's on the other side of the globe and we don't get to talk every day.

"You're doing well?" I ask.

"As good as can be. Missing you all."

"We miss you too." My family gathers around, Aunt Vi resting her chin on my shoulder. If I could have a birthday wish it would be for all of us to be together in person. It's been more than a year since Jaxon left for Japan.

"Let's get a picture before you go." Mom waves the photographer over.

They hired a professional? I know that should make me feel special, but—

I'm pushed to the center, and I hold up the iPad, keeping Jax close, wishing we'd been able to talk just the two of us. We do a photo with the Morgans then add Asher's wife, Rachel, and their girls—Poppy and Lily—and Luke's fiancée, Stefi. Obligatory pictures done, and tearful goodbyes said, I return the iPad to Philip.

My nieces tackle my legs then scamper off when Rachel tells them to shoo. She gives my hand a squeeze, her other hand resting on her extended belly. I still have trouble pairing my boisterous brother with the soft-spoken middle school guidance counselor. But maybe that skill is how she deals with him.

"Thank you for the flowers," I tell her.

"You're welcome. The purple tulips reminded me of you. Beautiful and unique."

Beautiful? Unique? I thrill at the compliment. It feels like I'm failing in the unique area, just existing in this thing called life. Not moving and shaking like my brothers and parents. Not exuberant, put together, or successful like Aunt Vi.

I opt for humor to hide my slide to melancholy. *Brain, why are you so bad at pep talks?* "I knew Ash didn't have a say in the flowers."

"Definitely not," Asher says with a snort. "I wanted to send you this but got shut down." He produces a small box wrapped in tinfoil.

"Should I open it now?" What if they make me open lots of gifts in front of everyone? What if there aren't any other gifts? What if someone gives me a Noah's Ark music box like Rachel received at her bridal shower, and I have to pretend to love it?

"Please put your brother out of his misery. He's been excited ever since this arrived weeks ago." Rachel winces as her stomach shifts.

I'm thinking baby number three isn't planning to wait for November. Also, he or she will be a soccer player or into kickboxing.

I fold back the tinfoil on the present to reveal a Funko Pop! box. The name Indiana Abbie is written on the front. Lifting the flap, I pull out the figurine. Two brown braids flow down from a hat like Indiana Jones, huge hazel eyes, tall black boots, brown pants, and a button-up shirt. Instead of a rope, there's a pen in one hand and a stack of books in the other.

"I had it custom made." Asher beams as he puts an arm around his wife. Their wide smiles are ridiculous.

I've ceased trying to explain to the brothers that I am not an archaeologist. The vinyl figurine is cute though. If I do take the job at the Westonia, I'm putting this in a place of honor on my desk. "This is great. Thanks."

"Well, you better go mingle. Dad especially wants you to meet Noah." Asher wiggles his brow. "I heard him talking about offering Noah's parents fifteen camels for you."

I groan. "Dad does know a man is not an acceptable birthday gift, right?"

"Mom even approves. Noah's the head coach of the Lady Knights. He could be 'the one.'"

I slug my brother's shoulder and, shaking my head, step off the deck to the crunchy leaf-filled grass.

With the exception of my brothers and my male friends at church who view me as "one of the guys," I have a hard time knowing what to say to men I'm meeting for the first time. I know sports, but otherwise my go-to info revolves around my work. Yet what guy wants to get an info dump on a seventeenth-century bowl or the process of restoring a painting? Then there's the "Pastor's Daughter" title, all the eyes on me, and the very real fear that I'll mix up my words and end up swearing.

Music with a salsa tempo blasts from speakers set up near a portable DJ booth. I wave at Gavin, who sits with his wife behind a table. He's another one Dad tried to "trade me for camels." Think biblical Isaac and Rebecca but with none of the romance.

The decibel level of the backyard increases as I greet my guests, thanking everyone who wishes me a happy birthday and pretending excitement at the surprise. So much for quiet and alone.

This is the point in every get-together when I wish a helicopter would fly in.

Blades whap-whap *against the air, growing louder until it hovers above the party. Abigail takes off running, unbuttoning her dress to reveal tactical gear—always ready like Wonder Woman. A ladder falls from the helicopter, and she climbs, calling to the crowd below, "Sorry, gotta go save the world."*

I'm about to head for a bacon cheeseburger when I spot Caleb and Philip and a stranger at a table with pictures, albums, and sports trophies. Not an antique in sight. A tribute to who I was before Gran's influence.

Wait? Why does Philip have my baby book?

Horrified, I shove Indiana Abbie into my pocket and hustle over, knowing exactly what's in that book. As a baby, I'd had the physique of a sumo wrestler. Thankfully, I thinned out as soon as I started walking. I'm barely five foot five, but I'm comfortable with my weight. Being active in sports helps.

I wedge between my brothers and yank the purple scrapbook from Philip's hands, maneuvering it out of reach.

"Hey! We were showing Noah how cute you used to be," Philip says with a pout.

"He doesn't want or need to see those." I focus on Noah, writing a placard in my head to calm my nerves. *Late twenties. Handsome. Great smile. Tight black curls. Dark skin. Dark, lively eyes. First choice for a jump ball tall.* My hands start to tingle as I try to form a coherent sentence. "I'm sorry they tortured were you." *Give me a B+ for that sentence. It was almost understandable.*

"I'm sorry to crash your party. Pastor Morgan—uh, your dad—invited me for dinner. Happy birthday, by the way." Noah's voice is deep and full of kindness that makes my heart sigh. He points to the plaque on the four-foot-tall trophy. 2018 MVP: 1003 BASKETS. "I've got one of those, but I only scored 1001."

I study him again for a beat before it hits me. "You played for West Mountain." I quirk a brow. "You played for the rival school, and now you're coaching at my alma mater?"

"I bet you could give me pointers." His smile widens, making his dark eyes almost disappear.

Wait. Is he flirting, or does he actually want basketball tips?

"Yeah, *three*-pointers," Philip says, elbowing me in the ribs.

"You still play?" Noah asks.

"She could totally take you," Caleb chimes in. My brothers' confidence in my playing abilities is endearing. I might not have played college ball, but I do enjoy a pickup game as often as I can.

"We should set up a game," Philip suggests.

"That sounds like fun." Noah gets an excited glint in his eyes.

My courage rises. Basketball. I know the rules for basketball.

"She plays dirty," Philip says.

"I do not. Just because you can't make a layup—"

Philip goes to ruffle my hair, but I evade his hands and knock into Noah. I barely get a whiff of his Old Spice bodywash before my nose smashes into his sternum. He steadies me, his body shaking as he chuckles.

"Aunt Abbie! Aunt Abbie! Come play with us. We wanna hear more of our story." Poppy tugs on my arm, and I step away from Noah. My face is probably redder than a Chicago Bulls jersey.

It's not a helicopter, but my rescue has arrived. My niece pulls me over to the kids' corner. Situated amid a pile of Barbies whose hair begs for fishtail braids, I pick up where I left off in the ongoing story about Gram Ninja. A fantasy story loosely based on my mom's ability to "disappear" whenever we go shopping.

⁂

I survive the party and cleanup that follows. The brothers all go home or, in Caleb's and Philip's case, disperse to play Ping-Pong in the basement game room. Their whoops echo through the house, happy at the moment, but that could change in an instant to wrestling about an unfair call.

Mom is holding Gran's shawl when I enter the dining room with a box of unopened gifts.

"Who gave you this? It looks like something my mother would've loved." Mom quietly fingers the fabric as I had done.

"Actually, it was Gran's." I set the box on the table and reach for the shawl. In my terrifying acceptance of the party, I'd forgotten the shawl. Forgotten the painting. Forgotten the note Gran wrote to Margaret Weston, fearing the consequences of her actions.

"Where did it come from?"

"It showed up at the Westonia. There was a box mix-up." I inhale the shawl's scent then wrap the fabric around my shoulders, drawing strength to ask about Gran's hometown. "Was Gran born in Hopalong, Ohio?"

"Of course." Mom's brow furrows.

Dad enters the room waving a manilla envelope. "Abbie girl, this came for you today."

At the sight of Donald Jenkins II, Lawyer, on the return address, words scroll through my mind's eye. *Sued. Summons. Court. Jail.* My ten-year-old self is still waiting to be hauled away for stabbing the plastic of a package of ground beef at the grocery store and not paying for it.

I try to keep my hand shaking to a minimum as I open the envelope. Inside is an official letter from Donald Jenkins II.

> *To Miss Abigail Rosiah Morgan,*
> *As per your grandmother's wishes, on this day, September 24, 2024, in honor of your twenty-fourth birthday, you are now the owner of Hyacinth Cottage. When you are able to go, please stop by Jenkins & Garmen for further instructions.*
> *All the best,*
> *Donald Jenkins II*

The other piece of paper is a deed. *24 Hyacinth Lane. Bridgeway, QLD, Australia.*

"Gran left me a cottage in Australia?" To verify that I'm not seeing things, I read both papers again.

"Australia?" Mom holds out a hand, and I pass her the letter and deed. Her eyebrows raise. "When was my mother ever in Australia?"

"Is it legit?"

Dad takes the letter and looks it over. "Donald Jenkins was your grandmother's lawyer. He did the reading of the will."

I vaguely remember the bald man with the enormous smile who declared Asher got Gran's house and the rest of us got money, crushing my heart at the thought that nothing tangible, no piece of Gran, was set aside for me.

"When you're able to go?" Mom mutters, shaking her head. "What game is my mother playing? It's not like you can just up and go to Australia."

"Why not? She can tag along with me," Aunt Vi says, joining our group. Her jeans and flannel have been replaced by black sweatpants and an IT's COFFEE O'CLOCK sweatshirt.

"Yeah, that's a great idea. The two of you—"

"I'm twenty-four," I say at the same time Aunt Vi says, "I'm responsible."

Mom rolls her eyes then looks at Dad. "Felix, say something."

"Well, she is twenty-four now." He winks in my direction. "And travel with my sister is never boring."

"Not helping, dear." Mom narrows her eyes at Dad then turns to me. "What about your jobs? You have obligations and responsibilities at church and your volunteer work."

"Actually, Mr. Romano offered me a full-time job at the Westonia," I say. "Writing placards. Well, rewriting them."

"Woohoohoo!" You can always count on Dad's "woohoohoo" when there's good news, especially when someone gives their life to Christ.

"That's awesome." Aunt Vi laughs with delight. "Watch out, world, there's another Morgan writer."

"Abigail is not an author," Mom says.

I cringe, but there's truth in that. Placards are not novels. I could never write a novel.

"You did accept the job, right?" Aunt Vi studies me, ignoring the heated look Mom's practically melting her with.

I shrug. "I wanted to think about it?"

Mom whips her gaze to me. "As you should. Seeking wise counsel is a mature thing to do."

"Sounds like the perfect time to go Down Under with your favorite aunt. Take some time to breathe before you start a new job. I'm sure Giovanni will let you." Aunt Vi bounces on her toes. The colorful glitter decorating her neon-green nails reminds me of Montreal Steak Seasoning. "I'll pay for your tickets. Consider it my birthday gift to you."

"Aren't you going to be gone until Thanksgiving?" Mom eyes Aunt Vi a little more on the distasteful side than normal.

"Thanksgiving?" I choke out. My fingers clench and unclench as my breathing grows shallow. Not this again. *I can't do this. What am I thinking? I can't get on a plane. And there's no way Mr. Romano will hold the job for two months.*

"This is a disaster waiting to happen," Mom says.

"It'll be good for her," Aunt Vi counters.

"What about praise team? Kids' church?"

"Breaks are always healthy."

"Says the queen of breaks. I know you can go off whenever, disappearing for months at a time because you can't 'deal with people talking to you when you're writing' but—"

"You know why I go."

"I don't want my daughter to be like you."

"I happen to think—"

"Stop! Please," I say louder than intended, cutting off the barbs Mom and Aunt Vi are shooting back and forth. Without another word, I leave the dining room, tears flowing unhindered. Thankfully, no one follows me up the stairs to my bedroom, where I collapse on my bed, blocking out reality with Gran's shawl.

Chapter Four

⊸——————◦——————⊱

I open the door to my office at the church as the phone rings. I reach for it, but my hand goes through. The ringing continues until Dad, frazzled and sweaty, enters and picks it up. "Abigail isn't here. She got a better offer than helping her church family."

Something touches my neck. My scream echoes around the office as spiders appear like stars in the night sky, their cobwebs infesting the space.

Dad's brown eyes lock on me. "Look what happened. You abandoned us. Choosing a job over ministry."

I turn and run from the room then down a hallway that dissolves behind me. I round a corner, my chest heaving, and find myself in the Westonia. It looks like a tornado touched down. The card catalogs are tipped, all the drawers open, typewriter-written cards floating in the air. Births. Marriages. Divorces. Deaths. Deeds. Odd files.

A card smacks into my face as Kasey waves a placard, Gran's shawl wrapped around her shoulders. *"These are terrible! You think you can write? You've ruined the Westonia. You're pathetic."*

Mr. Romano appears beside Kasey. *"I gave your job to Miss Fitzroy. You weren't worth waiting for."*

"Abigail?"

"Gran?" I search the room, trying to drown out Kasey's cackling laughter. A figure disappears up the stairs to the museum. I race up steps that have doubled in size.

The museum is still in pristine condition. Everything except the Weston exhibit. Cases are smashed. Dolls ripped apart. Pages torn from journals. A blood-like substance oozes from a hat.

There's a knock on the window. Glancing out, I find Gran in a field of weeds. The only light in a pitch-black world. Margaret Weston's journal and an ornate wooden box are clutched to her chest.

"You said you'd live boldly." Gran's haunted voice rings out as if she's standing next to me.

"I'm trying, Gran! I can't do this without you."

"Abigail Rosiah, find my story. You're the only one who can." Gran's pleading rips at my heart.

I smack the window. Instead of resistance, I fall.

I jerk awake before my dream-self hits the ground. My breathing is heavy and shallow, like I'd finished a marathon without being conditioned. It takes several moments to escape the clutches of the nightmare before I'm able to sit up. I grab my favorite stuffed camel, Gamal, clutching it to my chest as I scoot toward the headboard. It's been a while since I've had a "wrestling" dream. My subconscious knows I need to make a decision, and instead of offering helpful guidance, it's causing the stress meter to explode.

Live boldly. Gran and I had chosen that as our phrase of the year.

"It's hard to live boldly without you, Gran," I whisper.

Once my heart has settled, I set Gamal aside and gather Gran's letters I'd been reading before bed, tying the purple ribbon around them before sliding them safely into my nightstand drawer. Gran gave me stationery and a wax set soon after she moved next door, and we sent letters back and forth at least twice a month. Had rereading the letters triggered the nightmare?

I wince at the glowing red numbers on my alarm clock: 1:06 a.m. Wide awake, I climb out of bed and wrap Gran's shawl around my shoulders. If there's one thing I can take from the dream, it's that it's time to open the box.

The decorative box rests on the top shelf of my closet where I'd placed it six months ago. I couldn't bear to look at it then. Couldn't bear to open it or the envelope with my name written in Gran's beautiful, flowing cursive.

The night before she died, as I'd dropped Gran off at her house following a rather vigorous tango lesson, she'd said, "It's time to tell you a story." We agreed to meet at the café after I was done with work the next day.

That was the last time I spoke to Gran. I'd taken for granted that we'd have more time and hundreds of stories to create. Best we can figure, Gran was dropping the box off on her way to Bible study. Luke found her sitting in her car, which was parked in our driveway. A small blessing within the tragedy. The coroner verified cause of death was an aneurysm—unexpected, sudden, nothing could have been done.

Making myself comfortable on my beanbag, I remove the envelope from the top of the box. The tape still has a little fight left, but I win. Once the wax seal is broken, I unfold the piece of thick vellum.

I take steadying breaths and use my sleeve to wipe my eyes, careful not to let drops hit the paper and steal Gran's words.

> *My Dearest Abigail Rosiah,*
> *I'm leaving this box for you. We'll talk about these treasures at the café. For years, I've held these secrets. For years, I've prayed for the right time. This box holds many pieces of my heart. I pray that when you hear my entire story, you will know I kept things from you and your mother out of love, out of sacrifice.*
> *With love forever and ever.*

Setting the letter aside, I wipe my face once more before opening the box. My curiosity at knowing what was inside wasn't there six months ago. Not after the funeral. Not when the one person I'd shared stories with was gone. Keeping the box closed allowed me to pretend Gran was alive in some ways. I didn't want her story to end. But with all the new pieces appearing in the last twenty-four hours, it's like Gran's story has just begun. Her real story.

Inside the box is a well-loved leather-bound book. A compilation of poems by Eileen Duggan. *Odd.* Gran disliked poetry as much as I do.

The literary style frustrates me. I never understand what I'm supposed to think. Teachers say you can take whatever from a poem, but then I get the "not exactly what the author was going for" speech. How do they know what the author was going for? Were they there when it was written?

Biting back a smile at the memory of poetry discussions with Gran, I open the book to find an inscription written in a masculine hand.

> *My Rose,*
>   *The words filling these pages barely touch how I feel*
> *about you.*
>
>   *Roy*

Roy? While Rose was Gran's middle name, Grandpa's middle name was Mark and his first, Josiah. Could Roy be a nickname, or was there another man in Gran's life prior to Grandpa Brown? Regrettably, I'd only been around Grandpa a handful of times and knew nothing about my grandparents' love story other than that they'd met at a church function in Hopalong. After Grandpa died, Mom begged Gran to move to Westonia so she wasn't alone in Ohio, a plea I'm so thankful Gran listened to.

A decision that changed my life.

I flip through the pages, spotting passages starred and underlined as well as sketches of hearts and flowers and birds in the margins. A photograph flies out, and I tackle it like a fumbled football. Three names and a date are written on the back. *Hazel. Laurel. Rose. 1957.*

My hands shake as I turn it over. Three women stand at the end of a pathway in front of a sign that says *Hyacinth Cottage*. I study the picture with an intensity that matched what I felt during the pinnacle of an important end-of-season basketball game. Gran, age nineteen, stands in the middle. All three women wear skirts and blouses and matching looks of adoration. Friendship radiates from their eyes and smiles and the way their arms wrap around each other.

"Why did you tell me you never left America?" I whisper as I touch Gran's face. The woman I knew is there minus the years and laughter lines. The same smile, same lively, mischievous eyes. Poised and beautiful. I was wrong. Young Gran didn't look like Mom. She looked like me.

I don't want to, but I set the photo aside, eager to find more treasures. The only other thing in the box is a purple velvet drawstring bag. Inside is another wax-sealed envelope with my name on the outside. I break the seal to find Gran's pink diamond ring and a photo of my grandparents in 1959 in front of a small white church. Gran has the shawl wrapped around her shoulders, staring at Grandpa instead of the photographer.

Why hadn't I opened this box sooner?

I'd thought Gran's ring had been lost forever. She'd worn it to dance class, but she hadn't worn it the day she died. I try the ring on my fingers until it finds the perfect fit on my left-hand right next to my verse ring.

I hold up my hand, admiring the simple elegance. Three pink diamonds in a woven silver band. The gems smooth to the touch, not raised like most rings. *Is this what an engagement ring will feel like?*

Startling at the thought, I tug the ring off, thankful it doesn't stick. That's what I need—a single, wonderful guy not talking to me because he thinks I'm already spoken for.

Ring safely on my right hand, I undo the wax seal. It's addressed to me, but Gran didn't sign her name, just a crudely drawn hyacinth beside the reference of her favorite verse.

> *Abigail Rosiah,*
>
> *Life is as it is, and our paths never crossed. And even though we grew up so close to one another, it took running to America for us to meet. Unusual as it was, our love story began with Josiah pursuing me across an ocean. Romantically, at first, I wanted absolutely nothing to do with him. Especially when he gave up everything to stay with me. Love blossomed in Ohio. Constantly aware but living to the fullest, we learned each other's story, saw the other's heart. And then he bought me this piece of home.*
>
> *Mined in North Australia, Argyle diamonds are rare. Paid way too much for it at an antique jeweler. But every time I see it, I'm reminded of sacrifice and my true home. Everything I hold dear is right here, surrounding me in the present. Letting go of this ring is bittersweet, but I want you to have it. Like this ring, you are uniquely made—loved and cherished. Every time you see the sparkle of the diamonds, know that I am praying for you.*
>
> *Live boldly, dear Abigail. Love boldly. Even while you wait for God to bring you your own love story. Remember to trust God's timing and perfect plan. You deserve someone who holds you closer when they hear your story, your heart.*
> *Jeremiah 40:31*

I lean my head back and twist the Argyle diamond ring, wondering at all these things pointing to a connection between Gran and Australia. The ring. The cottage. The shawl. The painting. Pieces of home. The leaving and pursuit. All pieces of a puzzle.

God, is this a billboard answer? Should I go to Australia? What if I can't do it? What if I fail? I don't know if I can live boldly.

A soft knock on my bedroom door announces Aunt Vi right before she peeks her head in. "Hey, kiddo. Saw your light on. You okay?"

"I don't know."

Aunt Vi enters, shutting the door behind her. She sits in my desk chair and sips from a steaming mug of what I'm sure is espresso. Unlike the rest of society, the extra caffeine boost makes my aunt sleepy. *Melatonin* wakes her up.

"What's that?" she asks, and I hand her the picture of my grandparents. "Wow, you look so much like your grandmother. Stunning. And, swoon, you can feel the love she had for her man. Better than how I look at coffee."

"I wish I knew their full love story." I eye the poetry book. Roy had to be a nickname.

Aunt Vi sets her mug down and leans forward, handing me the picture before running her fingers along the shawl. "I can't stop staring at this."

"The last time I saw it, Gran said I wasn't ready, that I'd grow into the shawl and the story. But what if I'm not ready even now? Maybe I'm not supposed to have it."

"Is that what's keeping you from sleep?"

"I feel like maybe God has opened doors for me to go to Australia, but as Mom said, I do have responsibilities here—and a possible dream job." I take a deep breath, giving my aunt my best pleading smile. "Maybe while you're in Australia, you could—"

"Nope. Not gonna happen." She lovingly kicks me. "What are you afraid of?"

I laugh without humor. "Everything."

"What scares you the most?"

"Besides flying? Getting my dream job. What if I can't be witty and the Westonia closes because my placards are even worse than they are now? And taking the job means I can't be Dad's secretary. What if things fall apart at church? What if no one does the bulletins or worse, someone does them and they're riddled with typos? What if the church gets filled with spiders?"

"I was following until the spiders." Aunt Vi raises an eyebrow. "'What if' might be my favorite question but mulling that out in fiction is one thing. In real life, it can hinder you from living."

"I feel like a huge part of who I am got ripped away. I thought I knew Gran's story, but then, bam, she lived in Australia? And loves poetry?" I groan dramatically. "I wish my wrestling dreams would declare a winner and tell me what to do." Despite what Mom said, I do pray. And weigh. Sometimes to the point that I miss out on things because I'm waiting for that billboard answer.

"Look, I'm not going to tell you what to do. God knows I tend to do the opposite. Case in point, my English teacher telling me I'd never be a successful writer because I couldn't spell and had a hard time focusing." Aunt Vi's gleeful grin brings one to my face, stealing a bit of my anxiety. "But I also think you'd benefit from experiencing the research firsthand. Don't use fear as an excuse. I did that for far too long."

"But what if Mr. Romano gives the job to Kasey? Two months is way longer than a week."

Aunt Vi searches my desk, grabbing a stack of pink sticky notes and a black pen. "Here. Write down reasons why you want to go to Australia and reasons why you want the job at the Westonia. Not pros and cons, and definitely not why you think others want you to do it." She hands me the supplies then reclaims her mug as she stands. "Why do *you*, Abigail Rosiah Morgan, want to become the next author of placards? Why do you, Abigail Rosiah Morgan, want to go to Hyacinth Cottage?"

As the door shuts and she leaves me alone once more, my aunt's parting words become my personal mantra, one I know the answer to without having to write anything.

Why do I want to go to Hyacinth Cottage?

Gran needs me to tell her story.

AN AMERICAN DOWN UNDER

Kangaroos and emus and spiders, oh my!

According to research, everything in Australia wants to kill you, except maybe koalas who sleep twenty-two hours a day. Living the dream. Carry on, my sleepy friends.*

Postcard-worthy landscapes offer the reds of the outback to the blues of the shore. Beaches to deserts. Sun and surf. A whimsical theme park. An adventure playground—just don't try to pet a kangaroo. You're more than likely to be punched in the throat.

Australia is like a super chill friend who wears flip-flops all year long. Doesn't matter that they're a bit weird, what with Christmas in summer and mowing the lawn in the winter, they're super charming. Just keep them talking.

*I was just informed that koalas are mean. Sharp claws and teeth. Aggressive when threatened. Also, their growls were used in *Jurassic Park* as the T. rex growls. Maybe not so cuddly after all.

—*Abigail's Notebook of Silly Placards*

Chapter Five

I hate this. I hate this. I really hate this.

The dips. The feeling like the engine is cutting out. Ears filled with cotton. A thousand scenarios audition to be the star of my mind theater's production. Plummeting. Turbulence. Actually, the turbulence is rather reminiscent of driving over pothole-filled country roads. I'll pretend I'm on a Sunday drive...

I squeak when the intercom beeps. *Are we about to go down? I should have stayed home. I hate this. I hate this—*

The pilot announces that we've reached our desired altitude and can take off our seat belts. Yeah, no thanks. I'm good.

"I can't do this," I say through shaky breath cycles of in-out. I clutch my copy of *Howl's Moving Castle* like a security blanket.

"It's a little late for that," Aunt Vi says around a yawn.

I glare at her, wishing looks could destroy—or at least teleport me to Australia. Why has teleportation not been invented?

"Nothing is going to happen to you that God doesn't already know about." Aunt Vi opens her security blanket of choice, *Little Women*, signaling I should do the same with my novel.

Why didn't I ask for sleeping meds? A two-by-four? Anything to knock me out. Although, we are in first class on this plane and will be on the next. And these chairs become beds. I'm so glad I'm not sitting in economy, which according to my research would be like riding a school bus home from a basketball tournament—stuffed in, sweaty, noisy. Aunt Vi worked her magic, and I'm in the seat next to her. I'm highly suspicious that was due more to the fact that she'd already bought me tickets and less to do with her powers of persuasion.

I exhale slowly, allowing my reason for going to Australia to settle over me. *I, Abigail Rosiah Morgan, am going to Hyacinth Cottage because I want to know Gran's full story, not just the Jell-O she fed me since I was fifteen. Instead of digging online and in books for all the answers, I'm going to experience the research firsthand. Live boldly.*

I know I'm meant to be here. God opened all the doors. First with the tickets and then with talking to Mr. Romano. When my boss heard that I was debating going on a book tour with Aunt Vi, he practically shoved me out the door, reassuring me that the job would be waiting for me. I pray that my nightmare doesn't become reality and Kasey gets my job.

Okay, time to get my mind off all the unknowns and "what if" fears. I eye my new tote, a birthday gift from Luke and Stefi, where an envelope from Donald Jenkins II resides.

Once Aunt Vi and I made the flight official, I visited the lawyer's office. Mr. Jenkins gave me a packet and strict instructions to not open it until I reached Australia. But I am on a plane. No backing out. No escape plan.

Not knowing what's in this envelope made security checkpoints nerve-racking. I tried to catch a glimpse when my bag went through the X-ray machine, but no such luck. Part of me hoped they'd tell me to go home.

I glance at my aunt, but she's been sucked into her favorite book. Time to think things through.

Step 1: Get packet.

Step 2: Find out what's in the packet.

Step 3: Pass out until we've reached Hyacinth Cottage.

Setting my book aside, I manage to reach my tote without throwing up. With shaking hands, I unzip it, running my fingers over Gran's shawl. I'd chosen to pack it there rather than in my suitcase because to lose it would be unbearable, maybe even worse than the plane going down. After a dip in altitude, Scripture quotations, ring twists, and numerous deep breaths, I take out the packet from Mr. Jenkins.

The theater of my mind is blank. I truly have no idea what's inside this thing.

I unwind the thread holding the envelope closed. Inside rests another official letter from Jenkins & Garmen and an envelope with my name written on it in Gran's cursive. I skim the official document. The contract, which was written in 1960, was between Gran and Hazel Greer for the care of Hyacinth Cottage and witnessed by the first Donald Jenkins. A good-sized payment was wired every month from an account set up to stop "in the event that Hyacinth Cottage has a new owner."

An additional clause, added in 2016, states the cottage will pass to Abigail Rosiah Morgan on September 24, 2024. New terms and an agreement would be worked out for the care of the cottage after that date. A note attached via paperclip has a Bridgeway, Australia, address. Hazel Greer has the keys to Hyacinth Cottage.

I exchange the official letter for Gran's, breaking the wax seal. There are three hyacinths on this letter instead of her name.

> *24 June 2016*
> *My Darling Abigail Rosiah,*
> *If you are reading this, then I am HOME.*

My eyes cloud, and it takes a moment to regain my composure.

Aunt Vi squeezes my arm, letting me know she's close, before flipping a page in her book.

> *My Darling Abigail Rosiah,*
> *If you are reading this, then I am HOME. I longed to return to Hyacinth Cottage. But God wanted me with Him, and I can't say that I mind.*
> *The image of you in the shawl will forever be etched in my memory—you were breathtaking. Forgive my abruptness and leaving you without answers. Every one of my prayers was answered today. I'd long wrestled with who to share the cottage, the shawl, and my story, especially since your mother wanted*

nothing to do with my past. Then, there you were, wearing the answer.

Hyacinth Cottage was meant to be yours.

The journey to the cottage might have begun with fear, but it became so much more than that. Good and bad, the moments shaped my life. I learned about sacrifice, friendship, and true love. We gave up everything yet gained the world. It's hard to imagine life before secrets became a way of life. None of us knew what it truly meant. Our time at the cottage ended too soon. But I know you are the one to continue the story. Darling Abigail Rosiah, this is my gift to you.

We arranged for the cottage to be taken care of until you are ready. Hazel has been a faithful caretaker. Friendship with Hazel was an unexpected blessing. We were apprehensive of letting anyone know where we were, of letting anyone in. But Hazel became family—three women became one, inseparable. I didn't know much about domestic life. But Hazel helped us find our footing in the new life we'd been forced into. I long for even a fraction of her wisdom and strength. Real friendship is a gift, and I pray that you have found someone to guard your heart and keep your secrets.

Make sure you ask Hazel about our failures in the kitchen, which resulted in the patch on the shawl. I'm sure she can share other stories as well. Especially about the cottage's secrets. And about the care Roy put into the gardens.

We longed for Hazel to come with us to America. Pleaded. But in the end, she stayed to guard the cottage, which I am eternally grateful for.

As I write this, I pray that God uses my story to grow and stretch you. Loved getting to create stories with you. Remember every piece of art has a story ready to be heard. Be open to hearing. Accept that God has a plan even in the waiting.

I know you will do amazing things. I wish I were there with you to walk through the cottage doors. Can't complain about my new Home—surely, I'm lying in a field of wildflowers as you read this, listening to my Savior's voice.

Ask your questions. Listen to the answers. Embrace fullness of life.

There's a lot to unpack in that letter. Seeing me in the shawl. Secrets and treasures. Roy in the gardens. Gran a failure in the kitchen? She was an amazing cook and baker. Three women became inseparable. Gran. Hazel. Laurel.

What must it be like? To have someone to tell all your secrets to and not have them run away screaming or telling you, "You don't struggle. You're perfect."

What even is true friendship? Another pastor's daughter curse has me programmed not to get close to one particular person and to never play favorites. After my parents received a phone call from a church member saying I wasn't hanging out with their daughter because I was spending too much time with another girl, I've stayed back. Built a wall of sorts.

I've never had someone choose me. Never had anyone call me their best friend. Some days I feel that's more unattainable than having a boyfriend.

A bosom buddy.

A soul sister.

Jo and Laurie had that in *Little Women*. I cry the hardest when Laurie introduces Amy as his wife to Jo. Not because he should have married Jo—they were definitely better as best friends—but because they lost their special closeness. It wouldn't be the same. It couldn't, not with a wife in the mix.

I know that feeling of loss, even of something I've never had.

A tear hits my lip, and I lick it away. The altitude must be getting to me. I refold Gran's letter and return the manila envelope to my tote. Grabbing *Howl's Moving Castle*, I flip to where I left off, allowing Howl's and Sophie's quest to break their curses distract me from mine.

❧❀❧

We have officially landed at Brisbane Airport. Cue the "Hallelujah Chorus." Even though I feel like a flying expert now that I've spent more than twenty-four hours in the air and flown on two planes, if I'm forced to board another plane before we're scheduled to be in New Zealand, it'll be too soon.

While we wait for our suitcases—which in a nondescript luggage sea, neon pink will be easy to spot—I send a quick text to my parents and brothers. My parents gifted me an international SIM card with the caveat that I send lots of pictures and, as per Mom, give updates on Aunt

Vi. "Abigail, you need to be the adult. Make sure your aunt doesn't get arrested."

My phone vibrates with a reply.

JAXON: *Welcome to my side of the world. Proud of you for getting on a plane. Love ya.*
ME: *Love you.*

Two checkpoints for luggage, declarations, and a random drug check for Aunt Vi—because, of course, she'd be singled out to be sniffed by a dog—and I can see the exit path. Movies make leaving the airport look effortless, but Customs in Australia is super strict. I'm glad I knew what was in that envelope and that we didn't have food to claim.

We walk through glass sliding doors into a big open area crowded with people. Some hold signs welcoming family home, others hold clasped hands to their faces as their gaze skims past us in search of loved ones. With a squeal and a sleep-crazed wave, the college-aged girl who'd been walking near us runs into the arms of a couple I assume to be her parents, suitcase lurching behind her. It's beautiful and heart-wrenching all at once as I'm reminded again how far I am from my own family.

"Lisa said a car is waiting for us," Aunt Vi tells me, scanning the crowd.

I could kiss her personal assistant for taking away the hassle of finding a car to rent. Having someone familiar with the landscape is way less stressful than trusting my aunt to get us to Bridgeway. My aunt tends to get lost even in places she's been to before. Her GPS is possessed and has a mind of its own. Taking the "scenic route" is being kind, but Aunt Vi always discovers a hidden treasure for her wandering.

It doesn't take us long to spot VIOLET MORGAN written on a sign held by an older gentleman in a suit.

"Welcome to Australia," he says.

"He needs to keep talking," Aunt Vi whispers, so he can hear.

His lips twitch as he offers to take our bags. I hold my tote close but allow him to take my suitcase. We follow him down an escalator only to be met with a wall of heat when the doors open to outside. As my flip-flops touch non-airport, Australian soil—albeit sun-kissed pavement—I grin. If it wasn't weird, and the danger of being trampled wasn't a possibility, I totally would have kissed the ground.

"Feel that sunshine. Soak it in." Aunt Vi sighs, her face to the sky. "Winter doesn't get much better than this."

I inhale deeply, relishing the fact that my lungs aren't in danger of freezing. It was cold and rainy when we left JFK. Australia is the complete opposite. Not only are we in reverse seasons, we're in the future. I'm standing in October while America is still in September. It'll probably be snowing when we get back. Weather shock is going to be harder than jet lag.

The driver leads us to a black BMW. I'm not sure what year, but the sleek vehicle looks like it just drove off the lot. The brothers would be drooling.

He pops the trunk. "Lisa sent you coffee supplies. She said you didn't want to leave anything to chance when it came to your caffeine intake."

"God, thank you for Lisa. She gets me." I can tell Aunt Vi wants to hug the driver, but she resists, sliding into the back seat. I follow, keeping my tote on my lap.

The front right-side door opens, and the driver settles behind the wheel. Even though I'd been prepared for it, I'm still caught off guard. I'd read a blog post on the plane called "Things You Won't Find in Australia." The steering wheel is on the right, and they drive on the left side of the road. You also won't find Walmart or liquid cheese, and outlets are called power points.

"It's an hour's drive to Bridgeway, give or take traffic," the driver says once we're settled.

Lisa wanted to put us up in a hotel, seeing as the first book event is at a manor just outside Brisbane, but Aunt Vi is graciously heading straight to the cottage. I can't wait two days to see Hyacinth Cottage.

I retrieve the note from Mr. Jenkins and hand it to the driver. "This is the address I was given. Hazel Greer has the keys to the cottage, so we'll need to go here first."

As soon as we're on the main road, Aunt Vi leans forward and begins asking the driver questions, fulfilling her wish to keep him talking. By the time we reach the cottage, he'll probably give her the spare key to his house and an open invitation to come for Christmas.

I stare out the window, taking it all in.

I'm almost there, Gran.

A speed limit sign whips by, terrifying me. "Holy moly! Did that say ninety?"

"Kilometers per hour, not miles per hour." Aunt Vi's words calm my heart, but I'm too tired to do the conversion. She helps me out. "If I mathed correctly, we're going around fifty-five miles per hour. But you know me and math. We don't have a relationship."

My heart rate slowly settles as I enjoy every new sight. Trees. Flowers. Road signs with kangaroos. My eyes grow heavy.

I must have dozed because when someone shakes my arm, I whack my forehead against the window. Using a napkin, I remove the evidence of drool.

"We're here." Aunt Vi shimmies her shoulders as she exits the car.

I step out and slip my tote over my shoulder, eyeing the sign that reads GREER HOTEL.

White building with trim. Green roof. Wraparound porch. Lots of windows. People eating at tables on the deck. Laughter as well as bird calls permeating the air.

A menu board outside the door lists the specials. Chicken parmi. Crumbled Camembert served with cranberry dip. Prawn twisters served with sweet chili sauce. 250G Rump. Now that we've landed, my stomach alerts me to its unfed state.

The door opens as I'm reaching for it.

A handsome, muscular guy with short, curly dark hair and brown eyes steps through. He's mid-sentence. "You have to see this car." He's followed by another guy. They both head toward the BMW without noticing me or Aunt Vi.

Smile in place, I enter a world of heavenly smells, music, and energized charm. I don't know what to look at first, so I scan the restaurant like I'm watching a Ping-Pong match.

"Chicken schnitzel with avo and hollandaise," a waitress says as she puts a plate on the table in front of a customer we pass.

"What in the world is avo?" Aunt Vi's eyes widen. "I'm gonna investigate." She takes off after the waitress.

I debate waiting for her to return before asking for Hazel, but a dark-haired young woman behind the counter waves me forward. "Welcome to Greer's."

"Hi. I'm looking for Hazel Greer."

"That's my great-aunt. She's away from Bridgeway for a couple days." She holds her hand out. "I'm Jess. Are you the new owner of Hyacinth Cottage? Abigail Morgan?" She squeals when I nod. "You're here. We've been waiting and waiting. I can take you up to the cottage." She studies my tote. "Is that all the luggage you brought?" If I translated her wide-eyed expression correctly, she's equally impressed and horrified.

"We have suitcases, but they're still in the car." I motion over my shoulder.

"We? Are you traveling with a boyfriend?"

"Oh, no boyfriend." I laugh. "I'm here with my aunt."

Jess's eyes light up. "Violet Morgan? I was hoping I'd get to meet her. I've never met anyone famous before."

Aunt Vi scurries toward me, barely missing a tray full of drinks. "So, avo is short for avocado. I should have guessed. Oh, and we'll definitely have to try the chicken schnitzel burger." She chuckles. "That word is so fun. Schnitzel."

"That sounds good," I say then make introductions. "Aunt Vi, this is Jess. Hazel is her great-aunt. Hazel's away, but Jess said she'll take us to the cottage."

A glow worthy of hero worship takes over Jess's face as she studies my aunt. "Best day ever. I'll have my brother tell your driver to bring the car around. I want to take you up the path."

Jess steps from behind the counter and wraps her arms around me in a tight embrace.

My gut reaction is to pull away, but then I settle against her when she says, "I'm so happy you're here. We're going to be the best of friends."

HYACINTH

Origin story: eastern shores of the Mediterranean. Hyacinths are the fragrantly beautiful cousin of the asparagus. In the Victorian flower language, the hyacinth symbolizes sport or play. Heralds of warmer weather. Renewal, growth, and sincerity. Medicinal properties include alleviating coughing, easing digestive issues (could've used that after trying the food-that-must-not-be-named), and even a natural diuretic.

—Abigail's Notebook of Silly Placards

Chapter Six

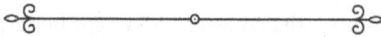

H ello, my lovelies," Aunt Vi says in a singsong voice. She's doing one of her live "Real Reel" videos on her phone as we walk. "As most of you know, I am in Australia. I'll be doing book-related events near Brisbane then heading to New Zealand to do more book events and, hopefully, cross more off my bucket list. I've been in Australia for three hours. I was gonna wait until I was rested, but you have to see this. Just look at those trees. My favorite color."

She pans the jacaranda trees, as Jess called them. They're worthy of being filmed and would be perfect for a romantasy photo shoot. Maybe Aunt Vi's Legolas sighting will happen before New Zealand. The path is hemmed on either side by the purple blossom-filled trees. And the ground beneath them? I can't help the wistful sighs flowing from me at the sight of the purple carpet. I expect the fragrance of lilacs, but they don't have a smell.

"We made a new friend. Say hello." Aunt Vi motions Jess into the frame. I book it up the path.

Jess obeys. "I'm Jessie Greer. My family owns the Greer Hotel."

"Don't you love that accent?" Aunt Vi coos. "And for my fellow Americans, Greer's is not a sleeping place like we'd call a hotel, but it's in fact a restaurant. And holy wow, I can't wait to try all the food."

Finished with saying hi, Jess catches up to me, linking her arm through mine. "You aren't going to say hi to all the fans?" She squeals quietly. "I bet there are thousands."

"Aunt Vi knows I'm camera terrified. At least when it comes to live videos. If I have a script, I'm a little better."

"I want to be an actress someday. I'd love to be in front of a camera."

"You'd be good at it." She certainly has the model looks and a vivacious personality.

"Stay tuned for mayhem and shenanigans. You ready, Australia?" Aunt Vi ends her live feed and reaches my side as the cottage comes into view. The backyard is an explosion of flowers that clearly have a "no boundaries" approach to gardening. And the cottage...

On the plane, we'd created our version of what the cottage would look like since the Google Earth shot angle was terrible. Was the cottage hidden on purpose? I chose to be optimistic while Aunt Vi imagined a leaky, saggy roof, creaky stairs, weeds choking the door, the stench of rotting animals—maggots and vultures circling—and a ghost named Hyacinth living in the attic.

While the perfect setting for a Faith Mackenzie novel, I'm glad my version is closer to the truth. The air is scented with Gran. Earthy. Spicy. Sweet. Hyacinths. The cottage and how it's situated among bushes and flowers is reminiscent of a Thomas Kinkade painting. It reminds me of the one that will forever hang in the ladies' bathroom at church. Even though the bathroom was updated, the painting remained.

"Why didn't Gran tell me about this?" I whisper to no one in particular. "If I'd known about the cottage, I would have asked to visit with her." *Maybe.* Guess we'll never know if I could've actually followed through with the travel even a year ago.

Aunt Vi wraps her arm around my waist. "We all have secrets. Sometimes, it's hard to share them, even with people we love the most."

"I wish Gran had been like you, open and honest."

Aunt Vi takes a sharp intake of breath, squeezing me a little tighter.

I wonder at her lack of response as Jess takes off a necklace with a skeletal key hanging from it. My inner antiquer begins happy dancing. This is the perfect way to unlock Gran's story.

The door swings in on well-oiled hinges. The kitchen has an open shelving layout, and a huge oak table with six chairs takes up most of the dining area. A bouquet of wildflowers sits in the center of the table. Given that no one lives here, it's bright, clean, and airy. Everything is polished timber: the floors, the beams, the twisty staircase leading to the second floor.

I close my eyes, imagining Gran standing here. Laughter. Tears. Friendship. Love. Music. Dancing. Good food. Dessert. Everything that should belong in a place like this.

"Isn't it great?" Jess says. "Someday, I'll own a house like this. Anything bigger would be too much."

"The bigger it is, the more there is to clean," Aunt Vi responds. "Which is why I don't have a house, although I've thought about buying one of those tiny homes. They're so cute."

"You could probably afford to pay someone to clean a huge house." Jess smiles as she ushers us inside. "My brother and I helped prepare the cottage for you. It's been nice to have spending money every month. I don't make much at Greer's." She pauses, her face scrunching. "Oh, any chance you'd still pay us to clean?"

I look to Aunt Vi. "I'm sure we can work out something to keep you on as caretaker. The lawyer mentioned making a new contract. Since I'm not planning on moving here, the cottage will definitely need looking after."

"What if you could move here?" Aunt Vi wiggles her brows.

"Not gonna happen."

"How long will you be staying?" Jess asks.

"We leave for New Zealand October 21," I say. *Three weeks at Hyacinth Cottage. Three weeks to figure out Gran's story.*

Someone knocks on the front door.

"That's probably Carl," Aunt Vi says. It hadn't taken her long to be on first-name basis with our driver. "I'll grab the suitcases."

"Come, I want to show you my favorite room. It's so big." Jess takes my hand and leads me up the stairs and down a hallway.

The room at the end is light and spacious. Wallpaper decorated with tiny blue flowers provides a backdrop to the full-sized bed and dresser occupying the space as well as a desk that's settled under a window overlooking the backyard and the jacaranda trees.

"My aunt will love this room." I touch the desk. *Did Gran sit here and write letters?*

"You don't want this one? Aren't you the owner?" Jess's brows lift.

"Aunt Vi stays up late writing, so having a desk, not to mention a view that screams inspiration, is a must. She needs this room."

"You are way too sweet. I don't think it's wrong to want the best."

"Is there another bedroom up here?"

"Yeah, but it's barely bigger than a closet. They should've widened it when they did renovations in the 1970s. At least they added indoor plumbing. Would have been nice to add more than one bathroom though." She motions down the hall.

This bedroom is half the size of the other, but it's perfect for me. I set my tote on the comforter decorated with hyacinths that covers a full-sized bed. There's only one window, which is round and up high, so not much of a view, but the rightness of being here, of choosing this room, brings me peace.

Was this Gran's room or Laurel's?

Aunt Vi is setting up her coffee station by the time Jess and I return downstairs. Three mugs rest on the counter beside a variety of bagged coffee grounds and a new coffee maker.

"Well, I need to head back to Greer's. I left the key on the kitchen bench for you," Jess says.

I file away the Australian word for counter.

She catches me by surprise again, wrapping her arms around me in a tight hug. "I'll see you soon. I'm so glad you're here." She doesn't wait for my response as she scampers out the back door.

"Quite the welcome," Aunt Vi says. "And this cottage is perfect."

"The room with the desk is yours. It overlooks the garden, figured you'd like the view."

"Don't ever let anyone tell you you're not the best." She arranges her coffee mugs on the shelf, sayings and pictures facing out. My aunt never goes anywhere without her mugs. They were protected in her carry-on, always within reach as Gran's shawl had been for me.

"I'm going to go explore." Time to put my Indiana Abbie nickname to work. Fueled by adrenaline, I wander the first floor. Besides the kitchen and dining area, there's a bathroom and a living room with a couch and two comfy chairs. No dust in sight. Not even behind picture frames. Yes, I checked. The Greers definitely can keep cleaning if it means I don't have to.

My search ends at a closed door right underneath the bedroom I chose. The door's creak startles me, but when I peer inside and spot the book-filled shelves on either side of a boarded-up stone fireplace, my excitement returns. I imagine Gran reading in the chair by the window. She loved a good book. Although, as far as I know, she never read one of Aunt

Vi's even though she bought them all to show her support. Gran couldn't stomach the crime or supernatural occurrences.

When I pull a book at random from the shelf, a cloud of dust follows close behind. I sneeze then raise my eyebrows. Were the Greers instructed not to enter this room?

The same dustiness ensues with the next book I remove. My heart flutters at the possibility that a secret could actually be hidden in here if this room was neglected by a rag all these years. Was Gran the last person in here?

I try every book, tilting them just enough in case it hides a secret. When no walls open, I check the books for inscriptions. Some have Laurel written in the front, while others have Rose. As much as I want to pull everything fully off the shelf, my eyelids are growing heavy. I should rest, or I'm going to be a mess at tomorrow's book event.

Retrieving my suitcase, I head up the stairs to my chosen bedroom and plop on the bed. My gaze roams until it lands on a painting of a cemetery. But instead of offering the sadness of loss, it evokes feelings of hope. Bright colors. Grass so green it sparkles. Crystalline water in the background. The mausoleum in the center reminds me of Queen Victoria's at Frogmore House and Gardens. But it's definitely not the former queen of England's final resting place.

Dragging myself off the bed, I move closer and search for the artist's name, finding it scrawled in the bottom right-hand corner.

Rose.

Gran painted this? Is this a clue to her story?

After snapping a picture of the painting with my phone, I do a reverse image search. An exact image pops up—a photograph of the Royal Brisbane Cemetery. I click on the link. It's not a cemetery in Brisbane as I'd assumed but rather located on an island called Northargyle.

Northargyle?

I type *Northargyle* in the search bar. Lots of hits. Sweaters and socks with the argyle pattern. An ad for a movie—*Argylle* spelled with two Ls. A town in New York with a space between *North* and *Argyle*. I scroll down a bit until I find a Wikipedia page for the Kingdom of Northargyle. All one word. Only one L.

Northargyle was established in 1843. The island is east of Australia and north of New Zealand and is ruled by a king. Charles Brisbane was given the throne by none other than Queen Victoria as a reward for saving her life. The current ruler is King Hamish I, a descendant of the first king of Northargyle.

Hamish, a handsome and kind king, takes one look at Abigail Morgan and whisks her away to his palace. She is so different than any woman he has ever met and will be the perfect queen because, after all, she is a church princess and can totally handle the pressures of the title.

I laugh at the super unrealistic scenario. That's what they get for not having a picture of King Hamish or even his age. License for my mind theater to put on a production of impossibility. The info reads like an elementary student's assignment. A student who'd rather be doing anything but schoolwork.

Two pictures of the tropical landscape, airbrushed in their perfection, catch my attention.

A gasp escapes when I see the map of the country. I take Gran's shawl from my tote and hold it next to my phone. The diamond shapes on the shawl have the same jagged edges.

"Were you from Northargyle?" I study the similarity between the shawl and map. Have I solved one mystery?

"Did you say Northargyle?" Aunt Vi steps into the room. "I thought she made it up."

"Who made it up?"

"Angie Thorne." Aunt Vi shudders as she says the name of her college roommate turned literary nemesis. Angie is also a bestselling author. Of romance.

"I thought she was from New Zealand?" During my research for *Inside the Oath*, Angie Thorne's name had come up under "famous people of New Zealand."

"That's what she tells the world. But back in college, she went on and on about living on a small island and eating dinner at the palace."

"It's a real place." I turn the phone so she can see. "Not that this site lends to its credibility. It's as mysterious as Gran, like it doesn't want to be found." I point out the shape of the country that's the same pattern on Gran's shawl then scroll through my pictures to find the one of the painting that had Gran longing for home.

Were Gran and Margaret Weston both from Northargyle?

Chapter Seven

M y brain would not shut off last night with all the new information, but I couldn't stay at the cottage when Aunt Vi pretty much begged me to come with her to the book event. I'd always planned on going, of course, but something in her worried comments of "what if no one shows up" had me scurrying to join her.

The car stops, and Carl announces that we've arrived at Sugarleaf Manor. I'm glad I came if only to experience more of the Australian culture.

When one says the word *manor* to an American, certain criteria must be met for the word to be applied. Mossy stone walls rising amid a grove of trees. Gothic windows. A gargoyle or five. Lights refracting off turrets. Crows sitting on magnificently spiked gates eyeing all who dare trespass.

Australian manors, not so much, although I do spot some crows about and hear the unmistakable caw of several more. The country is young, and gothic manors with their horrors and delights are nonexistent. In its place is a cheery yellow, two-story, very *Gone with the Wind* southern-style structure. It brings to mind sweeping gowns and men in uniform confessing their undying love before going off to battle.

With trepidation, she takes up her skirts, and with one foot in front of the other, she ascends the stone stairs to the front door. What secrets await, longing to be uncovered? Will she be accepted or forced to leave?

"This is splendid." Aunt Vi pans the manor with her phone.

"How perfect is it?" Lisa coos.

"You already know the answer to that."

Leaving my aunt and her assistant to chat about the perfectness of the event location, I move up the stairs. History pulses through my fingers as I run my hand along the stone.

The entry hall is a wide-open concept and smells of eucalyptus. A ginormous glistening chandelier dangles above me, and on a table to the left, there's a stack of brochures. I flip through the glossy pages, discovering the history of the manor. It was built in 1889 by Thomas Smith and was a family home until 1944. Much like the Westonia. A colorful map that includes a notation for a library rests on the last page. You can tell a lot about a place by what books are or aren't in a library.

"Yikes! I'm huge," Aunt Vi exclaims.

I turn, spotting a banner of her face positioned on the other side of the entry. It's a hair down, professional picture. Serious. So unlike my aunt who, at the moment, has her hair in a high ponytail, red sequined Converse on her feet, and black dagger earrings stabbed through her lobes just waiting to be pulled free by the next King Arthur.

"Welcome. You must be Violet Morgan." A woman in a blue power suit holds out her hand to me. A headset rests in her perfectly coiffed graying hair. Her accent is as French as her manicured nails.

Aunt Vi raises her hand. "Actually, I'm Violet. Vi to my family and friends."

The woman doesn't crack a smile, but her dark eyes do narrow. She looks between us, dropping her outstretched hand like she doesn't want to touch my aunt. She resembles a stoically focused palace guard.

I, on the other hand, bite back a smile as the "challenge accepted" look enters my aunt's eyes. She will make this woman like her by the end of the night. I've seen a hundred percent success rate in that area.

The seriousness of my aunt's writing doesn't match people's perception of what she's like in real life. Her avid followers know what to expect, especially if they follow her "Real Reels." Her books are full of quirk, but also quite a bit of blood.

Aunt Vi puts a hand on my arm. "This is my niece, Abigail."

"Glenna." The woman's glance to me is more acknowledged. My navy polka dot dress and tan heels are clearly what my aunt should have chosen as her attire instead of khaki capris and a black blouse.

Glenna peruses her clipboard. "If you'll both follow me."

She leads us down a hallway lined with the coolest stained glass I've ever seen. The top and bottom are solid colors and in between, with a gray background, are birds, trees, and different Australian animals.

Aunt Vi snaps a selfie with a kangaroo. I resist the urge to pull my phone out of my clutch and take one with a koala. Wait, I'm supposed to be sending pictures home. I pose with a koala and an emu then candidly capture Aunt Vi in the hallway, giving it the caption OFF TO THE BOOK SIGNING.

Glenna quirks an eyebrow but keeps her mouth shut. Pictures done and sent to my family, we proceed into the event room. Banners of all Aunt Vi's published novels line the wall like flags. A cardboard cutout of the actress who played Faith Mackenzie—who, I'll admit, sort of looks like me—stands beside a cutout of her partner Detective Leonard Irby. Unlike most duos, there never will be a romance arc even though the sparks fly. Faith is young and fiery. Leonard, thirty years her senior, is a curmudgeon who is oddly likable and relatable in his reaction to life. Their banter is my favorite part. They both lack filters.

A small platform has been positioned in one corner, and at least ten rows of chairs face it. Soft, classical music plays from the speakers offering a spa ambience.

"That's a lot of chairs," Aunt Vi says, not bringing up the music as I'd expected.

"There are more in the back," Glenna responds without looking up from her clipboard. "I will have the staff bring them out as needed."

"Wouldn't that be nice, but that's probably more than enough." Aunt Vi gasps. "A Sean Connery board!"

"Charcuterie," I mumble, shaking my head.

"I can never remember that word." She waves a hand in the air. "It's such a disservice to people everywhere that no one has made a Sean Connery charcuterie board."

"Ha! You do know that word."

Aunt Vi winks as she heads toward the platform with Glenna. I never know if my aunt does forget things or just enjoys being weird and hopes people think she's lost it. One need only consider the plotlines she concocts to know her memory capacity is gigantic. Or maybe that's the reason "normal" things are forgotten.

While Glenna and Aunt Vi chat, I do reconnaissance of the food table. Forget the charcuterie board. The table is an oasis overflowing with cheeses, meats, crackers, fruits, cakes, and other desserts. It reminds me of Gran's shawl in a way. I'd thought about wearing it tonight but didn't want to draw attention to myself. But if I'd stayed by the food, no one would have known I was here.

"The reading will begin at seven followed by a period of Q&A. Doors open at six thirty. Guests are welcome to refreshments and pretzels at any time, as you requested." Glenna motions to bowls with bags of pretzels on a table with Faith and Leonard merch, her lip curling.

It's not like my aunt asked for live animals. Food, especially pretzels, are a Violet Morgan staple. Mouths full equals less hangry heckling. It's nearly impossible to talk when you're eating pretzels.

"Can I load up now?" When Glenna nods, Aunt Vi grabs a plate and napkin.

I share a smile, which Glenna doesn't return as she focuses once more on her clipboard. She talks into her headset like her job depends on it. I'm not sure who's on the other end, since I haven't seen anyone else. For all I know, it's not even hooked up. Maybe she's writing a memoir, a speech-to-text deal. I'd definitely read the chapter on her impression of meeting the famous Violet Morgan.

At six thirty, the room is filled, as I knew it would be. A staff member appears with extra chairs, and I follow him on his return trip to a back room and help him lug out more. We end up adding an additional five rows. It's a good thing Aunt Vi ate before because the charcuterie oasis is reminiscent of a wasteland, well-picked over by a herd of locusts.

I find a place to the left of the stage, near the exit, leaving the chairs for those who aren't going home with Violet Morgan. Promptly at seven, Glenna moves to the mic and introduces my aunt to the crowd.

I've heard Aunt Vi's intro so many times. She holds the room in the palm of her hand with her antics and sparkling personality. I try to picture myself up there, making the crowd laugh and cheer, but it's never going to be part of my story. If only I had an ounce of her confidence, I wouldn't need to remind myself to live boldly.

Scanning the room's occupants, thrilling at their delight, my attention lands on a tall man probably in his late twenties, with mussed brown hair and a gray sweater standing in the opposite corner. At least fifty people sit between us, but I catch his eye from across the room. I don't usually care for facial hair, having grown up with a family of clean-shaven men, but this guy with the goatee is incredibly good-looking. He has what Aunt Vi dubbed "resting smirk face."

When he quirks an eyebrow, I flush and break eye contact. It's like Wizard Howl has stepped off the pages, straight from his moving castle. Dark and mysterious yet charming. Quirky. Endearing. A touch magical.

Several heartbeats later, I search the spot. He's still standing there but is now looking at Aunt Vi. She begins reading from her latest release, *Inside the Oath*. The excerpt is intense, the writing masterful, but I find myself opening the manor brochure to the map. Not that I don't love hearing my aunt read, but I'm in need of a turn about the room—well, more of a turn *out* of the room.

Glancing up from the brochure, I catch the guy watching me. He tilts his head as if guessing my desire to leave. Why must my hands shake so? I count my breaths. When I reach forty-two, I begin backing out of the room.

Once in the stained glass-framed hallway, I set my course for the library. They should've held the reading in here, even though it wouldn't have seated everyone comfortably. A rolling ladder straight from *Beauty and the Beast* is attached to the back shelves. One moment I'm at the library door, the next, I've placed one foot on the bottom rung.

Do I dare?

In my mind, I'm gutsy like Jo March. Daring like Mulan. Witty like Elizabeth Bennet. Passionate like Anne Shirley. Capable like Sophie Hatter.

The real me is an Ichabod Crane.

I plant both feet on the ground, resisting the urge only because a colorful painting entraps me, luring me away from the ladder. It's like every color was used. Normally, I wouldn't stare at a snake, but this one is gorgeous. Under the painting is a fat stone frog with a loopy grin.

"Tell me your story," I say, bending so I'm eye level with the frog.

Should she kiss the frog? Was the old woman lying when she spoke of the wrongfully cursed prince? Weren't curses meant for those who needed to learn a lesson? Abigail had rescued the old woman, helping her carry her water jugs up a steep hill, and was rewarded with the location of the frog. But could she—should she—trust the stranger's story? What if this wasn't the right frog? What if he transformed into an old man or even another animal? Or what if, in kissing the frog, she absorbed the curse and became a frog herself?

"Excuse me. Are you all right?" A deep Australian-accented voice startles me.

I spin to find the tall man who'd eyed me across the room. "Um, uh..." All words fly from my brain as his lively, light brown eyes twinkle. His grin is playfully magnetic, and a hundred percent amused.

Have you ever seen someone and instantly felt drawn in, desperately wanting to know them, to be part of their life? You know they'd be fun to spend the day with. Flying kites, skipping rocks, playing Twister, resting on a checkered blanket with a basket filled with all the proper picnic foods. That exact feeling washes over me.

I clear my throat. "Yes, I'm good."

"Actually, I was talking to Tiddalick." He points at the frog as he steps farther into the library. "Poor thing, being woman-handled and asked to reveal secrets without a proper introduction." He *tsks*.

"Tiddalick?"

"It is a fun name. I'll grant you that."

I bite my lip, trying to keep my smile hidden. I fail, so I turn toward the frog. My humor rising. Something about this man is disarming, calming. I take advantage of my body's stillness to play along, channeling Aunt Vi.

"Forgive me, Sir Tiddalick." I enact a perfect curtsy. *Thank you for the lessons, Gran.* "My name is Abigail Morgan."

"Morgan?" I freeze as the stranger repeats my last name.

Has he actually heard of my family? I thought I'd be safe. But even in Australia I can't get out from under the shadow of my family's reputation.

The guy releases a dramatic sigh. "That's a relief and also rather disappointing."

I deep dive for the courage to face him. "Why's that?"

"At first, I thought you were on staff. You were helping set up chairs when I arrived. But then you were lurking and slipped out of the room. I decided you must be a spy." He quirks an eyebrow. "I thought that if I were to apprehend you, maybe I'd be rewarded with an introduction to Violet Morgan."

"You were watching me?" I wait to be freaked out that a stranger saw me setting up chairs and sneaking away as soon as my aunt started reading. Instead, I'm charmed and eager for his response.

"You were pretty hard to miss." His smile deepens, skin crinkling around his eyes.

Knees, I did not give you permission to get gooey. Don't fail me. Hold me up!

"So, Miss Morgan—"

"Abigail," I correct.

"Abigail." Him saying my name is my new favorite thing. I wish I could record it and have it stick on replay. I stop myself from saying my middle name just to hear how it sounds on his lips. "What is your relationship to Violet Morgan?"

"She's my aunt."

"Ah! The famed niece that inspired detective Faith Mackenzie?"

"I'm nothing like Faith." He must really be a fan if he saw that interview.

He tilts his head, studying me like he doesn't believe me.

I rush on. "I mean, I am a pastor's daughter. But I'm definitely not bold and adventurous, even though they call me Indiana Abbie."

My laugh is tinged with something more giddy than nervous. "I live a very boring life. Adventure always happens to other people. Coming to Australia is the most exciting thing I've ever done. I actually got on a plane. Not that I could have traveled here any other way in so short a time."

"Are you on the book tour with your aunt?"

"Yes, but mostly because of the cottage my gran gave me." In true Abigail fashion, encouraged by the interest in his eyes, I rush on. "For my twenty-fourth birthday. I turned twenty-four on the twenty-fourth in the year twenty-four, a golden birthday. Gran told me she'd never left America, yet she was here in 1957. I have pictures to prove it. Also, I found this signed painting, which is funny because Gran didn't paint either. And if she was born in Australia, where'd her accent go?" That tidbit had taken some of my sleep last night when it hit me. "I feel like I didn't know her at all. She was a nurse who liked antiquing and dancing and baking."

"She sounds lovely," he says.

"Have you heard of Northargyle?"

"N-Northargyle?" He stutters the word, his brows rising to his hairline.

"I know, it sounds made up, or like a pair of socks. But I promise, it's a real place. Angie Thorne is from there even though she tells everyone she's from New Zealand. Apparently, she's had dinner at the palace." I make a face. "There wasn't much online about Northargyle. The Wikipedia page looked like a child had written it. My gran may have been born there, but I have no idea anymore. I'm not even sure if Christine was her real name."

He smiles. "Is your grandmother with you as well?"

I shake my head. "She passed away in March."

"I'm truly sorry to hear that. Grandmothers are special. I only had mine for six years."

"They really are. We did everything together. Well, except sports, and Gran didn't read any of Aunt Vi's books." A laugh escapes even as pressure builds behind my eyes. "We used to spend hours wandering museums and antique stores, making up stories about where things came from and what they had seen. I love stories. There's something inside me that gets so excited for the hunt. And now Gran's story. I feel like I'm doing a puzzle, and someone stole the box. Without the picture, how am I supposed to fit all the pieces together?"

He may not be giving me the "glazed doughnut" or "run for the hills" look, but I'm pretty sure I've overshared past propriety's limits. I wipe my eyes. "Goodness, I'm sorry. I blame it on the jet lag. I never talk this much. Ever. Especially to strangers." *Just stop already, Abigail. You already took home the gold medal in oversharing, no need to go for the silver and bronze.*

His lively brown eyes widen. Ah, there's the expected horrified look.

"I've been remiss and hypocritical," he says. "I never told you my name after I scolded you about demanding Tiddalick tell you his life story."

I giggle at his mock seriousness. *Giggle? Seriously? I do not want to channel flirty Lydia Bennet. At least I'm out of danger of crying with Gran memories.*

"My name is Colter."

Colter. I test it like I had Tiddalick's and like it so much better. "Nice to officially meet you, Colter."

"Likewise, Abigail. While I can't help you with your gran's story, I do know Tiddalick's." His grin is cheeky as he motions to the chairs. "Care to sit?"

A chance to listen to him speak so I won't? No question. "I'd like that."

"Tiddalick was a frog who caused a flood." As Colter settles in the chair, I catch a whiff of his scent. Sunshine with a hint of eucalyptus. Pure Australian bottled air. "He was so thirsty that he drank all the water in the land, causing a drought."

"A drought or a flood?"

"Patience, Abigail Morgan, I'm getting to that. Tiddalick drank all the water, leaving none for any of the other animals. Dying of thirst, they came together to figure out what to do, but none of them had any suggestions until the old, wise wombat suggested they make Tiddalick laugh so he would spit out the water." He shakes his head at my grossed-out noise before continuing. "They all tried. The kookaburra told silly stories, the kangaroos and emu played leapfrog. Frill-necked lizard strutted. Finally, the—" He cuts off and wiggles his brow.

"The what?" I lean forward, like one of my nieces, literally on the edge of my seat. Honestly, it's not as much fun being on this side of the story and not knowing what happens next.

"I don't know if I should give it away."

"What? You can't leave it there." I'm outraged yet laugh at the same time.

"Abigail," Aunt Vi cries in her "all hope is lost" voice.

Ready for action, I jump from the chair and hurry to the hallway. Aunt Vi stands against the wall like a cornered mouse. Her blouse is untucked, but everything else seems in order.

"You okay? What happened?"

"I sat in something and didn't bring my emergency clothes stash. I never go to any event without backups. But I was distracted and worried that no one would show up for the event. And...erg." She turns, showcasing a backside covered in—well, I'm not quite sure what. Chocolate? Berries? Coconut flakes?

Vi groans like she's dying. "I shall have to stand against the wall like Jo March, replacing my burned skirts for whatever it is I sat on."

"If I had to guess," Colter says, stepping beside me. "I'd say you sat on a lamington."

"I've been seen," Aunt Vi squeaks, twirling to hide herself.

"But like Jo and Laurie, friendship must come out of this." He sends a wink my way.

At the mention of her favorite book, Aunt Vi perks up. "You know *Little Women*?"

"Cover to cover." Before I know what's happening, Colter is removing his charcoal gray sweater. "For you, Violet Morgan. It should cover the cake."

"I can't take it." But she does. "Is this a Burberry?"

"It's from my sister. I don't know much about fashion. Sorry."

"Not like great literature."

"I'm always up to date on great literature."

"Looks like you're the hero without catching a spy," I say, indicating the sweater and the fact that Colter received his desired introduction to my aunt.

Aunt Vi puts on the sweater, rolling the sleeves that had covered her hands. Colter's height makes the sweater the perfect length for hiding all lamington evidence.

"To whom do I owe thanks for this sweater?" She bats her lashes, studying Colter. Her gaze shifts to me, approval flashing like an open sign. She's too old for him, right?

"This is Colter." I make the introduction before he can.

"I've never heard that name. Might have to add it to my next book."

"A dashing man, more handsome than any before, saves Faith Mackenzie from a group of pastry assassins bent on taking over the world one cake-tastrophe at a time." He grins, eyes sparkling like crazy.

Don't ask me to explain why I sighed.

"Not half bad," Aunt Vi mutters, the wheels of her writer brain churning. "Maybe he can be someone from her past. The one who got away."

"But you don't do romance," I barely get out. "I mean, your books aren't romances."

"Maybe it's time for Faith to find herself a man." Her eyes narrow, lasering on Colter. "And how do you know Abigail?"

"Your enchanting niece and I just met. I know we seem as if we've known each other for ages. It must be because I know Faith."

"I'm not enchanting," I say.

"Lies." Colter shakes his head.

The back of my neck heats as awkwardness creeps in.

"What shall we do with her?" He crosses his arms, his right arm holding his chin as he studies me. A tattoo on his forearm peeks out from under his partially rolled sleeve. Does that say Faith? Not likely. But...

"Do you have a Faith Mackenzie tattoo?" Aunt Vi beats me to the question. "Should I be worried or honored? I've thought about a tattoo, but needles freak me out."

Colter startles, uncrossing his arms. He tugs down his right sleeve then stops, rolling it up instead. The tattoo he reveals looks handwritten.

Faith. Service. Leadership. Romans Twelve.

The first verse of that passage scrolls through my mind. *I urge you, brothers and sisters, by the mercies of God, to present your bodies as a living and holy sacrifice, acceptable to God, which is your spiritual service of worship.*

"Sorry, not a Faith Mackenzie tattoo." Colter chuckles. "My father doesn't approve, so I usually keep it covered."

"It's beautiful," I say.

"It's from my mother's favorite Bible passage, the motto she lived by. The one I try to live by. It's in her handwriting. I got it a year after she passed."

Colter glances down the hallway, his smile dipping but not fully disappearing. I follow his gaze. A muscular man in black pants and a matching polo stands at the other end, arms crossed like a bouncer. Even from here, I don't see any laugh lines on his face, as if he's never experienced happiness or any other emotion. Maybe he's a robot.

"Well, Violet. Abigail. Looks like my friend is ready to go, and he's driving. Until next time." Colter bends low before straightening.

"Your sweater." Aunt Vi starts to unbutton it in a slow fashion, like she doesn't want to do it.

Colter holds up a hand to stop her. "What would your adoring fans do if you had to hide? Consider it yours."

He gives me one last silly grin then heads toward his friend, rolling both sleeves down as he walks. Colter clasps him on the shoulder as words pass between them. The man seems annoyed, like he's scolding Colter for running away. I strain to hear but nothing reaches my eavesdropping ears. With a glance our way, Colter offers a shrug and a nod before following the man around the corner and out of sight.

"Well, then," Aunt Vi says with a sigh, wrapping the sweater tighter around herself.

My sentiments exactly. I have no words.

Ladies and gentlemen, I just experienced a meet-cute worthy of its own chapter.

Chapter Eight

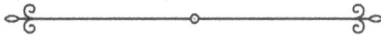

S *mile. Wince. Cringe. Smile.*
Cringe. Wince. Cringe. Cringe.
My interaction with Colter has replayed in my dreams. All. Night. Long. I've dissected the entire conversation every which way, oscillating between horror and charm. *They call me Indiana Abbie.* Had I really said that?

Maybe he didn't notice all my words. I release a breathy laugh as I sit up, scooting toward the headboard. Of course he noticed. I was the worst definition of bold. Just plain stupid. Naïve. I bet he's so glad his friend wanted to leave.

As soon as Aunt Vi and I returned to the cottage, I'd grabbed my Bible and read all of Romans 12 then did a quick social media search which failed before I finished typing Colter. He never told me his last name. Unfair. He knows mine. There's no way to stalk him. Not that I'd be obsessive about it, but he made an impression, and I want to see him again. Although, he probably has a girlfriend who wouldn't appreciate me dreaming about him. Guys like that always have a girlfriend. It's an unofficial law. A girlfriend, no doubt, who's gorgeous, tall, kind, demure, good with being in the spotlight, never oversharing to complete strangers.

Gran's shawl hangs on a hook beside the painting, looking right at home. If Gran had a problem oversharing, maybe I'd already know her story.

I rub my eyes and slip out of bed. No sense staying here marinating in my humiliation. After changing into shorts and a green tank top and sliding my feet into flip-flops, I gather my journal and phone and make my way downstairs.

Aunt Vi sits at the kitchen table, eyes closed as she sips coffee from a blood red *Murder of Mirrors* mug—her first novel in the Faith Mackenzie series. She resembles a mad scientist rocking the "electrocuted" look. I don't envy her trying to untangle her curls.

Her DONE PEOPLEING T-shirt seems appropriate for the situation. Colter's sweater is draped around the chair to her right as if lending moral support, removing every last hope that last night was a dream.

Aunt Vi's eyes pop open with jack-in-the-box quickness. She begins mumbling as her pen moves over the page faster than I can track. The ink is red this morning. Definitely a warning to steer clear. She may joke about me getting lost in research, but interrupt when she's in writing mode and you're likely to lose a finger.

Jaxon once asked a question when Aunt Vi was mutter-writing. The growl had him in tears. She yelled that she'd lost what would have won awards. Demon-possessed banshee bent on destruction had come to mind watching her. Good thing the pen she threw missed Jaxon. That one transformation had cautioned me for life.

"Childhood crush. Reunion. Funeral. Maybe if I kill him. Hmm, then I need her parents to go crazy." Aunt Vi whacks her head against the table and groans. Popping back up, she wads the notebook paper and chucks it across the room. A growing pile already exists by the corner shelf. "No, she should be the one who does that."

Choosing the gray INSERT EYE ROLL HERE mug, I fill it with coffee, adding a splash of cream and a spoonful of sugar. When Aunt Vi's ready to talk, she'll let me know. Her scribblings are interspersed with sips from her mug, which is almost empty. I jump in, refill, jump out. Thank goodness she drinks it black.

"Colter—"

I almost drop the coffeepot. Is Aunt Vi seriously contemplating adding him as a character? A love interest? My face heats. Figuring I should leave before I startle Aunt Vi by stepping incorrectly, breathing too loudly, or asking about Colter's role in her story, I head out back to mingle with the flowers.

Inhaling the fresh, non-freezing air, I settle at the small metal bistro table and open the journal Philip gave me for my birthday. He designed the cover: a tree made out of books and antiques. It's the perfect place to organize the mismatched pieces of this puzzle.

I create a list of questions that need to be answered:

- Why did Gran lie about not leaving America? Or say she was born in Ohio if she wasn't?
- Was Gran from Northargyle? Was Margaret Weston? How did they know each other?
- Why did Gran leave Hyacinth Cottage? Why did she never come back?
- Who owned Hyacinth Cottage before Gran?
- What happened to Laurel?
- Is Roy Grandpa Josiah? Or had Gran loved someone before Grandpa?
- Where did Gran get the shawl? Why did she hide it? Who is supposed to have it?

"What else didn't you tell me, Gran?" I say out loud, wanting to scream in frustration. I tap my pen on the page, eyeing the questions. So many questions.

Next, I write my to-do list, adding "make to-do list" as my first task then crossing it off as soon as I finish. There, I can honestly say I accomplished at least one thing on my list today.

- ~~Make to-do list~~
- Check deed to Hyacinth Cottage – previous owner listed?
- Find library for research
- Find a historical society
- Meet with Hazel Greer
- Find out more about Northargyle
- Find out what happened to Tiddalick

A brown and white bird lands on a tree branch at the edge of the garden. The second it opens its mouth and lets out a laugh, I recognize it as a kookaburra. Thank you, YouTube. Other birds twitter, ducking in and out of my vision. There are cicadas too. Cars in the distance. My focus is stolen by the symphony, my vision going hazy as I'm lured into creations of islands of beauty and secrets, of a handsome man with a playful smile. Without realizing it, I've doodled COLTER and ROMANS 12 all over the margin. In hearts.

Nope, not distracted at all.

I check the time on my phone and see I have an email from Libby.

Abigail,

Hope you're enjoying Australia. I wish I was there instead of here. It's supposed to frost overnight. Boo!

So, I was tidying the research room—as per Kasey's instructions—and found some of your notes. Your grandmother sounds interesting. I saw your list of questions about the connection between your grandmother and Margaret Weston. Would it be okay if I dug into Margaret and your grandmother some more? I'm so curious. Oh, and thanks for transcribing Margaret's journal. It was a big help.

Libby

I'm not sure how to respond. I want to be the one to discover the connection and solve this mystery, keep Gran and the shawl off the Brick Wall. On the other hand, Libby is a talented researcher, and she has access to the Weston side of things.

God, should I say yes?

I don't receive an audible answer, but the expected panic at sharing this isn't there, so I type a response for her to do so then hit SEND.

"Good morning, Abigail Morgan," a cheery voice calls.

I shade my eyes to see Jess making her way up the path. The sunlight adds veins of caramel to her dark hair, complementing her knee-length sunflower print dress.

"Good morning," I say when she reaches me. I start to stand, but she plops in a chair beside me and sets a basket on the table.

"I come bearing gifts. Some chocolates and other goodies." Her dark eyes sparkle. "I was going to bring it up yesterday, but I had to work, then I saw you leaving."

"My aunt had a book signing at Sugarleaf Manor."

"Oh, that's a beautiful estate. I've never been there—can't afford the dinner prices—but I know it's nice. I kinda wish I'd stopped by before you'd left so I could've tagged along. I don't ever leave Bridgeway."

"There's a book convention on the eighteenth at the Brisbane Hotel. Maybe you could join us for that. I'm sure Aunt Vi wouldn't mind, and I'd love you to come."

"That would be fantastic." Jess moves her gaze to the garden around us. "I hate that I'm twenty-six and have never done anything. The pub's great, but I want to get out of this town. Mom and Hazel never left." She releases a long breath. "Wish someone would leave me a cottage. You're so lucky to travel and not having to worry about money."

"This is the first time I've been out of the country." Unless you count the time Aunt Vi and I crossed the Rainbow Bridge into Canada. We almost ended up staying because the coin exchange machine was broken, and we didn't have any Canadian quarters to put in the turnstile. Aunt Vi ended up paying two lovely Koreans an American dollar for Canadian quarters to get out.

"Really? How old are you? Do you have a job?" Jess asks.

I laugh, feeling like I'm playing fifty questions with Aunt Vi. "I'm twenty-four. I've been working part-time at a historical society and part-time as a secretary at the church my dad pastors. But I was offered a full-time position that I'm hoping will be there when I go home."

"I don't really go to church, don't judge me. I haven't found one that will accept me." Before I can even think about how to respond graciously to that, Jess continues. "Do you have any siblings?"

"Five brothers."

"Five?" Her eyes widen. "I have one brother. He's the best, but I can't imagine having more. Are they all married?"

"Just the oldest."

"And your aunt isn't married? No kids?"

"She's not the settling-down type. She likes to say she doesn't need children because she has all of us. Along with two great-nieces and one on the way. Aunt Vi's quiver is full."

Jess swats at something unseen. "Ugh, the mozzies are out."

"Mozzies?" *Oh, mosquitos.* "That's sounds so cute."

"They're not cute. They're mean and horrible and should never have been invented." She stands, lifting the basket. "Anyway, I came to bring you this and to ask if you wanted to go into town with me. I can show you around. Introduce you to people. Show you what's fun. Not that we have too much. Please say yes."

I hesitate only a moment but surprise myself by saying yes for the second time today. Look at me go. I'd said yes to Libby researching and yes to Jess. Australia has kicked me out of my comfort zone, offering a clean slate. I'm ready to try new things and hang out with people and meet handsome strangers.

"Let me put this away and leave a note for Aunt Vi." I close my journal and lead Jess toward the house, stopping just before entering. "Just a warning: Don't talk to my aunt. She's mutter-writing and doesn't handle interruption at all." I hope Jess takes my upbeat presentation of the warning seriously.

Fortunately, Aunt Vi has vacated the table, even cleaned up the paper pile. The floor creaks above us. I pray she's broken past her writer blockage.

"Is that your aunt's? I bet she has a hundred." Jess sets the basket on the counter and takes Colter's sweater from the back of the chair, checking the tag. "Just what I thought. A Burberry. It's so soft. I bet it cost a lot."

"It belongs to a guy we met last night. He gave it to my aunt. She sat on a lamington and didn't have a change of clothes."

"Would his name happen to be Colter?" Jess returns the sweater.

"Do you know him?" I tamp down my desire to jump up and down. Maybe if she knows him, we can casually run into him.

Jess laughs. "You doodled his name all over your notebook. Someone has a crush. It's adorable."

My face heats.

"I don't know anyone by that name," Jess continues. "Not in Bridgeway. Judging by the quality of the jumper, he's probably from the cove. Posh houses, money to burn. They use and discard you. They don't mingle with us lowly people of Bridgeway."

"How close is the cove?"

"An hour's drive due east when the roads aren't flooded."

As soon as I finish scrawling a note to Aunt Vi, Jess grabs my hand and pulls me toward the front door. I barely grab my tote and hoist it onto my shoulder before we're outside.

The town isn't that far from the cottage. It's reminiscent of a Western village movie set. Colorful. Quaint. Perfect. If a cowboy stepped from an alley ready for a duel, I'd be delighted. Unless, of course, he was challenging me.

Jess has a long-legged, fast-paced walk. I keep up only because I don't want to get lost on my first foray with a new friend. Jess chats easily about clothes, the best places to shop, and the people in the town. I spot a café and make a mental note to tell Aunt Vi about it.

"Don't look," Jess whispers, linking her arm through mine. "We're being watched."

My heart stutters. Maybe it's...no, Jess said Colter's more than likely from the cove. But I did mention where I was staying. What if he decided to visit Bridgeway?

I look—well, I start to—but Jess yanks me down a side street.

"I said don't look," she giggles. "That was Ronald. He's a flirt. He keeps trying to date me. But he lives with his mum and has an even lower-paying job than I do. He wouldn't be able to maintain the lifestyle I deserve."

"I still live with my parents," I say.

"You're such a dear." Jess gives me a quick hug. "So, anything in particular you want to see?"

"Is there a historical society in Bridgeway?" I scan the buildings. "I need to do some research while I'm here."

"Research? That sounds boring." Jess laughs. "Sorry. I'm so blunt. I don't believe in holding back." There's a curl to her lip but also a spark in her eyes that I don't quite understand as she points across the street. "We have a bookstore."

Bookstore. Tiddalick! I'm already on my way to the door.

"Do you know the story of Tiddalick?" I need to know what and who made him laugh. Since Tiddalick caused a flood, I assume the animals were successful. But which animal won?

"The frog? Sure. Everyone knows Tiddalick. Well, everyone who paid attention at primary school." Jess opens the door, and I inhale deeply.

Bookstore air is a mix of magic and reality. A handful of people mill about, a couple sits close on the couch, books open but clearly not reading. Two tables are occupied. The patrons sitting at one table are on their phones, probably texting each other. A sign above their head announces that the bookstore now has free Wi-Fi.

"I've never seen it this busy," Jess whispers with giddiness. "Oh, Tim is working. I have to tell him 'told you so.'" She pulls me toward the counter.

"Jessie." A guy with a blond man bun swivels on a stool behind the counter to face us. I wait for Jess to comment, but it turns out she doesn't have to. "I was hoping you'd pop by today. You were right about adding a couch and some tables. And free Wi-Fi."

"I told you." She grins, fluttering her lashes.

"I got you a little something special as a thank you." He puts a long black velvet box on the counter.

Jess opens it to reveal a silver bracelet. "Oh, so sparkly. I'm never going to take it off." She slips it on her wrist, holding it up to admire. After a moment, she remembers I'm standing there. "Tim, this is *the* Violet Morgan's niece. You should set up a display of her books while she's in town."

Violet Morgan's niece. Pastor Morgan's daughter. Coach Morgan's daughter. Mayor Morgan's sister. Doctor Morgan's sister. I do have a name.

Tim's interest shifts from Jess. "Do you think she'd stop by, sign some copies?"

"Probably," I say with a shrug. Once again, my aunt's fame has preceded her. What would it feel like for people to get excited when they heard *my* name? I'd probably pass out if I was ever introduced as myself.

"Personal assistant to a famous author. That would be the best job," Jess muses. "Wonder if it pays well. Does your aunt have one?"

"Yes. Her name's Lisa."

"Bummer." Jess sighs. "Anyway, Abigail here wants a copy of *Tiddalick*. You have it, right?" She leans on the counter and touches the keyboard. Tim playfully slaps her hands away, taking over the typing. She rolls her eyes, slides back over the counter, and begins straightening and organizing the brochures and knickknacks she'd knocked out of place.

"By Robert Roennfeldt? Yep, one copy," Tim says, his tone bored, like I'm an inconvenience for asking. Maybe that's the real reason for less traffic in the bookstore pre-couch and Wi-Fi. "Kids' section. Over there."

Neither he nor Jess offer to take me. They keep up their conversation, laughing over something about someone they both know. I shake off the twinge of unrealistic expectations that Jess will stick close to me. I just met her. Of course, she has a life outside of me. I refuse to become one of those needy jealous friends.

The kids' area is through a doorway, pushed to the back, reminiscent of my desk in the research room. The adult section is colorful and clean. The kids' corner, in comparison, is dark and forgotten—like they want to pretend children don't exist. My nieces would join me in the hating of it. Kids should be the center of a bookstore. How will they learn the book smell if they can't find the stories themselves?

I locate the slim copy of *Tiddalick* wedged between two thick books. The top is dirty. There's nothing worse than dusty books at a new store.

Colter's voice plays in my head like a narrator as I start reading from page one, resisting the urge to flip right to the end. Colter does love this story. He'd shared it with me almost word for word. Maybe he's a teacher. He had that way about him—playful yet commanding. Engaging.

I stand in the doorway, watching unnoticed. My heart melts as he settles in a chair. The classroom is full of first graders. They all sit on a dragon carpet, eager to learn from their kind, wonderful teacher. His sleeves are rolled, showcasing strong forearms and his captivating tattoo as he lifts a picture book. "Once upon a time…"

"You find it?" Jess calls.

"Oh, yes." *Tiddalick* in hand, I make my way to the counter, backtracking when a display of colorful books catches my eye. *Northargyle?* I'd never heard of it, and now it's everywhere.

I pick up the book and realize my mistake. *Northanger Abbey* by Jane Austen. Returning it, I scan the bookstore.

"Do you have a travel section?" I ask, not seeing one.

"You just got to Bridgeway," Jess says with a laugh. "Where do you want to go?"

"Northargyle."

Is it my imagination or did the bookstore go quiet?

"You don't want to go there," Tim says, eyes widening.

"Why? What's wrong with it?" While I'm pretty sure Colter thought I'd made it up, Jess and Tim clearly know the place.

"I wouldn't wish a trip there on my worst enemy. Well, maybe my ex." Tim rolls his eyes.

Jess snorts. "Yeah, Ginny should definitely go there. She's so needy."

"Isn't that where your brother went?" a female voice says behind me. I turn toward the couple on the couch. The guy nods.

"He used to be so chatty, couldn't get him to shut up. Goes there then—bam!—doesn't say a word anymore." He shakes his head. "It's haunted."

One of the table patrons glances up from his phone. "Are they the ones with that deserted mental hospital?"

"Didn't the royal family die in a plane crash?" his table mate asks. "And the current queen jumped off a cliff?"

"I heard that the crown was stolen and whoever finds it is heir to the throne," the girl adds, her hand now gripping her boyfriend's. "But if you put it on and don't have royal blood, you die."

It's like children's church where one kid shares a prayer request then the others all suddenly have something to share, every request worse than the one before. Except these are adults. Their imaginations shouldn't be as wild. It is their imaginations, right? My heart rate accelerates.

"But the pictures are so beautiful."

I didn't realize I'd spoken out loud until Jess says, "First they lure you in, then they kill you."

"Maybe that's why Gran left," I muse to no one in particular.

"She's lucky to be alive," Tim answers.

Jess eyes him. "Her grandma is dead."

The harsh reality is like a slap. Had Gran barely escaped with her life? Is that why she'd kept her origin story a secret?

❧

Jess and I round a corner on our way back to the cottage when two cars race past, kicking up dust. I cough. Jess yells then takes off after them. Both cars stop as if listening to her. I fear she's going to lecture them, but she hugs the guy who vaults out of the red Mustang. A convertible. I've always wanted to ride in one.

Jess waves me over. "Abigail Morgan, meet my brother."

Her brother has the same dark eyes, hair, and smile. I recognize him right away. It's the guy who I held the door for at Greer's Hotel when we'd first arrived. With a car like the one he's driving, I understand his draw to the BMW.

"Well, hello. Abigail Morgan, was it? I'm Devon. That loser is Frank." He nods toward the black-haired guy exiting the blue Mustang. He punches Devon on the shoulder then gives Jess a hug.

"I hit 120," Frank says.

"I reached 140," Devon counters.

Jess catches my eye, rolling hers. I try to convert kilometers to miles per hour, once again not quite sure if I should be impressed by the speed. They'd blown past us quickly. I'm thankful no one had been on the road.

"What do you say, Abs?" Devon turns to me.

I cringe. Who gives a nickname to someone they've just met? Especially one that awful.

"Do you think I reached 140? Because I totally did."

I shrug, my face heating as they wait for my answer. Which I don't have. I grip the handles of my tote bag tighter.

"We should race, and Abs can declare a winner."

"It's Abigail," I say at the same time Jess says, "Abigail doesn't want to judge a race."

"Why not?" he asks.

Jess elbows her brother. She lifts an eyebrow, not so subtly motioning toward me. "Maybe she'd like to go for a ride."

"Do you? I'll take you for a ride," Devon says.

I eye the Mustang. "I've always wanted to ride in a convertible."

It's the right thing to say. Devon is opening the door for me, and before I know it, I'm buckled in the driver's seat…without the steering wheel. This will be an experience in itself, being on this side and not driving. Jess settles in the back, easing the fear of being alone in a vehicle with a guy that I've just met.

Frank revs his engine, and Devon reciprocates, pressing on the gas in neutral before shifting into Drive and tearing down the road. Maybe this wasn't such a good idea. But Frank turns in the opposite direction, and I'm relieved that the temptation to race has been removed. The wind whips my hair, and I can't stop the huge smile. I'm in a convertible in Australia. How's that for living boldly?

I'm someone special. Cruising down the road as if I own the car. The handsome man next to me thinks the world of me and will confess his undying love—

"So, you own Hyacinth Cottage now?" Devon asks as he turns down a narrow road.

I nod, the wind stealing my words. "My aunt and I are here for a couple weeks."

"Who's your aunt again?"

"Violet Morgan. She writes crime fiction."

"I don't read. No time. Give me a movie any day. Like *Murder of Mirrors*. Have you seen it?"

I check my laugh. "That's based on my aunt's first book." While the movie was pretty good and accurate—Aunt Vi had a lot of say—the books were so much better. As they should be and usually are. Except for *The Princess Bride*. Give me that movie over the book version any day.

"Your grandmother left you the cottage? Anything else?"

"Her ring." We stop at an intersection, and I lift my hand to show him.

"Argyle diamonds," Devon says. "Nice. Super rare, pink diamonds. Expensive too. Dad looked at getting a necklace with some for Mum once but…" He shrugs, leaving me to fill in the gaps.

Argyle diamonds. A piece of home. As if I'm holding the letter from Gran about the ring, those two words not in cursive appear in my mind. *North. Argyle.* The clue was right there before I even left home. Home was Northargyle. But how does Hyacinth Cottage fit into it all?

"Did she leave you a shawl by any chance?" Devon asks.

"Yes, she did. How did you know?"

"Hazel mentioned the beautiful lady with the shawl who was so kind to her."

"Great-aunt Hazel talks to herself, like, all the time." Jess leans forward, placing a hand on my shoulder. "Did you bring the shawl with you? I'm sure she'd like to see it again."

"It's what brought me here in the first place. I'm hoping to meet Hazel and talk with her about my gran." My desire to meet Hazel doubles. *The beautiful lady with the shawl who was so kind.* Yep, that's definitely Gran.

Devon accelerates, and I white-knuckle the door. When Jess cheers from the back, I ease up a little but keep my hold. I'm trying to embrace this. To experience the thrill of riding in a convertible.

Nope, I'm good. I don't like this hands-on research into living boldly. *God, please keep us safe. Help me survive this, please and amen.*

Chapter Nine

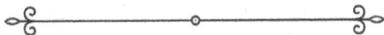

There was no way he would remember her, not after all these years. And even if he did, flirting across an open grave was crass at best.

The silence of the moment thundered in Faith's ears. Was she easing into the grave as well? She closed her eyes, half expecting to hear soil echo against wood, muffled by satin. Was this the death of a long-ago friend or the birth of a new life? How could these two collide?

She shook her head, inwardly scolding herself, then rushed a glance across the abyss. He smiled—shy and sweet—as the soft whispers of gears faded and the casket came to rest.

Not good.

She exhaled her own name to make sure she was grounded in this reality. Her timing had always been terrible.

But this was the worst. Yet... he didn't seem to mind, judging by how his gaze shifted, darkening—

So, what do you think?" Aunt Vi's question jerks me from the story. "It's awful. Admit it. Go ahead, I can take it."

Shaking my head, I look up into her hazel eyes, trying to orient myself. "It's good. I especially loved the pizza part."

"What?" Aunt Vi rips the notebook out of my hands and plops in the chair beside me, almost missing the seat.

I smirk and lift my mug.

I'd been enjoying what has quickly become my Hyacinth Cottage ritual of coffee, Bible reading, and welcoming the day outside when Aunt Vi found me. I'm glad she's writing, figuring out her story. I, on the other hand, still have way too many pieces. And brick walls. And fires. And KEEP OUT! signs. Literally.

The last two days have gotten me nowhere with Gran's story. The deed office was open, but a fire destroyed all the records I needed. I stopped by the library yesterday only to be told by a man in a hard hat and neon vest that it was closed for renovations. Hazel has yet to return to Bridgeway. And even after hearing the stories from the bookstore patrons, I still want to visit Northargyle. How else am I going to find out if that was where Gran was born? Online searches fail me.

"Goodness." Aunt Vi sighs and closes her notebook, snapping my attention away from my puzzle. My coffee sloshes on my Westonia T-shirt, and I set my mug on the table, wiping at the spot. "I thought you were serious about the pizza. Thought I'd gone insane."

"You haven't lost it. Yet."

She laughs then groans. "Adam's threatening to send a hit man if I don't send him pages soon."

"Just breathe. Your editor loves you."

She humors me by taking a huge, dramatic breath. "Also, now I want pizza. Maybe chicken bacon ranch. Extra cheesy."

My stomach growls in agreement. Pizza for breakfast sounds wonderful.

"What were you working on before I demanded you read my garbage?" Aunt Vi eyes my notebook and the ever-growing list of questions.

"Gran's story." I blow a raspberry, tapping my pen on the notebook. "I'm frustrated and struggling with organizing my thoughts."

"Too bad I didn't bring my rolling white board. You could've made a murder board to help you visualize the story."

"Ooh, I could still do that. Like the Brick Wall at the Westonia. Do you have sticky notes?"

"Do I have sticky notes?" She snorts then rummages through the front pocket of her purple backpack, handing me three packs, all different colors. "Use one color for questions, one for facts, and one for timeline. Get everything in order. You can stick them on your bedroom wall."

"I'll give it a try." It might not answer the questions, but I'm thrilled to be doing something. I start to stand, but Aunt Vi stops me and points toward the path.

"Morning," Jess calls, waving. She's not alone.

God answered my prayer, and I survived the convertible ride, even enjoyed it when my mind theater wasn't envisioning us crashing into a kangaroo. But I don't think I can handle Devon—

"Jaxon!" I'm up in a second, running down the path. My bare feet register stones, but I ignore them. He's here.

"I guess he is your brother," Jess says with a smile.

I tackle Jaxon in a hug. He lifts me off the ground, his arms tight and comforting around me. Tears fill my eyes at the happiness of being held.

"Indiana Abbie." He laughs as he twirls us. Jaxon's hugs are as good as Vi's. Even better because his hugs mean he's alive. Whole.

"When did you get so buff?" I playfully punch his biceps. His black T-shirt shows off his arms and toned abs.

"Army life. What can I say?"

I study him, committing his clean-shaven face, buzz cut, and hazel eyes to memory. Something about him is different. Leaner. Harder—not of body but of personality. Wiser, perhaps?

"Hey, Jax." Aunt Vi takes her turn hugging my brother. "Glad you made it."

My jaw drops. "You knew he was coming and didn't say anything?"

"Someone had to give him the details." She winks.

"How are you able to be here?"

"Remember that year I spent in Guam? Well, I had lots of leave time accumulated. A whole month. Figured I'd use some of it to visit my sister who's only ten hours away instead of two days."

"I'm so glad you did."

Jaxon glances at Jess, a smile on his face I've never seen before. My brother has been struck by Cupid's arrow. I've seen it play out on rom-coms and thought it cheesy. But seeing it in real life?

"I was wandering around, but Jess rescued me." Jaxon chuckles. "The soldier-in-distress in this case."

"I'm glad I spotted you." Color mars her cheeks as she studies her toes, which are painted a light pink to match her blouse. I never thought I'd see Jess flustered.

"I—I came to invite you to Greer's tonight. It's my mom's birthday." Jess returns her gaze to Jaxon. "You're all invited, of course."

"That sounds great." My brother answers for all of us. Not that I'd have said no.

Jess has this magnetism. A draw-you-in personality that makes you feel seen and special. I couldn't resist and it looks like Jaxon can't either. Friendship with Jess has been as effortless as Gran said friendship with Hazel was.

A sudden breeze kicks up, sending loose pages from Aunt Vi's notebook into the wind. We all jump into action. As scripted, Jaxon and Jess grab for the same page at the same time.

Aunt Vi and I share a look, shaking our heads but grinning like fools.

"Did that just happen?" she whispers.

Jess tucks a strand of her long hair behind her ears. "I'd better get back. I have to reorganize tables and set things up." She eyes my brother through shuttered lashes. "I'll see you tonight."

"Do you need help?" Jaxon asks.

"I won't say no." She spares me a glance. "Oh, and Hazel is back. You should wear the shawl." With that, she heads down the path. My brother follows, his backpack dropped on the patio, forgotten. Along with me and Vi.

"Good to see you too," I mutter, but I can't be upset that my brother has deserted me already for my new friend. He's here. I got to hug him, and I'll get to hug him again soon.

"That took the cheese award, but I'm glad I witnessed it," Aunt Vi says. She gasps then gathers her papers and heads inside, calling over her shoulder, "Plot twist!"

My cell phone buzzes on the table.

ASHER: *Is he there?*
PHILIP: *Have you stopped crying yet?*
CALEB: *You guys realize he might not be there, and you've ruined the surprise.*

Shaking my head, I sit before responding to the chat.

ME: *My favorite brother has indeed arrived at Hyacinth Cottage.*
PHILIP: *Mom says to send pictures to verify*
ME: *I will when he gets back.*
LUKE: *Thought you said he was there? Where'd he go?*
ME: *He met Jess, the neighbor girl.*

No more responses or questions come in. Like Jaxon meeting a girl isn't something they're curious or even care about. Brothers…

I'm about to put my phone down when an unknown number flashes with a text message. I jolt at the thought that it's Colter before reality brings me back to earth. *You're ridiculous, Abigail Morgan. He doesn't even have your number.*

LIBBY: *Hi, it's Libby. Found something. Call me?*

I check the time difference. Five o'clock. Yesterday evening. My hands shake slightly as I dial a number I've never called before. Libby picks up on the second ring.

"I hope you don't mind me calling. I'd rather talk than type every-thing," she says.

"I'm glad you called," I say truthfully. "You said you found some-thing?"

"An interesting request came through last week, which Mr. Romano handed me yesterday. I wanted to do some more research before I reached out."

I swat at a fly, glad it's not a mozzie. Giggling like I have every time since I learned that word. "What for?"

"Ownership of Margaret's brooch. Get this: Margaret's maiden name was Allen, not Collins, and she wasn't born in Colorado, but in—"

"Northargyle?" I say before she can.

"How did you know?"

"My gran painted the Royal Brisbane Cemetery, which led me to Northargyle. And since she gave Margaret a painting that reminded her of home, I deduced Gran was from there too. Thanks for confirming that." I sigh. "I haven't been able to find much about Northargyle. And the locals have all kinds of horror stories from murder to cursed crowns to deserted mental hospitals. I don't know what to believe."

"That's more than I found. There's nothing online."

"I know. That Wikipedia page is useless."

"You found an official site? My search results included a town in New York and two new sweaters." She chuckles. "I couldn't resist the argyle pattern."

I put Libby on speaker and check my browsing history for the site. ERROR FOUND.

What in the world?

"That's so strange," I say as I bring the phone back to my ear. "I mean, the site didn't have much other than the current king's name and a map of the island, but it was there. I swear I'm not making it up." If I was going to make up a king's name, it wouldn't be Hamish.

"Maybe it's being updated?"

"Maybe." I stand and begin pacing. Nervous energy is not conducive to sitting. "So, the brooch? It's not Margaret's?"

"They aren't accusing her of stealing it. They just want it back, along with anything else Margaret may have taken with her when she left

Northargyle in 1955. Prudence Ellery, the historian, was hired by the royal family to find all the items that disappeared from the palace."

"Whoa? The palace? Royal family?" My eyes widen as my knees give out, plopping me in the chair I'd just vacated.

"I know, right. The brooch belonged to Queen Charlotte Brisbane. Margaret was one of her ladies-in-waiting."

"I wonder if Gran worked at the palace, and that's the connection between her and Margaret."

Is that where you learned proper table etiquette and how to curtsy? Then again, if Gran had been a servant, why would she long to return?

"What else was on the missing items list? Was there a shawl?" I cough, instantly regretting bringing attention to that.

"Prudence didn't say. She got all hush-hush about it, actually. Asked me to be discreet in any inquiries."

Gran's note to Margaret.

I begin pacing again. Is Prudence who Gran was referring to? Should I return the shawl to the royal family? My fingers itch for my pen and list. Possible answered question ahead.

"Mr. Romano put this as a priority. The brooch has been sent to the jeweler for authentication, and I have a meeting with Samantha Weston as soon as she's back from her business trip. Mr. Romano wants me to get to the truth about who Margaret was. Sure would be embarrassing if we displayed lies about any of the founding family members."

⤜❦⤛

When Aunt Vi and I enter the Greer Hotel, I scan the other guests. A flush covers my cheeks as I finger my turquoise dress and the shawl, two items much dressier than the outfits the others are wearing. I should have worn shorts and a tank top like Aunt Vi.

My excitement to meet Hazel was the only thing that pulled me away from my wall of sticky notes. I'd covered a fair amount of it so far. It's a bit overwhelming, but it did help me set up my timeline and figure out more questions I need to ask. I also added the royal family and Margaret's—and Gran's, by association—involvement in the brooch fiasco.

"I don't want to stay too long," Aunt Vi says. "I need to get back to writing, but a brain break might produce some fodder. Also, I'm really only here for the food. Don't make me people. Deadlines make me grumpy and hungry."

My stomach growls as if agreeing with her. It smells heavenly. Yes, a brain break might bring something new to my puzzle as well.

Greer's is minimally decorated with the tables pushed to the edges, making room for everyone to gather in an open space. A lot of people are here. I twist Gran's ring, checking it's still there. What's the Australian version of a party extraction? Stampede of kangaroos? I guess I can still imagine the helicopter, complete with a good-looking Aussie pilot.

Jess sees us, her bored expression morphing to delight. She rushes across the room, my brother on her heels, and wraps me in a hug. Tight, like we didn't see each other this morning, or meet less than a week ago.

"Wow, look, my brother is here," I can't help saying.

"Hey, sis." His sheepish grin reminds me of Dad. Homesickness stabs my heart.

"What a beautiful shawl," Jess says, her fingers trailing along the fabric. "This is the one your gran used to wear?"

I nod as Devon approaches our little group. The smile on his face lights up his whole countenance, but I can't help imagining Colter's grin. There's no comparison between the two men. Devon is a little too shiny. To everyone else, he would probably earn a top-ten spot on "the world's hottest men" list, but to me, Colter's playful charm wins hands down.

"Abigail Morgan, you look amazing." Devon takes my right hand and kisses the back of it, his thumb running over Gran's ring as he releases my hand. "Is this *the* shawl?"

"Yes. Is Hazel here?" I scan the room, searching for a woman who could be Hazel. Every morning, seeing Gran's shawl hanging in my bedroom, I'm reminded that Hazel is my only real, living link to Gran. And maybe Northargyle. A country that's ghosting my brain and heart.

"Hazel wasn't feeling well. She had a long day of travel and was complaining about being held hostage or something." Devon shakes his head. "I can take the shawl to her."

"I want to actually meet her, ask her about Gran." I wince at my curt response, hoping I didn't sound mean or ungrateful. I'd rather not have to rely on a mediator. Things tend to get lost in the retelling.

"I can take you tomorrow," Devon offers.

"I'd like that. Thank you."

Aunt Vi moves beside me, and Devon's gaze homes in on her. "Violet Morgan, your niece told me I had to read *Murder of Mirrors* because I loved the movie. Would you sign a book for me sometime?"

Did he buy a copy of the book because of me? That's so sweet.

"I'm not supposed to say anything, but the sequel is being filmed at the moment." Aunt Vi wiggles her eyebrows. She hadn't told me that. I guess she likes and approves of Devon.

He makes a zipping of the lips motion.

She holds out a tote bag. "Speaking of my books, I brought a signed copy of my latest and a few other goodies for your mom. Jess mentioned she's a fan."

The music cuts off and applause erupts around the room.

"Mum's here. Come meet her, and you can give her the gift yourself," Devon says.

Mrs. Greer reminds me of the bust of Nefertiti—sharp angles, a rigid posture, and a neutral line of a mouth that could smile or frown at any moment. I hunt for traces of Hazel but don't find any evidence that she's related to the soft, carefree woman in the photograph. Mrs. Greer runs a shaking hand over her dress, which is a similar shade to mine.

"Happy birthday, Mrs. Greer," I say, hoping to ease her nerves if they are due to meeting the famous Violet Morgan. "I love your dress."

"I told her that color didn't work on her." Devon winks at me. "Definitely works on you, Abs."

"My children have told me so much about you both," Mrs. Greer says in a wispy, barely audible voice. Odd. Her children are animated, with voices that could easily be heard over a noisy crowd of sports fanatics. "And that Jaxon, he's such a dear already. He helped my Jess all afternoon, never taking a break."

"He's always been a hard worker," Aunt Vi says.

"So has my Devon. Cares about everyone else." She tenderly pats his cheek.

He reddens and pulls away. "Mum," he whines.

"Happy birthday." Aunt Vi hands her the bag.

Instead of being in raptures when she pulls out the book as Jess hinted, Mrs. Greer doesn't even crack the spine to see the inscription. She also doesn't check to see what else is in the bag. Or thank Aunt Vi.

"Look what your sister gave me. I told her she shouldn't have spent the money on it, but she said I deserved to have people spend money on me." Mrs. Greer holds out her hand to show Devon a silver bracelet similar to the one Tim gave Jess at the bookstore. Actually, it is the same bracelet. But, no, it couldn't be. Jess said she'd never take it off. "I couldn't believe how much she paid for it."

"Wait until you see what I got you." Devon crosses the room and returns with a small paper bag.

Mrs. Greer animates noticeably as she opens it, gasping when she removes something shiny. "Where did you get this?"

Devon shrugs. "I found it at an antique store."

My reaction is just as incredulous, in part because Devon went antiquing and in part because Mrs. Greer is holding a replica of Margaret Weston's brooch. The one taken from a palace.

"May I see that?" I ask, not realizing I'd stuck my hand out.

Mrs. Greer hesitates but places it in my palm.

I study the brooch. The same bird and silver sprig of flowers. I hadn't touched the one in the case at the Westonia, but if it was anything like this, it's got some weight to it. This isn't costume jewelry.

"Do you mind if I take a picture and send this to my colleague at the historical society?"

"Please." Mrs. Greer grants her permission.

I capture several angles, reluctantly handing the brooch to Devon's waiting hand when I'm done.

"Do you think it's worth something?" Devon lifts it to the light. If he were a cartoon character, I'm sure dollar signs would be flashing in his eyes. Is he going to give it to his mother, or keep it now that it might be worth something?

"It might be. There's a historian looking into one like it which disappeared—" I don't want to say *from the palace* or *Northargyle* in this present company's hearing.

Devon laughs. "I can't believe I found something in that junk heap."

Chapter Ten

The second brooch's appearance kept my mind reeling most of the night. When I'd texted the picture to Libby, she said she would reach out to Prudence Ellery—the royal historian—for answers. The mystery of the brooch and my excitement about meeting Hazel had vied for my attention while I waited for my brother to come home. I'd mulled over what questions to ask Hazel besides the ones mentioned in Gran's letter: kitchen exploits, secrets, Roy in the garden, their friendship.

I check the time. Before we'd left the party last night, Devon confirmed he'd pick me up around nine. It's almost eight thirty. I place the shawl safely in my tote then head downstairs.

Aunt Vi isn't at the table, and the blanket I'd left for Jaxon is folded in military precision on the couch. There's no sign of my aunt or brother. Jax tiptoed in around midnight, so we hadn't had a chance to talk. He'd stayed at Greer's to help clean up and, I assume, spend more time with Jess.

The back door opens, and Jaxon enters, sweaty from a morning run. I should probably try to squeeze in a run at some point while I'm here. The Winter in Westonia 5K is gonna be a killer if I don't.

"Morning, sis." He runs a hand over his head, the short hairs rasping against his callouses.

"Morning, bro." I've missed him so much. I can't help giving him a hug even though sweat mars his gray army tank. "Ugh, you stink."

He flicks the end of my nose then gathers his clothes and heads for the shower. The coffee is beeping that it's done when he returns to the kitchen.

"Take two," he says, wrapping me in a bear hug that lasts more than fifty heartbeats.

"So much better." I turn toward the coffee. "You still take coffee in your sugar?"

"Actually, I stopped drinking it." He holds up a plastic water bottle. "I'm almost a full-grown man." He purposely makes his voice crack, quoting a line from a family favorite movie.

"Don't let Aunt Vi hear you say that."

The floor above us creaks, and we start laughing. We'd both held our breath, waiting for our aunt to emerge and beat some sense into Jaxon for abandoning the elixir of life.

"Remember when Aunt Vi impaled me with a pen?" Jaxon's eyes widen in mock terror.

"I was thinking about that the other day."

"Our family is weird, isn't it?"

"The weirdest. But I wouldn't change any of them." We share a smile.

Jaxon eyes the cottage, taking it in as I had done. "So, this was Gran's? Didn't she say she'd never been out of the States?"

"There were a lot of things she didn't tell me." I eye my brother. "Speaking of not telling me things, I can't believe you didn't say anything about coming. You used to be my favorite brother."

"Used to be? Hah! Who always picked you first? Who helped you out of the tree when Caleb stole the ladder? Who took the brunt of the water balloons during our epic battle of 2018? Who untied you from that chair?"

"You did, but you tied me to the chair in the first place."

"Pretty sure that was Asher."

"Definitely you." I laugh. "Fine, you can still be my favorite. And we probably should take a selfie to verify you're here since we didn't get one yesterday."

Jax pulls his phone from the back pocket of his jeans, and we pose in several silly shots, sending them to the brothers and Mom and Dad. Having Jaxon here eases missing my family a fraction of an inch.

"So, Jess is pretty great." His statement gives me whiplash with the sudden change of topic. "We couldn't stop talking. She's something."

"She is," I say in time with a knock on the door. "That'll be Devon."

My brother straightens to attention like his captain has arrived. "Is Jess with him?"

"Not sure. Devon is taking me to Hazel's, so I can talk about Gran."

Devon's wearing shorts and a green T-shirt almost the same color as mine. *Twinsies.* I catch my giggle at the observation.

Jess barely registers me on her way to hug my brother. There's Jaxon's answer. Their voices are low, as if they're picking up exactly where they left off. What more do they have to say after hours together?

"How far is it to Hazel's?" I ask, not seeing Devon's Mustang or any other vehicle in the driveway.

"Figured we could walk. It's not worth the drive. Jess was hoping your brother would join us," Devon says, his eyes narrowing. "Do you have the shawl?"

"It's in my tote." I rinse out my coffee mug then sling my tote over my shoulder. "I'm ready."

Devon steps beside me as soon as we're outside, Jaxon and Jess falling in behind us. I try to think of something to say, but the need to overshare or get to know him isn't there. Besides, my brain space is limited given my focus on Gran's story and the questions I'm dying to ask Hazel.

Last night's rain has cooled the air quite a bit, and puddles dot the landscape. I jump over one, feeling like Jennifer Ehle in the BBC *Pride and Prejudice* adaptation. Good thing I'm wearing shorts, or my hem would be six inches deep in mud.

I glance at Jaxon. His gaze holds a "should I?" glint. I send back a warning glare. He'd better not splash me. He runs at a puddle, stopping just before jumping.

Jess squeals merrily.

"What do you think about going to the castle tomorrow?" Devon holds up his phone for me to see the screen.

"There's a castle in Bridgeway?"

"It's the closest thing you'll find around here. It was a disused movie set or something."

Unlike when I mentioned Northargyle, this creepy pile of stones warrants a haunted warning. Must've been a horror movie.

"Are you talking about the castle?" Jess says, closing the gap between the couples and pulling me from the scene in my mind theater. "You should tell your aunt to film a movie there, then I could be in it."

"My aunt isn't a director," I point out.

"You'd be the perfect lead," Jaxon chips in. "Like a Bond girl."

"You're so sweet." She grips his arm, drawing him closer as her eyes widen. "Honestly, the ruins scare me, but I don't mind going if you'll be there."

"I'm in." Jaxon would probably agree to be shark bait if she suggested it.

"It's settled then. We'll make a day of it," Devon says.

Hazel's isn't far past Greer's Hotel. It's a one-story tiny gray house positioned among gardens that aren't as well kept as Hyacinth Cottage's. The wear of the outside comes into focus the closer we get. Chipped paint. Broken shutters. Weeds. Vines choking the front door. It's like what Aunt Vi imagined Gran's cottage to be.

"The cottage isn't big enough for all of us," Jess says. "I'm going to take Jaxon for a walk."

Devon opens the door and waits for me to enter. It smells of onions and cabbage. Breakfast? That doesn't sound appetizing even for dinner. The only way I like cabbage is in coleslaw with lots of mayo and sugar. The cottage is jam-packed with shelves, furniture, crates, and cobwebs, although the path to the living room is clear enough.

"Hazel is going blind. Just a warning," Devon whispers, making the hair on the back of my neck flutter. The shiver is more reflex than chill. "Hazel?"

"In here," comes a crackly voice.

Hazel sits in a chair by an unlit fireplace, a worn and fraying patchwork quilt over her lap even though it's warm in the room. The window across from her is so dirty the sunlight barely squeezes through. The state of this house compared to Hyacinth Cottage is embarrassing. The urge to find a rag and bleach and start scrubbing almost wins.

Hazel lifts a trembling hand, which Devon takes gently. *So sweet.* He's shown himself to be loud and abrasive, but I'm glad for the glimpse of tenderness.

"Abigail Morgan is here to see you," Devon almost shouts. He'd said Hazel was blind, right? Not deaf? My ears ring with the volume.

"Abigail?"

"Her grandmother owned Hyacinth Cottage. The kind lady with the shawl."

"Lady Rose?" Hazel's voice cracks. "You came back?"

"Not Rose, Abigail." Devon rolls his eyes, motioning for me to come closer.

"I didn't think I'd ever see you again." When she holds out her hand, I step forward and accept. Her hand is small and rough, and tears glisten in her milky eyes. My heart twinges at this woman, so broken compared to Gran. "Come, sit, like we used to."

When she releases me, I remove my tote and sit on the sofa across from her, fighting the urge to sneeze as dust motes swirl. Devon stands behind me and rests his hand on the back of the sofa. I'm so aware of its proximity to my neck.

"I may not be able to see well, but I know you have questions." Hazel's sweet smile reminds me of a jack-o'-lantern's. "So curious, just like Rose and Laurel."

"If you were an antique, I'd ask you what your story was," I say, then realize what I've said. I hope she isn't offended.

"She's not far off," Devon mutters.

"Will you tell me about Hyacinth Cottage?" I say to get us started.

"Let's see. Roy was eighteen when he bought the cottage from my grandparents in 1954. But he didn't move right in as we expected. Rose and Laurel arrived in April, almost a year later. Roy didn't come until August. I was blessed to witness Roy and Rose's wedding."

"Wait, they married here at the cottage?" Something isn't adding up. Gran met Grandpa in Ohio, and they married in 1959.

"Such a lovely ceremony. Just the four of us. Rose and Roy. Me and Laurel. Oh, and the vicar."

"Was Roy a nickname? Was his real name Josiah Brown?"

Hazel's eyes lose focus as she purses her lips then finally shakes her head. "No. His name was Roy Currie."

Currie. My heart breaks. The inscription in the poetry book had been from Gran's first love. Had Roy's death and the memory of him at Hyacinth Cottage spurred Gran to leave Australia?

Devon yawns rather loudly, his jaw popping. How can he be bored?

He moves away from the couch and wanders the room, lifting items, checking boxes.

"I spent more time at the cottage after my family sold it than I did when we owned it." Hazel chuckles, which leads to coughing.

I wince at the rattling in her lungs as she breathes, wishing I could ease the cough.

When she recovers, she continues. "Your grandmother was the bravest, most talented person I knew. She was always painting. You all left so fast. I've been waiting. I didn't know if I'd live to ever see you again."

I share a look with Devon, who is across the room holding a wooden clock. The face he makes tells me he thinks his great-aunt has lost it. I turn back to Hazel. "Why did my gran leave? Were they in danger?"

"Her family didn't approve of the marriage, but they were so happy, so in love." A tear rolls down Hazel's cheek, the path slowed by the wrinkles like speed bumps. "I should have gone with you when you asked. I've regretted it every day. Forgive me."

"Why don't you show her the shawl," Devon says, returning to stand behind the couch. Positioning his hand even closer to my shoulder.

Hazel's reaction to it is instant and intense. Her body shakes as she embraces it like an old friend. More tears escape, leaving their mark on the shawl. "It was 1955, not long after your marriage...the first time I saw you wearing this. You were sobbing because your family had died. You were never without it after that. You always wore it while you painted, while you watched Roy in the gardens. While I tried to teach you how to cook."

Her fingers run along the patch, lingering on the hyacinth embroidered in the corner. "Your grandmother caught the edge on fire. So worthless in the kitchen. Couldn't even boil water." A laugh scrapes its way from Hazel's lungs. "I was the one who added the patch. Added the fringe and the hyacinth."

"Do you know where Gran got the shawl? Did she find it in Bridgeway?"

"No, no. It was made for her when she was born."

"Was she born in N—"

"No, no. Secrets. You...no." Hazel's eyes grow wide, her gaze skittering about the room. "Devon, get my box, please."

I expect him to return with a wooden box like Gran's, but it's a simple cardboard box instead. Hazel tries, unsuccessfully, to remove the lid, her hands shaking.

"Would you like me to open it?" When she nods, I take the box and open it easily.

Hazel rummages inside. "Where is it? I told her I'd keep it safe."

"What are you looking for?" Devon asks.

"The brooch. She gave it to me, friendship. We each had one."

"You gave that to me to give to Mother for her birthday."

"Oh…oh, did I?" Hazel stops rummaging. "I forget so easily." She begins coughing.

I look to Devon. "I thought you said you found it at an antique shop?"

"Look around you, Abs. This is an antique shop." Devon's phone rings, and he rolls his eyes. He answers, heading outside.

I focus on Hazel and the box, glad Devon's not hovering over my shoulder. I need space to think. Had Hazel given the brooch to him, or had he taken it? I don't want to contemplate that he's a thief. He wouldn't do that, would he? He lied easily enough. And if he's left his great-aunt to live like this, maybe that tenderness is just a lie too.

"I lost hope of ever seeing you again," Hazel says.

I relax my face, which I'm sure resembles a turnip, replacing it with a smile.

"But then that first letter arrived." Hazel glances toward the other room, lowering her voice as she removes a stack of letters from the box. "I've kept these letters safe. I didn't share. Didn't give it away. Didn't tell where they were. You're back now. You can keep them safe."

She hands me the stack of letters, and I open the first one. Definitely Gran's writing. Instead of a name, four hyacinths are sketched on the bottom. "Gran signed your letters with hyacinths too?"

"It was our code."

"A code? How? What?" My words come out in a splutter of excitement.

"The flowers." Hazel's gaze wanders from me.

I wait while she thinks. At least I hope she's thinking and will remember.

"Oh, yes. Well." She pauses again. The clock on the mantel ticks away the minutes that feel like years. "Five flowers means every fifth word? Every fifth letter? Or the petals or leaves mean something?"

Come on, Hazel, please remember.

Hazel's eyes become clear, and I think my plea was answered, but she grasps my hand, hard. "Keep those letters safe. Protect them. I'll always protect you."

"I promise I'll keep them safe." I place the letters in my tote as Hazel starts coughing. The box falls to the ground as she pulls out a handkerchief. I scoop up the box, setting it on the cluttered table beside her. Blood stains the handkerchief she uses to cover her mouth.

My heart aches. This broken woman has been through so much.

"Ready to go?" Devon asks as he comes back into the room.

"Thank you for coming to see me, Lady Rose," Hazel rasps.

Devon kisses her on the cheek, which startles Hazel. The shawl starts to slide off her lap, but Hazel clutches it to her heart, her eyes misty once again. How do I ask Hazel to give me back the shawl? What if Gran meant Hazel should have it and not Prudence?

"Will you keep the shawl safe for me?" I ask, knowing Hazel needs the shawl more than I do at the moment. If the royal family comes a knockin', I'll know where it is.

"Always, Lady Rose. I will always keep you safe." Hazel closes her eyes, a smile on her lips. It's not long before soft snores fill the room.

I follow Devon outside.

"Jaxon and I decided we should go on a picnic," Jess says as soon as she spots me. "He wants to see the park. There's a cute bridge and a pirate ship."

I clutch my tote, wanting to read the letters Gran sent Hazel. There's a hyacinth code that needs breaking. But the three expectant faces, especially my brother's, sway me into saying a picnic sounds good. I'll have time to read the letters after lunch.

Chapter Eleven

⟞⟊———○———⟊⟝

Lunch turned into a visit to the park, which turned into dinner at Greer's, which turned into making plans and reading all about the abandoned movie set castle ruins, which turned into not getting back to the cottage until ten. We ended up talking and laughing until midnight, my brother sharing stories about his buddies, driving his yellow Nissan Stagea, and his life on base.

Needless to say, I'd passed out before I could even think about the hyacinth code.

This morning, I am determined. The sun is barely up, and the letters from Hazel are open in front of me on the kitchen table. I'd commandeered it once again before Aunt Vi.

I rub my eyes for what seems like the hundredth time. Why can't I figure this out?

Five of the letters in the stack have hyacinths. Every letter is simple enough in its contents, stilted in writing compared to the ones without flowers. Talking about everyday things, books and poems they loved, flowers, and baking mishaps. Health issues and seeking second opinions are referenced as well. Nothing earth-shattering about why they had to leave Northargyle or Hyacinth Cottage.

"Morning, sis." Jaxon enters the kitchen in gym shorts and a sleeveless tank. "Whatcha working on?"

I hesitate a moment, but I'm dying to break this code one way or another. I have to know the secrets.

"Hazel gave me letters that Gran sent her throughout the years. She said there's a code but couldn't remember what it was. The number of hyacinths means something. This letter has four hyacinths. I've tried every fourth word in every fourth sentence and every fourth word in each paragraph. It's all a jumbled mess. Even if I rearrange the word order. I've looked at all five letters, taking the word that was the number of flowers for that letter. None of it makes sense."

"What about every fourth letter?"

I jot down his idea. It's a lot of letters, mostly vowels.

When I was seven, I'd bought a book on ciphers from the Scholastic Book Fair. I'd had grand plans of being hired by the CIA to solve the hardest puzzles when no one else could. Breaking codes was fun, but when I discovered how much math and brainpower was involved in writing codes, I abandoned that career path for sketching trees and sheep.

Jaxon picks up one of the letters, studying it.

I resist banging my head on the table. I'm missing something.

"What if you try the first letter of every fourth sentence?" Jaxon suggests.

Worth a try. With a sigh, I take back the letter. I wish my brother would stop hovering. I'm already under heavy self-induced pressure. A piece of Gran's story rests in my hands. What was so important to hide in code?

The first letter of the fourth sentence is S. I write it on the page in my journal. The next is an E. The next two are Ts.

At the end of the letter, I check the page. The message is there. *Settled in New York.*

"Woohoohoo!" I cheer in Dad fashion, instantly covering my mouth. Had I woken Aunt Vi?

Jaxon fist-bumps me. "You're smarter than you look."

"Haha."

"I'm going for a quick run. I'll be back in time to shower before we head to the castle," Jaxon says as he ruffles my hair on his way out.

I grab the next letter. Dated late 1958. This message reads *Relocated to Ohio.* Message three makes me sad. *Married Josiah.* Roy must have passed away between 1958 and 1959. The next message reads *Daughter born.* The date of the letter is Mom's birthday—1970.

The last letter with a hyacinth is dated 1971. *No more pain. Home in glory.* Laurel must have passed away as well. Poor Gran. Loss of her first husband and one of her dearest friends. And she never got to see Hazel again.

A scream rents the air then is followed by something hitting the wall. Aunt Vi. I've never heard that scream before. Frustration. Desperation. Pain. I grab my phone in case I have to call for help then run up the steps, tripping on the last one, acquiring a bruised shin.

The door to Aunt Vi's room is open. She's pacing, fluttering her hands, her fingers opening and closing like she smashed them and is trying to be brave.

I search the room. Clothes and shoes are thrown everywhere like my nieces had tried on every costume in their toy bin.

Aunt Vi begins tapping her chest. Hands fluttering. Words interspersed with deep stuttering breaths. "It's okay. I'm okay. Breathe. Just… br…breathe. She's…going…to."

"Aunt Vi—"

She holds up a hand, the universal sign to not come any closer. After a moment of deep, shuddering breaths, she goes to the desk. She tries to open the drawer but can't. "M-med. I need…" With a sob, she crumples to the ground.

I open the drawer to find an orange pill bottle and hand it to her. She can't get it open, so I squat in front of her, take the bottle, then open it in one try.

She swallows a pill without water then stands and ambles to the bed, making a cocoon out of her blankets. Her sobs punch me in the heart.

I snap a picture of the pill bottle before returning it to the desk. It's something called escitalopram.

She would tell me if she were sick. Right? Flashes of Gran healthy and dancing then gone the next day enter my thoughts. God wouldn't take Aunt Vi too, would He?

Aunt Vi never told anyone she was dying. One day she was there, and the next she was a shell of her former existence. The diagnosis came, and with it, the chance of survival slim to none. This trip to Australia will be her last. Her bucket list trip, crossing off so many things that she wants to do before she dies.

"Get a grip, Abigail," I mutter, shaking myself out of the morbid melancholy. I text a picture to Luke, asking him what the medicine is. I feel like I wait hours when my brother actually responds within a minute.

LUKE: *It's an anti-anxiety med.*

LUKE: *Are you researching for Aunt Vi?*
ME: *Something like that.*
LUKE: *Let me know if I can help with anything else.*
ME: *Will do. Love ya much.*

My relief is instant. She's not on some last trip. But medicine for depression? Not Aunt Vi. How is it even possible? She doesn't get rattled. She's the strongest, most joy-filled person I know.

"Abbie, Devon and Jess are here," Jaxon calls up the stairs.

"Go. Leave me," she rasps between shudders. "I—I don't even want to be around me at the moment."

"I'll be right back." I head downstairs. *I can't possibly go sightseeing. How can I pretend to laugh and be happy when Aunt Vi is wrecked? God, please let them understand.*

"Ready?" Jess asks, her arm already hooked through Jaxon's. "I can't wait for you to see the castle. Are you ready to be scared?"

I've already been scared enough for the day. "I'm going to stay here," I say. It comes out as a question.

Jaxon eyes me, brow lowered. "You okay?"

"Aunt Vi needs me. She…Well, she needs me." I don't want to share that my aunt is taking meds for depression with anyone yet. Not without her permission.

"Is she sick?" Jaxon asks, his lips quirking. "Or being overdramatic? Should we watch out for flying pens?"

I don't respond or join in the chuckles. Seeing my aunt in that panicked state is not even remotely funny.

Devon narrows his eyes. At least someone noticed I'm not laughing. "Of course you should stay with your aunt," he says. "Take care of her." The kindness of his words makes me think I'm imagining the weird glint in his eyes.

Jess tucks a strand of hair behind her ear. "Do you mind if we still go?"

"No. Go have fun. I'll probably just rest."

"We can't go to the castle without Abigail," Devon says.

"True. Maybe I'll take Jaxon to the zoo." Jess releases my brother long enough to give me a hug and kiss on the cheek. She takes Jaxon's hand and heads outside.

"Aren't you going to go?" I ask Devon, who hasn't moved.

"I'm not an animal lover. Take care of your aunt. She doesn't have children, right?"

I shake my head, confused as to why he'd ask that of all things.

"I'll see you later." He leaves without any other words.

Thank you, God, for answering my prayers of staying. No matter how weird that was.

The letters and my journal with the decoded messages are still on the table where I'd left them when I ran upstairs. I gather everything and head back up. I check on Aunt Vi. Her soft snores fill the room, so I continue to my bedroom. After setting my journal and the letters on my bed, I turn toward the wall covered in sticky notes, ignoring the peg where Gran's shawl used to hang. Hazel needed it.

With a weary heart and mind, I tear off the green sticky note with the question "What happened to Laurel?" and the one with "Was Roy Grandpa Brown?" My hand shakes as I write that Laurel died in 1971 in Ohio and that Roy Currie was Gran's first husband.

I add other notes to the timeline, filling in blanks for where Gran was and when. I also add what I learned about Gran's shawl—that it was made for her when she was born and that her parents had died in 1955.

Settling on my bed, I stare at the wall for a beat before grabbing *Howl's Moving Castle*. I clutch it to my chest for several heartbeats, needing comfort. Is this what it feels like to grow up? To know things that you wish you didn't?

I open the book to where I'd left off, finding the letter from Gran that I'd read on the plane. It has hyacinths. Had Gran left me a message like she had Hazel? I retrieve my pen and notebook, ready to decode another letter.

There are three hyacinths. Every third sentence, first letter. The message slowly appears on the page. *Behind fireplace.*

What fireplace? Gran must have meant Hyacinth Cottage, right? Why would she put that message in this letter if it were for somewhere else? There's only one way to test the theory. I almost trip down the stairs in my haste to reach the dusty room. The door creaks as I open it, a greeting this time, a celebration that a secret is about to be found.

The fireplace is boarded up. I run my hands over the cool bricks, the roughness catching on my skin. There's a loose brick, and I wiggle it. Instead of coming free, the wall to my left moves, outlining a door. I wedge my fingers in the seam and open the door to find a set of wooden stairs.

It's dark, but a pinprick of light comes from above. With a deep breath and a prayer, I climb the stairs, promptly sneezing five times. I push through cobwebs and acquire a coating of grit on my arms and face. The stairs lead to a room with a slanted roof. A small window, like the one in my bedroom, lets in enough light to see the space fairly well.

An unfinished painting rests on an easel alongside a paintbrush in an empty cup and a wooden palette with dried paint—like the scene was left quickly. A small desk with a chair is situated under the window, and to its right is a dust-covered trunk like the one I found in Gran's attic. I experience a déjà vu moment as I open it. Inside is a stack of canvases and oil paints long dried and cracking. The canvases are divided into two piles—blank on the right side of the trunk, completed paintings on the left.

The first is of a younger Hazel appearing how she looked in that photograph with Gran and Laurel. It's like Hazel will step off the canvas and wrap me in her arms. I set it aside with reverence and pull out the next. A man with light brown hair standing in the middle of a garden holding a bouquet of roses. This has to be Roy. He had such kind, wise brown eyes.

I'm blown away by Gran's talent. Why did she stop painting?

The next is Gran. A self-portrait. In a creepily cool way, it's like I'm looking in a mirror. I run my fingers over her face. Is this truly how Gran saw herself?

I've seen Philip attempt self-portraits. They always fall flat. He says it's hard to paint yourself well because we're blinded by our flaws. Can't see past our inadequacies.

There are no flaws in this painting.

I search through paintings of landscapes—most with that tropical feel that I'm guessing is Northargyle—hoping for a painting of Laurel. There isn't one. Why would Gran paint one friend and not the other?

Just to be thorough, I check the lid for secrets. My inner Nancy Drew cheers when I find a latch and a hidden compartment. This trunk is everything that I'd hoped the one in Gran's attic would be like. I discover a leather-bound journal with roses etched on the cover.

The handwriting is Gran's, but there are slight differences to the angle and swirl of the cursive. Maybe it's because the first entry was made on 16 April 1951. The day Gran turned thirteen. Handwriting tends to change as we age—mine morphed several times. That must be the reason for the differences.

Sitting cross-legged on the floor, I settle in to read about young Gran.

16 April 1951

 I was hesitant to write in this journal because it's so beautiful. But I've decided I'm going to fill it with all the good things. Today is my thirteenth birthday. Roy surprised me with this journal. It has roses on the cover! He travelled across the island to buy it. I'll never forget his smile when I opened it. He's so handsome. His eyes. His smile. I better stop because if someone ever reads this, they will think I'm crazy.

I flip to the end of the journal. The last entry is in 1954. Gran's sixteenth birthday. Only three years of words for me to savor. I try to stem the flow of disappointment and be thankful even for this much. Instead of flipping back to the beginning, I devour the last entry.

16 April 1954

 Today, Roy gave me a locket with his picture in it. The silver roses on the locket are so simple, so unlike the other jewellery gifted to me throughout the years. It's perfect. Especially since I can wear it without raising suspicions like a ring would have. I love Roy so much and want everyone to know. He truly is the best of men. I wish my parents would allow us to be together. I don't care that he's just a gardener. I'm just a girl. While I wait, I will hold on to the hope that someday I will be Mrs. Currie.

> "Research is a formalized curiosity. It is poking and prying with a purpose."
>
> —Zora Neale Hurston

Chapter Twelve

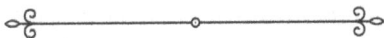

Oh, I wanna go to church..."

What in the world? The song plays through the wall, and I realize that the secret room is on the other side of my bedroom. That's the ringtone I chose for church.

Setting Gran's journal aside, I pull myself off the floor. I couldn't stop reading long enough to move to a comfier place. I perform stretches, toe touches, reach for the ceiling, massage my neck.

With Gran's self-portrait and her journal, I head down the stairs, dodging the few cobwebs that hadn't attacked me on the way up to the secret room. I close the door, thrilled to be the first person in that room in more than sixty years. A room filled with secrets for me to discover. I'm glad they waited. It's a wonder no one discovered it when the bathroom was added.

I catch sight of myself in the mirror above the fireplace. Cobwebs cover my hair and streaks of dirt under my eyes make me look like I'm about to rush onto the football field. I make a game face and head for the shower.

Once I'm cobweb and dirt free, I peek in on Aunt Vi but don't enter. Rest is the best thing for her, I'm sure. Also, my brain is in Gran's world. I'm not ready to re-enter reality.

Situated on my bed, I stare at the painting of Gran, thinking about all the things I'd glimpsed in the journal. She was a talented writer. Loved roses. Loved Roy. At times, I forgot I wasn't reading a young adult romance, getting weepy knowing that while they do end up marrying, Roy died in America.

As Gran said, she'd filled the journal with good things, but there were times when she struggled with loving Roy, with knowing the right thing.

Asking God to heal her body—for the physicians to find a cure. Begging God to change her parents' hearts, to have their prejudice be forgotten.

Sketches throughout the journal told their own story. Roses and other flowers. Kiwi birds. Sketches of Roy. I watched him mature through the pages like one of those flip-books. I agree with Gran. He was handsome, someone my thirteen-year-old-heart would have swooned over as well.

Roy would bring her flowers and pray with her. At that age, I was still trying to figure out who I was apart from a basketball playing pastor's daughter. Gran, though, knew who she was, what she wanted, and who she wanted to be with. Just as her self-portrait declared.

My phone vibrates on my nightstand. Seeing a text from Libby reminds me I never called to see what Dad wanted. I'll call him first then answer Libby. I check the time and do the math. It's a little before 7:00 p.m. Yesterday. Thursday. Worship team practice night. When there's no answer on Dad's cell phone, I call the church office.

"Pastor Morgan's office. This is Tabitha Peterson," a feminine voice answers, so professional. Did I sound like that when I answered the church phone?

"Hi, Mrs. Peterson. It's Abigail Morgan." An image appears in my mind's eye. *Short white hair. Piano player. Amazing baker.* She's basically an older version of me.

"Please, call me Tabitha or Aunt Tabby. That's what your father calls me." She chuckles.

"Is my dad there?"

"He just rushed out. Rachel and Asher are on their way to the hospital, and your father was going to stay with Poppy and Lily. Those girls are so sweet and so excited to meet the baby. We all are."

A stab of homesickness strikes. I miss my nieces. And hospital? A new niece or nephew is coming, and I'm not there.

"Do you know your sister-in-law's favorite dessert? I want to make them something special. Your father loved the lemon meringue pie I made him last week, but that's not everyone's cup of tea."

Lemon meringue is Dad's favorite dessert. I only tried baking it once. Convincing meringue to thicken and peak is not for the faint of heart. I'd gotten a lot of reading done. Book in one hand, electric mixer in the other, calling it good enough after more than an hour when it still didn't resemble the cookbook picture.

"Rachel loves banana bread with chocolate chips," I say, wishing I was home to make it. "She ate a lot of it during the pregnancy."

"Ooh, I have a wonderful recipe for that. It has coconut oil and tastes like an Almond Joy."

"She'll love that." I touch Gran's self-portrait, wanting to be back in the journals instead of dealing with the feelings bombarding me that I'm not needed at home, that I've been replaced, bypassed for something better. "Thanks for letting me know. Tell everyone on the worship team hello."

I hang up and read Libby's text.

LIBBY: *Have an update. Call me when you can.*

"So, what's the update?" I ask as soon as I've said hi.

"Samantha Weston found a journal hidden in a trunk. Margaret wrote in it when she was younger, before she left Northargyle. I'm about halfway through."

That makes two trunk discoveries this week. Why didn't Gran's have a hidden compartment? It's still in Asher's attic. I'd checked it after he inherited the house, thinking my younger self had missed something. Still nothing.

"Also, we're going to have to update the information we have on Margaret," Libby continues.

"How so?"

"Margaret was born in 1936 not 1938. She was orphaned at age thirteen and was taken in by a family friend who worked at the palace."

Why had she taken Gran's birthday? "Was my grandmother mentioned in the journal?"

"Not yet. I was able to verify Prudence Ellery's information. Margaret's maiden name was Allen, and she was Queen Charlotte's lady-in-waiting. Although Margaret longed to be chosen to care for the princess."

"What was the princess's name?" *Could it be Christine?*

"Margaret doesn't ever say. You might have to go to Northargyle to find the truth because no one seems to want to share. I'll email you as I transcribe. I'm hoping to work on it tomorrow, in between helping Kasey with prep work for the Founders' Day gala." Libby sighs. "I miss you being the one to help Kasey. You handle her instruction so much better than I do. Although, I lost a couple pounds from not indulging in the sweets you're always bringing in." She chuckles.

I'm about to say I'll be home soon, but I'm not ready. I still have so many questions. After I hang up, I face my wall of sticky notes armed with more names and facts. Queen Charlotte. A princess?

Libby is right. I need to figure out how to get to Northargyle.

❧⸙❧

I'm staring at a jar of Vegemite, wondering if I'm brave enough to spread it on toast, when Aunt Vi enters the kitchen. Jaxon texted that he was taking Jess to Sugarleaf Manor for dinner. What I wouldn't give for a charcuterie oasis right now. The current options are questionable.

"Do I smell coffee?" she asks, her voice groggy and crackly.

"It's what's for dinner. Coffee and either a—" I glance at the red and purple candy bars I'd discovered in the welcome basket Jess brought over that first day. "Chocolate Cherry Ripe or a Cadbury Dairy Milk. Unless you feel brave and want to try Vegemite." I wiggle the jar and pick up the Dairy Milk. "Oh, it's lamington flavor."

Aunt Vi chooses wisely, grabbing the candy bar out of my hand. "I'd much rather taste it than sit on it." She lovingly hip checks me out of the way and pours herself some coffee before turning to me with the candy bar unwrapped and the mug still on the counter. "Thank you for being there earlier. It's been a while since I had an attack. I had wondered if the medicine was doing anything. Now I know."

She takes a bite of the chocolate, closing her eyes. "Ooh, that's good."

"Are you truly okay?" Pressure builds behind my eyes. Things feel shifted. Not uncomfortable, but I'm seeing my aunt with new glasses.

"I will be."

"You scared me. I thought we were crossing things off your bucket list because you didn't have long." My voice cracks, and I have to force myself to continue. "I just, well, Gran hid so much from me and now…"

"Oh, kiddo." Aunt Vi sets the chocolate on the counter and wraps me into her arms. "I'm so sorry. I've been good for so long, but that's an excuse. I should have told you that I struggle with severe depression. I need the meds to think straight."

"How long have you been taking meds?"

"About five years. Your mom is the one who took me to that first appointment."

"Mom?" I pull back.

Aunt Vi chuckles as she retrieves her coffee, taking a long sip before continuing. "I know it seems like we'd like to mud wrestle at times, but your mom has been one of my biggest supporters. Your parents were the ones to show me I needed help and that it was okay."

"What brought on this attack?"

"I feel so stupid, but with the time zone change, and writing, and all the excitement, I forgot to take my meds." She takes another sip, wincing. "Finding out about Angie was one thing too much. The panic hit and I couldn't do anything. It's so silly, I know, but with my meds all messed up, I wasn't prepared."

"Angie Thorne?"

Aunt Vi nods. "She'll be on one of the panels with me at the Book Expo in Brisbane. It brought up a lot of things—insecurities, doubts. The comparing game never ends well. She has twenty books published and another releasing in December."

"But you have a movie."

"I know. And I know better than to compare too, but without my brain in the right frame, I took it way too hard. In college, Angie accused me of lying about the panic attacks. She said I was faking them to get out of doing things with her." She makes a face then smiles sadly, apologetically. "I've gotten used to hiding it. I have thought about doing a 'Real Reel' about it, but the thought of being so vulnerable and what the Internet trolls might say held me back."

"I think people need to hear your story."

"Probably. Especially since that's about as real as it gets."

"Live boldly," I whisper.

"Don't let fear stop you. I guess if I'm going to tell you to take a chance, I should too." She motions toward my notes, using it as a transition away from her panic. "What happened in the world while I recharged my batteries?"

"I found a secret room and paintings and Gran's journal. Oh, and Libby has a journal of Margaret's. Margaret used to work at the palace for Queen Charlotte. There's a princess, but we can't find her name."

Aunt Vi's eyebrows raise to her hairline. "I guess a lot happened."

"Do you think we could go to Northargyle while we're in New Zealand? It's closer to there than here."

"Definitely. Let's make it happen."

My phone alerts me that I have a video call waiting. I accept and am greeted by a hospital room.

"Say hello to Henrix Carey Morgan. I have a son!" Asher's face is brighter than lights on a night construction site as he pans to Rachel holding a sleeping miniature of him.

"Henrix?" Aunt Vi asks.

"It's a combination of Dad's name and Rachel's dad, Henry."

"It's perfect," I say. "So is he."

"Move the camera closer," Aunt Vi demands.

For the next ten minutes, we *ooh* and *aah*. Asher's call is perfect timing. The joy of new life is exactly what Aunt Vi and I truly needed to end this day with.

Hi all, Vi here. This "Real Reel" is going to be a little different. First, my niece is holding the camera, so no selfie arm in use. I can't get her to join me on this side of the camera, but her holding the camera steady is in line with this video. Bear with me. My niece is here in Australia trying to discover her grandmother's story, which has me thinking about my story.

I've always prided myself on these "Real Reels," that I'm one hundred percent authentically living. But I've been reluctant to get rid of one filter. After experiencing a rather severe panic attack in front of my niece—

Well, with Abigail's encouragement, a whole lot of praying, and coffee, I've decided to tell you my story. To remove this mask once and for all. So, here goes.

Before I came to Australia, I wondered if my antidepressants were working. Yes, I take medication for depression. I have for five years. It took me so long to go to a doctor and admit I needed something. I'd been raised to believe that as a child of God it would be wrong to take medications. Christians shouldn't get depressed, let alone take drugs for it! I just needed to have more faith.

The last few years I've come to realize how wrong that belief was. Christians, no matter how strong their faith, are still humans, with bodies that break and emotions that aren't always trustworthy. I need medication to think straight, and that's okay. Good, even. God gave us the knowledge and understanding to know how to treat these issues. For me, that means taking medication to fix a chemical imbalance in my brain. Kind of like taking Tylenol for a headache or insulin for diabetes. Of course, like a headache, medication isn't the whole solution, but it's definitely a part.

Even with the medication, every day I have to live intentionally. It's a daily—sometimes hourly—battle to speak powerful truth to myself rather than destructive self-talk. I try to set goals that I can obtain, even if it's making my coffee in the morning. In all honesty, there were days that I couldn't even put a K-cup in a Keurig.

I'm so thankful for my niece and the rest of my family. Their support, prayer, and love has propelled me through some dark days. And I'm thankful for all of you watching this "Real Reel." Praying you feel loved and a little less alone today. Also, I'd love to hear your story if you want to share.

Until the next "Real Reel." If you're near the Brisbane Hotel on the eighteenth, stop by the Book Expo and say "hi."

Chapter Thirteen

A re you sure I look okay?" Aunt Vi asks for the tenth time in the last five minutes. Her black dress balloons out like an umbrella as she spins. She's wearing low heels and silver drop earrings. No signature Converse. No signature quirky earrings. Her curly hair is down and shoulder length.

I didn't think she'd go through with it. I don't like it.

Two days ago, Jess suggested a spa day when Aunt Vi mentioned wanting a new look for the Book Expo, something a little more professional. Something that made her feel battle ready and more adult when she faced her nemesis.

I'd been happy to let my aunt do the makeover alone until she'd made the comment that maybe Colter would be at the Book Expo. I now have layers, highlights, and lowlights. While Aunt Vi looks younger, I look… well, not older, but a more mature and updated version of myself.

The cringe level when I think (and rethink) of our awkward meet-cute is at "maybe Colter thinks I'm cute?" rather than "maybe the helicopter could drop me in the Sahara." Antarctica would be nice, but my burning mortification would melt the ice and cause a flood. Kinda like Tiddalick.

"Are you sure I look okay?" Aunt Vi asks, bringing that question up to eleven times.

"You look classy," I tell her.

"I'm not used to adult clothes. But I have to say, these heels make my legs look rather fetching."

I'm betting she won't be able to survive the entire event in those heels, but maybe she'll prove stronger than I'm giving her credit for. She's already proven her strength since posting her "Real Reel." The comments and support rolling in are still going strong. So many people out there have similar stories. Of course, there are those telling her she's doing the Christian life wrong, but I'm so proud of Aunt Vi for not letting those few trolls stop her from sharing the truth with love.

"Makeup time." Jess enters the room with a bag in her hand.

I can't deny the tiny spark of excitement alongside the nerves that come with wearing makeup. When I told Jess I wasn't wearing any, she rushed home to gather her gear. The women in my life aren't big makeup users. Mom only wears mascara on Sundays and at special award banquets, and with five brothers, I never had anyone to be girlie with. Gran wore the bare minimum but didn't spend time coaching me on how to apply it. And Aunt Vi, well, she only wears makeup when she's on TV. Then spends weeks trying to remove the evidence. Rachel and Stefi wear it, but we're not at the "let's do each other's makeup" level.

Jess has me sit on a low stool. I eye her overflowing duffle that could easily double as a body bag. Nothing like the small case Mom keeps her makeup in. Why do I feel like I'm in the dentist chair?

"You have the perfect bone structure for makeup." Jess picks up a paintbrush. "I wish I could look as effortlessly beautiful. I'm not going to do too much, or you'll be prettier than me."

"Not possible," I say with a laugh.

"Close your eyes," she instructs.

I sit still, following her instructions of when to open my eyes, when to look up, when to suck in my cheeks. Not too much? Um, this is an intense process of brushes and colors.

"Limo's here," Jaxon says at the same time Jess says she's done. She squeals as if it's the groom come to catch a sneak peek.

Why did my mind jump to that? Jaxon and Jess are nowhere near ready to venture down the aisle. While I've never seen my brother like this, I do have some reservations about how quickly he's attached himself to Jess. Not that I'm comfortable voicing my concerns. Jaxon is wise, I trust his judgment.

"We'll be down in a minute," Jess says. "Okay, time to look, it might shock you since you don't wear makeup. But my work is amazing. I wonder if I could get paid to do it?"

With that warning, I take a giant step toward the mirror. A startled cry escapes. "Oh my, that's a lot of makeup. And my cheeks—I look like a Raggedy Ann doll." Or a clown.

Jess rolls her eyes. "The pink will blend in more as you wear it."

"You look amazing," Aunt Vi says as she takes her turn in the makeup chair. "I'd like to order the same."

I study my reflection, trying to breathe as I adjust the knee-length emerald green dress. When I'd showed it to Jess at the store, she said it was her brother's favorite color. I don't know why I gave in, other than it makes my hazel eyes pop closer to green.

"Do you have your emergency clothes?" I ask Aunt Vi when Jess finishes with her. Jess hadn't painted my aunt nearly as much as me. You can't tell she's wearing makeup at all. It's lovely, though, and very her.

"Sure do. Even put the jumper in there." She winks at her use of the Australian word for sweater. I hadn't wanted to say anything about taking it, but if Colter is there, we should return it.

Jaxon stands at the bottom of the stairs with Devon. Both guys asked to join us for the Book Expo. Devon, in shorts and a light blue polo, is casual to my dressy—a mismatched pair. But I hardly know him well enough to dictate his wardrobe. Not that I could see myself doing that even if I did know someone well.

"Wow! Look at you. You're hot." Devon whistles as I reach the ground floor. I try not to snort as he steps forward, offering his arm. "My lady."

Jess fixes Jaxon's collar. She whispers something only he can hear, and his grin grows. They've been sitting apart from people ever since their dinner at Sugarleaf Manor, whispering in corners, sharing secret looks and inside jokes. Spending every waking minute together. The direction they're heading—well, my mind wandering to the altar isn't that outlandish.

Devon escorts me to the BMW. Aunt Vi is already in the back seat, and Carl is behind the wheel. Lisa arranged for him to be our chauffeur. Secretly, I was rather happy that I had an excuse not to ride all the way there with Devon. He's driving separately, so he can stop by a friend's house near Brisbane to pick up something or other. I'm still not quite sure what he does for a job.

"Sure you don't want to ride with me?" Devon asks as he plays the gentleman and opens the door for me.

"I'd feel bad leaving Aunt Vi alone." I climb into the car. I was hoping Jess would ride with us, all the girls in one car, but my brother is more attractive.

"Okay, see you there," Devon says before closing the door. He taps the top of the car, a signal that we're good to go.

Aunt Vi sits quietly, wringing her hands.

I place one of mine on top of hers. "It's going to be fun. Breathe."

"I want it started already. Too much wondering." Her leg begins shaking.

"Angie might not even show up," I say, trying to offer something.

"Not a chance." Aunt Vi laughs. "She wouldn't miss this opportunity. It's too big, publicity and career wise. And I am gonna be there for her to torture."

<hr />

The event is at a hotel, one with rooms for rent, unlike Greer's. The main speaking event is in one of the ballrooms. There are three. Vendors are set up along the hallway, spilling into one of the biggest rooms I've ever seen. Like gazing upon Lake Erie, I can't see the other side. Chandeliers sparkle from the ceiling at differing heights. It takes my breath away.

I thought I'd be too dressy, but the outfits range from shorts and T-shirts to full princess gowns, steampunk ensembles, and Tolkien characters. Aunt Vi isn't the only one in costume for the event.

Devon, Jaxon, and Jess head toward the other ballroom to check it out. I want to join them in wandering through a world of authors and genres, but my place is with my aunt waiting for her assignment at the check-in table. I'm not leaving her alone no matter how many times she's assured me she's fine and did take her meds.

Glenna, the same woman from the Sugarleaf Manor signing, is at a table set up for Aunt Vi, complete with banner. There's no headset in sight, and her gray hair is down and loose around her face for this event. Glenna does a double take, approval this time instead of a sneer. Almost a smile. Looks like my aunt won her over. Or the outfit did.

Aunt Vi scans her schedule before handing it to me. Her drooping shoulders tell me nothing changed. She and Angie are on the same panel, talking about how to write great villains. Ironic.

"At least our tables aren't next to each other," she whispers, nodding toward the other end of the room, where I make out Angie's banner. Where my aunt's photo is natural, free, and fun, Angie's is akin to an eighties model glamor shot complete with poofy hair, shoulder pads, and makeup that will never blend.

I grab a book when Aunt Vi gasps, thinking she spotted her nemesis. Not sure what I'd do with the hardcover. A shield to hide us or a weapon for shooing Angie away?

"Is that Colter?" Aunt Vi asks, grabbing my arm.

"Where?" She'd better not be joking.

"At the door."

It's him. Commence full-body thrill. He's wearing a gray dress shirt with the sleeves rolled and dark jeans. His dark hair looks shorter, while his goatee is fuller, as though he'd started growing it when I met him.

Their eyes meet. Everyone else disappears as he crosses the room, the crowd parting as if by magic. He remembers her. He hasn't been able to stop thinking about her. He takes her hand, lifting it to his lips.

Then a tall, poised, gorgeous blonde moves next to him, and he dips his head to speak with her. His face lights up. I called it. Power couple right there. Happy, in love, with songs written about them, and turning the heads of everyone in a room.

Colter isn't going to rush across the room. Ever.

"I'm going to find the bathroom," I say. Nope, even my new look isn't going to work.

"Don't hide." Aunt Vi smiles, and I know she's seen right through me. "If I can't, you can't. Remember that, oh favorite, only niece."

"Not hiding."

She quirks an eyebrow.

"Okay, totally hiding, but I'll only be a minute. I need to mentally prepare."

In the bathroom, I study my reflection in the gilded mirror, thankful for a moment alone. Jess was right—the shock of seeing the makeup has dimmed, the pink of my cheeks blending to a more natural state. I look like summertime. Sun-kissed skin, hazel eyes glowing closer to green, hair highlighted. Not that I'd win a beauty contest, but I could compete.

I tilt my head. Maybe Colter won't recognize me. Ugh, who am I kidding. He won't glance my way, not with gorgeousness on his arm.

I adjust my dress and fluff my hair, pulling confidence back around me. "You can do this. You can say hi to Colter, at least return his sweater," I whisper to my reflection. "I can meet Colter's friend, be a mature adult—"

"Hello?" a voice calls.

I jump and whack my hand on the counter.

"Is someone out there?"

"Yes?" I respond, flapping my hand to alleviate the sting. Guess I should have looked in the stalls before assuming I was alone.

"Foolish me chose a jumpsuit. I can't get the zipper down. I've been here for twenty minutes. I have to pee. You'd be a lifesaver."

"I'd be happy to help."

The stall door opens slowly to reveal a sweaty-faced woman. No, not just any woman. Angie Thorne.

I hesitate a moment for Aunt Vi's sake then unzip the jumpsuit, knowing my aunt would want me to help. "Kill with kindness" and all that jazz. I wait while Angie goes, turning on the faucet so she doesn't feel self-conscious about the quiet, then rezip the jumpsuit when she's done.

"Thank you so much," she says, holding out her washed hand. "Angie Thorne. If I can do anything for you, please ask. How about a signed photo and book?"

Aunt Vi would love that.

Angie's eyes narrow as she studies my face. "Do I know you?"

I shake my head. "We haven't officially met. I'm Abigail Morgan. Violet's niece."

"Ah, that's why you're familiar. Well, I guess you won't be wanting a signed book," she says with a chuckle.

I put a hand on her arm before she can leave. With a deep breath I decide to just go for this. Be bold.

"Actually, my aunt told me you're from Northargyle. Could you tell me about it? I can't find any information about the country, and the website I had found disappeared."

"What would you like to know? I owe you one." She motions toward the stall.

"Is it haunted? Or is it a beautiful, normal island? Was the royal family murdered? Did the queen kill herself? What about the cursed crown?"

"Who have you been talking to? It sounds like a plot from one of your aunt's novels. Are you a writer too?"

"No, I'm in Australia trying to figure out my gran's story. It keeps getting tangled up with Northargyle, but there's no information anywhere."

"Northargyle is a beautiful island. It's had its share of heartache for sure. Lots of royals have died, but through accidents, not murder. As far as I know." Angie laughs like it's a far-fetched idea. "King Hamish's father took the throne when the entire Brisbane family was killed in a plane crash."

"Queen Charlotte?"

"Yes, and her husband, King Thomas, and children, Rosiah and Michael."

"Rosiah?" I gasp. "That's my middle name."

Angie studies me a beat as if mulling over her response to my declaration, her painted-on brows arching like boomerangs. Apparently, she decides I'm worthy because she says, "Not many know this, and I can't share how I do, but Princess Rosiah ran away days before her seventeenth birthday. Some say they found her, but I've always wondered if it's possible she didn't die with her parents and brother. Now there's a plotline for you."

"Do you think she could be alive? Are you talking like a Romanov situation?" The what-ifs pour in, producing Broadway-level scenarios on my mind theater.

"I like to think she is. Or was." Angie pats my arm. "This has been lovely, but I should get to my booth. My fans are waiting. See you around, Abigail." With one more pat, she exits the bathroom.

"Rosiah." I whisper the name I know so well. First Mom's middle name, then mine. I thought it was the combination of my grandparents' names. Josiah and Rose. Had Gran chosen the name in honor of the princess who died? Or had the princess survived?

Was Rose short for Rosiah? Was Gran the runaway princess? That would be an interesting plot twist. I feel like I've entered another dimension.

I need to find Aunt Vi, tell her—

I rush from the bathroom and smack into someone. Strong hands grip my arms, my nose smashed against a solid chest. I inhale. Eucalyptus and spearmint. I know *that* smell. It faded from the sweater, but here it is in full force.

"Are you okay?" a masculine voice says.

"Sorry, I was—" I'm scared to look up. What if it's not him?

But it is. Colter smiling, a glint in his eyes.

"Wait, are you talking to me this time?" I ask, mind cringing back to the awkwardness of our last meeting.

"Unless there's another frog around here I haven't spotted yet." He glances over my shoulder. "Any interesting artifacts in the loo?"

"Just Angie Thorne," I say without filtering. "She told me—" I catch myself before oversharing that my grandmother might be a runaway princess from Northargyle. It's not possible. "I'm still processing."

Colter laughs. "Hello, Abigail Morgan. I was hoping to run into you again. Not literally, as it happens."

He's still holding my arms. I find I don't mind, not one bit.

"You do recognize me. I got a new look. Cut my hair and added highlights. And Jess did my makeup. I don't wear makeup, and I don't look like myself. Well, I do, just—" I close my eyes and take a deep breath. *I need to be banned from talking around him.*

"You look as lovely as the first time we met." I don't get the sense he's being cruel. He seems amused by me, if anything. "I enjoyed our last encounter immensely and haven't stopped thinking about it."

"I was praying you'd wiped that encounter from your mind."

"Sorry, but no. I remember it all."

"So, she is real?" a sweet voice asks.

I had forgotten the reason I ran to the bathroom to give myself a pep talk. *Highlighted, styled blonde hair. Kind, light brown eyes. Classy blue dress with white butterfly pattern and heels.* I can't tell if she's wearing makeup. If she is, it's blended well. When she smiles, I know right away she must be Colter's sister. Her next words confirm it, easing my jealousy spree.

"When my brother told me he'd met Faith Mackenzie, I thought he'd gone crazy."

"Abigail, this is my sister, Eliana." Colter motions to her, releasing me but staying close to my side. "She's an Angie Thorne fan, but I plan on converting her to the right side of fiction. Not that there's anything wrong with romance."

"I thought you were his girlfriend," I blurt out. "I always wished I had a sister. I have five brothers."

"Do they all call you Indiana Abbie?" Colter's lips twitch then he full out smiles.

"They think I'm an archeologist. I have a degree in museum studies and love researching. In a way, I do 'hunt' for stories, but I'm not out in the field digging up lost cities."

"No wonder you two get along," Eliana says. "Colter is a storyteller like Mom."

My gaze goes to Colter's arm and the Romans twelve tattoo clearly on display today.

"Colt's told me so much about you." Eliana's voice is clear, precise—not forceful—and captures attention in the way she delivers her words. One of those voices that makes you hang on every word. Her accent is adorable.

"The crazy American in the library oversharing her life's story and talking way too much?" I wince.

"He never mentioned you were American, just refreshing. And that he admired the way you helped set up chairs at the event even though you weren't paid staff."

"Actually." Colter clears his throat. "I said she was refreshing and mysterious with a servant's heart."

"There's nothing mysterious about me."

"My brother felt he knew you because he knows Faith. He told me that you were, and I quote, 'picking up a conversation you've always been having.'"

My face heats. I'm pretty sure that was a compliment, but what if I understood him wrong? What if he's like this with every female? Maybe he's just nice. I mean, who gives their designer sweater to a stranger?

"Abigail," Jess calls before I can tell Colter I have his sweater. She rushes down the hallway and grabs my arm, crushing the tingles Colter caused with his touch. She doesn't even spare the siblings a glance before dragging me away.

I have to put quite a bit of effort into slowing us down.

"You have to come to the photo booth. We need pictures. Also, this place is crazy expensive to book a room," she says with a giggle. "Your brother is buying me a necklace. You have to come help me pick one out."

I shoot Colter and Eliana a wide-eyed glance. Leaving them is the last thing I want to do. I've only just found him again. He remembered me. And talked about me with his sister.

"Jess, that's Colter."

Jess stops and glances at them, eyes narrowing. "Just as I thought. Cove people. And clearly he has a girlfriend."

"That's his sister."

"You're too good for them. Come on, your brother and Devon are gonna spoil us."

"But—"

Jess is strong, pulling me so quickly I get whiplash when I send one more apologetic look Colter and Eliana's way.

Lord, please don't let them leave without giving me a chance to apologize. They must think me so rude. I can't stand the thought of them thinking I'm rude.

<hr />

I was right. The heels didn't make it to the end. Neither did the designer dress and carefully styled hair. As Aunt Vi takes the stage for the panel, sitting at the opposite end of the long table from Angie, I laugh. She's wearing jeans, a Faith, Gotta Have Her T-shirt, blue Converse, coffee mug earrings, and her hair piled on top of her head. There's the aunt I know and adore.

The emcee begins the "Writing Compelling Villains" panel by instructing the panelists to pass the mic and share their name, where they're from, and their favorite book that's not their own.

"Did your aunt sit on another lamington? I could've sworn she was wearing a dress." Colter moves beside me, bringing a sigh of relief.

I relax at the scent of him. Thank God for second chances.

"No lamington or any other kind of food. Oh, we brought your sweater. I was about to tell you that earlier. Ugh, you must think me so rude. I tried to get Jess to stop—"

"Abigail." Colter touches my arm, reigniting those tingles. "Don't give it another moment of concern. We'll say we're even. My friend took me away from Sugarleaf and yours from here." He glances around, his hand moving back to his side. "But to be safe, warn me if they're coming for you and I'll block them, if you'd like."

"They were heading to a concert or something." I smile at him. "I was praying that you hadn't left. I wanted to talk more with you and Eliana. Oh, and I should get your sweater."

"I wondered where that went," Eliana says as she appears on Colter's other side. She has an armload of Angie's books. The whimsical silhouette cover of the newest release makes me want to read it. "You may as well keep the jumper. I'll buy him another one."

"Or you could make me one." Colter trails off as Angie Thorne announces her name.

Angie proceeds with her introduction. As she's making eye contact with the crowd, she passes by me, but her gaze comes back, and she stutters on the part about where she's from, upholding her lie that she's from New Zealand.

The reaction is on par with Darcy seeing Wickham. Well, not the hatred, but the shock of seeing someone from your past that you never expected to see. Someone out of context.

Colter's easy smile returns when the mic passes to the next author.

"What was that about?" I ask Colter, not wanting to be nosy but really wanting to be nosy. "Do you know Angie Thorne? Let me guess—you're her spy?"

He puts a hand over his heart. "I would never betray Faith."

"He's always loved Faith," Eliana says.

I vaguely hear the rest of the authors' details, distracted by the man standing beside me. Finally, Aunt Vi is handed the mic and gives her information, ending with *Little Women* as her favorite book.

Colter chuckles then nods toward the stage. "So, besides your aunt's, of course, what's your favorite book?"

"*Howl's Moving Castle*," I say without having to think.

"I've never heard of that one."

"When I first saw you, you reminded me of Wizard Howl. Handsome, quirky, magical, handsome—" *Maybe he won't notice I said handsome twice?*

"And now that you've met me, do you still think so?"

"You'll have to read the book to find out. Do your own research." My grin is positively wicked. Ha! Two can play this game.

"Well played, Miss Morgan."

Eliana eyes us, so I explain. "Your brother was cruel and didn't tell me the ending and who made Tiddalick laugh."

"How rude, brother," she says with a shake of her head.

He shrugs. "Abigail likes researching stories."

"I sure do. So, what about you?" I ask, Colter. "What's your favorite book?"

"I'm partial to *The Scarlet Pimpernel.*"

"That's my dad's favorite." Dad's copy is about as worn as my favorite *Howl's Moving Castle* version. "Why do you love it so much?"

"The wit. The sense of justice. Sir Percy Blakeney had a great heart for the people and an unmatched love for his wife. Keeping his secret and distance in order to protect her. I admire Marguerite's drive to discover the identity of the Scarlet Pimpernel only to fall in love with his service and cause."

"I haven't read the book, but I've watched the movie." I wince at his playful eyebrow lift.

"For shame," he says in mock horror.

"And Dad's favorite scene wasn't even in the movie. The kissing of the stairs."

"Even more reason to read the book." He kisses his fingers before flicking them outward in the chef's kiss gesture. "And the reveal chapter—perfection."

"Maybe I can find a copy to read on the flight home."

"When do you head back to America?" Eliana asks.

"We're heading to New Zealand first. Aunt Vi has two book events—one on October 31 and the other on November 16. We fly home November 22." Aunt Vi's been planning her costume for the Halloween event but won't share. Guarding it like gold in Fort Knox. "Will you guys be going to the Halloween event?" A scene plays in the theater of my mind, wondering what costume Colter would choose.

A mask covers half his face, but she knows those lively eyes and that playful smirk. He's a cross between Zorro and Westley from The Princess Bride. *Her heart flutters, her costume compliments his, a damsel-not-in-distress but in longing. They stand atop a cliff, the wind flowing through her hair, coaxing her braid free. As the music swells...*

"Sadly, no," Colter says, pulling me back from myself right before I swoon. "And, sadly, my sister and I must get home."

"Already?" This moment was not nearly anywhere close to being enough. "You're not staying for the panel?"

"It's a long drive to our estate." He glances at Eliana, who nods. "My sister and I were scheming earlier. Feel free to say no since you already have friends here."

"I don't," I say quickly then catch myself. "I mean, I do have friends, but I would've stayed with you and Eliana if given the choice earlier."

"Told you so, brother." Eliana laughs. She tilts her head toward me. "He had a moment."

"I did not have a moment." He tries unsuccessfully to make a serious face.

"You were grumpy."

"Fine, I had a moment." He grins at his sister before turning back to me. "Eliana and I are planning on visiting our friends, Seth and Mia, tomorrow. They have a café that's part food, part art studio. Would you like to join us?"

"I would love to." My words come out in a squeal. Oops.

"Your aunt gave me your address earlier, so we can pick you up. Say around nine?"

"Perfect."

Eliana reaches out a hand, balancing her stack of books like a pro. "It was so nice to meet you. And I'm glad you're real."

"You too." *Glad you're his sister and not his girlfriend.*

"Until tomorrow." Colter offers a small bow then takes the stack of books from his sister before they disappear into the crowd.

Chapter Fourteen

Today, I'm spending the day with Colter and Eliana. There's a song in my heart and in my steps as I ready myself. I hum as I choose a café art studio-inspired ensemble—a colorful gypsy skirt and a dressier white T-shirt. I forgo the makeup, taking extra time to try a new hairstyle I'd seen demonstrated online. It actually turns out rather well. After tucking bobby pins into wayward strands, I continue humming on my way downstairs to check if Aunt Vi is in her zone at the table.

She stands at the bottom of the stairs with a smile and a steaming mug. "Good morning," she greets as she hands me the coffee. "Not that you need the caffeine injection this morning."

"Thanks." I take a sip, looking her over. She's showered and energized, her orange and ginger smell permeating the kitchen. "I heard you typing."

"I wrote 10,000 words." She's giddy in her delight. "I'm so excited about this story. I woke up writing but wanted to see you before you left."

I eye her, needing to know. "Did you actually give Faith a boyfriend?"

"It's a crush from the past. So not new. I'd been playing with this plot for a while, but the timing was never right. Keep being my inspiration. You and Jax both."

There's a knock on the front door as I'm finishing my coffee.

"He's early," I say with a yelp.

"Oh, I have a signed book for Colter. I sold out and promised I'd have one for him today." Aunt Vi hurries up the stairs.

I rinse out my mug on the way to the front door, which opens before I get there. It's not Colter. Or Eliana.

I refrain from groaning as Devon and Jess enter the cottage.

"The car's all ready," Devon says. "Get your purse. This is gonna be good."

"We didn't have any plans—" I start.

"We're going to the castle, since your aunt was sick last time."

"Oh, no. I'm sorry, but I can't. I already have plans," I say, seeking Jess's support. "I told you last night. Colter and Eliana asked me to go to their friends' café with them."

Jess's eyes narrow. "You didn't say anything."

Had I dreamed it? No, I told her. She squealed with me, making me promise to tell her all about it when I got back.

"Who's Colter?" Devon asks.

"Cove people," Jess tells her brother, keeping her eyes on me. "You can't forsake us for Cove people."

"I cleared my schedule for you," Devon chimes in. "I could've stayed in Brisbane making money."

"Can we go tomorrow?"

"I'm busy," Devon says.

Jess is texting as my brother appears. She holds up her finger as she finishes then leans his way to kiss him on the lips.

Maybe Jaxon will help me out here. He knows I have plans with Colter and Eliana. He wasn't too far from Jess when I'd told her.

"What's wrong?" Jaxon asks Jess, his fingers twining with hers. He lifts their connected hands and kisses the back of hers.

"Abigail says she won't go with us to the castle," Jess says with a pout. "She already kept us from going last time."

"Why?" My brother tilts his head.

My heart stutters, and I shrink back at the disappointment on his face. I hate that look more than anything. Like I'm a complete failure. That I shouldn't be allowed to exist.

"I'm spending the day with Colter and Eliana," I try to explain. "We're going to their friends' café."

"The sister I know would never abandon her friends. Her true friends who love her and want to spend time with her. I don't remember you being so selfish and negligent."

"But I promised—"

"I came to spend time with you. Come on, sis, don't be an idiot," Jaxon continues, firing away like he's on the battlefield. "Besides, I thought you had boundaries. I don't know how I feel about my sister going off with strangers."

Pressure builds behind my eyes. Colter and Eliana aren't strangers, at least not to my heart, but am I an idiot wanting to go with them when I've longed to spend more time with my brother? But never in my wildest dreams would I imagine my brother speaking to me like that. Cruel. Unkind. Who is this version?

A young boy with brown curls, probably about fourteen, rides up on a bike. "Abigail Morgan?" he calls out.

"That's her," Jess says, practically pushing me into Devon, who still stands in the doorway with an odd kind of twisted smirk on his face.

The boy hands me an envelope. Inside is a single typed line.

> *We hate to do this, but something has come up, and we are unable to go today.*

There's no signature, but there's no mistaking who it's from.

Jess looks over my shoulder. "Told you so."

My hope crashes, and I bite my lip to keep the tears at bay—the tears that had already been close to appearing after my brother's harsh words. I know life happens, but it still hurts that I won't get to spend time with Colter and Eliana.

I check the note again, begging it to have changed even though it won't. Something came up? So vague. Perhaps a friend unexpectedly arrived at their house. But what if Colter got hurt? What if Eliana got sick? Was something going around at the Book Expo? What if this is a ransom note?

Should I try calling? No, I couldn't do that even if I had the guts because I don't have either of their phone numbers. Unlike Devon and Jess, who seem to have one glued to their hands, there was never evidence that Colter or Eliana even had phones.

With a sigh, I turn to Devon and try to smile. "I guess I can go with you to the castle."

Devon cheers as he picks me up. My hand gets trapped between us, and I drop the paper. It crushes under Devon's feet. The disappointment at the loss of time with Colter and Eliana is replaced by a spark of interest in the castle. The day won't be a disaster. Maybe Colter and Eliana will be free tomorrow.

"I have the—" Aunt Vi joins the party with a book, a mug, and a T-shirt. Her eyes narrow when she sees my failure of a smile. "Where's Colter?"

"He backed out," Jess says as she picks up the crumbled note, ripping it to shreds before throwing it away. "Cove people are all the same. I told Abigail that they are users. They make you think you're special when you're really not."

I want to fight for Colter and Eliana, say that they are wonderful, but I can't push the words past my disappointment.

"Let's go have fun," Devon says, putting his arm around me.

I pull myself out from under him, saying I need to fetch my tote and will meet him at the car.

"You okay?" Aunt Vi whispers as she gives me a hug.

"I'll be fine. We're going to go see the castle ruins."

"Don't sound too thrilled." She chuckles. "I'm sure Colter and Eliana will be in contact."

"A girl can dream."

I slip my tote over my shoulder then meet everyone out front. Devon sits in his Mustang, the top down. There's another car behind his with Jess in the driver's seat. Unease builds within me. I stop my brother. "We aren't all riding together?"

"I want to spend time with Jess."

"But I don't feel—"

"We're all going to the same place. You're fine." He dismisses my concern as he climbs into her car. Jess drives off before I can beg to ride with them.

"Come on, Abs." Devon honks the horn, and I take a deep breath before settling in the passenger's side. "You can throw that in the back." He starts to remove my tote from my arms, but I tighten my grip.

"That's okay. I'll hold it." I need the security blanket.

"What's that?" He touches the image of Calcifer, the fire demon, screen printed on the front. "'I hope your bacon burns.'"

"It's from my favorite book, *Howl's Moving Castle*. Calcifer says that to Sophie because he doesn't want her to cook breakfast on him. He doesn't allow anyone other than Howl to do that, but Sophie forces him to cooperate." Calcifer is on par with Howl as my favorite character. I've underlined so many of his quips.

"Sounds like a kiddie book."

I manage a smile, reminding myself that we don't have to like all the same things in order to hang out.

Devon revs the engine, and we're off.

Closing my eyes, I breathe deeply, trying to enjoy the wind in my hair and the sunshine. Someone honks, and I open my eyes in time to see Jess waving as she turns right. Devon keeps going straight.

I twist in my seat, receiving a mouthful of hair as a reward. "Devon, your sister turned. You—"

"This way is quicker. We'll beat them there."

Nervousness ruffles the fringes of my control, but I force myself to resettle. Devon knows the area, and he's driving the speed limit. I have to trust him. Unless I'm willing to try my hand at jumping from a moving vehicle. If only I chose jeans…

A sleek, black car meets us on the road. I almost die when my gaze locks with Eliana's. Time slows as our vehicles pass like a special effect in a movie. I can see every detail of the confusion on Eliana's face.

Reality snaps back, and I twist once again. "Devon, stop!" I yell. "That was Colter and Eliana. Please, go back. I—"

"It couldn't have been them. They typed you a note."

"Maybe their plans changed again. Please, go back."

"I'm sure it wasn't them." Devon keeps driving, the speedometer slowly rising.

This is a nightmare.

"Please," I try again. "Turn around."

"Wouldn't it be nice if we could all be rich enough not to care about others' time and plans. Gotta love the luxury of saying one thing and doing another. Money. I hate rich people."

I clutch the door handle and try one more time. "Just stop. Please. I'll walk back. I need to make sure it wasn't them." Why did I get in this car alone? Why didn't I insist that Jaxon and Jess ride with us?

"Settle down," Devon says. "I'm taking you to the stupid castle. First you're demanding, begging me to take you there, and now you're all 'take me home.' Make a choice, Abs. You backed out last time. It's like you don't even want to go." Devon drives faster. "Women. Say what you want. Make it easier on us. Men aren't mind readers."

Is it just me or did I not tell him exactly what I wanted? For him to turn around? To stop. And when did I demand to go to the castle ruins? Yes, I did "back out" last time, but Devon had been so understanding.

Tears cloud my vision. The road before us swims. My hands are shaking, my body's shaking, my mind is even shaking—it's too cloudy. I might pass out. I can't be in this car. I sniffle, wiping at my face. I don't want to cry, but it's not looking like I have a choice in that either.

Devon glares at me. "Girls always think tears will solve everything. Pathetic. What a faker," he mutters.

"I'm n-not faking," I stutter. My grip on my tote is white-knuckled.

God, please. Please get me safely out of this situation. I can't believe I didn't stay home. I could've spent time with Aunt Vi. Why did I leave? Maybe Jaxon will take me back once we're at the castle.

A loud bang, like a gunshot, interrupts my prayer. *Clunk-clunk-clunk.* The car jerks to the side. A flat tire.

I hold in my cheer. That was a quick answer to prayer.

Devon swears as he pulls to the side of the road. He checks the tire then promptly throws a tantrum. He might be an adult, but there is no other description for the way he stomps around, swearing at the tire, the car, and the world in general. At least he leaves me out of the cursing range.

I vault to the grass, thankful that the car has stopped. There's no way I'm getting back in it. I might or might not have shut the door harder than required.

Devon's still yelling as he holds up his phone in search of service.

Time for me to do the next right thing. The obvious thing in this case.

"Pop the trunk," I tell him. My words are calm and measured even though I'm energized by God's answer to prayer. "I'll change the tire. Is there a spare?"

It's nice having something to do with my hands. I feel like a victim in Aunt Vi's novels, or maybe I'm the villain planning the demise of the convertible. Some villain I am, offering to fix the flat.

Dad made sure all of us knew how to change a tire. With five brothers, I couldn't be left out, and I'm glad for it. Although, I never expected my first chance to show off my skills would be in front of a guy who loves cars as much as Devon does.

It takes me a bit, but I figure out how to remove the old tire and put on the new one.

Devon walks over when I'm closing the trunk. Sweat drips down my back. If I'm lucky, my stench will repulse him. He spent the entire tire change talking to someone on the phone, not even pretending to help.

"Let's go," Devon says, already behind the wheel.

Goodness, not even a thank you.

"I'm going to walk," I say, grabbing my tote. The top down means I didn't have to reopen the Mustang door.

"Don't be stupid."

I scowl as I leave. Stupid would be getting in that car. Or in any vehicle ever again with Devon Greer. He calls my name, but I keep right on walking. I dial Aunt Vi's number when I find a signal but end up texting that I'm heading back to the cottage when she doesn't answer. Even if I'm fifty miles from Hyacinth Cottage, and even if I have to run away from snakes or other Australian wildlife, I'm not allowing even one stray hair back in that Mustang.

Sweating, crying, angry at myself. Frustrated. Relieved. Giddy. I'm the entire wheel of emotions at the moment. With greasy hands, a ruined hairdo, and sweatiness to boot. *Think of the good. You're not in the car. You're not wearing heels.* I move as far off the road as possible when I hear a car approaching.

The horn honks, but I am not giving Devon the benefit of acknowledgement.

"Abigail?"

That voice isn't Devon's.

I brush my face before I turn, wondering why I bother. The sight of Colter makes my tears escape. I let them fall as relief washes over me like a typhoon.

Colter parks and is by my side in seconds.

"Abigail? Are you okay?"

"I thought you had plans. That something came up," I gasp. "I was worried you were hurt. Or that you changed your mind and didn't want to hang out with me."

"Our plans were to be with you," he says. "When you weren't at the cottage, we figured you had changed your mind. Your aunt said you had been tricked into going with Devon to the castle ruins, but Eliana thought she saw you heading in a different direction."

"But there was a note."

"It wasn't from us."

"Then how…" I groan. I know exactly who wrote it. Starts with a D and ends with an N. Does Jess know what her brother did? I should have questioned the scene. Questioned the boy on the bicycle who happened to show up moments after I said no. I am an idiot.

"We never sent anything." Colter touches my arm. "We came to find you right away."

"I'm so embarrassed. You must think the worst of me for believing that note. You'd be right." I start to cry anew.

Colter's arms wrap around me, and I sink into his embrace, my ear against his heart.

"I could never think the worst of you," he whispers.

"I'm sorry. Devon wouldn't stop, and I was trying to make him turn around. Then there was a flat tire, which was an answer to prayer."

"I love it when God's answers are so clear."

"A billboard answer." I nod in wholehearted agreement. "I changed the tire." When I take a breath, it sounds like a strangled chicken. "I'm a mess."

"You can't scare me off with your tears. I'm quite fond of waterfalls." He shifts to retrieve a handkerchief, offering it to me. "I promise I just washed it. It's yours to contaminate and keep."

I wipe my eyes, transferring grease and dirt along with the tears. The handkerchief smells like him. Sunshine and eucalyptus. His kind smile reminds me of what happened. I proceed to "waterfall" some more. Colter holds me, not saying anything else. I'm not sure how long we stand there, but several cars pass. Part of me hopes one is Devon's. It would serve him right to see us. When I've exhausted my wellspring, I reluctantly take a step back from Colter.

"Eliana and I were heading to G'Day Café. Would you still like to go? Or we can take you back to the cottage."

"I'm probably not fit to be in public."

"Your eyes were brightened by the tears." Colter's smile brightens everything in me.

"I would like to go to the café, if you still want to hang out."

He squeezes my hand. "Always."

As we approach the car, Eliana steps out. She repeats her brother's concerns and reassurances before handing me a wet wipe and a compact. A true friend, helping even without asking.

Once my face is free of mess and my hairdo reassembled, Colter opens the passenger side door, his hand on the small of my back, ushering me in. Protected. Safe. Already this ride is a hundred times better, *especially* with Eliana in the back seat.

PSALM 121:1-2

I will raise my eyes to the mountains;
From where will my help come?
My help comes from the Lord,
Who made heaven and earth.

Chapter Fifteen

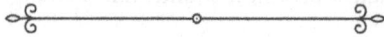

———⚬———

Forty-five minutes fly by even though all speed limits were obeyed. I don't want the ride to end. Eliana and Colter offer an easiness I've never experienced before in conversation. Yet the moments of silence were just as wonderful. Colter loves jazz music, and if his humming is any indication, he's a talented singer. More than once I missed what he was saying because I was imagining us singing a duet, our harmonies blowing the audience away. Winning that Golden Buzzer.

Colter parks in a paved lot then opens Eliana's door. Once she's settled, he helps me out of the car, winking before releasing my hand.

The butterflies are tumbling as I face G'Day Café. It's charming, and as soon as I step inside, I know I'll find it hard to leave even if I'm already anticipating another drive with Colter and Eliana.

G'Day is bright, colorful, open, and inviting. There isn't a line down the middle, but there are clearly two sides. The art studio is to the right, and the café part takes over the left side. The hint of paint and turpentine is overpowered by sugar and all the best kinds of carbs—fruity and chocolatey and filled with vanilla.

"Seth and Mia opened G'Day two years ago. Seth is a history teacher and artist." Colter indicates the perfect arrangement of paintings and sculptures and clay pots. "And Mia went to culinary school. This place is a combination of their passions."

"How long have you known them?" I ask as I'm drawn to a watercolor painting of a mountain stream bordered by trees.

"Seth and I went to uni together." He doesn't say it, but by his tone,

I'm guessing something British and exclusive. "He met Mia on holiday in New Zealand."

I study the words around the edge of the painting, delighting when I realize it's Psalm 121:1-2. "That's my life verse."

"Mine is Philippians 2:3-4," Colter says.

Do nothing from selfishness or empty conceit, but with humility consider one another as more important than yourselves; do not merely look out for your own personal interest, but also for the interests of others.

His choice of verse makes him even more attractive.

"Colter! Eliana!" I turn to find a tall man in his early thirties charging us. Blond hair. Dark blue eyes. Easy smile. He wraps Colter in a hug, slapping him on the back before offering Eliana a more subdued embrace. His attention travels to me, and I wait for an introduction only to find myself pulled in next.

He laughs as he steps back, grinning at Colter. "This had better be your good friend Abigail, or I just hugged a total stranger."

Your good friend. Why does that added word erase every bad from my day? The tears threatening this time are from overwhelm rather than brokenness.

"I'm Abigail."

"My father's joy," Seth says.

"Excuse me?"

"That's what Abigail means."

Colter shakes his head, but he's laughing. "I should have warned you that Seth randomly knows things. I apologize."

"Mia, they're here," Seth calls as he leads me to the food side of the café.

I eye the edible art on display behind the glass. Little cards with an artist's swirly font sit in front of each offering.

Lamington Sponge Cake with Strawberry Jam and Cream. Vanilla Slice. Neenish Tarts. Louise Cake. Custard Cream. Coconut Ice. Chocolate Ripple Cake. Jam Doughnut. Peppermint Slice. Pavlova.

"Ooh, what is pavlova?" The meringue-like substance is covered with fresh fruit and some kind of white frosting, giving no hint as to what's in the center. My mouth waters.

"You'll have to try it and find out." Colter wiggles his brow as he nudges me playfully with his elbow.

Eliana sighs. "Mia makes the best pavlova. I'm still hoping she'll share her secret with me. Maybe today."

"Mia!" Seth calls again. "I better go get her. She's been listening to the *Cyrano* soundtrack this week, nonstop. It helps with the magic of her baking, so she says."

"May I come with you?" Eliana asks with hesitance and shyness.

"Your apron is awaiting, my lady." Seth's words bring an eager smile to Eliana's face as she follows him toward the kitchen.

"Eliana loves to bake but doesn't get much opportunity to be in the kitchen," Colter says.

"Did you want to go help? I can fend for myself." *I'll be out here drooling over the desserts.*

"I'd rather spend time with you today." He motions toward a table vacated by an older couple who leave hand in hand. A chessboard with wooden pieces distracts me on the way by. The characters are all Australian animals. I pick up the king figure—a koala with a crown. The queen is a kangaroo.

"Do you play?" Colter asks.

"I have a chess trophy. That's how cool I am."

"What's your favorite opening?"

"Uh, the one where I win at the end?"

With a shake of his head, he slides out a chair. "For you, madame."

"Thank you, sir." I sit, chuckling at a man in his forties sporting a ball cap, a touristy I LOVE AUSTRALIA T-shirt, and a contented grin.

"I definitely recommend the pavlova," the man says, catching me eyeing his dessert.

"Thanks for the tip." Colter nods at the man's thumbs-up as he sits across from me. "So, Abigail, any other trophies I should know about?"

"Basketball. A shelf of them. Team trophies for winning state and a personal trophy for when I broke the school record of baskets made in my high school career."

"How many?"

"One thousand and three."

Colter whistles. "Impressive."

"My mom wanted me to play in college like she did. She coaches and teaches at the university and has played every sport there is. I may have followed in her footsteps, even played professionally, but Gran moved next door when I was fifteen. She introduced me to museums and antiquing. I still love sports. My brothers and I play pickup games whenever we can."

"Tell me about your brothers."

"Asher, Luke, Jaxon, Caleb, and Philip. Mayor, pediatrician, army, future lawyer, artist. You'll have to meet Jaxon before you leave." Although, I'm still a little miffed at how my favorite brother treated me earlier.

"Quite the family."

"They mean the world to me."

"I can tell. I—" His next words are cut off by someone calling his name. He stands as a black haired, pregnant woman waddles from the kitchen toward us.

"Look what your buddy did to me." She rubs her belly. Her eyes are the icy blue color I'd dreamed of having until I'd read Amy Carmichael's missionary biography and learned to be content with my hazel eyes.

Colter laughs. "You don't seem too upset."

"I can barely reach the counter."

"You're still lovely."

"Such a charmer." After hugging him, which involves lots of laughter, she turns to me, eyes narrowing.

I stand and run my hands over my skirt, hoping she doesn't notice the grease.

"Hi, Abigail. I'm Mia. I'm so glad you were able to join Eliana and Colter."

She glances at Colter, and I wait for her to say the cliché "He's never brought a girl here before," but she doesn't. Should I be happy about that? Or has Colter brought a lot of girls here?

A small wave of worried jealousy sparks. I push it down. *None of that now. I'm going to enjoy this moment and not think about the others who have come before me.*

"It's nice to meet you," I say, filling the not-quite-awkward-silence. "Do you know what you're having?"

"I sure hope it's a baby. Considering who the father is though…" Her delight and mischievousness causes an overzealous laugh to burst forth from me. Oops, that was loud.

"Did you decide on names yet?" Colter asks. "Or will you decide depending on the musical you're listening to at the time?"

"Nah, that plan went out the window. Seth wants to use his favorite Bible story for name options."

"So, Nebuchadnezzar, Shadrach, Meshach, or Abednego for a boy?"

"I so hope it's a girl." Her intense eyes lock on me again. "I hear you've never had pavlova."

As if by magic, Seth appears with two plates and puts them on the table.

Colter and I return to our seats. I pick up a fork and dive in without caring that I'm being watched and potentially judged because of the size of my first bite.

I was right. It is meringue. Kind of. The pavlova is crispy on the outside and sweet, soft, and spongy on the inside. What I thought was frosting actually is fresh cream, which tones down the sugar but makes the tartness of the kiwifruit and raspberries on top burst. "Wow, this is amazing."

"I love her accent. She's so cute," Mia says. "Can we keep her?"

I pretend I don't hear, which isn't too far from the truth because this dessert has created a monster. Pavlova is worthy of a woohoohoo! My serving disappears, and Colter, who hadn't even touched his, slides his plate in front of me.

"Oh no, I couldn't," I say.

"I believe you can." Colter sits back, crossing his arms, displaying his tattoo. He's nailed the service bit of the motto by giving me his slice without a fight.

I so would've fought having to share. And won.

"My ravishingly beautiful wife claims pavlova originated in New Zealand—" Seth starts.

"That's because it did. We made it first." Mia rolls her eyes.

"Pavlova was created in honor of Russian ballerina Anna Pavlova. She was touring New Zealand and Australia in the early twentieth century."

"Hon, Abigail doesn't want a history lesson."

"I don't mind, honestly," I say with a laugh. "I work at a historical society and love discovering interesting facts about the past."

"What's your favorite part?" Mia asks, rubbing her stomach.

"Besides the researching? The odd files." At their clueless expressions, I explain. "We house lots of records at the Westonia: birth, marriage, death certificates, and deeds. Then there are the odd files. It's where they put the blurbs from the newspaper that were odd. Snippets like 'So and so bought the first car in Westonia, but he still prefers his horse.'"

"That's amazing," Seth says.

"I've spent hours looking through them. There are so many. One of my favorites was about a man who lost his wallet only to have it returned by a dog three days later. With all the money still in it." I smile at their delight. "Reading them is almost as fun as writing placards."

"People write those?" Seth laughs, his eyes twinkling. "Somehow, I thought they just appeared."

"It's always been my dream job. Writing placards for a real museum. Like the Smithsonian."

"Where you work isn't a real museum?" Colter asks.

"It is, but it's small."

"Sometimes small isn't a bad thing."

I sigh. "I know, but I want to do more with my life. I want to make a difference. Like my family. Like my aunt. I wish I was more like her."

"You're more like her than you think." Colter's penetrating gaze heats me as if I were outside under the sun.

"Let's leave them be." Mia puts a hand on Seth's arm.

I forgot Colter and I weren't alone discussing my life.

"Yes, my beloved." Seth lifts her hand and kisses it.

When we're alone, Colter quirks an eyebrow. "So, Abigail, how goes the grandmother puzzle? Did you find the picture yet?"

"No, just more pieces. I found a secret room at the cottage full of paintings and Gran's journal. I've also talked to Hazel Greer, who knew my gran and told me some of the story." I breathe and have a second of thought before I spill. "Gran was born on Northargyle and ran away sometime before her seventeenth birthday with her friends. The three of them moved to Hyacinth Cottage. Gran and Roy married, but he died soon after they escaped to America. I'm still trying to find out why they left the cottage."

I unzip my tote and take out my notebook, showing Colter my list of facts. "Angie Thorne told me that the Brisbane royal line ended with the death of King Thomas, Queen Charlotte, and their children. But Angie says she heard rumors that Princess Rosiah ran away and may not have been on the plane."

Colter's eyebrows reach his hairline. He studies me as if trying to discover whether I'm insane.

I have to look away.

The pavlova man is wandering around the art collection. He's checking out the price tag on the Psalm 121 painting.

"Rosiah is a beautiful name," Colter says, clearing his throat.

I return my focus to him. "Mom and I share it as a middle name. I always thought it was a mash up of my grandparents' names. Josiah and Rose."

"Abigail Rosiah."

Okay, I should've told him my full name at our meet-cute. His accent makes everything sound so much better.

"That's me." I throw my hands out in a ta-da motion. "I am Abigail Rosiah, granddaughter, daughter of a pastor and a coach, sister, volunteer, researcher. Placard writer. History hunter. Indiana Abbie."

"You forgot muse and inspiration." The corner of his lip quirks.

"I'll add it to my list."

"My mother would have liked you. She was somewhat of an amateur researcher herself. She loved genealogies. She was working on our family's story before she died." His voice catches, and he glances away, his focus drawn from the present. "I've been hesitant to finish it, but you have inspired me with your love of your grandmother and your passion to find the truth."

"If you ever need any help, I'm here."

Seth appears again, setting a steaming mug of coffee and another slice of pavlova in front of us. Colter and I lift mugs then clink them together before drinking. I allow Colter to eat this slice even though he does offer to let me have it.

We chat for what seems like hours about everything and anything. Sports. The historical society. Researching. The founding family of Westonia project I was working on. Mr. Romano, Libby, Geoff, and Kasey. Siblings. My nieces and new nephew. Favorite foods. Our relationship with God, when we became His children—Colter was six. I was ten. We even talked about Aunt Vi's "Real Reel." Colter's gracious response was so quotable I jotted it down to share.

When Eliana, Mia, and Seth come out of the kitchen, I've won my third round of checkers. I'm a tad competitive. Eliana carries a bag of what I hope is full of edible goodness. My only regret is that I didn't try more while I was here. I'll have to return. Aunt Vi would love Seth and Mia. And the desserts.

"We'll see you on Tuesday at Kenwick," Seth says to Colter. "You ready to lose spectacularly?"

"Will you be there, Abigail? You can sit with me," Mia says.

"I didn't invite her yet, but I guess I'll have to now." Colter grins.

"Don't feel like you h-have to," I stutter, not sure what they're even talking about.

"Of course I was going to invite you. Seth stole my thunder. I had a speech all prepared."

"Your speeches are epic." Seth bows his head, an apology. "Sorry, Abigail, for stealing that privilege from you."

"You're still sore because I bested you in debate club."

"Too soon."

I'm missing something, but instead of being uncomfortable, I relax in the enjoyment of their easy, long friendship.

"My team is going to crush yours this year," Seth says.

Colter shakes his head. "We'll see about that."

"Maybe you should actually invite her. Make it official." Mia chuckles.

Colter's gaze meets mine. "Abigail, every year on October 22 we have a netball tournament at the Kenwick Estate. Would you like to come? I'd love for you to join us."

"Sure." I grin. "But what in the world is netball?"

Chapter Sixteen

C olter pulls up in front of Hyacinth Cottage, and I sigh. I don't want today to be over.

"I really like Seth and Mia." I clear my throat like I haven't talked in hours. Which is far from the truth. I've reached an all-time high of words spoken in one sitting. Intelligible words at that.

"They like you too." Eliana leans forward from the back seat to hand me a bag with the G'Day Café logo. "I made these. They're just cookies, but I thought you may like to share some with your aunt."

"Do I have to share?"

"Only if you want. I'll see you on Tuesday." Eliana squeezes my shoulder before Colter helps me out of the car.

We face each other as he closes the door. He's still holding my hand, his thumb moving in lazy circles. I wonder if he's as reluctant as I am for the day to end. The corners of his lips lift in his signature grin. "You, Abigail Morgan, lied to me when we first met."

"About what?" I wrack my brain, sifting through the things I over-shared, trying to find the lie. Is he about to tell me he never wants to see me again?

"You said you were nothing like Faith Mackenzie."

"I didn't lie." This conversation is becoming as repetitive as explaining to my brothers that I'm not an archeologist. Not Indiana Abbie. Not Faith Mackenzie.

"So, you're not brave, fascinating, strong, and beautiful?"

What's a girl's response supposed to be? "I—"

Jess rushes from the cottage, the front door slamming behind her. I will be strong if she tries to pull me away. But the tears streaming down her face stop me from telling her to stay back.

Colter must see them too. He nods. "Go to your friend."

"I wasn't a good friend today. Hopefully, she can forgive me for not going with them to the castle. I don't like when people are mad at me." I exhale. "I need to make this right."

"Be strong." He squeezes my hand. "I'll see you soon."

There's so much more I want to say, but I run after Jess. Is she mad that I didn't make it to the ruins? Was she worried that I didn't call? Had she assumed the worst when Devon showed up without me? Did Devon even go to the castle?

Jess is almost to Greer's by the time I reach her. Though she's sobbing, it's not hard to pick out that the tears are Jaxon's fault and not mine. A small relief, but I'm probably not off the hook with my actions today.

"Your brother," Jess gasps, "he's leaving me! He's going back early."

"He still has another week."

"He's choosing to go back early." She throws herself into my arms, and I barely keep us upright. "What am I going to do?"

I know how she feels—the looming deployment, the separation, the worry for his safety. I don't know what to tell her. The ache is there. It's part of loving someone who serves in the military.

"I don't know," I say. "But I'll be here."

"Sure you will." She snorts against my neck. "You couldn't even show up for me today. You abandoned my poor brother to go off with Cove people. Maybe that's your family's way—abandoning people to do whatever you want."

"I'm sorry for not being there, but—"

"The whole day was ruined anyway because of the call from base."

"Jess?" Jaxon arrives. He looks older, tired.

"I just can't." Jess's grip on me tightens. "You're leaving. You'll forget all about me. I'll be stuck in this town forever. Alone."

"I could never forget about you. I love you, Jess."

Jess's head pops up faster than a snapped rubber band.

I release my hold and step to the side as flabbergasted as she is. My brother said the L word, and by the expressions on their faces, this is the first time he's said it. If only I could be invisible and run. Back to Colter, preferably. I could've stayed talking to him for a few more hours.

Jess moves to my brother. "You love me?"

My mind wants to flee, but my body hasn't gotten the message.

"I do. I know it's only been a couple weeks, but I feel like I've known you my entire life." My brother gets down on one knee.

I gasp almost louder than Jess. What is my brother doing? What do I even feel at the moment? Happy? Disgusted? Leery? Elated?

"Jess Greer, will you be my wife?"

Jess squeals. "Oh my! Yes!"

❧

What a wild ride today has been—literally, in some respects. I'm at the Greer Hotel celebrating my brother's engagement to Jess.

I've decided to be happy for them. I'm excited, but of all my brothers, Jaxon was the last I'd expect to propose to a girl he just met. Whenever Jax would pick on Dad, Dad would respond that he hoped Jax's children did the same someday. To which, Jax replied that his children never would because they wouldn't exist. He wasn't ever getting married.

Mrs. Greer is in her element as she escorts my brother and Jess around the room. A room that is packed despite the speed of it all. Is the entire town here? I spot bookstore Tim, a redhead on his arm that I'm pretty sure I heard him call Ginny. Looks like they're no longer exes.

I don't spot Devon, and Aunt Vi isn't here. In her own plot twist, Aunt Vi and Angie Thorne met for coffee this afternoon and decided to eat dinner as well. I'm glad they're trying to mend and build a relationship.

"If only you had a ring," I overhear Mrs. Greer tell Jess while I'm choosing a drink.

"It's okay, Mother. I don't need anything fancy. You know me. I just need Jaxon."

"I know, darling. You never demand anything. But it would be nice to have a ring to show you're off the market."

Music starts playing, and Jess and Jaxon move to the center of the makeshift dance floor. You'd think we were already at the reception. I sip my ice water and watch, shaking my head every few minutes at the insanity of the whole thing.

Like a homing beacon, as soon as Devon walks in the front door, he sets his sights on me. I want to be anywhere but here. Run. Fight or flight? Fly. Fly. Fly.

Colter bursts through the doors of Greer's Hotel. White shirt billowing, black pants, a mask over his eyes. Sword raised, he points it at Devon. "To the death!"

Devon cowers as I rush into Colter's arms. "Take me away."

"As you wish." A vine appears and before we swing away, Colter presses his lips against mine—

"Abigail." Devon shifts on his feet in front of me, his eyes not meeting mine. "I can't handle thinking you hate me."

"I don't hate you." It's true. He scared me and lost my trust, but I certainly don't hate him.

"I wanted to spend time with you." His gaze lingers below my chin before trailing down to my shorts-clad legs. "I couldn't bear knowing you preferred someone over me."

A cheer goes up. Jaxon has dipped Jess, and they're locked in a PG-13 kiss.

Yikes. I used to dream about the hottest guy in school rushing the basketball court and kissing me passionately to the cheers of the crowd. All the mean girls' mouths hanging open in disbelief that he chose me over them. But the uncomfortable feelings attached to watching this experience have me rethinking the attendance of my first kiss.

"I can't believe we're going to be family soon," Devon says.

"Me neither."

"I'm going to help set up food. Don't leave." He leans in, kissing me on the cheek before I know what's going on.

My hand finds the spot, but instead of tingles, I'm repulsed. Where's the sanitizer?

My phone vibrates in my back pocket. I escape to the deck to answer, not even checking who it could be. Even a chat about my Jetta's extended warranty would be welcome.

"Abigail, it's Colter," comes the reply to my hello.

Colter. Best phone call ever. And I now have his number.

"Did my aunt give you my number too?" Honestly, I'm surprised my aunt didn't program his number in my phone with his own special ringtone. I wonder what song he'd get?

"Eliana got it from your aunt before we left to find you. We're back at Kenwick, using the landline."

I wish I could be with them instead of here where awkwardness resides.

"I wanted to make sure everything was okay with your friend."

"Oh, yes. I mean it turned out well. My brother has to get back to base earlier than expected. But he proposed, and she said yes, and they're all smiles again." My laugh comes out with a nervous shake. "It's fast, but I guess when you know, you know."

"My congratulations to them." Colter sighs. "Are you okay with your brother's deployment?"

"You'd think I'd be used to it now. In some ways, I am. I know God's got my brother, but there's always that fear that I may never see him again—"

"Abs, food's ready," Devon calls.

I hold up a finger.

"Is that Devon?" Colter asks, harshness in his question.

"He apologized."

Colter's laugh is full of disbelief. "Did he now?"

Hmm, come to think of it, Devon never did say the words "I'm sorry."

"I'll let you go," Colter says. "Tell your brother congratulations. I would like to meet him before he leaves if that's possible, maybe bring him to the netball tournament? Your friends are welcome as well."

"I'll see what's going on."

"Until Tuesday, Abigail Rosiah."

Before I can be rude and say I don't want to invite any of them, even my brother, the call ends.

As I'm sliding my phone back in my pocket, Jaxon steps onto the deck. "So, what do you think?" He motions inside with a glass bottle that smells like alcohol.

"Are you sure? Jess is great, of course, but you haven't known her for long. Have you talked to Mom and Dad yet?" It's hard being on the other side of the globe. They're all blissfully sleeping when I need to talk, need to share. Need someone to caution Jaxon about this speedy engagement.

"I'm an adult. I don't need their permission." He sighs, gripping the back of his neck. "I wish I didn't have to go, but I've been waiting for this assignment to open. Usually, I can't wait for a new place and adventure, but I feel like I have more to lose this time. Jess is perfect. So kind and sweet and the best person."

"She is one of a kind," I hear myself say, keeping my reservations about Jess's spiritual status unvoiced. I'm not quite sure how to word it without severing my bond with my brother. "When do you have to leave?"

"The twenty-first. Jess wants to elope, but I only have six months left. I'm thinking about not reenlisting."

"What would you do instead?"

"Teaching, maybe?"

"You'd be good at it." We share a smile. Adding teacher to the brothers' list would complete it. "Maybe we could spend the day together tomorrow, just the two of us?" I ask, hopeful that he'll say yes.

"Maybe you could help me find a ring." He takes a drink from his bottle then runs a hand over his head, turning to stare at the view.

Gran's ring. The thought pops in my mind and my heart misses a beat. A true love token.

There's a nudge in my soul. *God? Is that you?* He wouldn't ask me to give up the ring, right?

This symbol was pure love between Gran and Grandpa. It's only right that another couple should be blessed by it. I wait another beat but still feel that I have to offer it. Jaxon is the definition of sacrifice and love. He's given up so much.

I remove the ring from my finger and hold it out to my brother. "Grandpa Brown gave this to Gran. I want you to give it to Jess. Gran said that whenever I saw it sparkle, I would know she's praying for me. I'll commit to do the same for you and Jess."

He sets his drink down before pulling me into a long and deep hug. A real hug. "You are the best sister."

My eyes cloud, but I'm smiling. It's the perfect response to the ring. I know I did the right thing.

Jaxon releases me and heads inside to propose again.

I stay put, having already seen that once today. I stare at the view, mulling over the fact that I keep leaving pieces of Gran here in Australia when I came to find her. And soon I'll be heading to New Zealand then home. Empty-handed in so many ways.

"That was such a nice thing you did for my sister," Devon says.

I refrain from groaning at his invasion.

Giving my brother the ring was the right thing, a good thing, but I don't want to be congratulated when all I want to do is take it back.

Devon takes my hand, running his thumb over the empty spot on my ring finger. "I have to go out of town for a few days. When I get back, we'll have to go buy you a replacement."

Chapter Seventeen

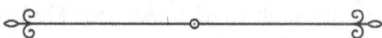

After watching videos on how to play netball—which is not the Australian word for volleyball, as I'd assumed—I'm confident about playing today. Spending time at Colter's home, however, is a different game I'm not ready to play.

We pass so many sprawling houses with pillars, porches, pools, and turrets that leave me speechless, and we haven't even seen the Kenwick Estate. Jess stops in front of large black iron gates with KENWICK MANOR on a golden sign that sparkles in the sunlight.

A man exits a guard shed and approaches the car. It's Colter's friend from Sugarleaf Manor. He studies us, and I guess we ace the test because the gate opens without me saying a word.

The driveway is tree-lined. The suspense is killing me. Oh, but it's worth it.

"Holy wow!" Aunt Vi says from the back seat.

"Maybe we shouldn't be here," I whisper.

Kenwick Manor is practically a castle, the architecture blending modern elegance with traditional elements.

Towering stone walls. Arched windows. Intricate detailing. Towering turrets rise at each corner, lending a medieval charm. Roof steeply pitched. Meticulous landscaping. Lush greenery, blooming flowers, and carefully trimmed hedges. A cobblestone pathway leads to a sweeping staircase and a massive door flanked by stone columns.

"They aren't any better than you. Don't let them make you feel undeserving," Jess says. "Besides, we were invited."

Regardless of the invite, my mouth stays open in awe as Jess pulls into a lot full of cars—mostly black, mostly sleek, and all sparkling in the sunshine, fresh from the car wash. We stick out in Jess's older, green Chevy. It's like the time I didn't get the memo that homecoming was eighties-themed, and I showed up in an elegant black ball gown. The amount of neon, teased hair, and spandex would've made the Go-Go's cringe.

"It's going to be fun," Aunt Vi says. "I'm determined to be your loudest cheerleader."

"Netball is not that exciting." Jess releases a long-suffering sigh. "I wish Jaxon was here. This is not going to be much fun for me."

I'd invited Jess to join us today so she wouldn't have to be alone. She's been moping about ever since Jaxon kissed her goodbye. I get it. I'm feeling a little mopey myself about my brother leaving without us having a heart-to-heart and resolving our differences. But the day is looking up.

With a deep inhale, I follow Jess and my aunt as they strut toward the door like they've been here before. Meanwhile, behind them, I'm sweating and shaking and trying to plan the best route for escape should the need arise.

When the huge front door opens, Eliana greets us dressed in a navy sleeveless dress and pearls. Okay, I am underdressed in my shorts and black tank top. Jess looks cute in a colorful summer dress, and Aunt Vi's sporting linen shorts. Her marigold Converse are the same yellow as the pencils on her T-shirt and earrings.

"I'm so glad you could all come today," Eliana says. She turns to Jess. "I hear congratulations are in order. Have you set a date?"

"Not yet." Jess's jaw tightens. "But Abigail and I are going dress shopping tomorrow. I have no idea where to start. You should join us. I'm sure you know some of the best places. Maybe there are some closer to you? We don't have any good shops in Bridgeway."

"That sounds lovely. I will see what I have on my schedule and let you know by the end of today." Eliana motions us inside. "Colter is around here somewhere."

Jess gives me a side-eye but remains silent as we follow Eliana to a low balcony overlooking a patio and a white tent. "It's grown so big over the years."

"How many games?" I eye the crowd. I'm itching to play, but that's a lot of people to observe my first attempts at netball.

"There's only one game. Colter and Seth's uni friends bring their friends and families, which are growing." She waves dismissively. "Neighbors showed up, and we didn't have the heart to turn them away either. If you'll excuse me, I need to play hostess. I'll find you later." She squeezes my hand on her way by.

"I'm gonna check out the food situation," Aunt Vi says, almost skipping away. I smile as she gets distracted talking to a group of people. Her hands move a mile a minute, and she shimmies her shoulders several times, constantly in motion.

"This is impressive. Although, I would have put the food tent on the other side. More convenient," Jess says, reminding me she's still beside me. "I hope Eliana can take us to some of her stores."

"I thought you said Cove people use and discard you."

"I never said that." Jess quirks an eyebrow. "Why must you lie? Come, let's go see who else is here. Everyone is so rich. Must be nice."

I keep my mouth shut as I scan the crowd. Colter is on the other side, way across the stone patio and yard. He's wearing a blue polo shirt and shorts. It's like he's in Australia and I'm home in America, an ocean of people between us.

Colter sees me, and everyone in the world disappears. A spotlight shines on us both as we move toward one another. His eyes glisten as he takes me in. I'm the most beautiful woman he's ever seen, and he doesn't want to look away. He can't look away. He never will look away, never look anywhere else. The crowd watches in awe, some shaking their heads that the wealthy Colter has eyes only for the pastor's daughter.

"Who's that?" Jess interrupts my fantasy. "Looks like Colter has a girlfriend."

"He doesn't have a girlfriend." But I look anyway. I sift through our café conversation. Huh. We never did talk about our relationship status during our lengthy time of sharing.

"Well, he lied, obviously."

A beautiful, petite Asian woman grips Colter's arm. She's definitely not his sister. She almost glows as Colter speaks to her. A young boy stands to the side of her eating cotton candy.

"Such a cute little family. The boy looks like Colter, don't you think?" I don't trust or like Jess's tone or insinuation.

No, I don't think the boy looks like Colter. I want to say that, but in the end, I say nothing.

"That's Lady Paige," a deep masculine voice with a British accent says. "And that's her son. She won't disclose who the father is, but we all know."

Jess and I turn toward a man average-looking in every way. *Dark blond hair. Clean-shaven. Brown eyes. White short-sleeved, button-up dress shirt. Khaki shorts. White slides.* Nothing about his outfit is right for netball.

"And who might you be?" he asks Jess. Cupid shot another arrow. I am invisible.

"Jessica Greer," she says softly.

"Lord Titus Danaby at your service."

I stifle a giggle at his poshness and the fact that his accent sounds so fake, like when I'm trying a British accent and failing spectacularly.

"Lord? I've never met a lord before."

"I've never met a Jessica before." The smirk plastered across his face sickens me, reminding me of the time I tried a Reuben sandwich. It had looked so good, but I'd had no clue that three of the ingredients were on my Do Not Eat! list.

Lord Danaby takes Jess's left hand and bows over it, flipping it at the last second to press a kiss to the inside of her wrist. "What a lovely ring, just like its wearer."

"It's from her fiancé, my brother," I say.

Why didn't Jess mention the importance of the ring?

I twist my verse ring, reminding myself to keep my words and heart pleasing to God.

"Too bad about the fiancé." His eyes light like he's been given a challenge and plans on winning. "Would you ladies like a tour?"

Who is he to Colter and Eliana? Who is he to offer a tour?

"We're good," I say, taking Jess's hand, the one released from Lord Danaby's grasp.

"I'd like a tour." Jess pulls away, giving me a harsh, unwanted look. "Why don't you go meet Lady Paige and her son." She emphasizes the lady part, highlighting my lack of a title.

Before I know it, Jess has left me alone. Abandoned me, her arm looped through Lord Danaby's. I lose all confidence. I don't belong here.

Instead of going down to where the people are gathered, I find myself inside. Like my feet and heart are on the same page, I discover the library right where it should be. The beating heart of the estate.

If I'd seen Colter's library before I met him, I would have liked him instantly. The collection of new and old books. The fireplace. Well-used blanket on a chair with an ottoman before it. Tasteful artwork. Fresh flowers in ornate vases. Window seat with decorative pillows in one alcove, grand piano in another.

An ocean-scented breeze swirls through the open window. I breathe deeply as I explore, gravitating toward the piano. At home, playing piano helps me decompress. Something about music soothes the soul. I sit on the padded bench and play a minor chord. The crispness of the sound rings around the library. A love song escapes as my thoughts wander to Colter again.

What if he has a son? I don't want to keep getting closer to him if he's with someone. But he's not with someone. He doesn't have a son. Seth and Mia probably would have asked how he was doing, right? A playmate for their expected child? But a lady? My title is nothing compared to hers.

"Abigail, you are such an idiot," I sing in place of the actual words.

"I've never heard that song before. But, encore, please."

At Colter's voice, I try to stand, twist wrong. Fall.

Colter is there, his lips settling into a grin as he helps me up. He keeps his hands on my arms until I'm steady.

"How long have you been listening?" I ask.

"You have an amazing voice." He chuckles. "Looks like I found the one thing you and Faith do not have in common."

"Yeah, that fact is one hundred percent Aunt Vi. She's all heart, though."

Faith went undercover as a stagehand for a musical. Both lead and understudy caught the "flu," and they'd heard Faith singing along under her breath at rehearsal. They knew she knew the part and forced her onstage. Where she promptly received a record amount of boos. Leonard had to step in and save the day.

Laughter floats through the open window as a group of kids run by with bubble wands. Lady Paige's son twirls and falls, much like I had.

"Man, I love that kid," Colter says.

"You should," I say, my heart dying a little.

Colter studies me, questioning. Clearly not knowing that I know. "What's this tone I detect?"

"I mean, fathers should love their children."

"Definitely agree with you. And someday when I'm a father, I will love my children quite differently from my father." His gaze drifts out the window then back to me. "What gave you the impression I had children?"

"Something Lord Danaby said about Lady Paige and her son, but it appears I misunderstood. I tend to do that."

"Let me put your mind at ease." Colter places his hands on my shoulders. His smile is kind, forgiving. "I don't have any children, and Lady Paige has never been my girlfriend. Dating her would be like wrestling a croc, I wouldn't know where to begin."

"Okay," I reply.

"Honestly, I've never had a girlfriend."

"Why not? What's wrong with you?" I gasp, covering my mouth.

Colter throws his head back in a laugh. "You are a delight, Abigail Morgan." Amusement still rolling through him, he studies me a beat. "My life is complicated. The type of woman I'm looking for, well, Lady Paige has never even been considered for that list."

"Okay," I say again, my face heating like an oven.

"I know what you need—a subject change and a ladder ride." He points toward the back wall, releasing his hold on me.

Once again, he's calmed the awkward, tamping down my rising anxiety. He takes my hand and leads me to the ladder then bows, motioning for me to climb. When I hesitate, he climbs a few rungs and rides it down the shelves then back.

I can't stop the bubbling giggles. What is even happening right now?

"Now you, it's been Colter tested and approved," he says.

I climb to the second rung so my behind isn't in his face.

"Hang on," he whispers in my ear, sending chills all over. I bite my lower lip as the ladder moves. Colter stays, holding the ladder the entire ride, adding his jubilant "Woohoohoo" to mine.

"Again?" he asks. His hands have moved to my waist, and I'm hoping they stay there. Safety first.

When we make it back, after three more rides, I turn on the ladder. At this height, we're nose to nose. He's so close.

"Thank you," I say on a whisper of happiness. "I've wanted to take a ladder ride ever since I watched *Beauty and the Beast*."

"I love how you take in everything, finding joy in the little things." He tilts his head. "So, why didn't you ride the one at Sugarleaf Manor?"

"You saw that?"

"I was hoping you would, so I could try it out, see how it compared to mine."

"This looks like fun." Eliana appears over Colter's shoulder in the library doorway. "Maybe we should offer ladder rides next year, start a new tradition."

"Nope, Abigail and I aren't sharing this." Colter winks at me before turning to his sister, one hand still on my waist. "I don't think our guests would enjoy it."

"As much as I'd love for us all to hide in here, we are the hosts. And there is a netball tournament to play and win."

Colter helps me off the ladder, not that I had far to go. His hand rests on the small of my back as we follow Eliana outside. High on ladder rides and Colter's touch, I could take on the world. Or single-handedly win this game of netball.

"Whose team am I on?" I ask.

"Oh, I didn't expect you to play," Colter says. "Seth puts together a team, and I have mine."

"But I watched videos. I know I'd make a great goal shooter or goal attacker." I motion to my clothes. "It's why I'm dressed like this. I thought I would be playing. I should've worn a dress."

Colter and Eliana share a look, both their lips curl in smiles.

Misreading situations is a gift.

"Come, let's find our seats." Eliana loops her arm through mine. "We'll cheer for Colter's team."

"You're actually going to cheer for my team this year?" Colter teases.

"Only if Abigail does."

Eliana leads me to chairs lined up under tents, so we're out of the direct sunlight. She excuses herself to take care of something or other before we sit, and I study the court that's just bigger than one for basketball, recalling the rules I'd learned from the videos.

The court is divided into three sections, with seven players on the court in their designated spots. The ball resembles a volleyball in size but has a basketball-like texture. Players cannot hold the ball for more than three seconds. Players cannot take more than one-and-a-half steps when in possession of the ball. If the shot is scored from inside the goal circle, the team gains one point.

"Abigail! You're here," Mia says with an enthusiastic wave. "Come sit with me."

I spot Aunt Vi in the crowd, but no seats beside her are empty, so I allow Mia to lead me to her section. Jess ends up in the row behind us.

A waiter walks around with a tray of lamington cake. My mouth waters as I take a bite-sized slice, trying to be polite as I shove it in my mouth. Oh, that's good.

"Serviette?" the waiter asks. He has both blue and green napkins in his hand.

"Take a blue one. That's Colter's team color," Mia says as she snatches a green one.

"I would have expected linen napkins," Jess huffs, declining either color.

"We only have linen at my estate," Lord Danaby says as he sits in the empty chair beside Jess.

"You're not playing?" I ask, annoyed that he's practically buzzing around Jess like a fly. I wish she would swat him away.

Lord Danaby chuckles. "I don't play that game."

"What are the rules again, Titus?" Jess asks.

I study her before saying, "I thought you already knew the rules. You said it was a boring game."

"It's called being nice, Abigail. You should try it sometime." Her words are for my ears only, and for Lord Danaby, since they share smirks.

I face the court, my brain screaming *shut up, shut up* as Lord Danaby explains the game, his voice grating like iron on iron. Two referees move onto the court and whistles are blown, cutting off the chatter. We all stand as the teams are announced, and I flap the blue napkin in the air.

Colter sees me, points, then waves.

I might have swooned if Mia wasn't standing so close. She's yelling for Seth to be careful.

The players take their designated positions. Mia grabs my arm as the whistle blows and the game begins. I can't resist a glance over my shoulder to see Lord Danaby and Jess with their heads barely an inch apart. I wish he'd leave so I can watch Colter and enjoy today without worrying about my future sister-in-law being seduced. I might not be thrilled about how fast Jaxon and Jess's relationship progressed but that doesn't mean I can't protect it on my brother's behalf.

The game is almost at the end of the first quarter when Seth jumps to block a shot. I know he's going to land wrong before he crashes to the ground, his ankle rolling beneath him.

Mia gasps, her fingernails digging into my arm.

"Oh no!" I'm up and running across the court. Not that I'm a medical person, but I know how to deal with a sports injury. *Thank you, Mom.* There's no blood or an obvious break.

Colter and another guy help Seth to the side.

"R.I.C.E," I say, repeating what they stand for. "Rest. Ice. Compression. Elevation."

Colter nods and an ice pack appears.

Mia crosses the court, whacking Seth on the arm. "I told you not to get hurt."

"I'm fine, I can—"

"You are not fine. You are done. I'm not going to have two babies to care for."

Seth groans. "We can't forfeit. I'd never hear the end of it."

"I'll play for you," I offer.

"She is dressed to play and did watch videos." Colter's eyes crinkle with delight.

Seth studies me, his smile growing. "You're in. Don't go easy on Colter just because he invited you to his humble abode."

"Not in my nature," I assure him, thrilled that I'm about to play. "I don't like to lose."

"I don't either." Colter wiggles his brow before jogging off to huddle with his team.

Seth's team congregates around him. Introductions done, we take our places on the court. The whistle blows, sending the thrill of the game coursing through me. It's not long before I get in the zone, adrenaline pumping through my veins as I run around, evading players, shooting, and scoring.

By the time the final whistle blows, I've won more than the game of netball. I've won teammates who trusted my abilities, allowing me to be one of them. Seth's team—my team—beats Colter's by five points.

I wipe my forehead, taking the offered water bottle from a teammate—the one who threw me the ball so I could make the last shot of the game. I'm a happy, blotchy, stinky mess. Netball is not quite the sedate tea party I'd dreamed up. It's just as fast and crazy as basketball even with all the rules.

I'm definitely going to introduce my brothers to netball.

Colter approaches, wiping his face with a towel. I can't look away. *God, you deserve a standing ovation for creating him.* I keep my lips shut, so I don't blurt out that thought in front of everyone.

"Maybe you shouldn't have watched those videos," Colter says with a laugh.

I return his smile. "I got the hang of it pretty quickly."

"I'd say you more than got the hang of it." Seth whoops from his spot on the bench, Mia by his side. "Told you we'd crush you this year."

"Your team only won because you weren't on the court." Colter puts his arm around my shoulders.

I experience a moment of panic of how awful I smell before settling. He's just as sweaty and sticky as I am.

"Abigail is amazing."

I soak up his praise.

"Next year, you're on my team." Colter realizes what he's said at the same time his words register.

I hurt that I won't get the chance for a rematch. But then...why not? Why couldn't I be here next year?

Australia and Kenwick Manor are now a part of *my* story.

Chapter Eighteen

Y ou'd think a store this expensive would offer a better selection," Jess says.

I heat on behalf of the salesgirl, but she's been well-trained and doesn't say anything. Although, I'm sure her mind is conjuring great comebacks.

Jess's comments are a little excessive. Ranging from "I could make this" to "I can't believe they'd charge this much for something so plain."

At the moment, she sways in front of a three-way mirror in an off-white dress that makes me want to belt out the lyrics to "Under the Sea." *Form-fitting. Mermaid-esque. Lacy. Sleeveless. Skirt flared from below the knees.* It's not a dress I would ever try on—how would I walk?—but Jess looks like she stepped off the pages of a bridal magazine. She's tried on more than fifteen dresses already. At least it's helped me decide on what my ideal dress would be. Flowy and simple, maybe with lace sleeves and a high waist.

"I thought Eliana would be here by now," Jess says with a pout as she twists to view herself from a different angle. Eliana knows the owner and arranged the earliest appointment of the day. "I want her opinion on the dresses. She knows clothes."

Clearly insinuating that I do not. "I'm sorry I'm not much help. I thought you looked amazing in them all."

"I'll try that one." Jess points to a pale blue dress. The salesgirl picks it up and follows her to the dressing room.

Beyond Dresses is like the costume exhibit at the Met. The various dresses, fabrics, styles, shoes, and accessories make for an overwhelming environment. I wander toward the bridesmaid dresses, wondering what color Jess is going to choose. My favorite is purple, like hyacinths.

The bell on the front door rings, and Eliana enters. She's wearing a flowing white sundress with blue flowers, and her blonde hair is in waves around her shoulders. Poised as ever, while I, despite the air-conditioning in the store, am sweating. I've been trying to think cool thoughts. It's not working.

Especially when Colter steps through the door. He's in a bridal shop, so of course my mind goes to aisles, "The Wedding March," and first glimpses. He even plays his part by lighting up when our eyes meet.

"I'm so sorry." Eliana kisses my cheek. "We got a late start."

"My fault entirely. Father called with a matter of importance." Colter runs a hand through his hair, his gaze scanning the dresses. "I'll be down the block at the café. Take your time." He dips his head in farewell and heads outside.

It takes a lot of effort not to run after him. Eliana is here, so Jess no longer needs me to *ooh* and *aah*.

"Forgive me." Eliana takes both my hands and keeps me from escaping. "I don't drive, and Colter wanted to come into town. He was hoping to eat lunch with us."

"No worries."

"You're here," Jess squeals. "Thank you for arranging an appointment. This store is amazing. All the dresses, oh, I can't choose. I love them all. Like they were all made for me. Abigail thought every dress looked amazing on me."

"I'm sure Abigail was right." Eliana offers a smile.

Another employee appears with a tray of glasses filled with champagne. I decline, as does Eliana, but Jess takes one, sipping daintily, hip cocked like she's posing for a photo shoot. When Jess finishes her drink, she lifts her skirts and heads toward the dressing room, telling me to come help.

"Unzip." Jess presents her back to me.

I reach for the zipper but catch Jess's eyes in the mirror. Tears fill hers when our gazes lock. "What is it?"

"I want to find the perfect dress, but I don't have the money. What was I thinking coming into this store? Your brother deserves the best, and I want to give that to him." She covers her face, her shoulders shaking. "I'll have to be married in a sundress."

"I don't think my brother will mind what you wear." I rub her back, careful of the material, praying I don't transfer anything to the extremely expensive silk.

"That's the problem. You don't care. How a girl looks matters, especially on her wedding day." Jess scans me then turns away. "You can leave."

"Everything okay?" Eliana asks when I'm back in the showroom.

"I said the wrong thing again." I sigh, feeling the need to share and have someone else help me dissect. "Jess can't afford any of these dresses. I told her my brother won't care what she wears, but she's not happy about that answer."

"Let me see what I can do." Eliana squeezes my hand. "I'll be right back."

Jess, in her red sundress, rushes from the dressing room. "I'm sorry, dear friend. I'm stressed. I'm so in love. I can't wait to marry your brother." She pulls me into a hug, giving me no choice but to accept. "But he wants to wait until he's done with his service. I just...I don't know if I can wait that long."

"It could be romantic, writing letters. Getting to know each other better. He only has six months left."

"Oh, Abbie, I love how clueless you are."

"Do you want me to pull dresses for your bridesmaids?" the salesgirl asks.

"I don't have bridesmaids," Jess says. "Do you have any more champagne?"

"Of course, madame."

I guess I won't be trying on dresses. I shouldn't have assumed.

The doorbell jangles, and my heart skips, but instead of Colter, Lord Danaby enters. What is he doing here? He appears shocked when he sees me. No, that's not shock, that's arrogance. He knew we'd be here.

Angie Thorne would gather the motherload of villain fodder from Lord Danaby, and Aunt Vi could create a monster.

"Titus." Jess gasps like she's surprised.

"Did I miss you in your dresses? I was hoping to catch a glimpse. Talk you out of marriage."

My stomach roils.

"You can't talk me out of anything," Jess coos. "Once my mind is made up, it's set."

"Where are you headed next?" he asks.

"We're meeting Colter for lunch," I tell Jess.

"I still have so much to do. I can't afford to stop."

"There's a shop around the corner that may have what you're looking for," Lord Danaby says. "I could take you."

I'm left standing, nonexistent.

Jess is puddle jumping in quicksand without a rope of escape. *God, keep Jess safe. Don't let Lord Danaby do anything to jeopardize my brother and Jess's relationship. Guard her heart.*

"Where did Jess go?" Eliana asks, returning with the owner. I'd briefly met Sarah when we'd first arrived.

"She left with Lord Danaby," I say.

Eliana turns to Sarah. "I'll be in touch. Thank you for opening your shop today."

"It was a pleasure to meet you, Abigail," Sarah says.

"You too, Sarah."

"Enjoy the rest of your day."

Eliana and I head toward the café. Her walk is slow, as she takes in the sights like it's her first time seeing them as well. A young man approaches, moving to the side to let us pass. His delighted, interested smile is all for Eliana, but she doesn't notice.

Jess would have been all over him.

"I'm sorry about Jess. She was so insensitive and harsh," I say. "I should probably bake cookies for Sarah and all the employees of Beyond Dresses."

"You don't have to apologize for Jess's behavior. You aren't responsible. How she acts is on her and not a reflection of you." She hooks her arm through mine. "That's something I'm still trying to teach myself. How I treat people is what matters."

"I don't understand men."

She smiles. "Neither do I."

"I've never had a boyfriend. I'm a pastor's daughter and dating me would be like dating the whole church." I make a face. "I've always thought of myself as the church princess."

"Church princess?"

I chuckle, shaking my head. I can't believe I'm about to share this fantasy out loud. "My dad is like a king of a small kingdom. So that would make me a princess. Lots of eyes on me waiting for me to mess up. Pressures. Obligations and expectations that come with the title."

"That is a lot to deal with."

"Do you have a boyfriend?"

"Not exactly. Nothing official." Her sigh is deep and would fill an entire book. It's a story I truly want to hear.

"What's his name?"

"Bradley," she whispers. I'd know how deeply she cared for him even without her mentioning her love. "My father arranged for me to meet Bradley's cousin, Silas. He thinks we're well-suited."

"My dad is always trying to hook me up too. He's not pushy, but he wants me to be married to add to his grandchildren posse."

"I met Bradley first by mistake and was already halfway in love before I was informed that my father does not approve. They do look a lot alike, but Silas doesn't make my heart flutter. Bradley is truly the best of me."

I wait for her to say more, but then I spot Colter at a table outside of the café. Reading. Would my father approve of him? Dad always said to find someone who is the same seven days a week. I've seen Colter in many different situations, and he is constant. Dad would like Colter.

When we're in range, I gasp. The sight of Colter chuckling while reading my favorite book does strange things to my heart. *Romantic notions: reading together, not talking, holding hands. Smiling back and forth every once in a while. A hand squeeze before a page turn. Release, then back, twining fingers, enjoying our separate worlds together.*

He stands when he sees us, doing the decent thing and using a bookmark instead of leaving the book open and unloved, the spine crying in pain.

"I started this delightful book," he says when he sees me eyeing it. He pulls out a chair for me then one for Eliana. "Is Jess joining us?"

"She's still shopping," I say, grabbing a menu and leaving off that she's with Lord Danaby. It's embarrassing and hurtful, and I can't bear to say his name.

As Colter takes his seat, I peek at him over the menu. A sign for the Antique Palace practically waves at me from across the street. My eyes widen, my fingers tingling with the desire to explore.

Colter glances over his shoulder. "Would you like to go antiquing after we eat?"

❧

Walking into the Antique Palace with Colter and Eliana brings tears to my eyes. The musty and leathery smells. The colorful hodgepodge of treasures waiting to be observed and admired. The creaking of the floor, the chime of clocks, the tinkle of bells.

While Colter stays close, I lose sight of Eliana among the treasures. Her excitement is reminiscent of my first antiquing experience. Before Gran's instruction, I'd always associated antiques with rich people and those who knew the value of things. I'd had no clue what was worth significant monetary value, so what was the point looking through a random assortment of items trying to find valuables? But Gran showed me that it wasn't about finding something worth millions shoved in a back corner. It was about the stories.

"Objects carry the stories of their owners," I say as I pick up a hand-painted teacup of two children sitting in the shade of a massive tree. I quirk a brow at Colter. "Do you want to play 'What's your story'?"

"How does it work?" Colter moves a book so it's in line with the others around it.

"We each pick an item. Then, without reading the tag, you create a story. Who made it? Who used it? Where has it been? Gran and I used to play all the time."

I pick up a large mahogany ring that has a kangaroo, emu, and a kookaburra sitting on a boomerang. "This was forged from a meteorite by three friends who were about to go their separate ways. They knew it wouldn't be possible to see each other again, but they'd heard of a legend where they could each give a drop of blood that allowed its wearer to transport them where their friend was whenever they needed to."

Colter takes the item from me and looks at the tag. "Hmm...a napkin ring. I definitely like your version better." He moves down the aisle, settling on a squat gold vase with a lid. He holds it up. "This is a magical djinn jar owned by a sultan of Persilla, of course."

I laugh. "What was the sultan's name?"

"Ali." He quirks an eyebrow, and I nod for him to continue. "Ali was at the Pools of Mamilla to perform ceremonial cleansing before his birthday. The sultan was exiting the baths when he saw the mystic being pursued by bandits. Their leader wanted to use the mystic to increase his fortune. They also wanted the djinn in the jar to perform miracles to be able to create their own country.

"The sultan ordered his men to help, and they defended the mystic. In return for his life, the mystic gave the sultan this jar containing the djinn. He warned the sultan not to open the jar, or the djinn would escape. Instead, he advised the sultan to write down his wishes and place them near the jar. The magic would ooze out of the djinn and the sultan would receive his heart's desire."

"What did Ali ask for?" I question, forgetting this is a story Colter is masterfully creating.

"What would you ask for?" Colter twists my question back to me.

"I…" I pause, holding off on saying Colter's name despite my rapid heartbeat encouraging me to do otherwise. "I guess I'd ask for the djinn to tell me Gran's story. All of it." I smile at him. "Thanks for playing along. I've never played 'What's your story?' with anyone but Gran."

"I'm honored you chose me. I like creating stories with you."

A stack of vintage postcards sits to the right of a green glass oil lantern. "Oh, I need to buy some. I collect vintage postcards. Aunt Vi sends me one from all the places she's been." I shuffle through the stack choosing one featuring a fashionable Edwardian couple holding hands with the sea between them with HANDS ACROSS THE SEA written at the top.

"You need this one too." Colter hands me a silly one with a koala, emu, and kangaroo. G'DAY FROM DOWN UNDER swirls underneath the animals.

We don't tell any more stories, just enjoy the items—books, lamps, wooden carvings. Colter asks me how to tell if an antique has worth or if it's a fake. I tell him all I know, which isn't much more than you could Google.

A small colorful kiwi wedged between a record player and a tea set practically calls my name. "This looks like the first antique I bought. It didn't have any value, but, now that I think about it, it reminded me of Gran's shawl." There's a tag on the bird's foot. "Weka? This isn't a kiwi?"

"People often mix up the birds. Weka are cheeky and like to steal shiny objects. But they are fiercely protective." Colter takes the bird from my hand. "Weka are the national bird of Northargyle."

"So the bird on Gran's shawl is a weka not a kiwi. Makes sense since Gran was born there." I look at Colter when I register his factoid. "Wait. How did you know the weka is the national bird of Northargyle? I thought you'd never heard of the island."

"Remember when I told you my mother was working on our family history?"

I give him a speechless nod and wait for him to continue, but Eliana joins us.

"I found this amazing fabric." She holds up a remnant imitating an autumn garden. "I can't believe I've never been antiquing before."

"That's why I love it," I say. "You never know what you'll find."

"What's the fabric's story?" Colter asks then explains the rules for "What's your story?"

I've trained him well.

Eliana purses her lips a moment then begins. "It once belonged to a girl. This is only a remnant of the fabric—a never-ending bolt. The girl made a dress which was admired by all. With each compliment, it absorbed the energy around her, amplifying her confidence. She inspired others just by wearing it. Confidence to become a designer, to marry the love of her life." Eliana's eyes take on that faraway look, her hands running over the fabric. A butterfly ring on her index finger catches, but Eliana "comes to" before it snags.

"I wish I had a dress like that." I could use confidence in life.

"Me too."

Colter shakes his head. "You both are inspiring without a magical dress."

"Maybe I'll wear it tomorrow." The siblings share a look, which sends a huge, instant smile to Eliana's face. Like she's been granted permission to share a secret. One that I'm not getting a sixth sense about. "Would you like to go with us tomorrow?"

"Another netball tournament? Did you just ruin another epic speech?" I tease.

"To the Glenmore Cove Museum." Colter runs a hand through his hair. "We have an appointment after church."

"Tomorrow is Sunday? Is the museum even open?" My Sunday has become Monday due to the time difference. I've been watching the Westonia Baptist Church service live online. It's not the same as being present, but I didn't want to miss out on Dad's series through the book of James.

"Not to the public," Colter explains, his expression as unreadable as a Hebrew manuscript. Where's Dad when I need a translation? "I'd love your thoughts on an exhibit."

"Where is Glenmore Cove?" I ask.

"Not too far from Kenwick Estate. Glenmore is where Charles Brisbane, the first king of Northargyle, was born."

THE CHURCH PRINCESS

Once upon a time, there was a girl who just wanted to be normal. She wanted to rip off her smiling mask of perfection and not have people gasp at the halo-less, plain Jane underneath.

She wanted to be able to voice her opinion and frown without causing a major disturbance. She wanted to mess up and not receive a sermon. She wanted to wear black without people assuming she'd joined the Dark Side. In reality, her rebellious preferences included running down the aisle in church, singing show tunes from the pulpit, learning to tango, and getting her motorcycle license.

She wanted to do things without everyone and their brother knowing about it. She wanted to have friends, close friends, without having to push them away when they got too close. She wanted people to like her because she was likable, not because they thought she had the "in with God."

She wanted people to hang out with her without hiding who they really were. To share their hearts and problems without telling her she wouldn't understand because she was a pastor's daughter and didn't struggle.

She wanted to sleep at night without worrying who was going to come to the door next, if her dad would be home at a reasonable hour after taking the town drunk to the hospital for the tenth time.

She longed to be held accountable to prayer and devotions instead of everyone assuming she spent hours reading her Bible and praying. She wanted to be challenged, kicked out of her comfort zone. She wanted people to ask her about her salvation experience and not tell her she was already saved. (Truth: God is not a grandfather.)

She wanted to get rid of her title, the expectations, and the rules. She wanted to be who she really was and not who she was expected to be. She wanted to be loved, remembered, and understood.

She wanted off the pedestal of perfection before it got too high, and she fell. She wanted to take off her mask and become normal.

Impossible. She would never be normal because of her role, her title, the people, and her dad.

—Abigail Rosiah Morgan, age 16

Chapter Nineteen

The Glenmore Cove Museum is real. I'd looked it up online, of course, but the low quality of the website along with a distinct lack of specifics about the Northargyle exhibit opening to the public next week had me wondering. If Colter and Eliana hadn't invited me today, I would've missed it since Aunt Vi and I are leaving for New Zealand in three days.

At least the name on the museum site was still there this morning when I looked again. Unlike Northargyle's mysteriously disappearing Wikipedia page.

I breathe it all in as Colter opens the car door and offers me his hand. *Dark jeans. Gray dress shirt. Sleeves rolled. Tattoo fully visible. Facial hair trimmed. Light brown eyes at half twinkle.* He maneuvers around me, keeping me close as he shuts the door. With his hand on my lower back, he ushers me toward the museum.

What museum? Artifacts smartifacts.

Colter lifts an eyebrow at my giggle, but like a true gentleman, he doesn't ask.

A man approaches as soon as we're in the foyer. At first, I think he's one of the museum employees, but he only has eyes for Eliana. He wraps his arms around her, sighing like he's home, resting his head on top of hers.

"Is that Bradley?" I ask yet know without the confirmation that it is.

Colter nods. "Bradley, this is our dear friend, Abigail." It will never get old that Colter introduces me as me, no titles or anybody else attached.

"Good to meet you," Bradley says, his voice deep with an Irish lilt. Fits with his red tinted hair, green eyes, and freckles. His love and care for Eliana is evident in the way he holds her, the way she clings to him.

I was already halfway in love before I was informed that my father does not approve. Bradley is truly the best of men. Eliana's words from yesterday come to mind. Has her father seen them together? How could he not approve of the way they look at each other with such respect and tenderness? Theirs is not the fleeting type romance novels are made of.

Colter must have the same desire to give them space that I do. With a little pressure on my lower back, we head down a hallway, leaving Eliana and Bradley in their happy bubble.

"My sister and I would be grateful if you didn't mention that you met Bradley," Colter says. "They're trusting God's timing, but it's hard for them."

Before I can comment, a woman in her fifties with a chic bob and sensible black heels greets us. The curator, I presume.

Elegant and timeless appearance. Confident presence, stylish yet professional wardrobe, reflecting the artistic environment around her. Black hair with streaks of gray like tinsel catching the museum lighting. Features defined and expressive, with thoughtful dark eyes that convey her passion for art and culture.

"Thank you for opening today," Colter tells her. "Eliana and I wanted Abigail to see the Northargyle exhibit."

"We are truly honored by your presence. Your mother is greatly missed. We are forever grateful for her work here and on the exhibit." She dips her head. "Enjoy your time. I will be in my office if you have any questions."

Colter leads me toward the north wing.

"Your mother did this exhibit on Northargyle?" I ask. "Was she born there?"

"Not exactly."

Not exactly? What does that mean? A strange excitement thrills me as we wander down the hall. I can't quite shake the feeling that something big is about to happen. That I might finally find some answers about Northargyle.

Colter is quiet as I take my time reading the placards and *oohing* and *aahing* over pieces of Australian culture on display.

A sign tells museum goers that they're now entering the CHARLES BRISBANE MEMORIAL WING—an exhibit on the history of Northargyle. I try not to run toward the archway designed like the cutout of a cliff. Flowers, birds, and jagged diamond shapes are carved into it like cave drawings. Pictures of the flag and crest hang above a placard.

NORTHARGYLE

Established 6 July 1843

Queen Victoria gifted the island of Northargyle to Charles Brisbane on occasion of his thirty-fifth birthday and as a reward for his part in thwarting an attack on Her Majesty. Charles became King Charles Brisbane I. His wife, Alexandra, bore him one son, Edward Brisbane, on 5 January 1845. And one daughter, Evangeline Brisbane, 4 September 1847.

Succession: In keeping with tradition, the throne passes to the oldest heir (male or female) on their thirty-fifth birthday.

5 January 1880: Edward Brisbane crowned king of Northargyle
8 May 1869: Evangeline Brisbane married Philip Wellesley

The next area holds paintings and artwork inspired by the people of Northargyle. Angie Thorne even has a display. It's like Northargyle wants to claim her even though she wants nothing to do with them.

Colter allows me space as I explore, hovering, hands behind his back. Every new display has me holding my breath as I approach. I want to savor, but I want to rush to find evidence of my grandmother. She's got to be here.

I study the portrait of the first Northargyle royal family. Their crowns could double as anchors for a cruise ship. "I wonder what Alexandra got Charles for his birthday," I mutter, laughing to myself. I quirk an eyebrow at Colter, but he's not looking at me. I turn back to the wall of paintings, pausing at every royal, noticing similarities. Strong family genetics.

(1880-1911) King Edward Thomas Brisbane and Queen Juliette
(1911-1937) King Andrew Charles Brisbane and Queen Katherine
(1937-1955) King Thomas Edward Brisbane and Queen Charlotte

Queen Charlotte. I know that name. Two separate portraits are on display—one for King Thomas, one for Queen Charlotte. Their death dates are the same.

"The Brisbane royal line ended with them. Their deaths paved the way for the Wellesley family," Colter explains.

I think of the Northargyle placard. "Didn't Evangeline Brisbane marry a Wellesley?"

"Royal family trees," Colter says with a shrug.

My breath catches at the next painting. King Thomas stands beside Queen Charlotte who holds a newborn wrapped in Gran's shawl. The shawl is missing the patch and the fringe, but that's definitely my grandmother's. The one made for her birth.

King Thomas and Queen Charlotte Brisbane with daughter
Rosiah Catherine Brisbane (16 April 1938 — 5 Dec 1955)

"That's my gran's shawl and her birth date," I whisper, covering my mouth with my hands. "Oh my."

Colter's intake of breath scares me, but he doesn't say anything as I study the next painting, this one of King Thomas and Queen Charlotte and Prince Michael. I'm guessing he's five or six years old. Why isn't Princess Rosiah in this family portrait?

King Thomas and Queen Charlotte Brisbane with son
Prince Michael Thomas Brisbane (10 Sept 1948 — 5 Dec 1955)

"Michael was seven when he died. So sad." I glance at Colter, tears threatening to fall at the loss represented in the painting. Colter remains mute as he motions toward a small nook set apart from the Brisbane family. A painting of a young woman who can't be more than fourteen wearing a simple tiara hangs above a wooden desk.

The painting is a twister touching down on my puzzle pieces and blowing every sticky note off my wall. Everything I thought I knew no longer exists. The veil has been burned.

This girl—although younger—*is* in the photo with Gran and Hazel.

Laurel is Gran. She was never Rose. Rose was the real princess of Northargyle. Every journal entry. Every painting. Every name. Every detail, even the shawl. I'd gotten everything so unbelievably wrong. I'm going to have to start from the beginning.

Gran hadn't been lying to me about her past, she'd just been protecting Rosiah's. *Some stories are too dangerous to tell.*

"I'm going to have to start my puzzle all over again. My gran was not Princess Rosiah," I say. "Her name was Laurel."

Laurel. Gran's real name was Laurel. Yep. This is big.

Colter releases a breath, and I glance his way. "I'm glad you said that."

He's glad I don't have royal blood? Why wouldn't he want me to have royal blood? Is it because we wouldn't be able to be together since he's a commoner?

I study the painting of a girl I feel I know more than Gran. "Angie was right," I whisper. "That death date is wrong."

"That's what my mother discovered as well."

"If Gran wasn't the princess, then who was she? Did she work at the palace? Was she her nurse? A lady-in-waiting? A scullery maid? I wonder if the palace would let me look at records." I blow a raspberry unintentionally in my frustrations. "I really need to go to Northargyle. Maybe Angie Thorne can use her connections."

Colter holds out his hand, which I accept. "Come, I need you to see the rest of my mother's project. This is what I would like your opinion on."

"I don't know how much help I'll be." My words are a squeak of emotion.

The archway to the right is flanked by two trees carved from the same faux material as the cliff cutout. Colter releases my hand but doesn't enter the room with me. "You shall not pass!" comes to mind as I look at him on the other side.

"I'll let you look." He offers me an encouraging smile.

With a shake of my head, I turn ready to face this exhibit. What other story-altering facts about Gran will I glean here?

The first painting is of a woman and man. Neither of them smile. Their postures are stiff, and they wear crowns set with matching green jewels. A vase holding silk roses rests on the table beside them.

King Frederick George Thomas Wellesley
(8 March 1931 — 5 June 1990)
Queen Ruth Selene Wellesley (nee Winthrop)
(6 June 1932 — 13 June 2000)

A painting on the back takes up half the wall. The current king of Northargyle. King Hamish Charles Wellesley I. Born in 1967, King Hamish is fifty-seven. He has a noble face. I tilt my head trying to figure out if I like his look. While handsome, he strikes me as hard and set in his ways.

The setup of this room is different. The feel is different, as if love has been trapped within these walls. Even though King Hamish doesn't smile, there are small lines around his light brown eyes. I'd like to imagine they are from smiling and not from squinting.

The painting of his wife, Queen Seneca, sits by itself. I admire the queen's gown and gorgeous wedding ring before studying her face. Dark blonde hair, amber-colored eyes, and a touch of a smirk on her lips. Not the Mona Lisa secret but one more pronounced. It doesn't leave the observer wondering if she's about to smile. You know she is.

> Queen Seneca Kathleen Wellesley (née Kenwick)
> (13 November 1970 — 2 June 2023)

A letter sits under the glass next to the plaque. It's Romans twelve. My pulse revs like an engine as I read through the entire passage. The last line stops my heart.

> Faith. Service. Leadership. Romans Twelve.

The handwriting. That motto. Colter's mother. Kenwick. Queen Seneca Kathleen Wellesley...

I whip around to see Colter framed by the trees like he's trapped in a Claude Monet watercolor.

In that moment, I know. Without a shadow of a doubt, I may not have royal blood, but Colter is the heir to the Northargyle throne.

ROMANS TWELVE

However, since we have gifts that differ according to the grace given to us, each of us is to use them properly: if prophecy, in proportion to one's faith; if service, in the act of serving; or the one who teaches, in the act of teaching; or the one who exhorts, in the work of exhortation; the one who gives, with generosity; the one who is in leadership, with diligence; the one who shows mercy, with cheerfulness.

Love must be free of hypocrisy. Detest what is evil; cling to what is good. Be devoted to one another in brotherly love; give preference to one another in honor, not lagging behind in diligence, fervent in spirit, serving the Lord; rejoicing in hope, persevering in tribulation, devoted to prayer, contributing to the needs of the saints, practicing hospitality.

Bless those who persecute you; bless and do not curse. Rejoice with those who rejoice, and weep with those who weep. Be of the same mind toward one another; do not be haughty in mind, but associate with the lowly. Do not be wise in your own estimation. Never repay evil for evil to anyone. Respect what is right in the sight of all people.

If possible, so far as it depends on you, be at peace with all people. Never take your own revenge, beloved, but leave room for the wrath of God, for it is written: "Vengeance is Mine, I will repay," says the Lord. "But if your enemy is hungry, feed him; if he is thirsty, give him a drink; for in so doing you will heap burning coals on his head."

Do not be overcome by evil, but overcome evil with good.

Faith. Service. Leadership. Romans Twelve.

—Queen Seneca Kathleen Kenwick Wellesley

Chapter Twenty

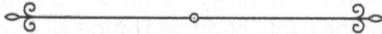

I n the space of two minutes, I've been hit with two life-altering truths, three if you count now knowing Colter's last name is Wellesley.

One: Gran was not Princess Rosiah.

Two: Colter is the crown prince of Northargyle.

And because of the second, I've claimed Colter's relief at the revelation. *Woohoohoo! We're not related!*

The theater of my mind is blank.

What girl doesn't long to meet a prince? There's a reason so many books and movies include that plotline. And yes, I've imagined this scene before, but the reality of such a situation is I don't know what to do with it. The impossible has become possible in a way I never imagined. Who needs to imagine the fairy tale when it's smiling hesitantly and expectantly at you?

"Your mother was the queen of Northargyle?" I can't believe I asked that.

"Yes." Colter sighs.

Trust, but verify. I spin toward the opposite wall and find two paintings. I charge over for verification of Colter's claim.

I study Eliana's painting and placard first, so I can park at Colter's.

Princess Eliana Kenwick Wellesley
(b. 10 March 1998)
Daughter of King Hamish and Queen Seneca
Patron of the Arts

Princess Eliana is everything a princess should be. Whimsical in style. Beauty radiating from every flawless pore. She looks so much like her mother.

Prince Colter's turn. The painting presents a clean-shaven version. I've been given license to stare at him without the nerves of full eye contact, although I feel Colter watching as I study his painted twin. I weave my fingers together to keep them at my sides. Probably shouldn't run my fingers over his face. One of the first rules of museums, don't touch the art.

Prince Colter Tilney Hamish Wellesley
(b. 26 April 1994)
Oldest son of King Hamish and Queen Seneca
Heir to the throne of Northargyle
Patron of Libraries

"I've wanted to tell you since I first met you," Colter says. "I wanted to help you in your search for your gran's story. But admitting I was born on Northargyle would lead to me confessing everything."

"Why didn't you?"

"You won't be able to tell anyone you're under a spell." The high-pitched, crackly voice scrapes along before turning into a cough. He grimaces as he clears his throat. "Well, that sounded better in my mind. I was trying to be the Witch of the Waste."

I quirk an eyebrow. "I broke your curse?"

"In a way. Keeping our identity quiet is my father's rule for Eliana and me to travel without a huge security team following our every move."

"You aren't protected?"

"Bishop is around here somewhere."

"Oh, the 'friend' at Sugarleaf and at your gate on netball day."

"Actually, that was Hugh. He's my father's faithful reporter of all things the royal children do." Colter winces. "We usually stay at Kenwick when we're away from Northargyle, but this time was different because of the museum exhibit and the book signing with Violet Morgan where

I met an enthralling American. Eventually, you would have discovered my identity in your researching, but I wanted to be the one to tell you."

"Does this mean you have to leave Australia? Did you give up your freedom for me to find out the truth?" How could he tell me if he's not supposed to?

"You're worth this. Definitely worth it."

"But if telling me means I'll lose you—"

"You're not going to lose me or Eliana." His playful grin is half back, one side lifted. I wait for the other corner of his lips to lift, but it doesn't. "You're not running or yelling at me."

"I knew something was special about you. In a way, I'm not surprised." I can't explain the calm. It's like the time I knew that Rachel was pregnant with Poppy before they told us. Just had the sense and wasn't as shocked as the rest of my family who felt blindsided. "Besides, every girl dreams the guy she falls for is secretly a prince."

"Falls for?" Now he's grinning full force. He reaches for my hand. "Just promise that when you see me in my princely attire, you'll still recognize and still be 'fallen for' me."

He gently tugs on my hand, and we're moving away from his painting. I don't want a time out from my staring. Then again, I don't need him to see me drooling.

"Now that I'm free to tell you my story, what would you like to know? You already know my favorite book and food and color," Colter says. "Do you have any questions about what it's like to be a prince?"

My mind empties. What do I want to know about the life of a prince? That hasn't exactly been on my radar. I understand his hesitancy—well, not hesitancy, but his lack of revealing anything—before now.

"I'm still me," he assures.

"Just with the word prince before your name and a crown upon your head." I have to add a crown to all Colter's facts. But also, I have to remove all the crowns from Gran's. "How many crowns do you have?" I hear myself saying.

He purses his lips and looks toward the ceiling, concentrating as he counts.

Goodness, he's still going. Does he have an entire crown room?

"Just one," he says with a wink. "So far."

"So far? Are you planning on stealing another one?"

"A special crown will be made for my thirty-fifth birthday. I'll wear that once when I'm crowned king, and then it will be locked away."

When he's crowned king...

Music swells, and we all turn as the doors of the cathedral open. Colter enters. The train of his robe drags behind him as he walks down the aisle. He kneels in front of the church official in charge of the coronation, and the room goes silent. The official approaches with a pillow on which sits a crown. But unexpected to all, Colter raises his head and extends his hand to the side. "I request that Abigail Rosiah Morgan have the honor of placing the crown on my head—"

"What's that smile for?"

I startle and heat. "Do I really smile so little that you have to ask?"

"You smile all the time. But when that smile appears, you radiate pure joy and excitement."

"I do?"

He leans forward, studying me. "Maybe I should be saying, 'What's your smile's story?'"

"I guess this smile appears when I'm in my mind theater." I shrug, heating again at the reality that I am voicing my craziness out loud. Maybe it's time for some running and screaming. But I continue, of course. "My mind likes to write silly placards about people, places, and things. I guess you could say I have an overactive imagination."

"I hope you never lose that smile." We've stopped in front of Rosiah's painting. "Someday, I'd like to move this painting and the entire exhibit to Northargyle permanently, but Father has yet to agree to it."

"Why would your father not want a museum on Northargyle?"

"I rarely understand my father. But in regard to a museum, this was my mother's passion, and Father never understood. I'm praying I can change his mind. Any tips will be helpful."

We chat easily about what I love in the exhibit and how it could be even better. The privilege of this preview is so exciting. Such an honor. Queen Seneca was talented, and Rosiah's items from the cottage, which I promised to bequeath to Colter, will only enhance what she started. Although, I will be keeping the painting of Gran—which Colter says is my right.

"I have one more confession," he says on our way out of the Northargyle exhibit, toward the main entrance.

I brace myself.

"I met—if you can call a passing on the stairs actually meeting, which I do—you on September 24 at the Westonia Historical Society. Not October 4 at Sugarleaf Manor."

"That was you! You were the handsome stranger in the sweater on the stairs." The scent of sunshine and eucalyptus hits me like we're there again. How had I not recognized him? Also, he remembers the exact dates? Swoon.

"I was waiting for you to recognize me, but you never did."

"I was in the middle of a heist, trying to be invisible."

He quirks an eyebrow. "Do tell."

"Margaret Weston's journal hadn't been transcribed, and I wanted to see if she'd mentioned Gran so I, um, borrowed it. But it worked out well." I circle back to the fact that I've known him longer than a month. "What were you doing at the Westonia?"

"Eliana and I were in New York City for a gallery opening. Prudence Ellery needed verification on a certain brooch, and I figured I was close enough to the Westonia to handle it."

Eliana and Bradley enter the room hand in hand. She glances between me and Colter, a sweet smile lighting up her face. Content. Happy. Not that she hasn't been before, but a visible weight has been lifted.

"She figured it out before I showed her our mug shots, as you said she would," Colter says.

"I'm so glad." Eliana releases Bradley to give me a hug.

"Are you secretly a royal too?" I ask Bradley. Wait, if King Hamish doesn't approve, then he must not be. If that's the case though, how will I even have a chance with Colter? Especially since Gran wasn't of royal blood?

"Not even close and of no importance," Bradley says.

"Hush, you," Eliana chides. "You are the one my heart loves and always will."

"So, one more order of business before we eat lunch in the gardens." Colter takes my hand. "I need a date to the symphony. Bradley is going with Eliana. Would you consider going with me?"

"Of course!" I answer.

Not only an official date with Colter—be still my heart—but the symphony with a prince? Oh, but wait. A prince. A real-to-goodness prince. And me, his date.

"I don't have anything to wear." Sometimes, I don't like being practical.

"Good thing you have me," Eliana says. "*That* I can definitely help with."

MUSICAL POTLUCK

Each instrument insists on bringing its favorite dish to share. The strings are in charge of pasta—comforting casseroles, rich and warm. (Although, the first chair violin insisted on bringing a four-tiered cake and the cellos brought Jell-O.) Percussion tap danced in with platters of fried chicken. Brass tooted their own horns offering up their famous cowboy beans—loud and demanding everyone's attention from the start. Maracas brought the tacos. Woodwinds show up late with a mysterious dip no one can identify. Piccolos brought pickles. Bass brought their signature bass, seasoned with Old Bay. Flutes are in charge of coffee—don't even think of suing them if you gulp instead of sip. Cymbals brought plates, which clashed with the napkins. Triangles, well they're just here for the fellowship—gotta watch that triangular figure. Once the conductor prays, let the silence be shattered and the symphony begin.

—Abigail's Notebook of Silly Placards

Chapter Twenty-One

I love the idea of evening gowns, but then the moment arrives, and I create scenarios of all that could go wrong. I'll spill something down the front of me. I'll trip on the hem and send someone *else* sprawling. I'll sweat so much that I will repel everyone. Nervous sweat smells so much worse than regular sweat.

Aunt Vi eyes me up and down, motioning for me to twirl. Eliana sent not only a dress for me but one for my aunt. I'm not sure who her date will be, but I'm glad she's invited.

"It's perfect," Aunt Vi says.

Despite my fears, I agree. It's as though a flower garden has come to life. *Black. Sweetheart neckline with capped sleeves. A floral tapestry covers the entire gown flowing over a layer of toile. Butterflies flit among dainty buds of white and red and pink.*

Aunt Vi's dress is a navy, one-shouldered gown that sparkles every time she sways. It's long enough for her to wear matching Converse that Eliana sent with the dress. I'm wearing black strappy heels a little higher than I'm used to, but wow, are they comfortable.

My aunt's hair is piled on top of her head, and several curls hang around her temple and ears, making it look salon-fresh. Mine's pulled back in a loose fishtail braid. We both decided against wearing makeup.

"I'm so nervous to see Colter." I make sure I have two earrings in.

"Nothing has changed, right? He's still the same amazing guy that you've fallen for." Aunt Vi shakes her head, her laugh as nervous as I feel. "I still can't believe that Colter and Eliana are royalty."

Colter had given his permission for me to tell my aunt when we got back to the cottage. After yelling "Plot twist! I've never played fifty questions with a prince!" Aunt Vi commenced with questions ranging from "What do you do all day?" to "Why aren't you in the news?" to "What's your favorite part about Northargyle?"

I allow one more glance in the mirror. "Okay, I think I'm ready."

"Go ahead. I'll be down shortly. I can't decide which earrings to wear."

"I like the silver musical notes."

"Good call."

While she puts them in, I grip my skirts, lifting them to reveal only my ankles as I make my way down the stairs. Colter said he'd be here promptly at five because the event starts at seven thirty and it's an hour drive. It'll give us leeway to not feel rushed in case the traffic is heavy.

A quick knock on the back door announces Jess half a second before she barges into the kitchen. Her smile falls as soon as she spots me. It's not awe of seeing something gorgeous and being speechless. It's more an anger that I dare look this good.

"Where are you going?" Jess eyes my gown. "Oh, right. Date with Devon."

"Actually, I'm going to the symphony in Brisbane."

"My brother said he had a date tonight."

"It's not with me."

Jess's entire face shifts. "It's Colter, isn't it. Don't lie and say it's your aunt."

"I didn't—"

"You're hurting my brother by spending time with this random guy. Devon has been nothing but adoring of you, and you're being rude and spiteful. But I guess you find people with money better company. No wonder you're always with them."

"I'm not with them because they have money," I say, brow lowered. "Colter and Eliana are good people." *Who also happen to be royalty.*

"Bet they bought you that dress too. How much did it cost?" Jess's eyes widen. "Wait, isn't that one of the bridesmaid dresses from Beyond Dresses? I swear I saw it on display."

"I—"

"It doesn't flatter you." Her eyes narrow. She's waving her left hand at my dress—a ringless left hand.

"Where's your ring?" I ask. *Please say you didn't lose it.*

"I had to have it resized. My fingers are so much smaller than yours." She rolls her eyes. "Speaking of rings, you promised Devon that he could buy you one. How can you go out with this guy when you're as good as engaged to another?"

"What?" I almost tip over. "I am not engaged to your brother, and I never promised I'd let him buy me a ring."

"Why are you lying? I don't like who you are anymore. I'll be having a conversation with your brother. He will take my side in this destructiveness." Jess scoffs. "I don't understand why you hate us. I thought family was everything to you. Yet you're spending your last days in Australia with them?" Her words spit at me like an irritated camel.

Get this girl some pretzels. I wince at my unfiltered meanness. I am not stooping to her level. Pressure builds behind my eyes. Why is she being like this?

"After all the cruel things you said about Eliana, I don't get—"
Okay, that's too far.

"Jess, I have not once ever said anything cruel about Eliana. I'm not going anywhere with Devon. If anyone is lying, it's him if he told you we were dating or engaged or whatever. It's not true and never will be. I'm going to the symphony."

"You're always leaving me. Everyone's always leaving. First Jaxon, then you and your aunt are going to New Zealand without me. Even Titus is out of town."

I'm glad for that tidbit. "Maybe we can do something tomorrow."

"You're not worth my time. When the Cove people tire of you, I hope my brother will still want you." She leaves without a backward glance, slamming the door behind her.

Part of my heart goes with her. Jess was my first real friend in Australia, my first real friend ever. She taught me to open up. To be okay with having a close friend. But did I force the friendship with Jess, see things that were never there, because I wanted so badly to have what Hazel and Gran had?

Two things hit me, and I laugh as a tear leaks from my eye. I've always had the mindset that I had to chase that one "sheep," that one person who didn't like me, to try to win them over. I needed everyone to like me. But one, I'm not God. Two, I have a herd of ninety-nine people who like me, encourage me, and build me up.

"Are you okay?" Aunt Vi asks as she joins me.

"Yes." I truly am.

There's a knock on the front door this time.

This is it. Nerves have returned. I can't move.

"Go, invite your man in." Aunt Vi pushes me gently toward the door.

A handsome man in a suit is revealed when I open the door. *Dark hair, sprinkles of gray in his beard. Early forties. Blue eyes.* He must realize I'm searching for Colter because he clears his throat, scans the area, and says, "The prince has been detained. I've been sent to fetch you and your aunt."

"How do we know you're not kidnapping us?" Aunt Vi calls from behind me.

"It is tempting. To spend time with the breathtaking and talented Violet Morgan would be any kidnapper's dream," he says. Wow, the schmooze is strong with this one.

"Did you call me talented? Just so you know, lines like that don't work on me."

"We'll see." He winks at me. "But, alas, there will be no kidnapping. My boss comes first, and he wants Miss Abigail Morgan by his side." He motions toward a car with a ringless left hand.

Had he done that to signal to Aunt Vi? Did he catch her looking as I had?

"Mind if I sit up front?" she asks. "I get carsick."

She gets no such thing.

The driver starts talking as soon as the cottage and Bridgeway are out of sight. "Prince Colter has informed me that both of you are aware of who he is, so we may speak freely. He told me to be prepared for fifty questions. I'm ready."

Aunt Vi's mouth falls open, but no words come out. She's as googly-eyed as a cartoon character. Any moment now, her eyes will fall out of their sockets. When she doesn't say anything, he grins.

"My name is Bishop Mills. I'm forty-two. I've worked for Prince Colter for three years."

"Who was the other man at the book event and at Kenwick Manor?" I ask then remember Colter had said it was Hugh, his father's spy. Bishop verifies the memory.

"Hugh was filling in while I was away. He was not happy that the prince escaped to go to the book signing."

I laugh. "I could tell."

"I arrived in Australia the day you and the prince went to the café. That pavlova is amazing." I catch his wink in the rearview mirror then shake my head. Pavlova man. "The prince likes to drive, but I was always close."

If I had the ability to scroll through all the scenes with Colter and Eliana, would I be able to spot Bishop like Waldo in a search-and-find book?

"I missed the netball tournament because I took my children to Greece for a quick visit with their grandparents."

Aunt Vi's eyes widen with every bit of information Bishop shares.

"My wife died about three months before the prince offered me the job as his personal driver. He reminded me that I had four wonderful children who needed me."

"Four?" Aunt Vi rasps.

"Tara, my oldest, is sixteen and a huge fan of yours. I allowed her to read your books with the promise she wouldn't sneak into bed with me because she was scared. I don't mind her reading them. They're better than Angie Thorne's." He wiggles his brow.

Aunt Vi laughs but doesn't comment.

"My middle two are boys. Gregory, who just turned thirteen, and Daved, who's ten. They don't like to read, sorry. They're more into cars, karate, and eating everything in sight. Then there's Molly." Bishop chuckles. "She's six and the spitting image of my late wife. I can't get her to wear anything but leotards and tutus. Purple, though. There's no pink for my Molly."

The ride is over too soon, the hour filled by easy and hilarious conversation. Aunt Vi eventually remembered she spoke English, and the two of them carried on a banter worthy of a spark-filled rom-com. They launched questions back and forth like a volleyball—bump, set, spike! They talked books and coffee and writing and how much Bishop likes

Leonard Irby. *When does Leonard's tragic past get revealed? What's next for Faith Mackenzie? How much can you bench press? Feel free to pick my mind for fight scenes.*

Bishop will probably show up on the page in the next chapter.

We pass a pillared building, driving around to a lot with only three other vehicles.

"Here you are, safe and sound," Bishop says as he parks beside a limo.

Had Colter arrived in that?

Bishop eyes my aunt, and I feel like I'm intruding. "I still have one question left, but you definitely used all yours."

"Guess we'll have to see each other again," Aunt Vi says, twisting the musical note earring dangling from her left ear.

"I'll have to make sure question fifty is epic." Bishop shifts his focus from Aunt Vi to the building. "I have strict instructions to escort you directly to the prince."

He opens the door and helps me out then moves around to help Aunt Vi. She waits patiently instead of vaulting out of the car. He offers his hand. As soon as she's out, her dress straightened, she links her arm through his and holds out the other for me.

Bishop leads us through a side door off the main entrance and straight to a handsome man about my age.

Wait! It's Colter. He's clean-shaven and dressed to the nines in a black tux. His playful smirk is missing, replaced by a serious, no-nonsense expression. Intimidating. Exactly like his portrait.

"Are you real, or did you escape from the painting in the museum?" I don't realize I spoke my random thought aloud until Colter answers.

"It's me." His words remind me that he may be a prince, but Aunt Vi is right—he's still the same, minus the facial hair.

"Hello, real Colter." Wait, should I have said Prince Colter? Your Highness? Do people know who he is here? Why didn't I ask Bishop?

"Abigail." He bows over my hand. His eyes give a little spark as he whispers, "I'm so glad you recognized me."

"I did promise I would." I don't admit that it took a minute. The lack of Wizard Howl charm threw me more than the facial hair.

Colter's lips twitch before he grows serious again. "I'm sorry I didn't come with Bishop." He pauses as someone approaches from another room. His eyes widen as he whispers, "Please don't think less of me tonight."

"I—"

"Is this the Miss Morgan whom I've heard so much about?" The booming voice sends shockwaves of panic through me and erases all mirth off Colter's face.

"Father, this is Abigail Morgan and her aunt, Violet Morgan. Ladies, my father, King Hamish Wellesley." The introductions come across as stiffly as a board. All traces of Colter's lively personality have been sucked away.

I curtsy. Aunt Vi wobbles a little but holds her own. Her hand settles on my arm as we both right ourselves.

Gran, again, thank you for all the lessons. Did you know that one day I might need them? Did you know I'd be introduced to royalty? Were you preparing me for such a time as this? My brain went to Esther quickly, but there's no way Gran could have predicted a chance meeting with a prince at Aunt Vi's book signing.

The king is handsome, a preview of what Colter will look like one day. Although, Colter already has more laugh lines. I pray he isn't reduced to whatever has taken hold of his father when he's king.

"Why didn't you retrieve Miss Morgan yourself?" the king asks Colter, a harsh look in his dark eyes. "You sent Bishop?"

"I wanted to arrive with you, Father," Colter tries to explain.

"Who am I when the lovely Miss Morgan is around? You should have gone with the car."

"I will next time, Father."

"Good, good." The king's smile lacks any hint of playful nature as he takes my arm and hooks it through his, leading me toward an archway and ushering me to a padded chair with armrests.

Colter enters the private box, seating Eliana and Aunt Vi before easing into the chair on my other side. Bradley is nowhere to be seen. Poor Eliana. I glance over my shoulder at my aunt. She gives me a finger wave then chats easily with Eliana. This is so weird. A commoner between royalty. A place of precedence over my famous aunt.

"So, Miss Morgan," the king says. "Tell me about yourself."

Trying not to shift in the seat, I take a deep breath and scroll through all the things I could say. I can't talk to the king in the way I've been talking to Colter. Music seems like an appropriate topic considering where we are. But what follows that? Sports? Research? Fishtail braids?

Sweat builds. *Breathe, Abigail. Just breathe.*

The lights dim, and the first notes save me from having to settle on a topic just yet.

Awe. Wonder. Tears. The songs, instruments, and the gifts and abilities of every performer held me captive from start to finish.

The emotion the music evoked made me forget that Northargyle's king was next to me. Almost. He occasionally asked questions, which I feel I answered well—as in, I answered the question and only the question.

Colter's leg brushed against mine at least once every song. During a particularly moving song, he leaned close to translate. He confessed he doesn't speak the language but knew the translation because it's one of his favorites by Erik Crusell, a composer from the country of Findlay.

When the houselights come up, the king stands and offers his arm, informing me that there is a reception for the royal family and honored guests. Colter pairs up with Eliana, leaving Aunt Vi to herself. As soon as we're in the ballroom and the string quartet starts a waltz, the king hands me to Colter, instructing us to dance.

Colter scowls but takes my hand.

"We don't have to dance, if you don't want to," I whisper once we're out of range of the king.

"Oh, I want to dance with you, Abigail. I'm just thrown by my father's forcing."

"So, because he wants us to dance, you don't want to? Stubborn much?"

Colter's playful grin tries so hard to make an appearance. "My father rarely does things without an ulterior motive. I can't figure this out. I'm not upset. Please don't think that. Father arrived as we were preparing to leave to get you and insisted on attending. I'm trying to be happy he's here, but I was looking forward to having you to myself. And because Father is here, Bradley couldn't stay."

"It's okay."

"It's not, but nice of you to say so." Colter leads me to the dance floor where we join numerous couples. "My father seems to like you. Which is odd."

I try not to be offended but it doesn't quite work. "You didn't think your father would like me? I mean, I'm not of royal blood—"

"It's not that. Well, a little. Father is different with you." Colter holds up his hands in waltz pose. "But now, we dance. Which I would have asked you to do regardless of my father."

I set up my frame. Colter pulls me a bit closer than any partner I've ever had. I'm supposed to look to the left, but I can't avert my eyes from his. Which is odd because I've never been good at making direct eye contact during dancing.

Our first movement together on the dance floor is seamless, like we've been dance partners for years. I realize that I've never fully trusted any of my partners enough to let them lead. Thinking I knew best. Thinking I could do it best. Colter dips me, and I don't pull or push. I just float. There is no fear that he will let me fall. He's not going to do anything to destroy my heart.

I'm not even tempted to lead. I'll happily follow.

By the end of the song, my head is resting against Colter's chest. We sway in our moment long enough for another song to start. A woman takes the stage, her voice throaty and deep. I look up to find Colter's eyebrow raised in invitation. I nod, and we thread through the other couples on the dance floor for another song.

Way too soon, we move off the floor hand in hand.

King Hamish greets us, clapping. Eliana offers a smile but doesn't say anything until the king gives her a pointed look.

"Abigail," she begins. "I know you've mentioned you'd like to visit Northargyle and that you and your aunt planned on visiting while in New Zealand. We're returning home in a few days, and we're wondering if you'd like to come with us then."

"We would love for you to be our guest at the palace," King Hamish adds. "If your aunt can spare you."

"She would love to spare her," Aunt Vi says, appearing suddenly as if summoned.

"Are you sure? You'll be okay alone?"

Aunt Vi waves off my concern. "Definitely sure. You go. Have fun."

"So, that's a yes?" Eliana asks.

"Yes."

NORTHARGYLE

Welcome to the island of Northargyle. A hidden gem in the Tasman Sea, just north of New Zealand. The island enjoys much of the same wildlife (not as many sheep) and weather as New Zealand (experience the four seasons all in one day).

NATIONAL BIRD: WEKA

Cross between a chicken and a small dino. Unlike the kiwi, whose wings are almost gone, this bird still has large wings. Flightless, but boy can they run! Bold personality. Curious nature. Beak made for mischief. Notorious snack thief—also likes shiny things. Likes to garden—will kindly pull out your lettuce plant to check its root health and to pick off any aphids, slugs, whiteflies, etc.

NATIONAL FLOWER: CRASPEDIA

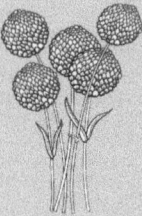

Also known as billy button, woolly head, golden drumstick. Ball-shaped cluster (wooly texture foliage) plus slim unbranched stems equals a drumstick. Colors range from white to green. Can reach the size of a tennis ball. Greek "*Kraspedron*" meaning "Fringed edge." Symbolizes good health.

Chapter Twenty-Two

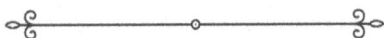

⬥━━━━━◦━━━━━⬥

W elcome to Northargyle." Colter takes my hand, helping me down the stairs of the private jet toward a waiting limo.

If I step on the shore, will it all disappear? Is it a façade? Will I pass through a screen and find myself on the creepy, haunted island the people of Bridgeway predicted?

When my foot hits the ground, I scan the area, expecting to see photographers jump out. I concentrate on my posture and make sure I'm smiling, hoping that if pictures are taken the caption won't read "Look at the awkward stranger who has no reason to be here."

"This is a private airfield, on palace property." Colter senses my questions, catching me not so subtly adjusting my skirt, making sure my bra strap isn't showing. "Not saying a photographer has never braved the high fence, but we're not worth their time. I'd be royally offended, but it helps me move around freely if my face isn't everywhere." He shrugs, offering his signature grin as we enter the limo.

As the scenery reminiscent of a kaleidoscope rolls by, my excitement builds at where this limo is heading. *I'm here, Gran, I'm really here. Soon*

I will be walking the halls where you walked. The song from *My Fair Lady*—"On the Street Where You Live"—lends accompaniment to that thought and a giggle escapes.

Colter quirks an eyebrow.

"I can't believe I'm going to be staying in a real palace." I'm still not sure my parents believed me when I told them I was going to Northargyle and staying at the palace with my new friends. Pictures are a must. "So, what's Northargyle Palace like?"

"Oh, the usual. Priceless art and furniture. Gardens. Fountains. Staff everywhere, forbidden wings, dungeons, the bodies of our enemies, drawbridge, moat."

"Wouldn't that make it a castle? Palaces aren't fortified."

"I love that you know that." He chuckles. "We are not so fortunate to have a drawbridge or moat. I probably would've gotten in trouble for raising and lowering the drawbridge and swimming where I wasn't supposed to."

Dark. Gothic. Towering turrets. Sliding panels that lead to lavish rooms. Secrets whispered in the hall by servants who never smile—who see everything. Who stop talking as soon as I approach. Faulty electricity, going off and on at random times. The chill of ghosts passing in the hallways.

"There's that imagining smile." Colter nudges me with his elbow. "What scene was playing?"

"I was thinking about hidden passages and ghosts. Gothic horror types of things. Are any of those in your palace?"

"Most definitely."

"Don't mind my brother." Eliana shakes her head. "The palace is a lovely place."

My jaw drops in awe as the limo rolls through the gates, and I catch my first glimpse of Northargyle Palace. It is the most beautiful building I've ever seen. Even my imaginings and dreams wouldn't have been able to create this. Lovely is way too tame a word.

Enchanting and dramatic. Eclectic architecture—Gothic, Renaissance, and Baroque elements. Towers and turrets giving it a fairy-tale appearance and an interesting silhouette. Façade of light-colored stone, adorned with intricate carvings, decorative motifs, and large, arched windows. Gardens in place of a moat. A captivating blend of history, art, and natural beauty.

There is nothing dark or dreary or mysterious. It's white and shining and happy. I don't know if my imagination is thrilled or upset. Was I hoping it would be dark and scary? Isn't being at a palace exciting enough?

"Do you like it?" Colter asks.

"You had me shaking, worried I wouldn't survive."

"Not everyone does," Colter mutters as the car stops at a grand staircase, the staff lined up on either side, ready to stick out their hands and coax us onto the field or court. *Go team!*

My giddy mood is rising. Actually, it could be panic. I'm not quite sure there's a difference. At least there's no jet lag to add to the relief of being off a plane this time. Even if the private jet was *very* nice.

King Hamish appears at the top of the stairs in a dark suit, but he descends as soon as my door is opened and my feet hit the ground. In a wave, the staff bows or curtsies as he passes. The driver doesn't even have time to offer to help me out of the limo.

King Hamish is there, hand extended. "Welcome to Northargyle Palace."

Colter and Eliana stay behind me as the king leads me up the stairs, the wave of staff dipping and rising again. "Zoe will be your maid while you are here. Good and fitting."

A young redheaded woman with tons of adorable freckles covering her face steps forward and curtsies. I stop myself from responding with one of my own. I'm not royalty, but I am a guest. The proper etiquette for meeting royalty is fresh in my thoughts. I was not going in unprepared since I love to research and being prepared cuts down on the severity of nerves. At least in theory.

"Get Miss Morgan settled. Dinner will be promptly at seven." The king releases me into Zoe's care. "Colter, Eliana. Come with me."

"Yes, Father," Colter and Eliana respond tonelessly together.

As Colter passes, he squeezes my hand. "I'll see you at dinner."

His father calls for him not to dally, his voice booming through the hall.

"This way, Miss Morgan," Zoe says.

"Abigail, please. Miss Morgan sounds way too proper, and maybe a little spinstery."

Zoe laughs as she motions for me to follow her through a hallway then up two flights of stairs. We pass paintings of landscapes and portraits intent on intimidating me with glares from where they perch on the wall.

When we reach a fork in the hallway, I take a moment to study the tapestry of vivid colors and shapes taking up the entire wall. It must weigh a ton. I'm about to touch a weka when a wailing screech sends me pole-vaulting at Zoe. My hands on her arms, my legs about to fly off the ground. Had I triggered an alarm? Will guards appear and drag me away?

Zoe's laughter brings me to my senses as does her explanation that the noise was just the palace talking. As I extricate myself from her personal bubble, I eye the long hallway where the "talking" originated.

"What's down that way?" The other end remains hidden in shadows, all dark and foreboding.

"That's the Brisbane Wing. No one is allowed to go there. It's off-limits."

I scurry to catch up to her. "Brisbane Wing? Why is it off-limits?"

Zoe's green eyes light up. I have found a kindred spirit. "That section of the palace was closed off when Frederick Wellesley was crowned king in January of 1956. Like the Wellesleys wanted to erase the Brisbane family, now that they were the rulers. It's probably falling apart, thus the 'not safe' bit. I've always wanted to go there. Now that I'm back at the palace, maybe I can."

"Back at the palace?"

"My mom used to be a lady-in-waiting to Queen Seneca. I'd come with her, play with the other staff children. But when the queen got sick, all her ladies-in-waiting were sent away. At least they weren't killed like Egyptian royalty."

"Was Queen Seneca very sick?" Colter never told me how his mother died.

"It was quite sudden. If you ask me, something wasn't right. I mean, who sends away those caring for a queen when she needs them the most?" Zoe stops in front of an intricately carved door, motioning toward it, instantly distracting me from the morbid directions my thoughts were headed. "This is your room."

"You're going to show me the way to dinner, right?"

"If you'd like."

"I would definitely like. I'd get lost and never make it. Then I'd starve."

Zoe opens the doors, lowering her head as I pass. The room is magnificent and not the least bit gaudy. It's sadly sterile and not filled with history, though. My suitcase is already in the room along with my tote bag.

"I will return before seven. Do you require anything else?"

"I'm good. Thank you so much, Zoe."

With a curtsy, she shuts the door, sealing me in.

The key turns, locking Abigail into the room. They don't want her to wander the palace, to discover its secrets. Stay away from the Brisbane Wing.

A history of deaths, early and unexpected, of disappearances, of forbidden wings?

Not everyone has made it...

Zoe returns as promised.

I barely had time to shower, change my clothes fifteen times, and braid and unbraid my hair. I'd spent most of the time exploring the room, knocking on the back of the wardrobe, and pulling on things, without finding any hidden doors or secrets.

I grab a lavender cardigan to put over the white sundress with purple flowers that won the clothes debate. The palace is a little drafty for being so modern.

"You look beautiful." Zoe points to her right ear. "You lost an earring though."

"Oh, thank you." I'd changed those five times as well. Finding the matching silver hoop, I'm ready. Shoes on my feet. Dress wrinkle free. Hair behaving itself in a fishtail braid.

"Prince Colter will approve, I'm sure of it. He certainly seems taken with you. I saw him squeeze your hand."

I'm quite taken with him, but I'm still not one hundred percent sure why I'm here. Yes, for research, but the king invited me to dinner like I'm part of the royal family and not just here to find Gran's name in the royal archives.

I follow Zoe down a grand staircase and to double doors that look like they'll take five people to open. Maybe they're automatic? Push a button and whoosh.

"I'll be back when dinner is over to take you to your room," Zoe says.

"I can show the way after we eat." Colter steps from an alcove.

My heart swoons. I have to put a hand on the wall, so I don't topple over. He is...wow. In casual yet formal attire, with the backdrop of a palace, he is every inch the prince. The only thing I don't like is that his tattoo is covered.

"Your Highness." Zoe dips low, straightens, then heads off, cheeks pink.

"What's for dinner? It smells amazing." My stomach grumbles, seconding my statement. Even though the comfort of the jet and Colter kept me distracted—holding my hand during takeoff and landing, multiple games of chess and checkers—I still hadn't been able to eat during the flight. Also, food might take my focus off how yummy Colter looks. *Stop, brain.*

"I hope you like wombat stew," Colter says with a face so straight, I know he's joking.

"So long as it tastes as good as it smells, I will eat the entire bowl. Don't worry, I know I'm not supposed to lick it clean." *I will make Colter proud with my table etiquette knowledge.*

We enter the dining hall. Our entire church could sit comfortably at this table that spans the length of the room. Only four place settings occupy the space, all at one end, thankfully, so we won't have to use our cheerleader voices to be heard.

Colter pulls out a chair, leaning close as he pushes it in after I sit. "You look lovely," he whispers before seating Eliana then rounding the table. He doesn't sit until his father enters and seats himself at the head of the table.

The king checks his pocket watch. "Dinner," the king bellows, making me jump.

The waitstaff appears along with covered dishes. That is the last word spoken until the soup arrives.

"This is cold. Why have you served this?" The king doesn't make eye contact with the waiter as the young man in a suit, white gloves, and a stony expression removes the offensive bowl. The one in front of me is taken as well.

I groan quietly at the lingering amazing smell. I'm relieved when another bowl appears, steam rising from it. Now, I have to wait. The rest of the meal follows suit, like a reenactment of *Goldilocks and the Three Bears*. Although, nothing is ever "just right" for the king. The meat isn't dry enough, the gravy isn't salty enough, the bread is too hard.

Where is the jovial king from the symphony?

Colter doesn't say anything, but there's definitely a wince or two or six. I catch his eye at one point, and he mouths an apology.

When dessert arrives, I hold my breath. The king better not send that back. It's pavlova. The room grows silent, or maybe I stop breathing, as he takes the first bite. His eyes close briefly. *And the king ate it and declared it good.*

I dive in, recalling that once the king is done with his food, I have to be done. It's so hard not to shove the whole thing in my mouth. I finish my pavlova right before the king does. Yes!

The king sets his silverware on his plate in the parallel "I'm done" position then looks at me. "Miss Morgan, how do you find the palace so far?"

I'm afraid to answer. Will it be accepted, or will he send me back to the kitchen like every dish tonight? "It's magnificent." That seems safe.

The king nods his approval. "Good, good. What would you change?"

Why would the king ask me that? He does know I don't have an interior design degree, right?

Would I change anything? Maybe the atmosphere. This dinner would've been so much more enjoyable if the ease of previous meals with Colter and Eliana had been allowed. But alas, no fun. No smiles. No laughter. The king would be appalled by my idea of a family dinner. When we're all together, meals often resemble a competitive game of Pit. Everyone talking over everyone, reaching across the table instead of patiently waiting for dishes to be passed, eating food off the floor, and chucking rolls like footballs.

"Father, Abigail has yet to see more than her room and the dining hall." Colter comes to my rescue.

"Well, what do you think of those?"

"I—"

"Father, maybe Miss Morgan would like to head to bed. It's been a long day," Eliana says. Her eyes remain downcast, reminiscent of Libby when Kasey is around. Does her father scare her or is it a sign of respect?

"Yes, yes. Colter, show her to her room. We will continue tomorrow. Perhaps I will give you a tour. Would you like that?"

"Very much," I say then have a moment of panic. Eliana and Colter will be there too, right? I'm not sure I could handle being alone with the king, especially if he's going to ask me how I'd change things. I'm just here to find Gran.

Colter moves behind me, pulling out my chair and offering his hand to help me stand. He gives it a squeeze before releasing.

"Good night, Father," Colter says.

"Make sure Miss Morgan is lacking for nothing," the king says.

"I will." Once we're outside the dining room, Colter's playful smile presents itself. "I'm sorry for Father. He likes things a certain way."

"He is king after all."

"That he is."

Instead of heading up the grand stairs, Colter leads me in the opposite direction. "I hope you don't mind taking the long way to your room. I'd like to show you the library."

Chapter Twenty-Three

I thought my reaction to seeing the palace was epic, but I swear I had an "Elizabeth Bennet seeing Pemberley for the first time" experience walking into the library. I can't help the happy disbelief that bursts from my very soul, or the way my heart wants to swoon. This library. Oh, this library. I'd move in if I could and never leave. It's like everything that makes me tick, besides a basketball court, can be found within these walls.

Who needs a djinn when you're friends with a real-life prince?

Chairs. A fireplace. A chessboard with glass pieces. A piano. Sculptures. Fake trees. It's like the estate library just a gazillion times bigger. Sadly, there are no rolling ladders, but twisty stairs to balconies make up for the loss. This is a "you can reach any book at any time" library.

Colter lets me savor the moment before motioning toward a room off to the side. "This is where my mother did all her research."

"It's like the records room at the Westonia, minus the creepy basement ambience," I say. "And it smells better."

Eucalyptus and cinnamon. Bookshelves filled with books of all sizes. Large table in the middle of the room with four chairs. Vintage record player between two comfy chairs. A landscape on the wall. A wooden tree that appears to have been broken, the cracks filled with different materials, colors, and gels.

"It's an Andreas Jarvela original. Part of his *Laconia* collection. It represents how even something broken and going in different directions can be beautiful when looking at the entire picture." Colter puts words to my awe and wonder.

"It reminds me of the Japanese art of Kintsugi."

"I bought it when Eliana and I were in NYC. A few days before I passed you on the stairs." Slowly, I move away from the piece, running my fingers over a tome so big I might need help lifting it. I'm flipping through the pages of a book by Eileen Duggan before I ask for permission for its shelf removal. Several passages are underlined but no sketches are doodled in the margins like Gran's. Wait, no, that was Rosiah's too. A gift from Roy. An inscription of love. *The words filling these pages barely touch how I feel about you.*

"Smile story," Colter says.

I hadn't realized my mind had wandered.

"Rosiah had this book, it wasn't Gran's. I'm smiling because Gran still hates poetry as much as I do."

"And why do you hate poetry so much?"

"I never know what I'm supposed to feel. Poetry experts tell you that you can take whatever from a poem, but then they wrinkle their noses and say, 'no, that's not it.' I'll never understand it." I shrug, making a face.

"You're allowed to think or not think, to feel or not feel. That's what I love about poetry. That you can think whatever you want. We've all experienced different things in our life, and that's what we bring to poetry, life experiences and ways of thought."

"Maybe I'm just heartless and emotionless."

"You just had all kinds of emotions looking at the artwork, so don't deceive yourself. And you have a lovely heart." Colter removes a ledger from the shelf, offering it in exchange for the book of poetry. "This is full of the research my mother did on the Brisbane family for the Northargyle exhibit."

I open the cover for a glimpse of Queen Seneca's now familiar handwriting. The last page ends with the royal family's death in a plane crash. The story that the exhibit told and got wrong. Before I can question,

Colter is in front of the record player. He removes several records from the stand, reaching behind them, procuring a small journal.

He straightens the records then hands me that book as well.

"This is Mother's research log of things she discovered about Princess Rosiah. I, like the rest of Northargyle, believed the princess died with her parents and brother, until Mother shared the story with me shortly before she died. Will you help fill in the blanks?" Colter sighs deeply. "Once the pieces are all there, I plan on sharing it with the world, but until then, this stays with you. Eliana doesn't even know this truth. I don't want her involved until the picture is complete."

"I'll keep it safe. Thank you for trusting me."

I clutch the ledger and journal to my chest as Colter delivers me to my door, thrilled that he trusts me with his mother's heart.

"Sleep well, fairest Abigail." He bows over my hand.

"You too, fairer prince."

"Until tomorrow."

In record time, even with a tingling hand, I'm in my lounge pants and sweatshirt, the books in front of me on the king-sized bed. Which do I open first?

Start at the beginning. "A very good place to start," I sing the rest of the line.

I open the ledger to read about all the kings and queens of Northargyle. Queen Seneca made detailed notes, listing facts about each royal member of the family, all the steps she took, where she researched, people she talked to. It's a historical society dream.

The stream of her cursive causes a swoony sigh as I think of Colter's tattoo. I read through the expanded version of everything that I saw at the museum, about Charles Brisbane and his heroics. About the line of succession. Most of the placards at the Glenmore Cove Museum were copied and pasted from this book.

With trembling hands, I set the family history aside and open Queen Seneca's journal, a sense of awe and reverence washing over me.

> *Princess Rosiah didn't die with her parents as the world believes. Rosiah left the palace in April 1955, only three days before her seventeenth birthday. Also around that time, five ladies-in-waiting went missing. Did Rosiah concoct the elaborate plan or one of her ladies-in-waiting? Every decoy princess was gifted royal items to lead any searchers astray. They*

all changed their birth date to 16 April 1938. Also missing from the palace were Rosiah's crown, the shawl and christening gown made for her at birth, and her Princess Box. Maybe Rosiah kept these with her?

Below is my list of decoys and the items they had. I have given the retrieved items to my trusted source to keep safe until the time when we are able to share our find with the world. These women gave up everything to protect Rosiah's secret. Talk about love and sacrifice. May I be such a leader.

Five decoys. Identifying royal items. The same birth date. I flip the page, eager to find Gran's name.

Joan Wilson (O'Leary): Bracelet and Emerald Earrings (Ireland)
* *Married. 6 children. 15 grandchildren. 2 great-granddaughters.*
* *Deceased.*
* *Retrieved the bracelet and earrings from Joan's grandson.*

Evelyn Martin: Royal Necklace (Greece)
* *Never married.*
* *Retrieved the necklace.*

Carol Kelly (Fisher): Tea Set and Coronation Spoon (England)
* *Married. No children.*
* *Deceased.*
* *Retrieved tea set, 1 teacup broken. Spoon missing.*

Doris Evans (Payne): Sovereign Orb and Cross (New Zealand)
* *Married. 5 children. 10 grandchildren.*
* *Retrieved orb.*

Margaret Allen (Weston): Royal Doll and 2 Brooches (USA)
* *Married. 2 children. 5 grandchildren.*
* *Location of the royal doll unknown.*
* *1 brooch in Westonia, Pennsylvania.*

No Gran. No Christine or Laurel. Gran wouldn't have had three names, would she? Anything is possible, but I'm leaning toward no. Especially when Margaret Weston's name was the same.

If I hadn't seen the exhibit at the Glenmore Cove Museum, I might still think Gran was the real princess. I lean my head back and close my eyes. *If Gran wasn't a lady-in-waiting, then what was she? Who was she to Princess Rosiah?*

Rereading Margaret Weston's items, it strikes me that there was a doll in the box that Samantha Weston delivered—part of the real items. Could that creepy porcelain doll be Rosiah's? Wasn't there also a christening gown?

Eagerly, I text Libby, hoping that the doll and gown are there. I set my phone aside but pick it up a minute later when the Faith Mackenzie theme song plays. *Aunt Vi.*

"*Kia ora!* This is your favorite aunt checking in. I just got to the Airbnb. We did an amazing job describing New Zealand for never being here. There really are a lot of sheep. Tell me all about the palace. How was your first day?"

I move out to the balcony as I describe the entire day, minus a few details like the decoys, of course. After hearing about Aunt Vi's travels and shenanigans, how she got lost but found an adorable sheep farm, I end the call and rest my arms against the balcony railing. The sun setting paints the sky with oranges, pinks, reds, and purples. I can't wait for my tour tomorrow to see everything.

A window-filled building, which I'm guessing is a greenhouse, sits near the palace on a weed-choked plot. A dark, unused, unloved stain amid blooming life.

A figure moves toward it.

I gasp when I realize it's King Hamish. The light he carries illuminates his face a quick second before he disappears inside.

Chapter Twenty-Four

Zoe shows up in the morning, appearing as soon as I step over the threshold of my room into the hallway.

Is there an alarm that goes off? I scan the area for a camera.

"Prince Colter asked me to bring you to the breakfast room." Her smile tells a story, like Colter said mine do. A story that makes out that I mean a lot to the prince of Northargyle. A smile that wants to know everything. A smile that says she heartily approves of my strappy, tan heels and ocean-colored sundress.

I only changed twice. Getting quicker.

With a nod, Zoe heads in a different direction than the dinner room. Windows bring in the morning sunshine, and I bathe in the beams as we pass through them. The room we end up in is smaller in size than last night's dining room.

Colter is seated alone at the table reading a newspaper. I'm glad to see this table seats ten instead of one hundred. He sets the paper aside and stands to greet me, retaking his seat once I've acquired mine. I could get used to this.

A maid places a plate in front of me before I can wonder where to forage for food. Eggs, ham, bacon, fruit, and toast. My mouth waters at the sight.

"How was your first night in the palace?" Colter asks.

"My last thought was 'I'm in a palace. I'm never gonna sleep tonight, no way no how.' That bed was so comfortable," I say with a dreamy sigh of someone who had the longest and best night's sleep of their life.

"Drat, you didn't feel the pea?"

I laugh. "I'm not a princess."

"I don't know. I don't even believe that girl was a princess." Colter hands me a steaming mug of coffee. "Maybe she was nosy and had to search everything."

"Ooh, I never thought about that. Maybe she had OCD." In between bites of food and sips of coffee, we talk about fairy tales and fables, making up reasons as to why the characters did certain things that have no rhyme or reason whatsoever. My favorite is Colter wondering if the wolf in "The Boy Who Cried Wolf" was in fact a shapeshifter. Making the little boy not a liar after all.

Our smiles are still there when King Hamish and Eliana enter the room. I reach for the silver urn, deciding to refill my coffee mug to give my hands something to do. Which is the wrong use of my nervousness.

"Why must Miss Morgan fill her own mug?" the king cries.

I set down the silver urn, my mug half filled. I want to say I can pour my own coffee, but the king's scowl is not something one should see this early in the morning.

A young man in a black suit and white gloves steps from the shadows and finishes filling my mug. I hope he can read the thanks in my eyes. His nose wrinkles, lips pinching as he sets the urn down before returning to the shadows. He reminds me of the woodcutters on a grandfather clock—come out, do their job, disappear until the bell tolls.

"Good, good." The king says that a lot. I'm not quite sure what he means by it. Is he talking to himself? "Son, I must deprive Miss Morgan of your company. There is a meeting with parliament this morning that we both must attend. Eliana will have to do."

"I can manage, Father," Eliana says.

The same maid that brought me goodness on a silver platter sets a plate in front of Eliana, uncovering it before bowing and disappearing.

"You may give Miss Morgan a tour of the palace. You know where is acceptable. Stay away from the grounds." The king leaves without eating anything.

"Why do we have to stay away from the grounds?" An image of the king yelling like the Beast isn't that hard to conjure. What does the king not want me to see?

Even though Roy Currie isn't my grandfather, seeing his handiwork at the cottage fuels my desire to see the palace gardens, the flowers, the trees, even the shrubberies.

"Father wants to show you the grounds himself," Colter says. "They're his pride and joy."

Typical me, searching for stories where there are none.

"He is rather proud of them," Eliana says.

Colter glances toward the young man in the corner, rolls his eyes, then pours coffee into an empty mug, passing it to Eliana. The rebel. The barista prince.

"Well, parliament calls. Enjoy your time together. I'm surely going to enjoy a meeting on my first day back." Colter gathers the newspaper and leather-bound book with a FAITH, GOTTA HAVE HER pen. How out of place in the hands of a prince. "Oh, and, Abigail, feel free to pour your own coffee. Stephen over there hates coffee and is liable to chuck it out the window."

I stifle a giggle as Colter bows to us, winks, then heads off.

"So, you don't have a gardener?" I ask Eliana once I've swallowed my last bite of bacon. My curiosity knows no bounds.

"We have hundreds of gardeners, but my father oversees the designs. Nothing is done without his knowledge or consultation."

After we've finished our breakfast, Eliana leads me from the room, prefacing her tour with, "I know my brother already showed you the library, but other than that and the grounds, there's not much to see."

"How can that be possible?"

"One room looks like the next, one wing like another, easy to get turned around. I don't want to not give you a tour, but I have a feeling you'd be bored."

"Do you have a favorite place?"

She lights up, taking my hand. I'm hoping it's outside, but the way Eliana behaves, it's unlikely she'd disobey her father. We pause a few times on our way, spending the most time in a hall of paintings. It's like walking through the museum exhibit. The last painting, even though there's about ten more feet of wall space left, is of Colter and Eliana as young children. Even at six, Colter's spark is there.

Queen Seneca and King Hamish aren't among the portraits. "What hung here?" I ask, wondering if that might account for the blank space.

"It was a painting of my mother. Father had it removed." Eliana glances around, lowering her voice. "The painting was supposed to go to storage, but I had it taken to my room. That's where I'm taking you, my favorite place."

Eliana leads me to her rooms, which are set up like the main floor of a house. My family could easily move about the bedroom without being on top of one another. The room has a fireplace, with two huge chairs positioned at the correct distance before it. There's even a bathroom with the biggest bathtub I've ever seen.

A sitting room off her bedroom holds the portrait of Queen Seneca. I can see why the king would want this removed, not because it's awful, but because it's so full of life. The artist painted the queen mid laugh surrounded by flowers. Her dress is plain white and her blonde hair loose, so different from the regal stoicism of the museum portrait. Her wedding ring is absent, replaced by a beautiful diamond ring with butterflies—the one Eliana wears now. Queen Seneca is sunshine personified amid a rainbow of colors. The joy is palpable.

"Wow," I whisper the word. "I wish I could have met her."

"I miss her so much." Eliana sniffs. "She was my best friend. I'm so lost without her guidance. The palace, and my father, have been so different. Mother held us all together."

"I wish I had that kind of relationship with my mom. There's been a disconnect since I chose to pursue history and a Museum Studies degree."

"Mother would always know what to do. This princess life with all the expectations, I just—I'm so thankful you're here. It's been a blessing more than you can imagine." She sighs. "My parents had an arranged marriage. And Father informed me yesterday before dinner that he is arranging mine."

"What about Bradley?"

"He is not royal enough for my father."

"There's hope though, right? Your father invited me here, and I have no royal blood whatsoever."

"It's hard to say why my father invited you here. I don't want to question it. But as a princess, my role is set out. I have obligations. The pretty face of the country, here to advance Northargyle's holdings."

"How do you do it? How do you balance the pressures of your title and expectations and what you want to do with your life? How do you be yourself when the world is watching?"

"You don't."

I laugh at the suddenness of her reply and the mock serious look on her face. She is so like Colter in this moment.

"In all seriousness, seek maturity and wisdom." Eliana plays with the ends of the tie on her dress. "It's far more difficult to step outside of your circumstances and be true to yourself if you're bogged down in the judgment and expectations of others. With maturity comes the wisdom to see that you can enjoy life to the full, and be yourself while still honoring the Lord, no matter what others say about you.

"Even if we weren't a princess and a pastor's daughter, we'd still have expectations and roles and titles. Sister. Employee. Wife. Mom. It's important to find creative ways to express yourself that fall under your responsibilities—if you love to paint, make your family Christmas cards. I express myself by sewing and designing things for Colter and palace staff. And being a patron of the arts allows me to enjoy the occasional fashion show and gallery opening."

As Eliana shares her thoughts, I realize my mom has been doing just that. She loves sports, and her way to fulfill ministry responsibility is coaching and mentoring. I love to research. How can I use that to help people, besides Aunt Vi?

"Come, let me show you my favorite place inside the palace." Eliana moves a painting first to the right then to the left, then right, and left once more. A door opens in the wall behind me.

We share a conspiratorial smile as we enter a secret room as big as the sitting room. It's like a sewing shop. Every amenity one would require, I imagine, to design and make clothes.

"This is where I can be one hundred percent me." Eliana releases a long breath, like I do when I tiptoe outside in the cool of the morning, sit with my coffee, and open my Bible.

Overwhelming peace as my worries and cares fade away into the silence. Into the knowledge that, before God, all I have to be is me. No trying, no façades, no second-guessing every word I say. Just loved. Free. I've read of His faithfulness in the past, time and time over, and just know that everything will be okay.

Much like Colter had at the museum, Eliana stays in the doorway as I wander about the room. In one corner is a drafting table, the sunlight illuminating it. The bolt of fabric Eliana bought at the Antique Palace is on a large table, waiting its turn to be cut into something gorgeous. *Sketches of dresses and suits. Sewing machine. Fabrics. Threads. A headless mannequin draped in a beaded fabric full of pins.*

"Was I wearing a Princess Eliana original to the symphony?" I ask, carefully fingering the silk of the unfinished gown.

"You were." Eliana colors prettily. "That one was always my favorite, and you made it look exactly as it should. I would love to share my designs with the world, but as a princess, I have duties and responsibilities that don't align with me hosting fashion shows."

On a shelf in the corner, I spot a decorative, wooden box. It's similar to the one resting on the shelf in my bedroom closet.

"My gran gave me a box like this," I say, admiring the woodwork. "But I guess it was Rosiah's. Although the things inside, minus the poetry book, were Gran's."

"It's a Princess Box. Queen Charlotte gave the first one to Princess Rosiah. This is where I keep my letters from Bradley and a promise ring he gave me for someday." Eliana presses the front then something on the back. A compartment slides out from the side. *Eliana Kenwick* is embroidered in the lining of the secret drawer.

She holds up the ring, emeralds and silver exquisitely sparkling, but I'm distracted by the secret drawer. Was there something more I'd missed in Rosiah's Princess Box?

One minute, Grandma is beside you, the next, she's three aisles over looking at stuffed unicorns. Little did her grandchildren know, every time Grandma disappeared, she was off saving the kingdom of Montour Falls. Her ninja skills and age—unsuspecting of someone "that old"—make her the royal family's greatest weapon against the forces of evil.

—Excerpt from *Gram Ninja* (Told to Poppy & Lily Morgan)

Chapter Twenty-Five

I have a few stolen minutes after lunch to call home. I wrestled with what to do, consumed with wondering what Princess Rosiah would consider her most treasured possessions. I want to know right now what she put in her Princess Box, but do I want someone in my room while I'm not there? To open the box and see its treasures before I do?

My curiosity wins over the fact that I won't be able to hold the box's secrets until I get home. I check the time converter app. Seven in the evening. Mom surprises me by picking up the home phone. Why isn't she at basketball practice?

"You're home?"

"They canceled after-school activities. Snowstorm. We're hunkering down, about to play Candyland with Poppy and Lily. Although, your father already fell asleep." Mom laughs, and I just make out Dad's snores.

"Wish I could be there."

"Everything okay at the palace? Thanks for the pictures." Mom huffs. "Still can't believe you're actually staying at a palace."

"I can't believe I'm here either. It's surreal." I clear my throat. "I just, well, I was wondering if someone could do something for me." Is Mom the right one for this job? Will she even want to help?

Eliana's talk about her mother being her best friend spurs me on and challenges me to find ways to express to Mom who I am. What if asking Mom to do this for me opens a way for us to reconnect? I would never trade my time with Gran, but I do miss Saturday gym time and doughnuts.

"Remember the box we found in Gran's car? There could possibly be a secret compartment in the bottom. It's in my closet. Top shelf. Behind the camels."

"A secret compartment." The excitement in Mom's voice throws me. "Hold on a second. I'm going up to your room."

I follow along on her journey to my bedroom: climbing the creaking stairs, opening my bedroom door, opening the closet door, grunting as she pulls down the box, dropping the phone.

"Got it. Now what?" Mom asks once she has possession of her phone again.

"There's a knob on the front and one on the back. Press the front one first then the back. A compartment should slide out from the side."

What if it's just a box? Something Gran found and not Rosiah's? I think back to Queen Seneca's list. Rosiah's Princess Box had disappeared.

"I'm going to put you on speaker."

I hold my breath.

Mom's whoop of delight confirms that it's a Princess Box.

I release the breath, and a smile replaces the worry.

"There's a name embroidered in the fabric. Rosiah Catherine," Mom says. "I've always loved that name. Although, it suits you far more. Who was she?"

"She was a princess of Northargyle who ran away when she was seventeen."

"Why do you have this box?"

"I'll explain, but first, what's inside the drawer?" *Please don't be empty.*

"There's a locket, a picture, and, huh—"

"What?" I stand, pacing the bedroom.

"A cassette tape."

Cassette tape? I bite back a laugh as Libby's hopes are fulfilled. An artifact to talk to me when I ask it to tell me its story. I hope Rosiah's story is on it and not some mixtape of radio copied music.

I pause but decide I can't wait. "Do we still have a cassette player?"

"I may have to go antiquing." Mom chuckles. "Actually, there's probably one in the basement. If this storm doesn't subside, I'll check first thing tomorrow."

"Will you send me pictures of everything in the compartment, please?"

"We're on it."

Forty minutes later, several pictures come through with a text from Mom saying Poppy ended up taking the pictures. Hurray for six-year-olds that know how to work technology. I smile, my heart aching a bit, at Poppy's expression as she wears the locket in one of the pictures.

The locket is on a simple silver chain. Roses are etched in the metal. It has to be the locket Roy gave to Rosiah on her sixteenth birthday. I zoom in on the picture resting inside. Rosiah and Roy together in the Hyacinth Cottage garden. Mom did a good job guiding Poppy, knowing exactly what I would ask to have included in the pictures.

Someone knocks on the bedroom door. Zoe stands outside with a piece of paper and a pair of black rubber boots. The king has requested my presence for a tour of the grounds. So official.

After putting on the boots, Zoe takes yet another path through the palace, this one ending in a room of windows that leads outside to a patio. The stones have a blue tint and all around are topiaries and pots of every size filled with flowers of all colors. Like a floral fiesta.

"Good, good," the king says when he sees me, eyeing the boots. He's wearing a dark green pair. Before I can panic about being alone with the king, Eliana touches my arm. I turn and offer a smile. Her boots match mine.

"Colter is still in a meeting," she says when I glance behind her. Ah, the life of a prince. I understand why Colter enjoys his time at the Kenwick Estate.

Unlike the inside of the palace, everything outside is different and new—I could spend the next fifty years wandering and never fully see everything.

The king acts like a professional tour guide. Although, he sternly berates the gardeners who have missed a weed here or put too much water there. I'm surprised when he plucks the weeds himself, leaving them in a pile for the gardeners to take care of. He never wipes his hands on his clothes though. A staff member appears with a towel for him to use and discard as he moves on.

He tells me the scientific names of the plants and flowers, paying extra attention to any I give more than a passing glance to. When I spot craspedia, the national flower, King Hamish gives me a full history lesson. The scents and sights are calming and energizing all at once. I can tell why the grounds are the king's pride and joy. He is as talented as I imagine Roy would've been.

We move around a corner and Eliana starts toward a path lined with trees. If I remember the view from my balcony, this is the way to the greenhouse.

"Miss Morgan does not want to go that way," the king says, the peace in his words replaced by an agitated, hard look. "It's too dirty. Come this way. You are to stay away from that path." He doesn't wait to see if we'll obey. As he said, so we must do.

"What's down that way?" I whisper to Eliana as we follow the king. "I'm not opposed to dirt."

"That was my mom's favorite path. It leads to the greenhouse Father commissioned for her. No one goes there anymore. In all honesty, I don't know if I could handle seeing it an overgrown mess."

⊱✦⊰

My legs ache from all the walking we did, and my belly is full from another huge meal that Colter didn't attend. Eliana caught me yawning and asked her father if she could turn in early. Covering for me and my desire to don comfy clothes and check in with Mom to see if it's still snowing.

At a knock on my door, I throw a hoodie over my tank top.

Colter stands in the hallway running a hand over his face. Though he smiles with his usual sparkle, weariness coats him like a flannel blanket.

"Hello, Abigail."

"You look tired," I say, not that I want him to leave, but if he falls over, I don't know if I'd be able to carry him to his room. And, just my luck, I'd probably be thrown into the dungeon for dragging around the crown prince.

"Parliament likes to say the same thing in different ways for hours on end. At least Chef made sandwiches for lunch and gave me an extra serving of pavlova for dinner."

I spot Zoe down the hall, peeking around a corner. She's basically fist-pumping. I guess I'd have help if Colter did pass out.

"How was your day?" he asks.

"Eliana and I had some lovely girl bonding time. She's talented and thoughtful and so wise. Then your father gave us a tour of the gardens."

"Thank you for being a friend to my sister. She's never been so fortunate."

"Neither have I."

As Gran had with Rosiah and Hazel, I've found connection and acceptance in Eliana and Colter both. I've overshared my heart and life and they didn't stop "reading," or "put me down" when they discovered the naïve pastor's daughter with an overactive imagination behind the mask. It's so freeing, yet part of me is waiting for someone to call and berate me for having best friends in the making.

Will I ever be free of that worry?

"I'm sorry I wasn't around." Colter's smile turns into a yawn that he tries so hard to contain.

"You should get some sleep," I say.

"I plan on it, as soon as I ask if you would like to accompany me to a library opening tomorrow."

"Where and when?"

"I've been overseeing the renovations of an old hospital into a library." At my raised eyebrows, he quirks his.

"A mental hospital?" Is this the one the bookstore patron mentioned?

"It used to be a children's hospital. They recently built a bigger and better one, leaving the old building unattended. It's the perfect size for room to read and imagine. The official opening is tomorrow."

"Patron of libraries," I joke, remembering his placard at the museum. "Keeper of books, protector of pages. What does that entail exactly?"

"Lots of reading."

"Sounds rough." I grin.

"It is."

"I'd love to go to the library opening, see you in action."

"Until tomorrow, then. Good night, Abigail." He starts to turn but stops as if remembering something. "One more question. Do you have a favorite picture book by any chance?"

"*Meanwhile, Back at the Ranch*," I say without hesitation.

Chapter Twenty-Six

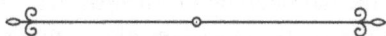

After breakfast, where I pour my own coffee because the king isn't in attendance, Colter leads me to a building that holds cars of every shape, size, and color.

"Pick one." He motions like I'm a contestant on a game show. "Keeping in mind that we'll both be chauffeured per Northargyle royal protocol. Annoying. Despite not being much of a car guy, I love to drive, but it has its perks. Like today. When I get to sit with you."

Aww…

A flash of chrome from the back corner yanks my attention away from the cars to a motorcycle with a side car. It's old but in pristine condition like every other vehicle in the building. "Do you have goggles and a flappy hat to go with that?" I point toward it.

"I knew I was missing out. See, this is why I need you in my life, to remind me of the essentials." Colter grins. "Can you keep a secret?"

"Of course." I lift an eyebrow.

"When Father's away, I take that for a spin."

"Is he often away?"

"Maybe once or twice a year. And since he made a trek already to the symphony to meet you, I missed my opportunity." He motions toward the cars again. "Anything but the motorcycle."

Once I select a black BMW, Bishop appears. "Good choice, Miss Morgan," he says as his phone rings. "One moment, Violet Morgan is calling."

Colter shakes his head.

"What?" I ask.

"I'm not sure if I should encourage them or demand they never speak again. I don't want to lose my driver."

"Aunt Vi isn't one to settle down. But they are super cute together."

"Your aunt says hi to both of you." Bishop returns to open the door to the car I'd chosen. I climb in and Colter follows after he says something to Bishop that I miss. Had Colter voiced his relationship concerns?

As we sit back and enjoy the ride, Colter tells me more about his role as patron of libraries, which is a lot more involved than just reading. This leads to talking about projects I've helped with, like being a part of Winter in Westonia, which leads to him asking if I'm homesick.

"At times I feel a stab of homesickness, but I've been enjoying my time away. I am looking forward to being home for Thanksgiving. What do you guys do?" The words are out before I remember Thanksgiving is an American holiday.

"Maybe we should hold a feast this year. Being thankful for what God has provided is never a bad idea. What do the Morgans normally do?"

"We start the day with an ugly sweater run to the mailbox and back. It's two miles round trip." At Colter's confusion, I explain why the mailbox isn't closer to our house. "We live on a mile-long dead-end road, and the mailbox is on the road, easier for the mailman to deliver."

"Understood."

"The uglier the sweater, the better. The two that finish last have to do dishes after lunch. Which is always enough food to send us into a food coma. Once we've recovered, we alternate between board games and napping. Then, if the pond is frozen enough, we'll play hockey. If it's not, then we'll play basketball."

"That sounds like a day to experience."

"I wish you could be there." A prince at Thanksgiving? Yep, that's going to happen never.

"While we don't celebrate Thanksgiving, we do celebrate Christmas. This will be the second one without my mother. The palace would be already fully decorated by now if she were still alive." Colter runs a hand over his hair. "But maybe I can talk Father into at least setting up a tree before you leave."

Abigail Morgan sings carols, bakes cookies, dances the waltz, and decorates the palace, giving gifts to everyone she comes in contact with. Her authentic living and passion help the king reclaim his Christmas spirit. In her honor, he allows her to place the star on the top of the tree. No need for a ladder, Prince Colter will lift her up...

"I'm sure the palace tree is humungous and perfect. We usually pick a tree out of the woods, the weirder the better." I laugh, returning to reality from my very own royal Christmas montage. "As the story goes, my mom was horrified their first Christmas by the tree Dad picked. Mom thought he was joking and told him to 'go get the real tree.' When he told her it was the real tree, she cried but decorated it. She fell in love with the tree and asked Dad to find one every year. We always had so much fun hunting for the saddest tree to love on. One year, we even tied two together to make a fuller tree."

I glance out the window as we drive past a house where a young boy is mowing the lawn. In no shirt. Not sure I'll ever get used to talking about Christmas when it's summertime.

"What other Morgan traditions do you have?" Colter asks.

"We do a White Elephant gift exchange where we compete to find the craziest gift. Last year, Luke found this portable toilet that played music when you lifted the lid. I still have no idea if it came like that or if he rigged it up." I feel tears building. "I guess I am a little homesick. I've been so focused on Gran's story. Then I met a prince who invited me to a library opening and started talking about team Morgan."

"He's especially glad that he met you."

"Here we are, Your Highness, Miss Morgan," Bishop says, bringing the car and the teary conversation of home to a stop. Time for librarying!

Colter touches my hand. "There will be photographers, so be prepared for pictures."

"Maybe Bishop should drive me around back? Or lower me through the roof?"

"You don't want to be in pictures with me?"

"I do. I just—" I wince. The fear of what people will say hits like a soccer ball to the face. "Do you want me in pictures with you?"

"Absolutely. If I surround myself with beauty, no one will look at me."

True to his word, as Colter helps me out of the car, flashes begin. I paste on a smile that I hope translates excitement rather than deer in the headlights. Colter releases my hand to button his suit jacket. I smooth down my dress, one that Eliana designed. Simple, flattering, comfortable. Pairs well with Colter's dark suit.

When Colter said that the library used to be a children's hospital, I was not picturing this lovely building with windows and light and cheery landscaping. Iron weka, kangaroo, and emu stick out of the flowerbeds as if calling readers home.

I gasp when I spot a huge stone frog in the middle of a fountain. "Is that Tiddalick?"

"It sure is." Colter puts his hand on the small of my back, guiding me down a path straight from an Italian villa toward an ornate, almost magical door.

Wouldn't it be wonderful if you could teleport between libraries? There's something so familiar about a library. Walking in and feeling at home, accepted, welcome no matter who you are or where you're from. A real community center. Although this library is nowhere near as grand as the palace or Kenwick Manor, or even Sugarleaf Manor, it holds its own quirky charm.

I've been in a lot of libraries this month. An entire range and scale that have all played a part of my story. Today is going to add another chapter to that guidebook. My library tour.

A man and woman greet us with a bow and dip of a curtsy. I follow Colter's leading in shaking their hands, telling them I'm so glad to be there. A photographer snaps a picture of my enraptured face.

The library is a colorful wonderland, a feast for all the senses. A place where imagination is released, and not just in the children's area. *Paintings of colorful landscapes and fictional characters. Multi-colored chairs and couches. Stuffed koalas, fuzzy kangaroos, and chubby wombats. Benches and beanbags underneath the branches of an enormous (fake) eucalyptus tree with rainbow bark. New and old book smell with a hint of coffee and spice. Laughter and chatter. No one telling you to be quiet while you enjoy a good book.*

Colter is led to a wooden chair. I hide my amusement as, instead of the grown-up chair, he folds his body in a colorful kid-sized chair, his tall frame dwarfing it.

He reads *Wombat Stew*, doing all the voices. Most of the kids gather on the floor in front of him and quote the book along with him. I'm going to have to buy a copy of this book as well to read to my nieces. I'm for sure going to add a wombat to *Gram Ninja*.

When Colter closes the book, he looks over at me then back at the children. My senses tingle at the unknown, but I trust Colter. "Now, what do you think about my friend, Abigail, reading a book to you? She's from America."

The kids cheer, while I take a very familiar book from the librarian. *Meanwhile, Back at the Ranch* by Trinka Hakes Noble. How had they acquired a copy so quickly?

I try to tamp down my nightmarish, recurring dream—the one where my brain isn't attached to my voice, and I can't read. Where I mess up the words and become incoherent as if speaking a different language.

"Would you like to read to them?" Colter asks, consideration personified.

Do I dare?

"Yes, I'd like to," I say right before a little boy grabs my hand and escorts me to the adult chair Colter was supposed to occupy. The anticipation in the boy's eyes is all the encouragement I need. Who cares that there are fifty adults sprinkled throughout the room?

I hold up the book, letting the familiar words suck me in, and all my doubts and nervousness escape. I confidently do all the voices, delighting at the kids' laughter at my Southern accent attempts.

Colter stands in the back, like a proud teacher observing his pupil. I try not to look at him. Every glance costs me a stutter. The kids clap when I reach the end, their excitement infectious as they scatter to discover more of the library's treasures.

After eating several cubes of cheese and bite-sized lamington squares from a large gathering room, I wander, not lost at all. Colter finds me in the nonfiction shelves. An older woman steps easily beside him. The sense that she's familiar rises as I study her.

Early eighties. Silver-gray hair, styled in an elegant way. Skin shows signs of age, with wrinkles that add character and tell stories of a life well-lived. Bright, expressive eyes, reflecting warmth and curiosity. Colorful dress, sensible shoes. Grace and resilience, embodying the beauty of her experiences.

"Abigail, I'd like to introduce you to Prudence Ellery."

"Prudence?" I know that name. "Oh! You were in contact with the Westonia." I lower my voice. "You were interested in the brooch."

"Your coworker has been so helpful." Prudence holds out her hand, and I accept it. Her grip is strong. "Prince Colter told me that he gave you Queen Seneca's notes on the royal family, and that you're writing a story about your grandmother and Princess Rosiah."

"I'm just compiling the research. I'm not a writer." I wave my hand dismissively, ignoring Colter's knowing look.

Prudence glances around before moving closer to me. "Queen Seneca contacted me about researching Princess Rosiah. She'd found something and wanted my opinion since I had helped with the Brisbane royal tree. I told her about my brother and the others who were sent to find Princess Rosiah. And I confirmed Queen Seneca's suspicions that the princess didn't die with her family."

A thrill rushes through me as I follow where this is heading.

"Three months after Rosiah disappeared, one of the gardeners also went missing, one my brother knew loved the princess with all his heart. No one believed my brother's theory, but he pursued that lead even though the others laughed."

"Roy Currie, right? Do you think he could still be alive?" I hadn't considered that possibility when I rewrote Gran's story with Rosiah as the star. There was never any mention of Roy dying.

"He very well could be, but I have no clue where to find him." Sadness softens Prudence's eyes. "When the Brisbane family died, the searchers all returned. Except for my brother. The last letter from him stated that he'd found Roy and Princess Rosiah. That was 1957. I never heard from him again."

"Do you have a picture of your brother?" I need to confirm or deny my suspicions.

"On my desk. I don't officially work here anymore, but they've been so kind to give me an office to do my research from." She moves through the library, a spring to her step, reminding me of Gran in her fullness of life.

Colter's hand brushes against mine. "Prudence is right. You should write this story. You have such a way with words."

"I definitely say a lot of them, especially around you." Hah, if only he heard the full stories. The theater of my mind would terrify him.

I play the suggestion over as we duck around two tables piled with books waiting to be catalogued. Rosiah's mystery, and the potential to see Prudence's brother, keeps me from stopping to read all the spines. Could I really write a book?

"I'm not qualified," I confess. "Books are Aunt Vi's thing."

"So, you haven't been researching? You haven't been pursuing leads? You don't have letters, artifacts, memories of the shawl? You don't have an entire research room in the palace library? You, my dearest Abigail Rosiah Morgan, are overqualified."

"But, why me?" I whisper the question.

"Why not you?"

Prudence opens a door and invites us into a cozy office full of books and colorful Aboriginal artifacts. There's even a didgeridoo. She takes a framed picture off her spotless desk and passes it to me. "This is my brother, Josiah Ellery."

I take a deep breath before I look.

The black and white photo shows a handsome man with dark hair and a strong build. I touch his face and smile. "I know exactly what happened to your brother," I tell Prudence. "This is my grandpa."

ISAIAH 6:8

Then I heard the voice of the Lord, saying,
"Whom shall I send, and who will go for Us?"
Then I said, "Here am I. Send me!"

Chapter Twenty-Seven

Why not you?

W I sit in the pew next to Colter, trying to focus on the service. If being in a church in Northargyle with Colter beside me isn't distracting enough, add in the question from yesterday and all the encouragement Prudence gave me after I told her the truth about her brother...

Yeah, there's no hope of me remembering the key points of this sermon.

God, is this you telling me that I need to do this? The topic of me writing keeps coming up, positive and negative. Mom telling me I'm not a writer. Me telling myself that. *Placards aren't novels.* Mr. Romano said I was creative. Colter said I was talented—even though he's never read anything I've written. Angie Thorne even asked if I was a writer.

"Then I said, 'here am I, send me.'"

My head snaps up, my hand hitting Colter's as the pastor reads from Isaiah 6.

Colter grunts, fighting back a grin as he repositions his Bible so it bridges our legs. His Bible is well-loved. Verses highlighted. Notes in the margins.

He taps a written note. "Why not me?" He wiggles his brow then refocuses on the message. I stare at Colter's writing, running my fingers over the words as if they'll transfer, the ink a tattoo on my soul.

As we stand for the benediction, an older woman stares at me while everyone else faces the front. I glance at Colter, thinking she's watching him. But when I smile, she startles and turns away.

I touch Colter's arm to ask him about the woman, but she's no longer there. Colter pats my hand, leading me from the private box.

The wonderful members of Westonia Baptist Church would be aghast at how quickly we exited the building. Meet and greet time—lovingly dubbed hug and howdy—is an event all its own after we've been dismissed to "Go forth and make disciples."

Eliana is already in the car when we get outside, the sunshine quite warm but welcome. Colter hands his Bible to her through the window but doesn't get in.

"I usually walk back to the palace if you'd like to join me," Colter says.

"A Sunday stroll instead of a Sunday drive? Yes, please." I hook my arm through Colter's offered elbow, adjusting my tote to my other shoulder.

We don't make it far before someone calls my name.

"Abigail." Zoe motions to the woman with white streaks in her red hair—an older version of Zoe. "My mom wanted to meet you."

"You're looking well, Mrs. Talor," Colter says as he releases me to take her hand.

"Your Highness." She curtsies.

"Thank you for allowing your daughter to assist Abigail." He turns to me. "Mrs. Talor always snuck me cookies when my mother wasn't looking."

"You were such an angel. I couldn't help it." Mrs. Talor's smile lights up her face.

Colter laughs. "Well, I think I'll go speak with Pastor Greyson. Give you ladies a chance to chat about me." He nods to Zoe and her mom before heading toward the front steps of the church, greeting people as he passes.

"He is so like his mother." Mrs. Talor smiles, and I follow her gaze. Colter takes a flower from a young girl, ruffles the hair of a boy, and bends to talk to an elderly woman using a walker.

Smiling, I focus on Zoe and her mom. "I wish I could have met Queen Seneca."

"She would have liked you. I can tell you're as strong of character."

If only she'd seen my total lack of focus during the service.

"Zoe said you used to care for the queen, and that King Hamish sent you away before she died?" I ask.

"We were all sent away. The king brought in the best doctors, but no one could figure it out." The emotion builds on Mrs. Talor's face as she continues. "Queen Seneca suffered from headaches and nausea and would collapse at any given moment. Once she coughed so hard there was blood. It was hard to watch someone so strong fade away."

"Were Co—the prince and princess home?" *How dreadful to see your mother like that.* That was one blessing with Gran, at least. My last memory is of her dancing with our instructor. The picture of health. I can't imagine having to watch her fade.

"Princess Eliana was away, and I think Prince Colter made it home the week before she died. The week leading up to our dismissal, the king acted as if the queen had already died." Mrs. Talor's gaze shifts toward Colter then back. "We were told not to talk about it. The king didn't want the kingdom to know how sick she was."

"I wish you'd been allowed to stay and care for her."

Mrs. Talor takes my hand, her gaze shifting toward Colter once more. "Take care of yourself. Zoe is always close if you need anything. There are secrets in the palace that have long been covered."

Her words send chills coursing through me, but Colter ruins my chance to respond by returning and giving Mrs. Talor a hug. After goodbyes are said, Colter holds out an arm, and I accept the steadiness.

Secrets in the palace that have long been covered. Is there more to Queen Seneca's death? Was the "suddenness" brought on by something other than actual sickness? I keep my face neutral so Colter won't ask about my thoughts. He won't appreciate the direction.

As we make our way past the church graveyard, the old woman who'd eyed me during the service peeks around a headstone. I direct Colter's gaze, hoping there's actually a woman and I'm not hallucinating.

"Do you know who that woman is?"

"That's Old Mary," Colter says.

"She was staring at me during the service."

"Seems I'm not the only one." Colter nods a hello, which sends Old Mary ducking behind the stone. Gone again. "I once got stuck in a bougainvillea bush, and she helped untangle me from the thorny branches, patching me up. I haven't seen her in a while. I'd feared the worst. But looks like she's still among us."

❧❀❧

An email from Aunt Vi waits in my inbox when I settle in my room for the night. The subject reads *It's About Time!*

I'd texted her about her writing process, admitting that I wanted to pick up where Queen Seneca left off. Compile all the notes I have about Princess Rosiah and Gran—even though there are still some holes.

I open the email with shaking hands. Why had I emailed her? I am a researcher. I write placards.

> *Abbie,*
>
> *Nonfiction isn't my wheelhouse, but I know you can do this! Told you you're a writer. Here are a few forms and work-sheets that I use—timeline tips and outlining (which I know you like to do, so stop making that face). Have so much fun! Saying a prayer that the words pour out. I'm so proud of you. Listen to your prince. You are overqualified. Go forth and write!*
>
> *Your Favorite Aunt*
>
> *PS: Say hi to Bishop when you see him.*
>
> *PPS: Bishop sent me a picture of you and the prince at the library opening. You are glowing. Has the prince kissed you yet?*

I'm so glad I read that in my bedroom. Alone.

With a shake of my head, I open the attached document. Aunt Vi is right—I do love to outline, and I am good at timelines. Maybe I can do this. I arm myself with a notebook and pen then drop both to grab my cell phone when it dings.

> **RACHEL:** *Awake with Henrix. God brought you to mind, and I asked the Holy Spirit for a word to pray over you. The word was CAPTURE. That's a new one! Usually, I get joy, peace, grace, etc. But now and then, I get an unusual one—fluidity and acceptance, for example. So there you have it! The Spirit knows its purpose.*

Capture. I wish I could capture this story. Capture my thoughts. I make a mean to-do list, and write amusing placards in my spare time, but writing a long piece? I want to make Colter proud by writing this story, his family history that his mother wanted to complete.

Someone knocks on my door, and I welcome the invite to procrastinate a little longer. It's Colter.

"I found this in my mother's room. I often find myself there on Sundays." He hands me a small journal. "I only looked at the first page, but there are notes about our family. I'd forgotten about it until I saw it on her desk. Maybe it will help you as you write."

"I still don't know if I can do this. I'm a researcher. A dreamer."

"You are a writer." He lifts my hand to his lips. "Until tomorrow, Abigail."

Alone again, I scramble back on the bed and open the hand-sized journal—the perfect size for taking notes at a crime scene or during church.

Queen Seneca starts with random notes about the palace staff. Talks about Mrs. Talor and her kindness. Mentions her other ladies-in waiting.

An entry about halfway through stops me.

> *Hamish does not know that I have continued this search. He forbade me from continuing. "If you find an heir, you are taking away your children's birthright. Think of Colter, think of your family." I started this project because of family. I have wrestled with what to do, but I cannot rest until I find out what happened to Rosiah. She did not die with her parents and brother. The Wellesleys have known since the beginning, keeping it a closely guarded secret, so they wouldn't lose the throne. Now that I know, how can I be queen knowing that I might not have the right? That there could be an heir, someone more deserving than I? God, I want to respect my husband always, but in this… In this, I must continue. Hamish must not know, until I have found the truth. I don't know if the Brisbane Wing is the right place, but I know my research will be safe there. For now.*

The Brisbane Wing. I have to go there now. Off-limits and all. I'll sign a waiver. Take a Sunday stroll through the palace that leads to the Brisbane Wing. It's not like it's locked. And the king never said I couldn't go there, not like the path to the greenhouse.

I throw on my basketball sweatshirt and set out. When I reach the tapestry and the fork in the hallway, I search for cameras. Do I dare? My insatiable curiosity as to what Queen Seneca hid in the Brisbane Wing overrides any fear.

The tapestry ripples, the drafty moan not making me jump, but I do glance over my shoulder. *Please don't give me Faith Mackenzie's luck. I can't handle a ghost.*

"Miss Morgan," the king says.

So much for not freaking out again. At least I harnessed my scream. *Proud of you, Abigail.*

King Hamish stands at the end of the hallway like a Georgian-era clock. Arms crossed. Face hard. Shadows weighing him down, making him both relic and ruler—untouched by the passing of the moments, but bound to them nonetheless.

I curtsy rather shakily.

"You should not be wandering around here." There is no "good, good" offered.

"I'm sorry, Your Majesty." I curtsy again.

"Go back to your room where it's safe, Miss Morgan."

"Good night, Your Majesty," I say, and after I give him a third curtsy, I return to my bedroom and shut the door. A nervous, panic-laced giggle escapes, although there is nothing funny about this. Guess I am banned from going to the Brisbane Wing.

I grab *Howl's Moving Castle* and go out on the balcony, my hands still shaking. I'm not going to be able to focus on writing.

Something moves in the garden, the same as my first night here.

King Hamish is entering the greenhouse.

Chapter Twenty-Eight

Enough is enough. I tried to sleep. Tried to forget that King Hamish was sneaking into the greenhouse. Is it considered sneaking if you own it?

I pace back and forth in my bedroom, dressed all in black. Who do I think I am? Harriet the Spy? Nancy Drew? Lara Croft? Walking toward the Brisbane Wing was one thing, but this...

Strapping on her thigh holster, grabbing her rope and super top-secret grappling gun, pulling her hair into a bun. Indiana Abbie is ready to infiltrate the greenhouse. Where secrets lie.

I scrub a hand over my face. What am I thinking? I'm not going to go. Yes. I. Am.

I will not rest unless I take a peek. Just walk around the building. I don't have to go inside. If my morning run happens to take me by the greenhouse then so be it. I want to like the king, but there's something going on. I'm doing this to understand the king's story. For my book. Yep, that's why. Blame it on my famous aunt telling me I needed to experience the research firsthand.

With my plan settled, I open the door and check the hallway. Empty. The sun has barely decided to appear. A few staff mill about. I smile and motion like I'm going for a run. And actually tell a few that I'm doing just that.

Nope. You aren't acting suspicious at all.

It's round two of the Westonia heist. But I did meet Colter last time. If I survive this caper, maybe I'll find him.

But do I want him to know I'm sneaking about? Did his father tell him he caught me headed toward the Brisbane Wing last night? Colter is pushing me to write his family history, so I'm adding him to the blame list as well.

The morning is lovely, and I take advantage of breathing the fresh air, a mix of tropical smells all its own. The waist-high weeds in front of the greenhouse door are trampled down the middle enough that I don't feel the need to stay away from the front door. It's locked. Of course. The weeds on the farthest side stand tall and untampered, but I stay as close to the building as possible, hoping they'll bounce back after my quick steps on them.

At the back, a window is open as if waiting for me to look through. A low stone wall is perfectly placed to give me a boost.

It's the Garden of Eden remade. Immaculate and cared for. And the scent. Roses. Hyacinths. Eucalyptus. Quirky craspedia. Sweet. Earthy. Talk about a sensory overload.

I haul myself through the window. Dropping to the ground, I make my way along a stone pathway toward a fountain that's a replica of Northargyle Palace. Water trickles merrily, evoking a sense of calm and timelessness.

I've soaked in maybe ten minutes of serenity when jangling at the front door alerts me to someone else about to join me. Nope, not going to happen. I step off the path and hide behind a tree, crouching low, praying I blend in.

I am a tree. I am invisible.

King Hamish approaches the fountain. He sits on a bench, staring. Lost in the same trance I'd fallen into moments before.

I turn my head trying to catch a snore, but he's not sleeping. After forever, he stands, taking a trowel from a metal bucket and disappearing around the side of the fountain. The stone palace blocks him from view.

He soon returns to the bench with an envelope in his hands. The trowel clangs against the bucket, and I gasp at the suddenness of the sound.

Covering my mouth, I try to replicate a statue. *You are stone. You are still. You are one with your surroundings.* I use these tactics when we play hide-and-seek—I'm still the best hider in the family. My talent of finding the perfect hiding place has finally come in handy.

King Hamish leaves, locking the door behind him.

I release a breath and ease myself up, my elbow smacking a potted plant to my left. I grope, catching the pot before it topples.

My heart rate is faster than a turbo engine as I make my way to the back of the fountain. *She spotted the fresh earth praying hard that she wouldn't find a tibia...*

Chuckling at my imagination, and hoping this scenario doesn't ever become a reality, I kneel in front of the dirt patch. Should I grab the shovel? It's not like the king hid a body. According to research, digging a grave with a shovel takes about four hours, not like in the movies where it's like thirty seconds.

I test the depth of the dirt and discover there isn't much before I hit a metal box. Scraping away the dirt, I lift the lid.

Inside rests a single envelope. Thankfully, it's not sealed with wax or any other deterrent. The paper inside has a heavy, masculine hand, inked as if with a fountain pen.

> *Cadence,*
>
> *My love, I am at a loss as to what to do. Do I proceed? Do I ignore? Do we celebrate? You were right. Everything we know could change forever. I'm not ready, but I know having you with me will make this bearable.*
>
> *You've always held my heart.*

Who in the world is Cadence?

❧

Everything is back and buried before I extricate myself from the greenhouse and make my running ruse a reality. The mundane event eases my brain into productivity. With every question, my feet hit the path I've chosen. I'm not sure at all where I'm going.

The sun is fully up—and the questions I've asked myself exhausted—when I hear the distinctive sounds of basketballs hitting pavement. That's what I need. A good layup. Several three-pointers. The feel of a basketball releasing from my hand and the whoosh of the net.

Colter and a group of guys dribble balls on a crack-free court. I do a quick count for team purposes. Uneven. Colter's smile lights up his face when he sees me. He bounces a basketball toward me, and I grab it, charging in for a layup.

"She's on my team," Bishop calls from the sidelines where he and another man are stretching.

"Nope, prince's choice," Colter says.

"You aren't captain today, Your Highness." Bishop bows, exaggerating a hand wave.

"Rock, paper, scissors it out," I say with a laugh. Hey, it works with my nieces.

Colter and Bishop play best out of five. Colter wins, which thrills me.

"Prince luck," Bishop mutters.

Colter introduces me to the other members of our team. It's a mix of kitchen boys and gardeners. I eye the other team. One huge man wiggles his fingers at me in a wave, his grin growing right before he sinks a three-pointer.

"Who's that?" I ask Colter.

"Chef." Colter elbows me playfully. "Don't let him scare you. He only makes one out of every ten shots, so we'll be good for a while. Let's show them what we've got, Miss MVP."

The basketball in my hand and the court beneath my feet is exactly what I needed. It only takes four three-pointers—like they thought it was pure luck and not skill that I made it each time—before the other team guards me heavier. And as Colter said, Chef misses two of his attempts. One because I blocked it.

I'm going in for a layup when I hit a wall and find myself on my butt, the breath knocked out of me. I flop on my back, arms extended and groan for added flair. My brothers and I give extra points for the dramatics—rating the flop, moans, and amount of tears. I start laughing when I remember I'm not with my brothers. Oops. Wiping the sweat from my eyes, I sit up. My cheek is tender, and I wince.

"I'm so sorry," the "wall" says. *Chef.*

"It's all good. I have five brothers—"

"What is the meaning of this? Why is Miss Morgan on the ground?" King Hamish's booming voice cuts off my laughter. "She could have been hurt or killed."

Now who's being overdramatic?

I'm still on the ground with the wall's hand outstretched. Chef helps me up as the king approaches, fire shooting from his nostrils and eyes blazing.

"You are done. Off the palace grounds. Now." The king points at Chef who tenses beside me.

I guess my performance was stellar if the king believed I was actually hurt. *One hundred points to Abigail!*

"Father," Colter says in a warning tone. King Hamish whips his focus to his son. A silent conversation takes place.

I study my fingernails, the dirt caked underneath reminding me of what I'd been doing this morning. Does the king know I was in the greenhouse? Had he been with Cadence before coming here?

"You can stay," the king says following an eternity of glares.

Chef keeps his rigid posture, but the ease is back.

Would the king really have fired someone over knocking me to the ground during a game of basketball that I chose to play?

"Are you okay? Truly?" Colter asks, his thumb rubbing gently over my cheek.

I jerk back, not because I don't want him touching me, but because it's tender. "I'm fine." My heart is skipping. "That was nothing compared to my brothers deciding I needed to be smashed between them. At least this wasn't my eye. Sorry for the dramatics. My brothers and I award points for performance."

After a tense interval of waiting, the king nods. "Hopefully, it will be gone by the ball."

"Father?" Colter glances his father's way once more.

"I've decided to hold a ball in Miss Morgan's honor." With that abrupt, left-field announcement, King Hamish leaves me wincing in a totally different way.

Chapter Twenty-Nine

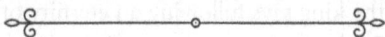

Why not you?

"Well, because I can't do this." I rip a page from my notebook and chuck it across the room. It's boring with a capital B. Followed by a capital O-R-I-N-G. And fifteen exclamation points.

I understand Aunt Vi's frustration and focus and wanting to throw things. Maybe I am a real writer—at least by Violet Morgan's standards.

For two days, I've been attempting to write. All I've accomplished is feeling like an imposter while taking over the entire table in the library office. The surface is covered with index cards, sticky notes, notebooks, and pens. The index cards are color coded. Dates in pink. People in blue. Interesting facts in green. Questions in white.

So many questions. And I've yet to find Gran's name in any official palace record. It's like she was a ghost. At least Mom entered the basement "closet of no return" and is searching for a cassette player. Maybe that will bear some fruit.

I smell coffee right before a steaming mug is set on a coaster in front of me.

"You spelled *traveled* wrong," Colter says as he taps my notebook where I'd scrawled *Josiah Ellery traveled to America.*

"You're back." I stand and hug Colter, my back cracking at the movement. He's been gone for two days finishing up details for a monument reveal on his mother's birthday, thus the reason I was able to focus enough to frustrate myself completely with the writing of the royal family story. I glance at my notebook. "And I did not spell *traveled* wrong. It only has one L."

"You Americans and your one L." He shakes his head as he touches my cheek, raising an eyebrow, before lowering his hand. "Glad to see you're bruise free."

"I'm made of tough stuff."

"Yes, you are." He eyes the table. "Eliana said you've been spending a lot of time here."

"You've created a monster." When I wasn't in the library, I spent time with Eliana, ate meals with a king who likes to yell, and chatted with either Libby, my family, or Aunt Vi. Libby sent a picture of the doll, confirming that it is the royal doll. The christening gown on the other hand, had belonged to Margaret's daughter. Rosiah's is still MIA.

I sip the coffee Colter brought me, savoring the chocolate and toffee mix that I've been chugging like it's going out of stock. "Thank you for this."

"You're most welcome." Colter shifts a stack of pages in his hand, a green clip on the top.

"Princely reports to peruse?" I ask.

"Faith Mackenzie biggest fan duties. Your aunt sent me her mess draft. She wants honest feedback."

"Just don't correct her one L spelling, and the kitchen counter is not called a bench. People sit on benches. They don't cook on them."

"I shall try my hardest." With one more grin, he snatches one of my gel pens before settling into a chair across from me.

Great. My focus will be truly tested now.

Sipping the coffee, I scan my list of pieces still missing. I need to visit the Brisbane Wing, but that's never going to happen unless God provides a miracle. I have no desire to run into the king again. He'd probably push the eject button. *Goodbye, Abigail.*

"I rather like this new character," Colter says with a chuckle.

I narrow my eyes. "Aunt Vi didn't actually name him Colter did she?" I haven't been privy to my aunt's new book. I'm not even sure of the plot. I'm usually one of her first readers, but I'm thrilled she asked Colter since my attention is very much elsewhere.

"No, although, I'm suspecting it's his middle name." He writes something before flipping to the next page.

"What did you write?" I can't help asking.

"Just noted that her new man now has a different eye color." Colter wiggles his brow. "He's starting to sound like Bishop. My character has been upgraded."

Colter continues reading, flipping pages at a fast pace, marking things here and there. He catches me watching him and lifts the page, blocking his face, his eyes peeking over the top.

"You're distracting me," he says.

"You're distracting me," I fire back, sticking out my tongue.

Eliana enters at that moment. I put my tongue away, but she doesn't seem to notice. Animated is a tame word for the glow taking over her face. She's almost jumping up and down.

"Abigail, Father wants me to help you find a dress for the ball," she says in a hurry.

"I thought you were designing one." I'm partial to the one that looked like a night full of stars. Her offer to be my designer made the fact that I'm going to be the center of attention at the end of the week a bit more bearable.

"I was, but Father wants you to pick a dress from Mother's closet."

"One of Mother's dresses?" Colter raises a brow in pure disbelief.

Eliana nods. "Father also said I could pick one for myself."

"Now?" I ask, gathering my mess.

Colter waves a hand, shooing us from the library. "Go, I'll care for your things."

Out of habit, I slip my tote over my shoulder then follow Eliana as if in a daze. Other than looking at possible dresses, I've been trying not to think about a ball that's being given in my honor. At least it wasn't like my birthday party where I knew nothing about it. I have some time to mentally prepare.

"Father is being so generous," Eliana says as she opens the wooden door to her mother's suite. Unshed tears sparkle in her eyes. "He must love you as much as we do. And letting me wear one of Mother's gowns…"

The king keeps surprising me in his acceptance. He is kind and courteous, even if it's in an unsmiling way. At least to me. With Eliana, he's a nitpicker. Nothing she does is ever right. The comments intensified at every meal without Colter in attendance. He adds a filter that even I couldn't offer. Eliana is graciousness personified.

Queen Seneca's rooms are dust-free, but I can tell they haven't been lived in. The air is cool, but too fresh, like a hotel. Sterile. Bleached. I do catch a whiff of Colter, must be from his Sunday visits.

Eliana allows me to wander the room. She's doing her own slow lap, touching things here and there. Having read through Queen Seneca's notes and journal, I've entered a friend's room. Book-filled shelves and paintings and a window seat. Dried flowers rest in a blue and white vase.

"Mother's closet is through there."

I nod and let Eliana show me the way. The closet, which includes a room off the side full of shoes and jewelry, is bigger than the Westonia reference room.

"Mother loved pretty dresses," Eliana says. "Too bad we only get one each."

"Being able to do outfit changes throughout the ball would make it easier to decide." I run my hand hesitantly over the fabrics. "I can't possibly choose."

So many dresses. In every color imaginable. A rainbow of silks, satin, and tulle. Beading. Embroidery. The Westonia could create a Threading through Ball Gowns exhibit with these gowns alone. I might have to suggest that to Kasey.

Eliana starts hanging dresses on a bar stationed in the middle of the closet. Ninety-nine percent are a shade of green. The color of my eyes on a green day.

The last dress she pulls is white with an overlay of lace covered in red roses. She doesn't hang this one, but instead, drapes it over her arm. "I'll give you a moment. I've already made my selection." Eliana squeezes my hand, tears in her eyes, before leaving me with so many choices.

I choose a pale green gown to get the fashion show started. It looked better on the hanger. I rehang it then go for a darker green dress with huge skirts. Again, the hanger wore it better. Before I try on a third, I do a lap around the closet. What if none of the dresses work?

As I'm reaching for a sage green dress, I catch sight of a Princess Box. It's on a shelf off to the side, hidden from direct view. Checking to make sure I'm still alone in the closet, I open the lid first. Secret drawer after.

The box is full of pictures. I flip through the stack. Colter, Eliana, and Queen Seneca. Silly faces. Serious faces—even though I can tell they were seconds away from laughing. A picture of Colter on a tire swing and a young Eliana in a sparkly dress and tiara. Definitely what I'd expect a loving mother to treasure.

King Hamish doesn't make an appearance in any. Odd.

Under the pictures, I find a birth announcement and first official baby picture for both Colter and Eliana along with a postcard with their names and the meaning typed on them. Colter means "he who cares for the herd." Eliana translates to "my God has heard." I turn over Colter's card and find a blessing written in Queen Seneca's handwriting.

"He who cares for the herd."
May Colter grow to have the heart of worship of David and the faithfulness
of Paul. May he grow in knowledge of You, loving and caring for the people
of Northargyle as You do.

Eliana's follows.

"My God has heard."
May Eliana grow to have virtue and courage like Ruth and Esther, and
wisdom and leadership like Deborah. May she know her identity rests in
You as a child of God.

With a heart overwhelmed by Queen Seneca's love for her children, I put everything back and close the lid before pressing the buttons for the secret drawer. *Seneca Kathleen* is embroidered in the fabric. The only thing in residence is a folded piece of brown paper. If I'm reading it correctly, behind the tapestry that hangs beside my workstation in the library office is a passage to the Brisbane Wing.

"Abigail, were you able to choose?" Eliana calls, and I drop the map.

"Not yet." I pick up the paper, refold it, and stuff it under my discarded dress before realizing I didn't shut the Princess Box. I put everything back to rights and grab the only purple dress on the rack, stepping into it.

"I'll need help with the zipper," I say. I'm just pulling the fabric up to my shoulders when Eliana enters.

Tears fill her eyes. It takes several moments for her to collect her emotions before she zips me up.

I step in front of the full-length mirror, trying not to give away that I hadn't looked at myself yet. I gasp.

The deepest violet shade. The gown drapes off my shoulders into a sweetheart neckline with elbow-length sleeves in tulle. Paper-thin petals in the same deep violet cover the neckline and cascade down the sides of the sleeves to just above the elbow. A fitted waist with a full-length tulle skirt flows from the waistline.

"It's perfect," Eliana whispers, her hands clutched to her chest.

> "I cannot help imagining how it would be to be a heroine."
>
> —Catherine Morland, *Northanger Abbey*

Chapter Thirty

I didn't try on any of the other dresses. One, because I didn't want to, and two, because Eliana called for a maid, who took our choices away to freshen to ball ready status.

Claiming the emotions of the morning gave her a headache, Eliana went to lie down. So, I find myself in my bedroom, staring at the map.

Only three words are written on it, written in Queen Seneca's hand. *Study. Rosiah. Charlotte.*

Is this your answer, God?

The map is a gift. An answer to prayer, a way to find out what Queen Seneca kept hidden in the Brisbane Wing. I've already snuck into one place this week. What's another?

I change into a pair of jeans and a dark gray T-shirt, not wanting to ruin my dress. It's going to be dusty. This isn't my first Brisbane secret room.

Armed with the map and my phone—what I wouldn't give for the flashlight, multi-purpose tool, and Oreos in my Abigail the Spy kit stashed in my bedroom closet—I open the bedroom door. The hallway is empty. I head toward the library, relieved that Colter isn't in the chair. My workstation is neat and orderly, the coffee cup gone, though the scent lingers.

A small tapestry with the Northargyle crest hangs right where the map says. I push it aside wondering that no one knew this was here. That the tapestry never was updated. The outline is barely visible. Checking over my shoulder one last time, I run my hands along the line until my nail fits in enough to pull.

The door opens and overpowering mustiness seeps out. I'll have to shower five times to make sure there's nothing lurking in my hair before dinner.

"Abigail?"

I twist at the voice, tangling in the tapestry, to find Zoe. I put a hand to my chest. At least it's not King Hamish.

"What are you doing?" She sets down a tray and moves to my side. "Is this a secret passage? Where's it lead?"

"The Brisbane Wing," I say. If I wasn't standing in the doorway, she'd probably be halfway down the tunnel already. "Do you want to come with me?"

"Yes!" She catches herself, repeating the word in a whisper. "Yes, please. I love detective shows. Give me a good mystery, and I am so there."

I smile at her eagerness and confidence in her ability as an amateur sleuth based on her hours of "research," comforted that I won't have to do this alone. I take out my phone, shaking it for the flashlight, and we begin down the tunnel, dodging cobwebs.

"This is so exciting. Like Enola Holmes," Zoe whispers, gripping my arm.

At the end of the tunnel is another door. I turn the knob and discover a replica of the library office complete with floor-to-ceiling shelves full of books. Though this room is far more muted. Likely due to the dust and cobwebs. Two years' worth if Queen Seneca was the last visitor.

Unlike the "modern" library office, this one is full of antiques. Vases. Paintings. Sculptures. I resist touching anything yet. My beam of light becomes unnecessary with the sunlight filtering through the dusty windows. The drapes are parted, and I long to close them fully to protect everything in this room from sun damage.

After promising the study that I will be back to explore it more in depth, Zoe and I head down the hallway to the staircase leading up to the rooms marked ROSIAH and CHARLOTTE. The scent of dirt mixes with the dust, wafting from the long-dead plants on pedestals that line the hallway. Altogether, it reminds me of some of the unkempt antique shops Gran and I stumbled across. We never stayed long at those.

I keep my hand off the banister, so I don't leave a trail. Does King Hamish visit this wing? Is that why he was lurking at the entrance?

"We mean you no harm," Zoe whispers as the walls "talk" to us. She's once again clutching my arm. "We're looking for clues."

I'm not exactly sure what clues she's looking for, but I don't pause to ask as I step into Rosiah's bedroom.

"It's empty." Zoe states the obvious.

No bed. No furniture. No decorations. No dresses in the closet.

While Zoe exclaims over the nothingness, I move through a doorway to an antechamber.

This room is empty too, except for a single painting hanging above a fireplace. A garden. A young man, with his back facing out, bends to pick a single flower. A rose. It's a grander scale of the one in the cottage, but without Roy—pretty sure it's Roy—facing the viewer. Among the flowers but not identified. A crown peeks out from the bushes.

No X marks the spot, but Abigail knows this is the place. She'd followed the clues in the painting. Rosiah's crown never left palace grounds, and she was going to prove it. Her smile grows when her shovel hits metal. Kneeling in the dirt, she lifts the box from its prison and opens the lid.

"Abigail, you have to see this wardrobe," Zoe calls, stealing my focus from the crown hunting fantasy.

I wish I could take the painting with me, but alas, nothing says "visited the Brisbane Wing" like a gigantic painting with a coating of dust.

Queen Charlotte's room, in comparison, is well stocked. Furniture galore. A closet filled with dresses and shoes. Artwork on the walls. A tall wardrobe looms in the corner. I ignore the dresses in favor of inspecting it. The scrollwork is intricate. When I touch a weka, a drawer extends from the front whacking me in the stomach.

Inside is a journal. I lift it carefully, wishing I'd thought to grab a pair of gloves. Charlotte Brisbane is stamped into the cover.

Zoe screeches as something scrapes along the window sending my heart into erratic beating.

What if the king is here? What would he do if he caught us?

I wait a beat, but when the sound grows louder, I take that as our signal to leave. Journal in hand, Zoe and I scurry back to the study and down the tunnel.

Cracking the hidden door just enough to ensure the library office is empty, I make quick work of exiting, shutting the door, and straightening the tapestry.

"That was so exciting. Thanks for letting me tag along." Zoe dips an unnecessary curtsy then picks up the tray, the fresh cup of coffee she brought now gone cold. "Oh, I was on my way to tell you that tomorrow is Queen Seneca's birthday, so there's no formal dinner tonight. I'll bring a tray to your room."

Once I'm alone, I face my workstation, finding it an unorganized mess. My notebook is open to the page I'd started on Queen Seneca, a blue index card resting on top. The question I'd written flashes like a neon sign.

Did Roy Currie return to Northargyle after Princess Rosiah died?

Chapter Thirty-One

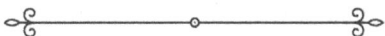

I brought everything from my workstation back to my room. Once I'm showered, I'll sort through it all. Make sure nothing's missing.

I must calm myself first. The spray of the water erases the dust and cobwebs and sweat. *Breathe, wash, breathe, rinse, breathe.* Repeat. My brain catalogs everything in my notes that someone snooping would have seen.

Who would go through it? One of the king's spies? Hugh?

I hadn't written down Cadence's name on anything or any hint that I'm questioning the cause of Queen Seneca's death, so that's good. I didn't want to chance Colter or Eliana seeing it and being crushed by their father's unfaithfulness.

After the longest shower of my life, I put on a comfy T-shirt dress then remove everything from my tote bag, laying it out on the bed. It's all here. All the index cards, no pages ripped from my notebook, and all my pens—even the one Colter was using.

I lean my head back against the headboard. Maybe a strong wind blew through the window? Maybe no one actually messed up the neat piles Colter had created.

At ease, for the most part, I slowly crack the spine of Queen Charlotte's journal. It's not as brittle as it first appeared. The passages on the pages are short. It starts with a quick jotting about her wedding and the birth of Rosiah. Queen Charlotte wasn't a consistent journalist. Were the gaps evidence that nothing exciting happened, or was her life made of secrets too great to record?

The words on the page from 1953 stop me, while ink splotches indicate tears likely fell during the queen's writing.

> *The hardest thing is feeling completely helpless. There's nothing you can do to take your daughter's pain away. What I wouldn't do to trade spots with her. Rosiah is a fighter, but I fear for her life.*

The next pages chronicle the care Rosiah received. The anguish Queen Charlotte faced at seeing her only child suffer. The questions. The treatments. The secrecy. Trying to keep from the staff and the country that their beloved princess was sicker than the royal family let on. Rosiah had good days and bad. Queen Charlotte was looking into an experimental treatment, but she wasn't sure how effective it would be. She wrestled with the fact that it could cure her daughter—or kill her.

The last entry is only a few short sentences.

> *10 April 1955*
> *The surgeon arrives next week. Dr. Gillespie assures us this is the correct course, the only way to save our daughter. Lord, is a lobotomy the answer?*

Lobotomy? Grabbing my phone, I enter the familiar-yet-not word in the search bar. *Brain surgery.* What was wrong with Rosiah that this was the course of action? Also, did Rosiah run away before she had the surgery? Or was she sent away because it hadn't worked?

Maybe I'll give Luke a call once I get this journal safely back to where I found it. After someone going through my notes, I don't want it to be discovered in my bedroom.

I pull a sweater over my dress, slip on ballet flats, grab my tote, and head toward the study. I keep an eye out for Zoe, but my sleuthing partner is not lurking around any corner. I'm a bit relieved. I want to be alone this time. Soft music comes from the library office, and I hesitate, but recognize the piece from the symphony—the one Colter translated.

Colter sits in a corner chair, his head resting against the back, eyes closed. His arms are crossed. Sleeves rolled. Tattoo visible. A notebook and pen rest balanced on his knees.

I try not to be creepy, but I can't look away from the scene.

A tear rolls down his cheek at the crescendo of the song. When the music ends, Colter breathes deeply then opens his eyes. And spots me.

"Hello, Abigail," he says, wiping his face.

"Sorry to intrude."

"You've caught me in a state of melancholy. Feel free to run or join me." One corner of his mouth lifts, an attempt at playful, even though it's evident he's hurting.

"Definitely joining you. Feeling a bit melancholic myself." I settle in the chair next to his, the record player between us. The violin melody of the next song stirs my tear ducts that were already loose from the anguish of a mother's heart.

"I was trying to write my speech for Mother's monument reveal tomorrow. Nothing like last minute. But I find I'm without words," Colter says.

"I'm sure you'll find them." I should hire myself out to be an author pep talker. If only it worked on myself. "Your speeches are epic, after all, according to Seth."

Colter smiles. "I was able to escape for most of the day with Violet's book, but the return to reality hit me hard."

"How was the ending?" I ask, curious as to what he thought.

"It's your aunt's best one yet. There's so much heart and soul to it."

"I can't wait to read it."

Colter studies me. "Did you find a dress?"

"I did. Eliana said it was your mother's favorite."

"Mother had lots of favorites. I look forward to seeing which one you chose. Speaking of, do you have a date for the ball?" He wiggles his eyebrows. "Because I know a guy who's interested in taking you."

"Who? Chef?" I can't help saying.

One of those laughs where you're trying to be sad, but you can't help it bursts forth as Colter tips his head back. "Sadly for you, Chef has a wife. But I am without a wife and would love for you to be my date."

"I'd love to be your date to the ball." Wife too, if we're being honest, but he didn't ask that. "I can't believe I'm going to ball, and not a basketball. I feel like Cinderella."

"But unlike Cinderella, your prince knows who you are. And if you do run away at midnight and lose one or both shoes, I will make sure to return your footwear in the morning."

"Such a gentleman," I joke.

"Were you going to do more research?" Colter motions to my tote. "I won't be in the way, just over here listening to this record. Possibly falling asleep where I sit."

"No, I—" Do I ruin his smile by sharing the pain of Queen Charlotte? Before I've listed the pros and cons, I take the journal from my tote bag. "I found Queen Charlotte's journal. It's so sad. Rosiah was sick, and the surgeon had been called to do a lobotomy."

"Where did you find that journal?"

I heat but confess. "The Brisbane Wing."

"And why, Mrs. Snoop, did you go to the Brisbane Wing?" he says, referencing Howl's nickname for Old Sophie.

"I found a map in your mother's room when I was picking out my dress."

"I knew it," he chuckles. "The passage is in here somewhere, isn't it? There were times I'd stop by to say hello, and Mother wasn't here even though I knew she had been."

"The door is behind the tapestry." I motion toward it, and Colter lifts the tapestry before I say anything more, reminding me of Philip when he gets an idea for a piece of art and is called to action.

"This has been here the whole time? Huh."

I hold the journal up. "I was on my way to take this back."

"I think I'll join you."

"Zoe went with me before. She's an avid watcher of detective shows. I might still have her nail marks in my arm."

Colter takes my hand. "Just so I don't lose you, and I don't want to add marks to your arm."

The walk down the tunnel is a hundred times better with Colter. Protected. Safe. I know he won't let anyone, namely his father, yell at me if we're discovered. The study is how Zoe and I had left it. But the sun is almost set. We find a lamp and plug it in.

As promised when Zoe and I were here earlier, I take the time to study the room in depth.

Spacious. High ceilings adorned with intricate moldings. Rich, dark wood paneling. Ornate, mahogany desk with a plush, high-back chair. Inkpot with quill. Floor-to-ceiling bookshelves. Ornate globe. Collection of maps occupy one corner. Luxurious rug covers the polished wood floor. Artwork includes several landscapes featuring weka and craspedia.

A ledger rests on the desk, and I open it to find a list of palace staff during the Brisbane era. Scanning the list, I come up empty with any proof of a Laurel working at the palace.

"Gran is still not here. It's like she didn't exist." My finger stops toward the bottom of the page. "Oh, there was a Mary Campbell who was nurse to Princess Rosiah. Could that be Old Mary?"

"Hmm, could be," Colter says absently. He's lifting books off the shelf, reading the titles, putting them back straighter. He stops suddenly, removing a thick leather-bound book. "I wondered what happened to Mother's Bible."

He runs his hand along the cover then opens it. Something flies from the pages. I squeal thinking it's a bug—not that I'm scared of them, but I don't like being surprised—before grabbing it. It's an envelope with Colter's name on it. I hand it over.

"My mother wrote me a letter?" The awe in his voice is reminiscent of an angel visitation. Wonder. Disbelief. Horror. Joy. He moves to the desk and sits in the chair without removing the dust, his hands shaking as he pulls out a folded piece of paper.

"I'm going to take the journal back." I don't think he heard me, but I don't mind. Colter deserves the same space he'd offered me at the museum—space to digest, space for silence. I'm so curious as to what his mother wrote, but in this, I'll practice patience instead of asking fifty questions. When he's ready, I'll be ready.

Retracing my steps, I return to Queen Charlotte's room, finding the knob and replacing the journal in the drawer. I stop by Rosiah's bedroom to look at the painting again. I allow myself time to stare, discovering new little things here and there. Flowers. Birds. Colorful patterns around the edges. The light from my phone illuminates a shape under the crown. Had Rosiah painted herself watching Roy? I guess my fantasy of finding the crown buried in the garden was off. Right?

I snap a picture in time to that scraping noise that sent me skedaddling earlier. Time to get back to Colter. Alone time is over.

Colter is smiling, his eyes noticeably tear-filled. Without a word, he stands and pulls me into his arms. Curled against his chest, his head resting on top of mine, we sway in the silence, holding each other.

"Thank you for bringing me here," he whispers against my hair. "I now have the words to share."

Chapter Thirty-Two

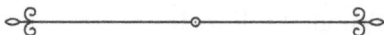

King Hamish isn't here. A service dedicated to Queen Seneca Kathleen Wellesley, his late wife, and he's a no-show?

Searching the park and growing crowd once more with the same king-free results, I turn my focus to the monument that's covered with blue cloth. The green where the monument takes center stage is small but well kept. A slice of the palace gardens for everyone to share.

I resist the urge to cause a scene and wave at Colter. Or give him a thumbs-up when he does glance my way after he and Eliana take their seats on the raised dais to the right of the green. Bishop drove me here separately, so I haven't seen Colter this morning. I saw Eliana briefly when she arrived at my bedroom with a breakfast tray and a request not to wear black. I chose the pink dress I wore to the museum. The deep purple of Eliana's dress matches Colter's sash. The sash, dark suit, medals, and hat mark him every inch the crown prince.

A trumpet sounds and a man moves to the podium. He gives a brief opening then Colter steps to the microphone amid a round of applause. I try but don't really succeed in keeping my clapping dainty.

"Ladies and gentlemen, honored guests, and beloved citizens of Northargyle," Colter begins then pauses to make eye contact with the crowd.

I don't know about everyone else, but I feel seen. Appreciated and cherished.

"Today, we gather to honor the extraordinary life of my mother, Queen Seneca Kathleen Kenwick Wellesley, whose love and wisdom continue to inspire us. All who knew my mother know there are so many wonderful things that could be said about her, about her love for the people of Northargyle and her family. Of her service and sacrifice.

"As I prepared for today, I found myself wondering what my mother would say to you all if she were here. I struggled to find the words. But then last night, I was given the gift of a letter that my mother wrote to me before she died." Colter finds me, and we share a smile as he takes the letter out of his suit coat.

A low hum moves through the crowd, silencing just as fast when Colter continues.

"I'm not going to read the letter, it is rather personal, but this charge that she left for me, I pass on to you all. My mother taught us that faith is the foundation upon which we build our lives and our relationships. It empowers us to reach out to those in need and to extend a hand to those who feel forgotten. My mother understood that true leadership begins with a heart full of agape love. Agape love is defined not by feelings, but rather on a conscious choice to love others without expecting anything in return."

I catch movement among the trees as Colter starts reading Romans 12. The king has arrived. He watches from the tree line, unmoving. Better late than never, I guess.

A trumpet blasts Northargyle's anthem, the crowd singing words to a tune that's familiar. I hum along, making a mental note to find and memorize the words so I'm ready for the next event. Two uniformed men move to either side of the covered statue. With a tug of the ropes, the fabric peels away to reveal a statue of Queen Seneca mid laugh, hair flowing free. It's the painting in marble.

The gasp of appreciation echoes around the park, mine included. The queen's motto is chiseled in the stone at the top of the pedestal. If King Hamish hid the painting of her like this, no wonder he was hesitant to be here.

I glance over at the tree line. King Hamish is no longer alone. A woman in a dark suit places a hand on his arm.

Is anyone else seeing this?

The king covers the woman's hand with his, and they stand connected for several seconds before turning and disappearing from view.

I take a step in their direction, but someone stops me.

"If I hadn't seen it with my own eyes, I wouldn't have believed it. Abigail Morgan in Northargyle," Angie Thorne says.

When I turn, I'm greeted by a less painted version of the bestselling author. Thankfully, she chose a skirt and jacket instead of a pantsuit.

She narrows her eyes. "Why are you here?"

"Colter invited me—"

"Not at this event, on Northargyle, and staying at the palace."

"I'm here researching. I'm picking up where Queen Seneca left off with the royal family. Your comment about the princess not dying with her family made me think my gran actually was the princess."

Angie's painted-on eyebrows arch.

I rush on. "But Gran wasn't royalty, she'd just left the palace with Rosiah and cared for the princess until she died in 1971. They were best friends."

"So, I was right?" Angie says rather smugly. "Princess Rosiah didn't die in the plane crash?"

I bite my lip, my eyes widening when I realize I just shared research that I was supposed to keep quiet. My heart rate picks up. "Please," I plead, "don't say anything. Prince Colter asked me to keep it quiet until the full story is known. I still have several holes to fill, and we don't want details getting out yet."

"I won't share anything. You have my word." Her gaze moves to the monument. "Queen Seneca was truly an extraordinary woman."

"She was." I glance at the vacant tree line then back to Angie. "Why do you tell everyone you're from New Zealand if you were born on Northargyle?"

"When my books started making news, Queen Seneca asked me to claim New Zealand since my father was from there. I agreed because I wanted to keep Northargyle from becoming a tourist destination for avid Angie Thorne fans. I'm protective of this island and its history. And its royal family." She studies me with the intensity she had in the bathroom at the Book Expo—peering into my soul to see if I'm worthy. "Are you vying to be our next queen?"

"I—"

"Your Highness." Angie dips in a curtsy.

I shut my mouth and smile at Colter, praying he hadn't heard Angie's question.

"Hello, Angie," Colter says.

"The monument is lovely. It captures your mother's beauty and spirit."

"The artist did an amazing job." Colter looks at me. "Did Angie tell you her brother is the one who created it?"

I shake my head but don't say anything. Angie's comment is still bouncing around like a pinball. I am not vying to be queen. Absurd. Out of the question. Worthy of a fairy tale…

"Speaking of, I'm going to go say hello to my brother." Angie dips in another curtsy. When she straightens, she pats my arm, a sweet, genuine smile on her lips. "Good luck, Abigail, on all fronts."

Colter leads me toward the car, and Bishop opens the door. I slide in, ready to tell Colter I'll see him back at the palace, but he surprises me by removing his hat and climbing in beside me.

"Oh, I thought I was riding back to the palace alone," I say.

"Since we're so close, I'd like to show you my favorite place on the island."

Colter takes my hand but doesn't say another word as Bishop pulls away from the park. The scenery reminds me of a color wheel, spinning through the entire rainbow as we drive. My mind imagines all the places that could be his favorite. *A park? A restaurant? Another library? Castle ruins?*

Maybe five miles from the park, the road narrows and the car passes under a wrought iron archway—stone pillars on either side like sentries—and into THE ROYAL BRISBANE CEMETERY. A cemetery is Colter's favorite place?

Bishop parks in a gravel lot and helps me out of the car. I decide to leave my tote so I don't have to keep track of it, trusting Bishop will protect it and not snoop. Colter removes his suit coat and rolls the sleeves of his white shirt, boldly displaying the motto as the monument to his mother had.

Colter resumes the handholding as we stroll among the headstones. The air holds the crisp smell of mold and upheaved ground. The detail, craftsmanship, and various colors and shapes of the stones and monuments leave me speechless. My fingers itch to care for the older, neglected stones covered in lichens and caked-on grass trimmings. What I wouldn't give for a toothbrush, cuticle sticks, and a spray bottle of water or D/2 solution.

"When I was younger, I used to close my eyes every time we passed a cemetery or a graveyard," I say as we loop back and forth along a packed-dirt path.

"Why's that?" Colter asks.

"I was scared I'd die if I looked at them." I chuckle at my younger self. "But since I fell in love with research, I've come to appreciate the history. There are so many stories and reminders to live life to the fullest while God has me here."

We make it to the center of the cemetery where the mausoleum from Rosiah's painting presides on a knoll as if keeping watch. Bushes and flowers planted around it act like a moat of fortified beauty. Did King Hamish have his hand in the landscaping?

Instead of stopping, Colter directs me up a steep path, away from the cemetery. A lone tree sits at the top of a cliff with a bench positioned underneath. We sit in silence and gaze at the sun-sparkled water below. The peace and indescribable beauty definitely give off favorite place vibes.

I catch my gasp. This is the scene from the painting Gran gave Margaret.

This view reminded me of our home. Oh, how I long to return.

"I come here when I need to think," Colter says. "When something happens that requires prayer and a chat with God. The last time I sat here was after I met you at the book signing. I came home to retrieve Eliana before heading back to Kenwick."

I glance at him then away, not knowing what to say. Not wanting incoherent words to destroy this moment of euphoria.

"My life was set. I love my country and was preparing myself to become king at thirty-five. I knew my role. The expectations. I was ready to marry whoever my father chose." He sighs deeply. "Don't take this the wrong way, but I knew what to expect before I met you. Now, I'm not so sure."

Our hands are entwined on the bench between us, his thumb running over my knuckles.

"Besides Seth, Mia, and Eliana, I've never allowed anyone so close. I don't know how to be close to someone without thinking about the life I'd put them through. What woman who's not already royalty would want the added pressures of being queen?"

I want to say I volunteer, but humor at this point would be inappropriate. Silliness has no place here.

"I often wonder if it's worth it." Colter squeezes my hand.

"If what is worth it?"

"The price tags that come with loving full blast."

We sit in silence, breathing, thinking, praying. At least I am. This is the most serious conversation I've ever had. It's serious and exciting, and I don't know if Colter is hinting what I think he's hinting.

"Sorry to unburden," he says, his eyes focused out to sea.

"Anytime," I whisper. "You and Eliana have become my closest friends."

"I'm honored, Abigail. I know you need to go home in a week, but I would love for you to come back to Northargyle. Our time together will never be enough."

⁂

We've arrived at the palace when my phone buzzes. I dig in my tote for it as I maneuver out of the car, seeing that I've missed three calls from Jaxon. I haven't heard from my brother since he went back to base, and his quips on the sibling chats have been nonexistent.

"Everything okay?" Colter asks.

"Jaxon called several times." *Please, Lord, let him be okay.* "Do you mind if I call him?"

"Not at all." Colter leads me toward the palace gardens.

My hands shake slightly as I dial my brother. Until I hear that I'm being ridiculous, there's always that fear that something is wrong.

Jaxon answers on the first ring. "I've been a fool."

"What happened? Are you okay?" I sit on a bench, my legs wobbly.

Colter gives me space but stays close.

"Jess has been seeing Titus Danaby."

"Lord Danaby? Jess wouldn't—"

"Apparently, they're eloping. She called me from a hotel in Spain."

"Are you sure?" I stand, covering my mouth.

Colter is by my side in a second. He puts his hand on my shoulder, offering support.

"She said marrying a pastor's son who was 'quitting' the military would be way too hard." He growls. "Then she had the gall to accuse me of lying about being rich. Titus told her that you weren't an heiress and that I'd never be able to give her the lifestyle she deserved."

"Why would she think I'm an heiress? Because of Gran?"

"He filled her head with all these lies. I guess I'm just not good enough for her."

"Don't talk like that. You're amazing."

"It doesn't matter. I'm done with her, Abbie. I'm done. I never want to see her again." He hangs up, ending the conversation, closing that chapter completely.

"What about Titus?" Colter asks.

"It's awful." Tears fill my eyes. "My brother broke it off with Jess. She's been seeing your friend, Lord Danaby. I shouldn't have invited Jess to Kenwick."

"He was never my friend, and now he won't have that option."

"They're eloping."

"Titus will never marry her," Colter says like it's a done deal. "He has a mistress on every continent."

"Jess accused us of lying that we're rich. I mean, yes, Gran did leave me a cottage, but that doesn't mean anything. How could Jess be so cruel?" Even as I say it, Jess's words way back to the first day we spent together come in quick bursts.

I let out a frustrated cry. "I've been as much a fool as my brother. I was so excited to have someone who didn't know about my family choose me. But I ignored all the unkind things she said and did, latching onto her promises of best friend status. I so wanted to say I had a best friend."

I take a deep breath and berate myself for good measure. "Way to be a good judge of character, Abigail Morgan."

Chapter Thirty-Three

*M*y pen moves though I'm not in control. The ink turns black to red, the words "I Wsa Psinode" marring the page, followed by the sketch of a single hyacinth.

A rustling in the bushes draws my attention to Queen Seneca. Her hair blows loosely around her shoulders, the purity of her white dress a stark contrast to the rainbow of flowers behind her. She beckons, her wedding ring flashing like a lighthouse to wayward ships. I set my journal and pen in the grass beside her crown, meeting the queen at the greenhouse window. She points inside.

King Hamish dances with a woman, a bouquet of vibrant pink flowers hiding her face.

"Abigail Rosiah." I turn to find Colter in a tux, standing on the palace terrace. My purple ball gown shimmers like a resting place for fireflies as I run to him. As soon as I take his hand, we're in the ballroom, surrounded by a crowd.

Colter gasps as King Hamish appears on the stairs overlooking the dance floor. A woman steps beside him and kisses him on the cheek. She looks right at me with a smirk, her face a blur that I can't get a read on. The woman *morphs to Jess and the king to Jaxon. Lord Danaby appears and hands Jess a bouquet of pink flowers which she hands to my brother.*

As soon as Jaxon touches them, he falls to the ground, tumbling down the stairs to land at my feet. Unmoving. Dead. Whispers of poison increase in volume.

"Get away from me," Colter yells, backing away, eyes wide and horror-filled like I'm a monster. My ball gown has become my maroon Lady Knights uniform, my lucky knee-high basketball socks and black high-top sneakers on my feet.

Lady Paige puts her arm through Colter's, offering me a pink bouquet. From the corner of my eyes, I see the basketball hurtling toward me before it smacks me in the head...

I wake feeling unsettled and out of whack. The word "poison" stuck on my mind loop. What is my subconscious saying? And what's with the bouquet of pink flowers?

Was Queen Seneca trying to tell me that she'd been poisoned? That her illness wasn't what we'd been told—just like a lot of other things going on in and around this palace and my life in general.

Rubbing my eyes, I retrieve my phone and search "poisonous pink flowers." Number one is oleander. My hands shake as I read through the list of symptoms of oleander poisoning, making a mental check mark next to each one that Mrs. Talor told me Queen Seneca showcased.

Stomach pain. Dizziness. Vomiting. Weakness. Trouble breathing.

Had the king and Cadence poisoned Queen Seneca?

I laugh at the absurd thought, but the evidence isn't so far away from the possibility. Removing her painting, not allowing anyone to decorate for Christmas, not showing up for her monument reveal with everyone else, yelling at his children, having his own rooms, forbidding anyone to enter the greenhouse yet leaving love notes to another woman.

Does oleander grow in the greenhouse? I won't be able to rest until I know.

In record time, I'm dressed all in black and at the unlocked greenhouse window. I'm about to climb through when I'm jerked back and tackled to the ground. My grunts break through the quiet. I'm roughly rolled over, coming face-to-face with the mystery woman from the monument reveal. The one who held hands with the king.

Dark eyes. Dark hair. Strong, muscular build. Sinister, stone face...

"You?" I ask.

She doesn't speak as she yanks me to my feet. From across the park, I'd thought she was older, but she's got to be in her late thirties. The woman grips my arm hard enough to leave marks and begins marching me toward the palace.

"Are you taking me to the dungeons?" I ask in a breathless rush. "I don't want to be locked up. There's an explanation. It's not what you think."

The woman doesn't respond.

"I mean, yes, you did find me about to climb through the greenhouse window, but I was trying to find oleander. Did you poison Queen Seneca?" Oops, I hadn't meant to say that out loud.

That stops her, and I topple to the ground, landing hard on my knees, rocks biting into my palms.

"What?" she grinds out, eyeing me so fiercely I swear I can taste blood. She has her hand around my bicep when Colter appears.

"What's going on?" he asks. "Abigail?"

"Your Highness, I found her trying to climb through the greenhouse window," the woman reports.

Colter nods. "I'll take her. No need to tell Father."

"Yes, Your Highness." She releases me and backs away.

I glance over my shoulder, but she's already gone. I wish I could master that skill. Especially in this moment.

"So, trying to climb through a window?" Colter crosses his arms, quirking an eyebrow. "You didn't think the front door would work? First the Brisbane Wing and now this? Any other places you've been snooping?"

My face heats like a petulant child, and I can't look him in the eye. "Did you know that woman? She was at the monument reveal with your father."

"My father was at the park?"

"Hiding in the trees all suspicious like," I say. "Does your father love her?"

"I don't understand that question." A strange look crosses Colter's face. "Helena is one of my father's bodyguards. She's married to Hugh."

"Wait, if that's Helena, then who is Cadence? Was your father having an affair before your mother died? Did they plan to get rid of your mother, so they could be together? I saw oleander in the greenhouse." *At least I think I did.* "And Mrs. Talor listed all the symptoms of poisoning when I asked her about your mother's illness."

Colter holds up a hand, taking a step away from me like he craves the distance. "Let me see if I understand this story you've concocted. Stop me if I'm wrong. My father was in love and having an affair with a woman called Cadence before my mother died."

"Yes, and he still is. He writes to her, leaves the letters in a box in the greenhouse."

"Those letters are private, Abigail."

"So you knew your father was having an affair? Did your mother know?"

He laughs without humor. "What comes next in the story? I'm sure you did the research."

"I don't know."

"You don't have all the facts, yet you're accusing my father of being unfaithful and what, having his bodyguard kill my mother? With a poisonous plant growing in the greenhouse?"

"Your mother had all the symptoms of poison. Headaches, nausea, dizziness. Mrs. Talor said her death was sudden, and Zoe said it was very suspicious."

"It was sudden, but my mother was already at stage four when they discovered she had ovarian cancer. We couldn't convince her to try treatment. Mother chose quality of life over quantity."

"Why did your father send everyone away, threatening them if they said anything?"

"I was there."

"But your father—"

"Abigail, please think about what you're saying. What would my father gain by harming my mother? My father loved my mother more than life itself."

"I thought maybe she discovered something about Princess Rosiah. In your mother's notes, she said that your father forbade her from researching. But she didn't stop. She discovered Rosiah was still alive. Your father didn't want her to search for heirs because he didn't want to lose the throne."

"You think Father killed my mother to keep her quiet? Or because of an affair? Which is it?"

I shrug, cringing. "Both?"

He shakes his head, narrowing his eyes. "There isn't some huge conspiracy here, Abigail."

"But you told me when I arrived at the palace that not everyone has survived."

"You're being ridiculous. Life isn't like your game of 'What's your story?' Can you even tell the difference between fiction and reality?"

"I—" I can't be here anymore. I run from Colter, from my humiliation and utter childishness, not stopping until I'm in my room. "Stupid. Stupid." Tears are pouring. I've been so foolish. So stupid.

There's no way I'll be allowed to stay at the palace. No way I'll be allowed to attend the ball tomorrow night. No chance of ever telling Colter that I think I'm in love with him.

Heartbreak.

Crushed.

No breath.

Colter's right. I am ridiculous.

Chapter Thirty-Four

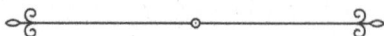

M iss Morgan." I swim toward wakefulness and the sweetly accented voice. "Abigail."

What day is it? What time? I fight my way out of the blankets covering my head, the sun hitting me in the face. *Hiss!*

"Abigail?"

Once my eyes have adjusted and my brain catches up that I'm still at the palace, I spot Zoe near the wardrobe.

"Have you come to help me pack?" I ask in a raspy old woman kind of voice. It would serve me right if I was cursed to be old like Sophie Hatter. I could go find another palace and just clean all day, talk to the fire, and eat bacon.

Zoe's brow scrunches. "I've come to help you get ready for dinner." She sees me glance at the time. "The king wanted an early dinner, so everyone is well-rested for the ball."

"Are you sure they want me? That Colter wants me there?"

"Prince Colter sent me to get you ready."

"I'm not sure I should go. I've been a fool," I mutter. *What if King Hamish knows what I accused him of? How can I face him? How can I face Colter?*

"The prince said you might hesitate. He asked after you earlier, but then Prince Silas arrived, and Prince Colter told me to leave you to rest." Zoe whips the covers off me and forcibly removes me from the bed, helping me stand. "I'm sure whatever it is, you'll work it out. I've been watching the two of you. The prince is smitten."

"I don't think he is anymore."

Zoe rolls her eyes, and before I know it, I'm wearing a white dress with vivid pink flowers on it and standing in the doorway of the dining room. The table is full, someone at every place setting. Where did they all come from? Paid actors to witness my demise?

King Hamish greets me with a kiss on both cheeks then directs me to a chair on his left. He pulls out the chair himself, acting like I'm some visiting dignitary in need of impressing.

A relieved breath escapes. Colter didn't tell him. Or is this the calm before the storm? Will he crush me in front of all the guests?

I chance a look up. Eliana is across from me listening intently to a man with curly red hair. At first glance I think it's Bradley, but then I remember Zoe saying Prince Silas had arrived. The cousins could easily be mistaken for brothers. Although Prince Silas is slimmer and definitely doesn't respect or cherish Eliana the way Bradley does.

Every time King Hamish addresses me, I wait for his anger. But he's laughing, jovial. Reminiscent of the symphony king. And, suddenly, Eliana's biggest fan. He talks her up in front of Prince Silas, giving her a glowing report that is so deserved but odd coming from the father who's done nothing but nitpick his daughter like a hen.

I sense Colter several seats down from Eliana and catch his eye briefly. Nope. Can't look at him. Pressure builds behind my eyes. *No crying at dinner, Abigail Morgan.* I'm so thankful for royal table etiquette and the rule about only talking to people on your left or right.

If I shift a little, the huge candelabra blocks my view of Prince Colter entirely.

❧

Following the longest dinner ever, where I have to dive so deep for a smile and manners, the king herds us to a large music room where a stringed quartet is set up. He's off playing host, so I'm able to stay near the back, like a wallflower of old, hoping not to be noticed. Waiting to be sent away.

I'm not brave enough to look about the room in case I see Colter. This carpet is rather lovely, the swirls, the flowers—

"Abigail, come with me."

My shivers have shivers at the sound of Colter's voice. He wiggles his fingers. Despite my hesitancy, I take his outstretched hand, which he squeezes before guiding me outside.

The setting sun transforms the sky into a canvas of rich, changing colors—vivid oranges and fiery reds that gradually blend into soft pinks—graciously offering enough light to see the garden path.

"Wait," Colter says, sensing my urgency to say something.

What am I waiting for? Is he about to yell at me? I'd deserve it, of course. My eyes flood with tears, and I sniffle as quietly as I can so I don't give myself away that I'm losing control.

Colter remains silent, not stopping until we've reached the start of the trail his mother loved. The one his father warned me to stay away from. Why would Colter bring me here of all places?

After a deep exhale, Colter says, "I owe you an apology, Abigail."

"What?" I startle, glancing up then away. "I should be the one apologizing."

"I owe you many apologies. I projected my frustration on you because I was upset with my father for inviting Prince Silas to the palace to close the marriage deal with Eliana. No matter what, I should have listened instead of laughing at your concern. I've failed you, and I am sorry." Colter stops my need for space with a hand on my arm.

I stare at it, unable to make eye contact with him.

"Please forgive me. I was out of line."

"You were right. I'm ridiculous," I sputter. "I accused your father of murder. Of having an affair. You have a right to hate me. I—I am so embarrassed."

"Abigail, please look at me."

"I don't think I can," I whisper.

Colter lifts my chin with his fingers. "Abigail. I truly am sorry. I shouldn't have said what I did. Your imagination is refreshing. You have such a unique way of seeing life. Your creativity, service, and passion drew me to you. You pour so much into everything and everyone around you. I want to be someone who replenishes you, who fills your bucket to overflowing instead of sapping you of all that makes you so special."

"You should tell me to go—"

"You're not going anywhere." He shakes his head good-naturedly, releasing my face in exchange for my hand, not letting me get away. "I tried to see my father through your eyes, thought about it all afternoon. Coming from someone who didn't know the full story, I could see how you may be led the direction you were. Palace secrets do abound. The severity of my mother's condition was covered up, as was Rosiah's illness and disappearance."

"That still doesn't make it right."

"I know you don't have nefarious purposes. That you didn't make those accusations out of spite."

His kindness is too much. My eyes fill again.

"Regarding my father, come, I want to show you a story."

Taking my hand, he starts down the path toward the greenhouse. If I dared, I would dig in my heels. I've already potentially angered the king by my accusations. What will he do if he finds out I disobeyed his order and stepped foot on this path? Which is definitely not any dirtier than any other path in the garden.

Colter stops us in front of a eucalyptus tree, the bark a rainbow of color that matches the sunset behind it. It's one of those trees that begs for twinkling lights, a blanket, and a good book. A minty-fresh haven away from the world.

"My parents' love story began with an arranged marriage, but my mother started writing Father notes," Colter says. "They weren't long— sometimes even one word. The first one may have been 'Hi.' Father soon responded, so the story goes. Mother told me about them but never did share what they wrote."

I make a noise that tries to be an "aw" but gets lost. It's like the mailbox Laurie bought for Jo and her sisters so they could write back and forth.

"Their mutual love of gardening and the hours they spent out here ended up bringing them together." Colter motions toward the tree. "This is where mother left the first note, and Father carved their names."

Cadence and Hamish are etched into the trunk, a heart around their names. Like it's a piece in a museum, a wooden plaque is on display in front of the tree. I move closer, and before I realize it, I'm reading poetry.

My rise and fall
My beat and pulse
My tempo, my time, my measure.
My birdsong
My steady stream
My hope, my rock, my rhythm.
My joy and peace
My rest and ease
My love, my light, my anchor.
My eternal flame
My constant heart

My Cadence e'er surrounds me.

"Cadence was my mother's nickname, one that only my father used," Colter says quietly. "Father lost his cadence when Mother died."

A barrage of emotions builds as I read the poem again. Like a veil has been ripped off, the wall between my heart and brain explodes. Turns out I don't hate poetry. I just needed the right one to get me started.

Colter doesn't say anything, but he knows.

"So, the greenhouse? He's been writing to your mother this whole time?" I say in awe. "That's the most romantic thing I've ever heard."

"Ever since I can remember. Although, I've never been daring enough to read any of them. I guess they could have been trading recipes."

"No, they are definitely words of love."

Colter takes both my hands, his thumbs skimming across the top. "I can't stand the thought that I've hurt you. You've come to mean so much to me."

"You mean so much to me too," I whisper.

"I've tried to be a prince, but I'd really like to kiss you, Abigail Morgan."

"I've never been kissed," I admit. "What if I'm bad at it? I don't—"

"Breathe." Colter turns my hand and kisses my palm.

A nervous laugh escapes at the tingles coursing through my arm down to my toes. He hasn't even touched my lips yet.

"I never thought I'd actually make it to this moment. I've always lived on the sidelines, watching everyone else date and experience romance. While 'sideline dating' was informative in helping me know what I didn't want, it wasn't exactly fun—" I wince. "Oversharing, sorry. Can you tell I'm nervous? You probably don't wanna be anywhere near my lips right now."

"Honestly, I'd like to be closer." He shrugs, his eyes twinkling merrily as he fights a grin. "And, if you're awful, we'll have to practice."

"What if you're the one that's awful?"

He tilts his head, one eyebrow quirked in mischievous amusement as he takes my face in his hands. He runs a thumb along my jaw then his lips are pressed against mine. Slowly, then deeper. Hesitant, yet sure. Giving and taking in equal measure.

Nothing I imagined prepared me for kissing. Tears build in response to this precious gift. At his forgiveness and mercy and acceptance. He's choosing me, even though he had every right to kick me to the curb.

When he pulls back, he catches a tear making its way down my cheek.

He kisses my forehead, lingering a moment before circling me in his arms.

"You're quite talented," I whisper against his heart, which is beating in sync with mine.

"So are you."

Chapter Thirty-Five

"Y ou are ravishing," Aunt Vi says, rolling the *r*.

Zoe holds up my phone so Aunt Vi can see my entire outfit. Queen Seneca's gown. Her favorite because it was the king's favorite. I've been transformed into an exquisite creation of shimmering purple.

Eliana's stylist is a miracle worker. My hair showcases the loose, elegant style I've always wished to achieve. A silver headband, not quite a tiara, and real hyacinths are woven in. The flowers match the purple of my gown, like the dress was made from hyacinth petals.

"I wish you were here," I admit from a well of nerves.

"Part of me wishes I was too, but mostly I'm good. Already in sweats and the bra is off. Planning on watching *Little Women*." Aunt Vi smirks. "No matter how late, you better call me with more kissy details."

Colter and I hadn't stayed much longer post first kiss even though we both wanted to. Our walk back to the palace was sloth-paced.

I'd called Aunt Vi in a state of delirium as soon as Colter said good night. We giggled and squealed for thirty minutes, me rehashing the moment, dissecting my first kiss every which way. Of course, I hadn't told my aunt about the murder charges that preluded the romance. Ain't nobody got time for that nonsense.

"Love ya much, kiddo." Aunt Vi blows kisses. "Oh, and make sure Zoe takes pictures of you to send to your parents. I know your mom will want to see you."

"I will. Love you too."

Zoe snaps several pictures of me, which I send to my parents, and only my parents. The brothers would make snarky comments, and I don't want anything to ruin how I feel or shatter the calm, even if I know they'd be joking.

There's a soft knock on the door before Eliana enters. "Colter said I should come make sure you're ready. I—" Her eyes cloud up, her hands going to her heart. "I know I saw you in the dress already, but Abigail…"

I cross the room and, careful of both our dresses and hair, pull her into my arms.

"I'm so glad you chose this dress," she whispers.

"Me too." It's then I realize Eliana is not wearing the dress she'd chosen from her mother's closet.

Instead of the white gown with rose-covered lace overlay, she's wearing a green and purple tartan-looking dress. While gorgeous, Eliana shifts uncomfortably.

"Where's the white dress?"

"Father sent this one because Prince Silas is here. It's in honor of the kingdom of Ardach." She sighs. "My only comfort is in knowing that Father will not use your ball as a means to make an engagement announcement between me and Prince Silas. Father may be cruel and oblivious at times, but he would not ruin the purpose of this ball. Which is you."

"I still don't understand why your father thinks I deserve a ball."

"You are worthy to be celebrated. And even though Bradley isn't in my cards, Father is not opposed to my brother pursuing you."

My face heats.

"I'm sorry you couldn't wear your mother's gown," I say.

"I'll wear it to the next ball that Silas doesn't attend." Eliana takes my hand. "Are you ready to be introduced to everyone?"

"Wait, did I need to study titles and names and what everyone looks like?" *I should have spent time watching videos instead of playing spy and being overconfident because I know how to waltz.*

Eliana laughs softly. "Father wanted this to be more informal, so no receiving line. Even though the food, music, and dress are on par with the normal procedure."

Zoe adjusts my skirts and straightens a tendril of hair before giving me a thumbs-up and allowing me to leave my bedroom. I follow Eliana toward the grand staircase where King Hamish waits. *Black coat and pants. White shirt. A medal with the Northargyle crest on his right lapel. Purple sash. Dark hair with streaks of salt and pepper—freshly cut, freshly shaved.*

I search for Colter, for his playful grin. Eliana's hand tightens on my arm, but she doesn't speak.

"Good, good." The king's second "good" cracks, like he can't push it past the lump growing in his throat. His dark eyes are noticeably moist as he kisses both my cheeks. "A vision. Both of you." He turns from me, giving Eliana a single cheek peck on his way toward the doors. He's announced and disappears, the doors shutting behind him.

"Where's Colter?" I whisper.

"Father wants Colter's first view of you to be descending the stairs."

"No pressure." *King Hamish might as well hang up his crown and become a matchmaker.*

"I'll be next to you the entire time. Once the introduction is over, it'll be smooth sailing." Eliana hooks my arm through hers as we approach the doors. "Together, we will conquer."

The doors open to reveal a balcony overlooking the ballroom, music ascending to heighten my awe. I don't have much time to take in the activity below before we begin our descent. True to her word, Eliana doesn't release her firm grasp as she whispers encouragement.

One step at a time.

Colter waits at the bottom with his father in a similar suit minus the medal and sash. When my name is announced, Colter freezes, his eyes widening. I've mesmerized him. The rest of humanity forgotten. I can't stop the thrill, knowing that I've inspired his world-stopping speechlessness.

"Good, good," King Hamish says when I successfully reach the bottom. *First mountain conquered!* The king places my hand in Colter's then offers his arm to Eliana, leading her to the dance floor.

Colter still hasn't moved. On contact, he shudders—in a good chill way, not repulsion—and his crooked boyish smile appears.

"Hi," I say, looking him over. Be still my heart.

"I have no words," he says.

My face heats as his gaze dips to my lips inciting all the memories of our kiss. Thankfully, the first strains of a waltz fill the room.

"Shall we?" Colter asks. I nod, and he leads me onto the dance floor. With deliberate slowness, he slides his hand down the length of my arm then up to my back where it rests in waltz-pose.

He keeps a greater distance between us than at the symphony. More people are here. I am on display. Up on a pedestal, free to be judged and critiqued.

"Here we are again," I say, nervousness stuttering my chuckle.

"No place I'd rather be."

My greatest fear fades as I focus on Colter. There's no place I'd rather be, either, because I'm not alone in the spotlight. If getting to dance with Colter means I have to be the center of attention, so be it. It's worth it a hundred times over.

"I wonder what people are thinking," I muse.

Colter studies other couples around us. "They are curious. They are envious. They are hungry." Colter nods toward an older gentleman who is hiding a yawn. "They are bored and tired. But overall, they are in awe of your beauty."

"You need to stop saying things like that. I don't deserve them."

"Sorry, but I don't plan on ever stopping." With those words, he's dipping me as the song ends. Colter lifts my hand to his lips once he's righted me, pressing a kiss there. "Would you like something to drink? I could use one."

"Sure. Hydration is important."

"That it is. Hydration first, then we are dancing again."

"What will people think?"

"Thankfully, we aren't in the 1800s. And if we were, I'd be playing my prince card." He winks before heading off.

I'm waiting for Colter to bring my drink when Lord Danaby enters the ballroom. No. Not here. Not tonight. My answer to whether Jess is with him is answered as she hooks her arm through his. She's wearing Gran's shawl over a low-cut black dress.

I'm glad I don't already have my drink because my hands tremble uncontrollably. I can't see her, not tonight, not for a while. What if she tries to talk to me? Are they already married? Why is she here?

This is my ball, and I did not invite her.

Jess makes eye contact as if her only goal is to find me and flaunt her status. She whispers something to Lord Danaby. He smirks my way then they disappear to the outside section of the ballroom. Mission accomplished.

"What is it?" Colter sets the drinks down, so he can take my hands.

"Jess," I breathe out. Pressure building behind my eyes.

Colter's jaw tightens as he searches for them.

"They went outside," I barely get out. I want to run and hide. Where's the closest bathroom?

"I'll be right back." Colter's grip on my hands tightens then he's off like an avenging angel, even though he didn't actually see Jess.

Should I follow or continue my escape? No, this is my party. I am not leaving. I need to face this and not run—no bathroom pep talks, no helicopter extractions. I need to speak up for myself. For my brother. Jaxon deserves a champion. Also, I want Gran's shawl back. And her ring.

I skirt the ballroom, acknowledging those who greet me, praying they excuse my quick responses. When I make it to the outside ballroom, it takes me a moment to find Colter. He's on the farthest edge of the dance floor speaking to Lord Danaby and Jess.

"You can leave by choice, or you can be escorted," Colter says. "Neither of you are welcome to stay."

Everyone looks at me when I slip my hand into Colter's, letting him know I'm here.

"Well, look who it is," Jess scoffs. "Just going to Northargyle to research? You are such a liar."

"Are you married?" I draw strength from deep within. "Who invited you? Why are you here?"

Jess ignores my first question going right for the second. "I had to come warn the prince. Abigail isn't who she says she is. She thinks she's so much better than everyone, thinks she's perfect, thinks she actually deserves a prince." Her face twists into an awful expression, her eyes blazing as she zeroes in on Colter. "Did she tell you she's already engaged?"

"No, I'm not." I plead with Colter to believe me.

"You're so fake. Everyone sees it. She used my brother, and she's using you. She promised to marry Devon then, oh, something better came along."

Jess has confused her story with mine.

"She's an imposter who doesn't deserve to be here."

Bishop appears along with Helena. Warrior stances. Stern, no-nonsense expressions. I huddle closer to Colter. He squeezes my hand, my whole body shaking.

"I'd like my gran's shawl and ring back," I say.

"Here, take it. It's not worth anything anyway." Jess rips the shawl from her shoulders and throws it on the ground.

"The ring," Colter reminds her.

"I sold it."

"No!" I cry out.

Helena puts a hand on Jess's arm.

Sparing the king's bodyguard a rage-filled glare, Jess throws one more barb at me. "You'll be sorry."

While Helena escorts Jess, Bishop manhandles Lord Danaby down the stairs. The situation is taken care of without much notice from the gathered crowd.

Colter picks up the shawl and wraps it around my shoulders.

"I'm not using you," I whisper as I pull the shawl tighter, thrilled to have it in my possession once more. "And I was never engaged to Devon Greer."

"I know." Colter kisses the back of my hand, then wipes an escaped tear off my cheek.

"But she's right that I don't deserve to be here—"

"Abigail, do not believe her jealous lies. That's all they are. Those who know you know the truth, that there is nothing fake about you. Besides, this ball is for you, so if anyone doesn't have the right to be here, it's me." At his smile, tension ceases to exist. "Let's forget about them. They can't ruin this night unless we let them. It's over and they're gone. They will be off Northargyle within the hour." He studies my face. "Okay?"

I nod.

"Now," Colter tucks my hand into his arm, "we are going to go give everyone enough fodder to last a lifetime and only dance with each other the rest of the night."

Chapter Thirty-Six

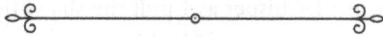

bigail! Not a second to lose." Eliana's excited voice cuts through my dreaming bliss.

I peek over my covers to find a different Eliana than the one I've seen every day since we arrived at the palace. Like she's been on the beach. Relaxed. Radiant. Barely attempting to contain her giddiness. She's lost her reserved control.

"What's going on?" I ask as I jump from the bed with all the expectancy of Christmas morning. I hope I'm not reading Eliana's excitement wrong.

"All the guests are gone, and my father has left the palace. Colter is waiting for us."

In record time, I'm showered, my hair piled on top of my head. Eliana is wearing shorts and a simple blouse, so I follow the casual dress code.

The palace air is charged with excitement. The staff all smile openly, moving about as if in a musical. If they start singing, I'll probably join them. I didn't realize King Hamish's presence—knowing he could appear at any time—affected the entire palace and not just me.

"It feels like when Mother was alive. I've missed this," Eliana says, as if reading my thoughts. Instead of heading to the breakfast room, Eliana leads me outside to the back patio then into the gardens and to Colter.

Wizard Howl charm and mischievousness. Sparkling light brown eyes. Goofy grin. No hint of facial hair. Brown hair trimmed. Dark jeans. Black short-sleeved polo. Tattoo on full display.

"Good morning." He stands, and for a moment I wonder if he'll kiss me in front of Eliana, but he presses his lips to my cheek instead. First one then the other. Ending with a wink before he pulls me down on the blanket beside him. "Behold, brunch."

Once he's offered a gratitude-filled prayer, he hands me a mug of coffee and uncovers the bowls and plates. Bacon. Eggs. Toast. Fruit. Pavlova. The lack of formality is refreshing as we forgo all silverware, Colter shoveling the eggs into his mouth with a piece of toast. I can almost imagine I'm with my family and not on an island with royalty. Our easy banter and laughter is back.

After brunch and a stroll through the gardens, where Colter holds my hand the entire time, Eliana announces she's going to go call Bradley.

"And we, my dear Abigail, are going to find you a piece of your puzzle."

"Which puzzle?"

"Your gran's." Colter slings his arm around my shoulders, and I anchor mine around his waist.

His answer doesn't narrow it down much. I shift through the possibilities as he leads me to the garage. Once we're inside, he hands me a flappy hat and goggles.

"Are we going for a motorcycle ride?" I don't hide my excitement.

"Yes, my lady, we are." Colter dons a matching leather hat with flaps and goggles.

I can't help the laugh that bursts out. "You look so goofy."

"Join me in the goof." He points to my hat and goggles.

I accommodate him.

He adjusts the hat, taps my chin, then helps me into the sidecar. I can't believe I'm about to do this. I've never thought much about my bucket list until I saw things that I've always wanted to do.

Colter climbs on and starts the bike, the seat rumbling beneath me. "Hold on."

I grasp the bar in front of me, my stomach jolting like I'm at the top of a steep roller coaster. I've never been a fan of them, but this is magical and amazing. Maybe I'll have to give theme parks a second chance.

Bishop pulls out behind us in a light gray BMW, and I return his jaunty wave. Good to know if we run out of gas, we'll have a ride back.

Talking isn't really possible, but we grin loopily back and forth. The gentle speed. The sunshine. The fresh air. Colter's steady control. My hat flapping in the wind. I didn't realize riding in a sidecar could be so romantic—especially with the silly hats and goggles. I raise my hands and let out a loud "Wahooo!"

Colter parks in front of a small house that sits between a matching row of others. I take off the flappy hat. I'm about to put my hair back up, but Colter steals my scrunchie.

"I haven't seen your hair fully down." He touches one of the pieces that, since it was twisted up from the shower, has a curl to it. "It suits you."

I decide to let him keep my scrunchie as I bend over and fluff my hair, whipping it back up to hang unhindered. Once righted, I eye him, quirking an eyebrow. "Your goggles and hat are still on."

"Disguise." He grins. "She's expecting us."

"Who?"

"Mary Campbell." Colter knocks as I process the name, recalling where I'd read it. Mary Campbell was a nurse to Princess Rosiah. But what does that have to do with Gran?

The door opens to reveal that Mary Campbell is in fact Old Mary. Her smile is endearing as she waves for us to enter. The sense that I know her hits me just like it had with Prudence. Could Mary be related to Grandpa Brown—Ellery—as well?

"Come in," Mary says. "The tea is ready."

"After you." Colter ushers me inside to a kitchen that reminds me of the healer's cottage at the Renaissance festival Aunt Vi and I visited while researching *The Façade Beneath*.

Bunches of drying herbs—sage and rosemary—hang from iron hooks filling the air with potpourri. Wooden shelves lined with jars, mismatched glass bottles, and cookbooks with pages curling at the edges. An old-fashioned stove, its copper kettle gently steaming. A basket of fresh fruit. Hand-painted tiles on the walls depicting scenes of harvest and feasts.

Colter takes off the flappy hat and goggles, setting them on a rough-hewn table before running a hand over his hair. I bite back a giggle at the sight of my colorful scrunchie still on his wrist.

Mary starts to lift the tea tray, but Colter beats her to it. "I'll get this, Mary."

"Come in where it's comfortable."

He carries the tray to a cozy sitting room. It's neat and tidy with more dried flowers hanging from the ceiling in lieu of decoration. The walls are bare except for a painting of a garden that I know is by Princess Rosiah. I check the signature, confirming my guess, before joining Colter on a brown sofa with claw-foot legs.

Mary takes the matching chair across from us, handing us each a hand-painted teacup. The steaming liquid smells like pumpkin pie. Mary studies me as she had in church. I take a sip of the tea to break eye contact. Cinnamon? Ginger? It's so different from any tea I've ever tried to like. For one thing, it doesn't make me gag. I take another sip. Just as good as the first.

"When I saw you that day at church, I thought she had returned." Despite her age, Mary's voice is strong.

"Who?" I come out of my tea musings to pay attention.

"My sister. Laurel."

"My gran was your sister?" My tea sloshes in my excitement. Colter hands me a napkin, exchanging it for the teacup. "Laurel Campbell. I know Gran's last name."

"A piece of your puzzle." Colter squeezes my hand then addresses Mary. "So, you used to work at the palace. I only recently made the connection."

"My mother was Queen Charlotte's nurse, and she would bring me with her, training me to eventually care for Princess Rosiah. Laurel came with us to the palace one day when she was thirteen, the day Rosiah had her worst attack. My sister was able to calm the princess when the rest of us failed. I don't know if it was because they were the same age, but they became inseparable."

"Do you know what was wrong with Princess Rosiah?" I ask. "Queen Charlotte wanted her to have a lobotomy."

"The doctors never diagnosed the issue, but I knew the lobotomy wasn't the right option." Mary's gravelly laugh is full of delight. "Rosiah showed them. She left the palace instead of allowing them to operate, taking my sister along with her."

"So, she didn't leave because of Roy," I whisper.

"Well, not fully. Roy Currie was such a nice young man. But he was staff like the rest of us. King Thomas did not approve of the friendship. Roy left the palace three months after Rosiah. I knew they were together, but I never knew where."

"Did you know about the decoys?" Colter asks.

Mary nods slowly, like she doesn't want to admit it. "My sister was the one who thought up the plan. Having them all take Rosiah's birth date, giving them items to throw anyone who searched for her off the scent. I was brought into the confidence because I overheard their plan."

That's why Gran feared the consequences of her actions. Understandable.

"My mother and I were dismissed. On penalty of treason, we were told not to tell anyone that Princess Rosiah wasn't safe in the palace. Royals and their need to present a perfect face." She winces but doesn't apologize to Colter.

"When King Thomas, Queen Charlotte, and Prince Michael were killed in that plane crash, the entire country was told Rosiah died with them. I believed the story, thinking they must have caught up with her, never knowing what happened to my sister. If Mother and I were threatened with treason for sharing, what would happen to Laurel?"

Mary's hands shake and she clasps them together, picking at the fabric of her gingham skirt. "I did wonder if Laurel was on the plane, but then Queen Seneca showed up at my door."

"I didn't know my mother was here," Colter says softly.

"She was talking to people who had worked at the palace, gathering information for the royal family tree. Your mother was a rare woman, and I knew I could trust her with my secret about the decoys and that Rosiah had run away almost eight months prior to the plane crash."

Colter makes a noise. "My mother shared that information with Father, who already knew that Rosiah didn't die with her family."

Mary nods. "I've prayed every day that Rosiah received the treatment she needed, and that I'd see my sister again." Tears cloud her muted hazel eyes as she studies me. "Then there you were at church. You look so much like Laurel. Please tell me what happened to my sister."

❧⁂☙

Two hours later, Colter and I return to the palace in Bishop's car. Someone will retrieve the motorcycle later. The storytelling and tears took a lot out of me. And being in the car gave us an excuse to hold hands, even though we didn't talk.

I realized, as I told Mary all about her sister and the journey she and Rosiah took after they left the palace, that I was telling Gran's complete story for the first time. All the pieces are in place. The final image is of a woman who gave up everything to care for a princess. Laurel Rose Campbell also known as Christine Rose Ellery Brown. Conspirator. Caretaker. Secret keeper. Sacrificial. Faithful. Unknown by everyone but ever present in the life of the princess. Friend.

No greater love.

"Everything is set up, Your Highness."

I startle out of my musings. "What's set up?"

Zoe curtsies and not so subtly winks at me. "I will bring dinner in a little while."

Colter takes my hand and leads me up. And up. And up winding stairs to a round room of windows. A table is set with two chairs, candles lit. A doorway leads out to a balcony, one that circles the turret.

I do an entire lap, taking in the palace grounds from every angle. "What is this place?"

I'm not sure if Colter hears my whisper, but he responds as he rests his hand on top of mine on the wooden rail. "We call it Stargazer Perch," Colter says. "At least I do. The Tallest Turret rolls off the tongue weird."

I laugh then turn to face him. "Thank you for today. Thank you for helping me complete Gran's puzzle."

"In some ways, I wish it weren't over. But I know we still have other stories to share." He cups the back of his neck then hands me the package he's been carrying. "For you."

"What is it?" I ask, but am already removing the wrapping, which Colter takes and places in a garbage can so my hands are free. It's a copy of *The Scarlet Pimpernel*. I hug the book to my chest.

"I figured since I've read your favorite book, you should read mine." He smiles then sighs. "I've been trying to forget you're leaving in two days. I'm not ready."

"Neither am I."

"Let's pretend, use our imaginations, nothing holding us back, for the rest of the night that you're not leaving. That I'm not a prince who can't follow you to America because he has a schedule and so many duties this time of year. You are Abigail, the beautiful researcher who loves stories, and I am Colter. Just Colter. Two best friends sharing dinner, pavlova, dancing, and maybe some kissing."

"Best friends," I whisper the words, my heart soaring. Uncaged. Free. In that instant, everything else fades, and I realize I've never truly felt this alive, this unburdened. "Yeah, I can join that dream."

Colter full out grins as he grips the upper part of both my arms, tugging me toward him. *The Scarlet Pimpernel* rests between us. He kisses my forehead then my jaw.

I lift my chin hoping he's going for my lips next.

With one more smile then several heartbeats of him staring deeply into my eyes, he finally presses his lips against mine, sealing this beautiful moment with a kiss so magical I don't ever want to leave.

Chapter Thirty-Seven

One minute I'm blissfully floating on a cloud of happiness, the next, it's two a.m. and Hugh is escorting me to the king's office, Gran's shawl in his hands.

Zoe woke me, all wide-eyed and terrified, telling me to dress as fast as I could because the king was demanding to see me. I'd thrown on a dress and slid my phone into my pocket, not coherent enough to know what I needed to be prepared for.

I'm led down a desolate hallway I was never introduced to, where Hugh opens a door and motions for me to enter. I can hear a drum beating in time to my steps, an ominous march toward my awaiting judgment, toward a mahogany desk where King Hamish waits. Imagining a black robe and gavel in the king's hand isn't hard to do.

Had he heard about my accusations? How do I explain my way out of that one? I mean, I did accuse him of having an affair and murdering his wife.

Hugh hands over the shawl, bows, then stations himself at my side like he's ready to restrain me if I put one toe over the line.

"Miss Morgan, it has recently come to my attention that you are not of royal blood," the king starts.

Wait? What? *Hadn't that already been established?*

"That your grandmother stole this shawl and has been masquerading as a princess her entire life when she was, in fact, the daughter of a servant." He sets a crown on top of the shawl.

"Is that Rosiah's?" The question escapes. Followed by another one. "Where did you get it?"

"You kept vital information about Roy Currie's whereabouts to yourself. You stole my wife's research, papers that are precious to the royal family."

"Roy's alive? I knew it. I—"

"Impertinence. Do not forget in whose presence you sit."

I open my mouth but close it when the king holds up a hand.

"I invited you to Northargyle Palace as an honored guest, only to find you are not who you claimed to be either. You are the unemployed daughter of a pastor and a coach. Going nowhere in life. You disregard rules, trespass, and twist the truth to fit your agenda. You have betrayed not only my trust but also the entire kingdom of Northargyle."

My jaw tightens as I try to keep tears from pouring down my face. Jess's accusations I could deflect. The king's? The king's words strike deep, reaching all the way to my core. I deserve this.

"You have manipulated me. You have manipulated my children. Because of you, my daughter informs me she will not be marrying Prince Silas. And my son, you have bewitched him, using his good nature for your own devices."

Hugh shifts beside me, gripping my arm tightly.

"There is no longer a place for you here, Miss Morgan," King Hamish says. "Effective immediately. You and your maid are never to step foot on Northargyle again, and I forbid you to contact either of my children."

At a flick of the king's wrist, Hugh leads me from the room.

Zoe stands on the other side of the door with a leather bag slung over her shoulder, tears marring her freckled face. Jeans and a T-shirt have replaced her maid uniform. A young man stands beside her with my suitcase and tote.

"Oh, Zoe, I'm so sorry," I say.

Instead of anger, she drops her bag to the carpet and tackles me in a hug.

I haven't just messed up my life. I've ruined hers. "I deserve this. I knew it was too good to be true. But you, you don't—"

"You deserve no such thing," Zoe says.

"I got you fired as well."

"It'd be no fun at the palace without you anyway." She tightens her hug.

"I feel so horrible. What will you do now?"

"Maybe I'll go to uni and get my detective license."

I chuckle at her humorous attempt even though my heart aches.

"Take care of yourself, Abigail."

"You too, Zoe. Thanks for being the best maid a commoner could ask for."

"It's time to leave, Miss Morgan," Hugh says, brooking no argument.

I receive my suitcase and tote and follow Hugh down staircases and passages that must be how the staff moves about unseen, through a quiet kitchen, and out a back door. Welcomed in honor, escorted away in shame.

A car waits, the engine a low purr in the darkness and stillness of an hour when I should be sleeping. I search for Bishop but know I won't find him. Does he know what's going on? Will he let Colter and Eliana know?

I glance up toward the Stargazer Perch and let myself remember.

Laughter. Playfulness. Friendship—true and best.

Colter's gift, and the sweet kiss at my bedroom door when he'd said, "Until tomorrow, Abigail."

The bliss I'd felt in our moment of pretend has been ripped from me, my heart twisted in agony, my soul aching.

Oh, how far I've fallen...

Chapter Thirty-Eight

A n air horn rips me from sleep. Not that it was deep or sweet or dreamless. Nights of blissful slumber belong to my past. As does waking up on my own time and in my own way, apparently. I've been hibernating for two days, trying to figure out how to adjust to my new normal. Trying, as Aunt Vi's realest "Real Reel" encouraged, to speak powerful truths to myself rather than destructive talk and set goals I can obtain.

Morning coffee. Bible reading. Unpack suitcase. Afternoon coffee. Nap. Avoid rom-coms. Reorganize bookshelves. Cuddle with Gamal. Avoid checking phone every five seconds to see if Colter or Eliana texted. Keep mind theater blank. Early bedtime.

My bedroom door slams open seconds before my nieces jump on top of me.

"Aunt Abbie! Aunt Abbie!" they chant as one. "It's Thanksgiving!"

The air horn blasts again. Closer this time.

I pull the covers down to find my nieces inches from my face. Behind them stands a wall of my brothers decked in their ugly sweater finest. Laughing, I grab my nieces, blowing raspberries on their necks to their squealing protesting delight. They scamper out of my reach, a trail of giggles following them from the room.

"Time to rise from the unshowered ashes and run," Asher says. He lifts the air horn, fingers moving for the trigger, but Rachel deprives him of the torture device. She acts like she's going to chuck it down the stairs, but ends up putting it behind her back, out of my brother's reach.

"Get out, all of you." Rachel motions for the brothers to exit. "Give Abbie space to get ready."

"Yes, boss." Asher leads the way, the others filing out behind him with fake petulance.

"Downstairs in ten, Morgan, or we'll be back," Luke threatens before closing the door.

I pause and reflect, taking stock of my life before joining the revelry. Today is a day of thankfulness. And, despite being kicked out of Northargyle, I am thankful to be home surrounded by my family.

My journey from the palace to home involved a car, a boat, another car, three planes, and two full reads of *The Scarlet Pimpernel.* Hugh had driven me to a boat dock, where I'd been secreted away to New Zealand and Aunt Vi's rental cottage. I'd cried myself dry that night, sleeping an entire day of my life away. We could've flown to America from New Zealand, but I wanted to spend at least one more night in Hyacinth Cottage. A sort of full circle ending to what brought me to Australia in the first place.

I study the painting of Gran now hanging next to my wall of vintage postcards. I've yet to add the two I'd bought at the Antique Palace—they're somewhere in my tote. The pink sticky note that I'd written "I, Abigail Rosiah Morgan, want to go to Australia to discover Gran's story" still on the wall where I'd left it.

"I discovered your story, Gran," I whisper. I also added so many chapters to mine. The good, the bad, and the wonderful. I'm definitely not the same person who wrote on that sticky note.

When the air horn goes off again, I jump out of bed and dress in sweats and the sweater Aunt Vi and I found in an Australian thrift shop. It has kangaroos and emus wearing Santa hats. It's not exactly ugly, at least not to me.

"Morgan!" Someone bangs on my door.

I whip it open and jog past Asher. "Ready to lose, biggest brother?"

"Do you even remember how to run, little sis?" He pulls a travel mug out of the pocket on the front of his Christmas cow sweater and takes a sip.

"I'm gonna annihilate you and your dad bod!"

We elbow each other on the way down the stairs. Mom and Dad sport neon athletic headbands and matching dinosaur sweaters. Aunt Vi is rocking leg warmers and an ugly Rainbow Brite sweater. She gives me a thumbs-up then does several speed runs before collapsing in the recliner breathing heavily.

Yes, I'd left pieces of my heart all over Northargyle and Bridgeway, but there's no chance to take up residence in the pit of despair. Not that I want, or should, dwell there.

The morning is crisp and cool, and my breath swirls in puffs as I step outside. Caleb, the serious runner, is stretching. Poppy and Lily hold hands, their tinsel-covered sweaters flashing with light bulbs, their hair standing straight up on top of their heads like geysers. Stefi and Luke chose bedazzled bride and groom sweaters. But Rachel wins for the ugliest. Every item one would expect to find in a Christmas junk drawer has been sewn to a sweater the color of puke. Bells. Cardinals. Tinsel. Ornaments. Fake snow. Snowmen. Flashing-nosed Rudolph. Nutcracker with an impressively bushy mustache.

"Same rules as last year," Mom says, organizing us as usual.

"There are no rules," Philip whoops.

Mom gives him a look before continuing her speech. "To the mailbox and back. The last two across the finish line win dish duty."

Once I've staked out my position behind the starting line, I check out the competition to my right. Philip yawns. Caleb squats, one hand on the driveway. Luke and Stefi are pushing back and forth, trying to get the other to step over the line. Aunt Vi has her serious face but breaks concentration to send me a wink.

"On your mark," Rachel yells. She's been designated as the race officiant because Asher wrote her a "just had a baby" excuse. Henrix is bundled up in the stroller sound asleep, unfazed by the zoo-like chaos. Morgan babies are conditioned to wake in the quiet. "Get set. Run!"

The exercise is somewhat foreign, but I soon find my rhythm, my grin growing. Philip elbows me on his way by, and I pick up my pace. Aunt Vi and I run side by side for a bit, but I put on my "rocket boosters," touching the mailbox the same time as Philip.

On the way back to the house, I pass Vi, Mom and Dad, Asher and the girls, and Luke and Stefi. We call out jeers as is the custom. Bashing everything from their running form to asking if they need their Depends changed.

Caleb wins. Philip and I cross at the same time. Then Mom and Dad. Asher and Vi, each of them carrying one of the girls. Last to cross the finish line are Stefi and Luke, hand in hand. They share a kiss in celebration of winning dish duty.

My breath catches and I have to look away, blaming my sudden tears on the chill in the air. Is this what my future will be like? Moments of memories that flip my *okay* status to *not okay*?

❧

Three hours later, turkey coma has officially been achieved. I'm curled up on Asher and Rachel's couch under a fuzzy blanket, my head resting on Dad's shoulder. Snow is falling gently outside the living room window. Praise music flows from the kitchen, where Luke and Stefi are finishing the dishes. It'll be several hours before I'll be able to dribble a basketball without groaning.

Being in Gran's old house, surrounded by those who love me unconditionally, brings overwhelming gratitude this year. Tears prick my eyes as I gaze from one person to the next, treasuring the scene. All that's missing is Jaxon, who sent a very impersonable "Happy Thanksgiving" text minutes before we sat down to eat. I take several deep breaths, trying to keep my status as *okay*.

"Ew! Philip!" Caleb cries from his corpse pose on the floor, waving his hand in the air.

Philip pulls the collar of his shirt over his nose and mouth. "It's not me."

"It's Heni," Poppy says matter-of-factly as she flicks the Chutes and Ladders spinner.

Aunt Vi stops rocking, the antique rocker creaking as she lifts Henrix. "Guess my record is intact. Every time I hold a baby, they poo."

When the smell hits me, I gasp and untangle myself from the couch. Looks like my nephew just handed me something to blame my tears on. "I'll change him," I offer, taking Henrix from Aunt Vi.

"Good luck," Asher says from the love seat, tightening his arm around Rachel. "Might need a hazmat suit."

"Henrix takes after his father." Mom smirks at Asher as she slides her piece down the gameboard. "I'm sure the delivery nurses still talk about the stinky baby who made them pass out whenever they entered the NICU."

Keeping Henrix a safe distance from my nose, I head upstairs to the forest-themed nursery and settle my nephew on the changing table.

By the time I remove his diaper, I'm second-guessing my kindness. "Man, kiddo, that's impressive."

Henrix makes a noise that I translate as "Why, thank you."

Once I've locked the grossness in the garbage can, liberally sprayed air freshener about the room, and acquired hand sanitizer, I pick up Henrix and hold him close, breathing in that newborn smell. I walk back and forth in his bedroom, humming, eventually moving to the padded rocking chair and positioning my nephew on my knees face up.

"I am thankful to be home," I whisper, repeating my words of thankfulness from dinner. "But I don't know what to do next."

Henrix blinks at me, his tiny fingers wrapping around my pointer finger. Babies make great therapists.

"I know I'll be okay I just…I feel numb." My words catch on a cry. "I miss him so much. Why hasn't he tried to reach out? It's been almost a week. I know his father forbid me from having contact, but why can't he reach out? Why can't Eliana? Have they forgotten all about me already?"

Rachel taps on the door alerting me to her presence in the nursery.

I start to stand but she stops me. "Stay where you are."

"Sorry I didn't come back," I say. "I needed a moment."

"It's all good. I needed one too. Your family can be overwhelming at times." She smiles lovingly, a true sister-in-arms. "I'm here, you know, if you ever want to talk about what happened."

I told my family that I'd been asked to leave the palace because I wasn't of royal blood. Aunt Vi knows the entire story, of course, even my unfounded murder and affair accusations against the king. I'm still processing. Weighed down by embarrassment and shame and loss.

"I'm barely holding it together," I whisper.

Rachel understands my unspoken invitation to stay and sits on the floor, pulling a stuffed fox onto her lap.

"I wish he would reach out. Does he wonder why I'm not there? Did his father lie to him?" My breath catches. "I love him, and I never got to tell him."

"Maybe Colter is sorting through the same questions. He may have to work through what he believes. Princely responsibilities, pressures from his father." She eyes me. "What specific reasons did the king give for sending you away?"

"He told me I was an unemployed manipulative nobody—"

"What? Give me the king's number, I'll call him right now and set him straight." She snorts at her outburst. "Sorry, that's not helpful right now."

I can't help a small chuckle as I shift Henrix up into the crook of my arm. He's sleeping, his chest rising and falling, not a care in the world. Lucky boy.

"Look, I know we're not besties, but I've been a part of your family long enough to see your heart. You're the farthest thing from manipulative and fake. You have a true servant's heart. You did just offer to change an explosion."

"I was hiding."

"No matter what, you notice the needs of those around you. You're the first one to clean up, the first to arrive, the last to leave. You've watched my kids and made time to stop what you're doing to braid their Barbies' hair whenever they ask."

"I love doing all that." I press a kiss on Henrix's forehead.

"We all have seasons in life where the best of who we are is not on stage. When we're doing the backstage work. I've struggled all over again with my change in roles since Henrix was born, being at home with the kids. It doesn't make what I'm doing less valuable. There will come a time when I'll find a place on the stage again. It's the backstage phases that help prepare us."

"I'm definitely backstage," I say. "Perhaps maybe under it. Oh, or maybe I'm the one with the spotlight, training it on the actress."

"The right man is going to want your heart. You'll be his leading lady no matter what role you're playing." Rachel's eyes light up. "I'm such a dork. Just wait, I have more cheesy lines."

I offer a half-hearted laugh on the heels of a sniff. "I wanted it to be Colter. I thought God brought Colter."

"Maybe He did. The story is still unfolding. I'm not sure where it'll end up. But the only way for the story to keep going is for you to stay in it."

Rachel grabs a box of tissues, setting it on the table beside the chair after I pull one free. She returns to her place on the floor, choosing a stuffed raccoon to pull into her lap this time.

"When I first met your brother, I didn't even like him. He was so loud and didn't understand personal space. But over time, God—and let's be honest, a determined Asher—wore down the walls around my heart. Then, as I'm opening up, everything blows up in my face. I had no idea if we would ever end up together at that point. Love felt like an exercise in cruelty."

"I didn't know that part of the story," I say on a sniffle.

"During that time that we were on a 'pause' in our relationship, I realized something. With a man as high quality and godly as Asher, it was better to have known and loved him than to have not ever had that privilege. He challenged me, helped me learn about myself, and taught me about what kind of man I one day would want to love forever—and I could not have learned those lessons without the high-risk adventure of falling in love with him."

High-risk adventure. The price tags that come with loving full blast.

I pull Henrix closer as Colter's words meld with Rachel's. "That part makes sense to me," I admit quietly. "I can already see so many ways God's using all this uncertainty and pain to teach me about myself. It sure would be a lot easier if I knew how things would end. But, I know, that isn't how faith works."

"It's definitely hard, but so worth it to hear God's whispers of love along the way. That's a love, a security, that far outweighs any human love or happily ever after. It'll get you through the rough days. You just have to keep going. Keep trusting. Even when it is rough.

"You love stories. Picture this as a story. The greatest story. With God as the Author and you His beloved character He's dreamed up to bless the world with. Until you see yourself through the Author's eyes, as someone worth loving, you aren't going to be able to accept another human's love. Not fully, anyway. You'll always be second-guessing and waiting for them to find out who you really are then reject you."

I feel that wrung out weariness one has after a good cry, but I also feel underneath Rachel's words a bedrock of hope to grab hold of and slowly climb back up. "So, sometimes the waiting parts of a journey make the adventure better? The parts where you thought you swerved off the cliff and ruined your story could be the best chapter just getting started?"

Rachel flashes a full-watt grin. "Sleeping Beauty's long nap sure seemed like a detour, but it allowed the prince to test and prove his love for her. Thomas Edison called his hundreds of 'failed' attempts at a light bulb merely steps to his groundbreaking invention, essential to lighting up our world today. The hungry caterpillar gorged on colorful food for days then disappeared in a quiet cocoon food coma before he could ever break free as a butterfly."

Now it's my turn to laugh. "The hungry caterpillar? That's your example of a great adventure? Is that because you saw me eyeing the pumpkin pie and apple crisp and planning to gorge myself on colorful Thanksgiving treats to distract me from my sorrows?"

Rachel reaches for Henrix, whose eyes are open. He's spotted his mom, heard her voice, knew exactly where to look. "Nope. That's because all my counseling examples these days revolve around Dr. Seuss characters and illustrated board books."

Chapter Thirty-Nine

For the second morning in a row, I'm up early, sitting in the sunroom window seat with my coffee, notebook, pens, and printed pages of writing from the day before. Since my chat with Rachel, I've gotten some real sleep, my mind excited to wake and work on the history of Northargyle. While I'm in this backstage "pause," I can be productive. I am going to stay active in my story and finish what Queen Seneca started. What I'll do with it when I'm done, I don't know. Maybe I'll send it to Angie Thorne.

I'm flipping through the printed notes about Rosiah's childhood when Mom sets a box on the dining room table, motioning me over.

"I planned to give this to you as soon as you were home, but the timing was wrong."

Uncurling myself from the window seat, I move to the table. Rosiah's Princess Box rests inside as well as a Walkman with a headset.

I'd forgotten about these finds.

I start with the Princess Box. The purple drawstring bag that once held Gran's ring rests inside as well as the letter Gran had written me about her love story with Josiah Ellery. Grandpa really had been her one and only love. A pang strikes my heart all over again at the thought of Jess selling the ring as if it meant nothing.

"It's such a beautiful letter. I read it several times," Mom admits. "My parents told me they'd met at a church function. I never questioned it, but the truth is sweet."

"The hyacinth code," I whisper as I run my fingers over the single hyacinth.

Mom asks if she can decode the message following my explanation that one hyacinth means the first letter of every sentence. Pretty soon the message appears. Gran's true name. *Laurel Campbell Ellery.*

I give the locket with Roy and Rosiah a second, but I really want to skip to the cassette tape. So I do. Mom disappears to the kitchen, reappearing with a box of tissues.

"You'll need those. I went through an entire box."

"I can't believe I forgot about this. What's on it?"

"It was hard for Rosiah to write so Roy bought her the tape. My mother actually did a lot of writing for the princess."

The handwriting puzzle piece shifts into place. "That explains why Rosiah's handwriting looked like Gran's. It *was* Gran's."

"I saw an entirely different version of my mother through Rosiah's eyes." Mom laughs. "I even make an appearance on the tape."

"Does this have all of Rosiah's story? About why she really left Northargyle?"

"Why don't you listen then we can talk about it." Mom eyes the stack of printed pages. "What are you working on?"

"The history of Northargyle. Colter's mother started to write it before she died. I'm trying to make her dream a reality." I hesitate a moment then ask, "Would you like to read what I have so far?"

"I'd love to."

Mom heads for the living room with my pages, and I return to the window seat with the cassette player. Leaning my head against the wall, I put on the headphones and press play. Rosiah's accented voice reminds me of Eliana's. Instead of a crushing blow at thinking her name, I smile at the friendship we shared.

> *"Laurel, or Christine as she is called now, encouraged me to tell my story. She's always been passionate about people's stories. Roy bought me these tapes, so I could record it, since most days my hands no longer work without pain. Arthritis has taken so much from me. Christine writes for me, one more thing that she does without complaint. I miss painting. I miss writing. I miss the feel of the sun on my arms, being with Roy in the gardens. It's too hard to get outside now. Oh, I'm supposed to be telling my story..."*

The tissues form a mountain at the end of the window seat, burying my feet like I'm on the beach beneath a pile of sand. That was an emotional ride, even knowing the journey Rosiah took to live boldly. Talk about tears. My woes are nothing compared to Rosiah's.

My questions have all been answered, the edge pieces of Rosiah's puzzle have been added. The story is complete.

After cleaning up the tissues, I gather my things and move to my bedroom. I need my laptop so I can transcribe the cassette tape. Easier access to Rosiah's words will be essential to my writing. With a freshly opened tissue box within reach, I open my laptop and once again don the headphones.

Before I can push play on the Walkman, there's a knock on the door, and Mom comes in, setting a mug of hot chocolate with whipped cream and a dash of cinnamon on the desk beside me.

I take off the headphones, but Mom doesn't say anything. She crosses to Gran's painting, touching the frame before settling on my beanbag, my pages tucked close to her heart. Mom's gaze tracks around my bedroom, her mouth opening and closing several times. Once she's looking at me again, her lips curl up slightly.

"I've never been good at talking about my feelings." The breath Mom inhales could keep her underwater for a record-breaking amount of time. "It's probably why God blessed me with boys. Then you were born, and I was determined not to repeat my relationship with my mother. Mom was so distant. I thought it was me, that I was unlovable, and I never wanted that for us."

"Gran loved you so much." Rosiah's observations confirmed that. "And I never doubted you loved me."

"I dealt with jealousy for years when you connected to my mother in ways I never did. Listening to those tapes opened my eyes to my mother's true story. Everything she did was to serve and protect those she loved." Mom smiles. "You are so much like your grandmother. She would be proud of you."

Wiping my eyes, I motion to the pages still clutched to her chest. "What did you think?"

"I know I can speak this truth with love."

I lower my brow. As far as segues go, I'm not sure where this is heading. I brace myself. She doesn't have to say she hated them.

"You are so quirky. Full of heart and life. But what I read was boring."

"Mom—"

She holds up a hand. "Honey, it's well-researched and very informative, but where is the heart?"

"It's right there." I wave my hands like I'm trying to get the point guard's attention. *Hellooo!* "It's in the notebook. All the facts. The time-line. I can add in what I've learned on the tapes. Everything is there or will be."

"I was wrong when I said you weren't an author. You are. You always have been. I've listened to you with your brothers. Listened to you when you created stories with Gran and with your father and aunt. I may not join in, but I'm always listening. Maybe it's time to stop focusing on the facts."

"But Colter's mother wanted to write the history," I say, gritting my teeth, tears building. "History is facts."

"No. History is stories. It's right there in the word. And you aren't Queen Seneca. Stop forcing yourself to be anyone but yourself." Mom winces as she extracts herself from the beanbag. She sets my pages on the desk.

Looks like a bonfire is in my future. I hope we still have marshmallows and homemade chocolate chip cookies. At least I'll get a s'more or ten out of my failure.

"What do I do now?" I whisper. My momentum to write has been driving me from my bed. Will I be able to get up without a purpose?

"What about writing it as fiction based on a true story? Truth through fiction?" Mom touches my face. Tears pool in her blue-gray eyes. "I'm so proud of you, Abigail."

I didn't realize how my heart longed for those words to be said—not in relationship to sports. Craving them like Tiddalick did water. Mom kisses the top of my head, then leaves me alone, the journal in front of me filled with words I've been laboring over since Colter asked, "Why not you?"

Truth through fiction. Based on a true story? Where's the heart?

I realize I just had a reverse Jo March and Professor Bhaer moment. He told her that the fairy stories weren't her, to write real life. Mom just gave me the opposite advice. Yes, I love the research, but creating stories is where my heart lives. I'm passionate about imagination.

My eyes widen as if a dam has burst. I can see clearly now the Brick Wall is gone. I know what to write.

Faith. Service. Leadership.

Friendship. Sacrifice. True love.

I grab a pen and a fancy journal that I've been saving for something special. As if my purple gel pen is being controlled by someone else, words appear until I'm flipping to another page then another.

Some stories are too dangerous to tell, mine was one of those...

TRANSCRIPT OF PRINCESS ROSIAH'S STORY
RECORDED ON CASSETTE TAPE IN JANUARY 1971

Laurel, or Christine as she is called now, encouraged me to tell my story. She's always been passionate about people's stories. Roy bought me these tapes, so I could record it, since most days my hands no longer work without pain. Arthritis has taken so much from me. Christine writes for me, one more thing that she does without complaint. I miss painting. I miss writing. I miss the feel of the sun on my arms, being with Roy in the gardens. It's too hard to get outside now. Oh, I'm supposed to be telling my story.

I was born the sixteenth of April 1938. Rosiah Catherine Brisbane, Princess of Northargyle. My parents, King Thomas and Queen Charlotte, were loving parents, and I lacked for nothing. Growing up in the palace—I knew nothing different.

I met Roy in the gardens officially when I was ten. I got turned around on the grounds, and he rescued me. I admit, I was there throwing a tantrum because my baby brother was getting all the attention. Michael was such a sweet baby, but I was not happy in the beginning.

On my thirteenth birthday, I had my first seizure. My parents hid me away from the world like Rapunzel in her tower, safe from the world's knowledge. Many doctors cared for me throughout the years, but it was Mary Campbell and her sister Laurel whom I trusted. Laurel was there with Mary on one of my roughest days. While I don't remember much of that particular episode, I remember Laurel's care. She didn't offer me rote comfort that "everything would be okay if I just trusted God." I knew that. Laurel held me. Prayed for me. Never once treated me like an invalid. She saw me, spoke to me with complete truth and love.

I had good days and really bad days from that moment on. Due to my illness, the doctor said I would never be able to have children. Father did not take this news well, but he kept it from the world. More doctors with more opinions were brought in until one suggested a lobotomy. I overheard this rather than being told directly. I admit, I had the habit of eavesdropping. My parents agreed the lobotomy was the best course of action. I knew I had to leave; the risk was too great. I'd rather live a shorter, yet fuller life then be confined to my bed if the worst happened.

My brother would be king, so the Brisbane line was safe. Laurel came up with the plan for the decoys. We chose five ladies-in-waiting close to my age, giving them each a token that would lead searchers away. Laurel was to come with me. She didn't work at the palace, no one would know she was missing. And, though I hated to admit it, I needed someone to care for me.

When I shared the plan with Roy, he told me that he'd bought a cottage in Bridgeway, Australia. It was his plan to move there by himself in the event that I married another. His "jealousy" offered us a place to escape to. Laurel and I left three days before the scheduled surgery. Roy waited three months before joining us at the cottage where we married the next day. I didn't want to waste a single second of my life without being his wife. He married me even knowing we'd never have children. Roy used to say though, "Who knows what God will do?"

We were happy at the cottage, settled into a new life of learning. But then my parents and Michael died in a plane crash. I did think about returning to the palace, but it was said I had died on the plane as well. I gave up that life and decided to stay hidden.

My cousin Frederick and his wife Ruth would take the throne. She was a godly woman I'd met several times. They were recently married and both healthy, with no reason why the Wellesley line wouldn't continue through them. Unlike me. Even if I did return, the crown would pass to them soon enough. Going home would only prolong the inevitable. Northargyle needed strength, and I didn't have it. So I stayed silent.

We spent two glorious years at Hyacinth Cottage. At times, I was too sick to do much, but I relished my role as a wife. And my friendship with Laurel and Hazel deepened to something so beautiful I knew I would not survive without them. But then Roy saw Josiah Ellery in Bridgeway, asking questions. Why was he still searching when I'd been declared dead? Fearing he would inform the world I was alive, Roy, Laurel, and I fled in the night. Hazel decided to remain with her family. We promised to write, not knowing if that would ever be a possibility. A piece of my heart stayed at

Hyacinth Cottage, but we had to leave. I sold some jewelry for money to get us to America.

But Josiah pursued us across the ocean. By the time he confronted us and heard my story, he'd already fallen in love with Laurel. My dear friend was hesitant to marry, but Josiah graciously allowed her to stay close to me. Both so bound by duty and love and protectiveness—they were a fierce sight to behold. Having them care for my safety even though the palace was far behind us is more than I deserved. They gave up everything, even their true names to protect me. To keep my identity a secret from the world, they surrendered theirs. Giving them the deed to Hyacinth Cottage for their wedding never seemed enough, but it was all we had.

A well-known American doctor finally diagnosed me with lupus. Even though I am in pain, I am thankful to be alive. Thankful that I get one more day with Roy and Christine and Josiah. And now Heather.

One of the greatest joys was holding Christine and Josiah's baby girl for the first time. I needed help, but Roy was right there with me. They named her Heather Rosiah. I cried when they told me. Heather is so precious, and I'm counting her as my legacy as much as theirs. Christine loves her daughter more than life itself. But to protect me, I know she will keep things from her daughter. Maybe one day, Heather will hear my story and understand. God, may it be so.

I don't know how long I have left, but I thank God every morning I wake up with breath in my lungs. I've lived fully. Loved completely. God's goodness has been unmeasurable. Who knows what God will do.

Chapter Forty

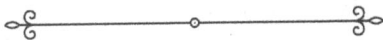

Today's to-do list brings me to the steps of the Westonia. Goal: acquire job at the Westonia Historical Society and Museum. Even if it means I'm relegated to a life of untangling Slinkies and wearing ironic graphic tees.

I hadn't realized how much I missed the atmosphere and people until Aunt Tabby offered to let me have my secretary job back. No offense to Dad and the good people at Westonia Baptist, but there's only one boss I want. Is it possible that Mr. Romano's offer of a full-time job is still on the table?

God, please let it be available.

Adjusting my tote, I open the door. It's been a long time since I entered the Westonia through the front. Even with my volunteer status, I had access to the employee entrance in back.

My heart misses a step when I see a silver-haired woman at the information counter knitting. My first thought is that I've been replaced. Then she looks up, and I realize it's Erlene. She's retired at least four times already.

She sets her project aside when I approach. If I'm correct, it's going to be a purple dragon. "Abigail, what a delight to see you this morning."

"If I'd known you would be here, I would've made snickerdoodles." I indicate my tote, where a container of peanut butter no-bakes rests. Erlene doesn't like peanut butter, but they happen to be Mr. Romano's favorite. Sweetening the begging with sugar is not beneath me.

"Oh, that's fine, dear." She pats my hand. "Then I'd have to say no thank you, and I don't know if I'd be able to. Your baked goods are addicting."

We chat about food, family, and Thanksgiving for several minutes, but when the conversations shifts to Australia, I proceed with my mission. "Is Mr. Romano in his office yet?"

"He should be. Go on back." Erlene waves her hand like she's conducting a symphony then picks up her crochet. "And, Abigail, we're all so glad you're home."

"I'm glad to be back," I say as I skirt the desk, careful not to whack the glass case that holds the weathered map of Westonia on my way by. Ruining that display would not win me full-time status.

Mr. Romano's door is open, and he's behind his desk reading today's *Westonia Gazette*. I take the container of cookies out of my tote and set them in front of him. His eyes light up as he tosses the paper aside and opens the lid. The nutty sugar aroma wafts around me, masking the Italian-laced air.

"Abigail Morgan, what can I do for you this fine morning?"

Cue the begging.

"I'd like to apply for the full-time position. The Westonia means so much to me. The people, the work, this town. The Westonia is home. I know I've been gone a long time, and you said the job would be waiting, but I understand if you gave it to someone else. I will go back to volunteering. Although, I'll have to find a paying job because I'd like to move out of my parents' before I'm eighty."

Mr. Romano grins as he takes a slim box from his desk drawer and hands it to me.

Inside rests a nameplate. An actual nameplate with just ABIGAIL written on it. Not a Morgan indication anywhere.

"I should have given that to you a year ago. It's been sitting in my desk for months."

"I have the job?"

"If you want it." Before I can yell "of course I want it!" he holds up his hand. "Not that I want to talk you out of it or take back that nameplate, but there is one thing you need to consider before accepting. I received an interesting call from the Smithsonian. I didn't know that you applied there."

"It's my dream job." I shrug. "I applied knowing it was highly unlikely they would ever call. I don't have enough experience. But I'm hoping that I'll get it by working here, and maybe someday I'll apply again."

"Someday is a lot closer than you think."

His words bring a deluge of thoughts, so fast, I can't latch on to any of them.

"Why don't you have a seat?"

I obey setting my tote near my feet.

"My friend at the Smithsonian reached out. I'd sent her your silly placard on the Westonia, and she loved it. They see what I do, that you have a gift for bringing history to life. Marianne is currently working on an exhibit on the history of the Smithsonian. They could use an extra set of hands."

"Me? Really?" I stand and pace. I can't sit down while I process. I just got home. What will this mean? Do I stay at the Westonia? Do I take my dream job? Am I ready to leave again? It's like a Choose-Your-Own-Adventure novel without the fear of getting eaten by a yeti or being buried by an avalanche. I hope.

God give me a billboard, please, oh, please!

"I forgot to mention a small detail," Mr. Romano says rather jovially. "You will be able to write the placards from here."

"What?" I slam the brakes on my pacing, eyes wide, staring down my boss. "That's not a small detail. You mean I can have my research and write it too?"

Mr. Romano nods then hands me a tissue as tears release. That was some billboard. I don't have to choose, not really. I wipe my eyes. Maybe I should take stock in tissues, I've used enough of them in the last couple weeks.

"I'll have Marianne send you details," Mr. Romano says. "I have complete faith that you can work for them and still serve the people of Westonia."

"I won't let you down."

"I'm confident you won't." With a smile, he picks up his paper.

A question nags my brain, and I stop, turning back. I don't want to ruin this moment, but I have to know. "Did you hire me because of my family? My aunt?"

Mr. Romano chuckles. "A professor at Gettysburg College reached out to me, telling me about an amazing researcher living in Westonia. I was about to hunt you down when, lo and behold, your application arrived on my desk. You asked for volunteer work, and I delivered, but I wanted you full-time. I figured you'd ask when you were ready. The full-time job has always been yours." He motions to the nameplate. "Better go see how that looks on your new desk."

Instead of turning left toward the research room, I turn right. My hands shake with excitement as I fish my cell phone out of my tote. There's a new group chat labeled TEAM MORGAN. The brothers plus Mom, Dad, Rachel, and Stefi.

ME: *I'm an official full-timer at the Westonia! I get a desk and a nameplate!!*
DAD: *Woohoohooo!!*
ASHER: *Knew you could do it, Indiana Abbie!*
RACHEL: *So excited for you!*
LUKE: *Way to go, sis.*
STEFI: *Exciting!*
PHILIP: *Next up, world domination bay-be*
CALEB: *I'd vote for you.*
ME: *Also, don't know all the details, but I'll be helping the Smithsonian with a project.*
MOM: *The Smithsonian???*
ME: *They want me to write placards for an exhibit!*
MOM: *But you just got home.*
ME: *That's the best part. I can work from my desk at the Westonia.*

The texts that follow that announcement are pretty much copy and paste. I'm about to put my phone away and go find said new desk when my phone vibrates one more time.

JAXON: *I'm proud of you. Love you, sis.*

I gasp. Jaxon messaged. I feel like jumping up and down even more. Since Jess broke his heart, I've been sending "I love you" and "praying for you" texts, all which have been ignored. Giving him space has been so hard. If it were feasible to go to him, I would've been on the next plane. But I'm not even sure where he's been stationed. Hearing from him on top of everything else is icing on the cake. A double chocolate with whipped coffee cream and so much caramel it's beyond a food coma cake.

With a huge smile on my face, I head toward my new office. Libby is at one of the two desks, a pair of glasses perched on her nose as she reads through a stack of papers. I take a moment to stand in the doorway and observe my new digs.

Two desks with computers. Windows with cute curtains. A view of the main street of Westonia. Smells of cinnamon and ink. A bookshelf with vases, knickknacks, and leatherbound journals. A rolling chair behind my desk—must resist rolling down hallway. Office mate, Libby. Bedecked in a purple argyle-patterned sweater and matching scarf that's corralling a hundred braids.

"Hey, roomie," I say.

Libby whips off her glasses, jumps up, and charges me like I'm holding a red flag. *Olé!* "You're here! I missed your face!"

"I missed yours too," I say honestly, enjoying the life being squeezed out of me. "I'm sorry I didn't answer any of your texts."

"I knew you'd reach out eventually. I wasn't going anywhere." She laughs merrily, shaking us both. "Jet lag is no joke, and then there was Thanksgiving. I didn't look at my phone for a few days myself."

"Knowing you were there means more than you'll ever know." I give her one more hug then remove my tote, taking out the nameplate. "Thanks again for all your research help while I was away."

"It was a blast." She sits on the edge of her desk, watching as I position my nameplate, stepping back to get the full effect. "I'm so glad you're a full-timer. We're going to have so much fun researching everything."

I laugh at her enthusiasm as I retrieve Indiana Abbie to keep my nameplate company. Something told me I would need her.

"So," I say, turning back to Libby, "an artifact actually talked to me."

"What did it say?"

"A lot actually. I'll bring it in so you can listen." Still on my high, I tell her about the dual timeline story about Rosiah and me that I've been working on. It's been entertaining fictionalizing myself. I named my character Amelia—a name I've always loved.

"Knock, knock." Kasey raps on the doorframe then steps into the office, as pristine as ever in a navy power suit. A clipboard rests in her hands. "Giovanni told me you're back."

"The Westonia is home." I repeat my words to Mr. Romano. "I'm meant to be here."

"I could have used you earlier, but you're here now. Time to earn your first paycheck." She motions for me to follow her, leaving without another word.

I share a look with Libby.

"Good luck." Libby rolls her eyes then slides her glasses back into place.

Kasey leads me to the ballroom that's in the stages of being decorated. Fabric is draped from the ceiling with white lights that will be magnificent when they are turned on. Ten high tables are set up around the edge, the perfect height for standing and eating finger foods.

"In light of the recent information about Margaret Weston, the family would like to hold a gala here that coincides with Winter in Westonia. As if we didn't already have enough going on that weekend. But what the founding family wants, the founding family gets."

"What can I do to help?" I ask, wandering around the room. The vision of what it could look like takes over my imagination.

"I need you to write up a brochure featuring Margaret Weston's revised story. Giovanni said you were the expert. He wants to exhibit the brooch and that horrid porcelain doll before handing them over to the people of Northargyle."

Northargyle. I startle at the word.

"Is it true? Were you at the palace?" She eyes me, a hint of respect evident. "What was it like?"

I don't want to be like Angie Thorne and start bragging about having dinner with the king. Especially since that same king scored a field goal punting me straight off the island. "It was magnificent. Until I got kicked out," I add because it's me.

"That's impressive. I've only been kicked out of bed. Several actually."

I barely catch the laugh at her bluntness. To distract from my near miss, I run my fingers over the sparkly fabric in a box yet to be draped.

Kasey moves beside me, and I meet her narrow-eyed gaze. She studies me for a beat like she's waiting for something. A comment? A scream? A hundred-meter dash of no return?

"You know, when you first started here, I was not a fan of you." Kasey puts her hands on her hips. "You were this perfect, bubbly pastor's daughter who would do anything for anyone without complaining even though you were just a volunteer. I kept waiting for you to snap at me and break, but you never did. The thing is you're consistent, and I don't have that in my life."

She sighs, her hands dropping from her hips to motion around the room. "I need your help finishing up this event. Honestly, it'll be boring without your input. I've tried to emulate you, but I'm just not that funny."

"Maybe we could go to dinner and talk about what needs to be done still. Or you could come over, and I'll make us something." A menu runs through my mind of what I could make to "show off" my culinary skills. Burgers? Mac and cheese? Would I have time to make an apple pie?

"You'd actually let me in your door?" Kasey draws my attention away from mentally locating the apple-corer-slicer-peeler.

"If you stand on one foot and knock out 'Jingle Bells,'" I say, forgetting that I'm having a conversation with Kasey Fitzroy. A normal one with all the Abigail Morgan flair one could ask for.

Several seconds pass before Kasey allows a small smile. "I think I'd like to see the Morgan compound."

Chapter Forty-One

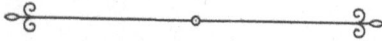

A little to the left," Kasey says as I adjust the strand of icicle-shaped lights accordingly. My arms ache from holding them above my head, but I stay strong. Tonight is the Weston event and the start of Winter in Westonia. It has to be perfect.

"How's that look?" I ask.

"Actually, put them back where you started."

After hooking the strand, I climb down the ladder and stand beside Kasey.

"This turned out—" Rendered speechless, I survey the ballroom that's been transformed into a winter wonderland, offering the serene beauty and magic of the season.

Frosty white linens resembling blankets of snow. Sparkling icicle-shaped lights dangling from the ceiling. Tiny LED candles twinkle like stars in the night sky. Unadorned pine trees line the perimeter. Crystal vases filled with white roses, silver pine cones, and delicate twigs. Soft instrumental Christmas music setting the mood. Winter spiced air.

"Amazing," I finish.

Kasey's cheeks redden as she takes a sip from an insulated Westonia tumbler. Since we've started over, I haven't seen her use the Smithsonian mug. At times, she tests me to see if I'll snap. Some days I want to, but then I remember her comment about needing consistency, and I grin and hang yet another strand of Christmas lights.

"Hot off the presses." Libby enters the ballroom and hands me a manila envelope as she takes off her black knee-length parka. "It's starting to snow. It's going to be the perfect backdrop for Winter in Westonia."

I open the envelope to find the small pamphlet I'd put together on Margaret Weston.

The picture on the cover is of a painting George Weston III commissioned in honor of her fiftieth birthday. Margaret never let on that in 1988 she was actually fifty-two. The caption underneath uses all her names as well as her real birth date and death date.

> *Margaret Dawn Allen Collins Weston: a remarkable woman who bridged two worlds. December 13, 1938 – January 7, 2024.*

The full display is up in the museum for the Westons to view as well as any town members. Hopefully, the excitement will build for the Founders' Day celebration in May.

I'd kept the quirk of Margaret's story low but tried to make it worth the read—full of heart, inspiring that love of history my placards provide.

> *Margaret Weston was born on the island of Northargyle December 13, 1936, to Ralph and Flora Allen—both passed away in 1946. Orphaned, Margaret found herself a ward of the palace. When she turned sixteen, she began training as a lady-in-waiting to Queen Charlotte Brisbane. In her time in this role, Margaret also cared for Princess Rosiah Brisbane. Margaret's life took an unexpected turn in 1955, when in a daring act of royal subterfuge, she became a decoy princess, tasked with hiding the true identity of Princess Rosiah.*
>
> *Margaret left the palace, taking on Princess Rosiah's birth date and identifying items, agreeing to go even though she was not told the entire story. In selfless service to her country, she gave up her life at the palace to protect her princess.*
>
> *Margaret's journey led her to America in 1962. She met and married George Weston III, embracing a new role as a beloved member of this close-knit community. Her true legacy lies in her contributions to her new home, where she is known for her kindness, charm, and deep connection to the land that her husband's family helped establish.*

Margaret was rarely seen in the public eye, but her behind-the-scenes attention to detail is the reason Winter in Westonia is what it is today.

Kasey takes a pamphlet and flips through the glossy pages. "These turned out well."

"Thank you." Praise from Kasey is on par with Mom's.

I'm particularly proud of the end result, especially since the timeframe to produce it was miniscule. It's colorful and includes lots of pictures that came courtesy of Prudence Ellery. Pictures of Margaret at a young age and one with Queen Charlotte. I may personally be banned from Northargyle, but the Westonia has contact through the brooch inquiry. Mom connected with Prudence—her father's sister—and has convinced her to come for a visit in the new year. I'm looking forward to seeing her again.

I organize the pamphlets on the designated table—which Kasey comes behind and fixes. I smile at her need for perfection. Her need, even though we knew we'd be working today, to show up dressed to the nines. Meanwhile, Libby and I are twinning in sneakers, jeans, and sage green Winter in Westonia T-shirts.

"I'm going to take the ladder back to the research room," I tell them. "Then home to nap and change. I'll be back around five."

"See you then. I can't wait to see your dress," Libby says.

I'm about to cross through the foyer when my hackles rise. Something isn't right. Erlene isn't at her post, just the life-sized pangolin she's crocheting for her grandson. I scan the rest of the room.

A man stands at the odd files, his back to me. He's in jeans and a charcoal sweater. His low and familiar chuckle steals my breath. My heart leaps like a kangaroo, bouncing with excitement and energy, ready to propel itself into the unknown with joyful abandon.

Colter.

It's him. It has to be. What do I do? I just got my life organized again. Sorta. Kinda. Okay, not fully, but I'm trying.

I shift the ladder and start toward him, opening remarks running through my mind. The spinner of options lands on an epic line, but what comes out is, "A prince in Westonia, definitely odd file material."

He stiffens at my voice, pushing in the drawer he had open before turning to face me.

All noise ceases to exist. I forget how to breathe. Forget how to think. Forget that I'm not a wax figurine in a museum.

"Hello, Abigail." Colter breathes my name. A playful glint enters his eyes as he looks the ladder up and down. "Are you planning on riding that? Or is this another heist?"

"What are you doing here?" I blurt out.

"Short answer, I'm here for you, Abigail Rosiah Morgan."

"She's unavailable. Well, she's not not available. She's still single all the way." I almost lose my grip on the ladder, the sweat building on my hands and my neck as my focus seeks out anywhere but Colter. What am I even saying? And why am I referring to myself in the third person?

I clear my throat. Take two. "I've been busy trying to live intentionally and stay active in my story. To set goals I can obtain. To not overshare with strangers."

"I hope I'm not a stranger." Colter's whispered plea captures my gaze for the briefest of seconds.

I jump, keeping hold of the ladder but releasing a strangled scream when a hand squeezes my shoulder.

"Is this man bugging you?" Geoff asks.

"He's not a man, he's a prince," I say.

"I think she's debating whether she's going to whack me upside the head with that ladder. I'd deserve it." Colter eyes never leave mine. *Unnervingly wonderful.*

"Oh, yeah? What'd you do?" Geoff crosses his arms, acting all menacing even though he's wearing a History Buff tee that features a muscular George Washington lifting weights.

"I didn't go after her when she left Northargyle."

"Well, you're here now." Geoff nods, prying my fingers off the ladder. He elbows me in the side. "I highly recommend breathing. Oh, and thanks for those brownie cookies. Don't change anything, but keep practicing." With a wink, Geoff removes himself and the ladder from the foyer.

I greedily acquire several deep breaths before closing the distance between me and Colter, the floor creaking as loudly as my heartbeats. It's time for me to take the stage, to be the leading lady. To live boldly. To obtain answers.

"What's the long answer?" I ask, stopping two arm's lengths from Colter. Close but not too close. Yet. What I really want is to tackle him in a hug. Bury myself in the strength of his arms.

"I learned the truth about why you left the palace." He takes a step toward me, but I hold my position.

"Your father didn't give me much choice. He practically called me a vixen who put you under my spell of manipulation." I shrug. "I'm just a commoner going nowhere."

"There's nothing 'just' about you. Unless it's coupled with 'just perfect.' You're beautiful and kind and unique." He motions around the room. "The jewel of Westonia."

"Did you memorize an entire chapter of cheesy pickup lines on your way here?"

"It was a long flight."

"Oh, I know. It's days of my life I've erased."

Colter releases a long breath. "I'm very sorry for not coming after you. For allowing my father's lies to take hold. He said so many things, so many untrue things. But then he answered a prayer, granting permission to turn the Brisbane Wing into a museum. He was hoping to distract me from you, but by giving me the project, he kept you foremost in my mind."

"So, you're here for my museum knowledge."

"I'm here to apologize. Can you ever forgive me? Forgive Eliana. Your friendship is so dear to us. To me." He chuckles. "My sister allowed me a week of anger."

"Lucky, my family only allowed me two days. Not that I am over you—" I cut myself off.

"While I had my moment, Eliana discovered the truth that Father had kicked you out. Lied to you. Accused you of things that are not in any way true. When I confronted my father, he forbid me to contact you or ever think of you again. I told him I couldn't do that. I could never forget you. I never want to."

I step forward hoping to encourage his confession to continue.

"I was a fool for believing my father—believing that you didn't want me or the palace, that you couldn't handle the royal responsibilities."

"That's not true. I love you," I say, then cover my mouth.

Colter removes my hand. "I was hoping to say that first."

"I wanted to tell you so many times. I even wrote you a poem."

"I'd love to see that." He smiles as he reaches into his pocket. "I have something for you."

Gran's ring.

I snatch it from Colter's hand, tears blurring the gems. "Where did you find this? I thought Jess sold it?"

"She actually hadn't." He runs a hand through his hair, cupping the back of his neck. "I went to Hyacinth Cottage. I knew you wouldn't be there, but I guess I was hoping for something, some reason to follow you to America. Jess approached me with the ring. She's been discarded by Titus."

"Poor Jess."

"She asked me to have you call her. She believes there was a misunderstanding, that Jaxon got the wrong impression."

"I don't think I'm ready to talk to her. Not yet. And probably not for a long time unless God works a miracle. I'm still in the anger stage of grief." I fit Gran's ring on my right hand, running my fingers over the pink Argyle diamonds. "Thanks for bringing this to me. It means so much."

"Actually, I need it back." Colter holds out his hand.

"Why?"

"Abigail." He beckons with his fingers. "Please."

I slip off Gran's ring and place it in his palm. Much as I don't want to ever let it go again, I trust him.

With the grin I love so much firmly in place, right there in front of the odd files, Crown Prince Colter Tilney Wellesley gets on his knee.

Several gasps force me to glance over my shoulder—Erlene is herding Kasey, Libby, and Geoff from the doorway—but Colter takes my left hand, effectively returning me to my kneeling prince.

"Abigail Rosiah Morgan, I know we haven't known each other that long, but I want to spend the rest of my life loving you full force. The risk is worth it. I don't want to do life without you." He slides Gran's ring on the finger it was meant to be on all along. Left hand ring finger forever. "Would you stoop low enough to marry a prince?"

"Is this real?" I whisper. This scene is everything I prayed for. I've imagined this moment since before I knew Colter's name. Before Northargyle. Before Tiddalick. Before I knew how many secrets there were to find.

"Very real." He tilts his head, eyebrow quirked. "So, will you marry me?"

"Well, you did already put the ring on my finger." I drag him to his feet, wrapping him in a fiercely tight hug. "Yes, a thousand times yes." My words are muffled against his chest, but I know he hears. As I breathe in his scent of eucalyptus and sunshine, I detect a hint of hyacinth.

My heart will never be calm in his presence.

Colter's arms tighten around me, and happy tears well, leaving their mark on his shirt. We stand clinging to one another for several minutes before his hands move up to my shoulders, allowing some space to build between us. He swallows, his light brown eyes searching mine. What is he waiting for? Is he nervous?

I, however, am not nervous. Nor do I have any patience left.

Cupping the back of his neck, I draw him to me until our lips connect, producing an entire-body sigh. Oh, how I've missed kissing Colter. Every time I think a kiss couldn't be more perfect, it somehow gets better.

He holds me with tenderness, love, and a care that fills the hole in my heart, a hole that's been there since the night his father ripped me apart and banned me from Northargyle. Colter's touch overflows every crack in me with healing gold. Just like our first kiss, there's a hint of awkward, but I pray that never changes.

Colter ends the kissing way too soon. He's such a prince. But before I can protest, he takes my hand. "Let's go talk to your parents."

> "Instead of searching for a person worth marrying, become a person worth marrying."
>
> —Pastor Felix Morgan (Abigail's Dad)

Chapter Forty-Two

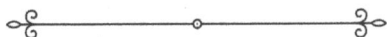

No," Dad says.

"What?" I wait for his smile, for a "gotcha!" For a woohoohoo! Colter's hand tightens around mine.

"Mom? Dad? You've been pushing me to find a godly man. Offering camels left and right to every eligible bachelor." My nervous laughter falls flat. "Colter has a personal relationship with God. He's everything that I've prayed for. He's the same seven days a week. I love him so much."

"It's not because we think you aren't suited, that you wouldn't make a great team. That we doubt your love for one another." Dad links his fingers through Mom's—still a united team after thirty-one years of marriage—and all the elation I'd felt at Colter's proposal drains from me. "You've informed us that King Hamish doesn't give his consent, so we in good conscience can't give ours."

"You've known each other such a short time," Mom adds her thoughts. "Honey, he's a prince. Not that we think you don't deserve him, but what about protocols?"

"I can learn," I say. "Aren't you always telling me to practice? I know I can be as good a princess as a basketball player."

"And like on a basketball court, you need a supportive team, especially when you make mistakes. And the probability of you making mistakes as you learn protocol is inevitable." Mom turns to Dad as if passing the relay baton.

"Marriage is hard," Dad continues. "As I'm sure, is royalty, given you haven't had instruction from birth. Learning all that without the grace and kindness from the king will be a lot to take on."

I glance at Colter and find hesitancy in his eyes that's reflecting mine.

"Your father's right. The royal world can be a lot," Colter says. "There's no guarantee you'll even want to be part of it a month or two down the road."

"Of course I'll want to be part of it. That's who you are and where you'll be. I want to serve Northargyle with you." Ugh, I'm heading toward whiny, a child who's not getting her way.

Though I hate to admit it, Colter's world and all the protocols that come with it—even with the more relaxed laws of Northargyle—exists outside of my comfort zone. And the thought of King Hamish yelling at me, calling me names every time I mess up...

God, please let King Hamish come around sooner rather than later. Soften his heart.

"Love is patient," Mom says, patting my knee. "And in the waiting, you'll give us time to get to know Prince Colter. Love him as you do."

"I'm sure your brothers will appreciate the time to test him." Dad chuckles.

I groan, leaning my head back. "Why did God give me such wise parents?"

Colter's suppressed laughter shakes the entire couch.

I open one eye to half glare at him.

"It'll be okay, Abigail. I promised to love you no matter the risk. That hasn't changed even though marrying you right this second isn't an option." He winks then lifts our connected hands, pressing a lingering kiss to the back of mine.

I eye the ring he'd placed there when he proposed. "Does this mean I have to remove the ring?"

He shakes his head, his gaze soft. "Keep it right there as a symbol of my promise to you. A promise to learn and grow together. To pray for one another, to build on the relationship we've already started. A promise to make the waiting worthwhile and fun."

Rachel's thoughts on how the pauses in a journey enhance the experience align with the advice I'd given Jess. Didn't I suggest that growing closer during the time apart—writing letters—could be romantic? Looks like it's time to put action to my words.

"How long are you able to stay in Westonia?" Dad asks Colter.

"I will need to head back on the sixteenth." He turns to me. "But I'm all yours until then."

"Did you bring a suit and tie?" I ask.

"Royal 101. Always travel with a suit, or in your case, it'd be a ball gown."

"Noted. See? I'm learning already." Only a million more protocols to perfect. "Be my date tonight, and then tomorrow, I'll show you Winter in Westonia."

❧

Colter wearing a glittery green tutu with a TEAM MORGAN shirt replaced the formal photo we'd taken last night as my phone's background. For his personal contact photo, I snapped a picture of us, Colter kissing my cheek. Very swoon-worthy.

Yes, Colter now has a phone. We can text whenever we want. He'll also be able to text with the brothers. They added their numbers attached to menacing selfies lest he forget that, even though he's a prince, they could and would make him disappear.

I love my family.

Experiencing Winter in Westonia through Colter's eyes made it the best one yet. Snow covered the ground, making the wooden village set up on the green Christmas movie perfection. The vendors were brilliant too. I'm still a bit giddy over ordering a Sean Connery charcuterie board for Aunt Vi. I can't wait to give it to her at Christmas.

After the full morning and afternoon, we congregated at Asher and Rachel's for shenanigans and snacks.

"Colter's been gone a long time," Luke observes as he lays down a set of three aces, winning yet another game of rummy. Philip wanted to play Monopoly, but Colter cashed in on some "royals aren't allowed" rule. The rest of us have adopted that as well.

Last I knew, Colter was chatting with Dad about *The Scarlet Pimpernel*. I search the living room. Dad's in his favorite chair, but there's no sign of my prince. Where did he go?

"He said he needed the loo," Caleb adds to the conversation, "but I think he climbed out a window."

"Ha-ha. I'm gonna go find him." I motion for Dad. "Take my spot. Just don't lose."

"Where are the girls?" Rachel asks as she picks up the pile and shuffles for the next round. "It's too quiet."

"Maybe they have the prince tied up." Philip crunches a pretzel. "Or they're letting him try on their tutus."

When I find Colter, he is not tied up or sporting a tutu, but he is with my nieces in the attic playroom. The three of them are wearing foam crowns and curled up on a beanbag reading *Tiddalick*. Gran's trunk is open, dress-up clothes piled inside, ranging from princess gowns to superhero costumes and capes. Evidence of a tea party covers a small table, Poppy and Lily's dolls still drinking.

"He doesn't need our help at all." Asher comes up behind me and puts a hand on my shoulder. "Any man who can survive that is a real prince."

Colter glances our way. I could punch my brother for disturbing perfection. My handsome prince bestows a wink upon me but finishes the book. Unlike how cruel he was to me.

"Girls, it's time to get ready for bed," Asher says.

"Will you come play with us tomorrow?" Poppy asks Colter.

"I'd love to attend another tea party, now that I know the correct way." His smile is all sweet admiration as he hugs both my nieces.

Talk about swoon-worthy!

"Rarrr!" Asher roars, holding up his hands in monster pose. "The last one to bed will be gobbled up and turned into a snoring potato!"

Poppy and Lily scream delightedly as Asher stomps after them, leaving me alone with Colter.

I'm drawn into the playroom and toward Colter like he's the Hope Diamond—rare and shining with an undeniable allure. The foam crown covered in jeweled stickers makes him irresistible. "Love the crown," I say.

"Totally my color." He takes it from his head and puts it on mine. "Although, it suits you much better."

"Maybe I'll wear it to my first princess lesson." When we'd asked Eliana if she'd help me with the princess protocol, she hadn't hesitated with her yes. Even more than the lessons—which we'll do online since I'm still banned from Northargyle—I'm eager for the strengthening of our friendship. "Did you have fun with my nieces?"

"They are a delight, just like their aunt." He glances at the tea party. "Also, I'm pretty sure Baby CeCe Paprika is wearing Princess Rosiah's christening gown. Her initials should be sewn in the lining."

"What?" Poppy's favorite doll is in my hands faster than a fish on a baited line. RCB is stitched right where Colter said.

My hands shake, partly with excitement, but mostly at the horror that such a priceless antique has been used as a child's plaything. I carefully remove the gown and replace it with a shirt and flowered jumper. An actual jumper, not a sweater.

It doesn't seem any worse for having been Baby CeCe Paprika's ball gown. To my absolute relief.

"Looks like a christening gown as well as the brooch and royal doll will grace your museum." I take out my phone and send a quick text to Rachel about the find and an apology to pass along to Poppy for the wardrobe change. Grinning, I slide my phone back in my pocket.

"What's that smile's story?" Colter asks.

"Just thinking about you in a tutu." I hook my arms around Colter's neck. His hands settle on my waist, making my stomach zing. "Maybe we can enlarge the photo to display on the palace wall. People of North-argyle, behold your future king."

"As long as you're there to hang it, you've got a deal."

Chapter Forty-Three

I know Christmas time is when normal people write those "our year in review" letters, but today is September 24, 2025, and if there's anything I've learned, it's that my life is not normal or boring, and that is more than okay.

It's been one year since I held the shawl and received the deed to Hyacinth Cottage.

Eleven months since I learned Colter's name and added prince to it.

Ten months since I was invited to the palace, attended a ball, discovered an understanding of poetry, received my first kiss, accused the king of murder, and got kicked out of Northargyle for life. That was a busy month.

Nine months since Colter proposed, and my parents said no, and we listened. We vowed to make the waiting fun, and it has been. Sending pictures of items back and forth playing "What's your story?" Working on the Royal Northargyle Museum—which King Hamish allowed me to be involved with through the Westonia Museum filter. Sending Colter odd files of the day. Participating in princess lessons with Eliana.

Eight months since Hazel Greer passed away, and Zoe moved into Hyacinth Cottage to become its new caretaker.

Seven months since Luke and Stefi married. I got to be a bridesmaid. Also, Seth and Mia welcomed a baby girl. Hannah. A name that means "Grace of God."

Six months since Colter arranged a video call with Roy Currie. I'm looking forward to my ban being lifted from Northargyle, so I can give him a hug.

Four months since a very successful Founders' Day celebration and the reveal of the Smithsonian exhibit.

Three months since Jaxon came home for good. He's taking classes to earn his teaching certificate, and in his spare time, he's coaching varsity soccer at Westonia High School. He runs practice like basic training. Those kids can "Yes, sir!" with the best of them.

One month since Bishop asked Aunt Vi question number fifty. She said yes. I sent Colter a sympathy card.

And exactly one second since I hit send. The message pops up on the screen that my email has successfully sent. An email to Prince Colter Wellesley with my finished manuscript attached. A story that I've poured my whole heart and soul into.

I took today off because it's my birthday, and I wanted to do one more read-through of my story. And after I agreed to a dressy family dinner to celebrate me making it to twenty-five, my family respected my wish to spend the morning alone. The dressing up was a weird request, but Eliana sent me an original gown from her Kenwick Collection, and I can't wait to wear it tonight. She also gifted me a friendship bracelet and a certificate from "Princess School."

Colter sent me a copy of *Howl's Moving Castle* with a hand-painted cover done by Seth. Howl and Sophie Hatter look a lot like me and Colter. I opened them last night because it was the twenty-fourth in Northargyle. I wish he could be here today, but we made plans for him to join us for Thanksgiving. Two months until I get to hug and kiss him.

At four thirty, I unzip the garment bag from Eliana. It's an evening gown that reminds me of fall, my favorite season. *Ombré tones of dusty pink and a touch of purple to add richness. The shoulders boast the most exquisite rich chocolate-colored flowers, and the pin-tucked bodice is sparingly encrusted with small jeweled and pearl-centered buds that trail across and down the side.*

After my shower last night, I'd put my hair up in a messy bun. When I pull the hair tie out, my hair looks like it was professionally curled. Yay for a good hair day. Stepping into the dress, which, thankfully, has a side zipper, I ready myself for the evening shenanigans.

Deciding against shoes, I head for the stairs. At the bottom, my entire family waits. Suits and ball gowns for all. Even Henrix sports a miniature bow tie. Aunt Vi has on the navy dress and Converse she wore to the symphony. She holds Bishop's hand, her engagement ring—five diamonds on a woven band—winks at me from her finger. His kids are here as well. His youngest is twirling in a dress with Poppy and Lily.

"This is the best birthday ever," I holler, forgetting the "inside voice" lesson. I've decided that for my birthday, I will be small-town Abbie who doesn't wear shoes or use silverware. Napkins optional. Huge bites—definitely happening!

We gather around the table, dressed in our finest attire, devouring French toast with strawberries and whipped cream, mounds of bacon, and coffee. Stefi surprises us all with homemade pavlova and lamington cakes.

Aunt Vi's phone rings, and we all boo and fake glare at her.

"I know, no phones at the table." She kisses Bishop soundly then leaves the room, returning within seconds with a wrapped present. "Time for your first present."

I take off the bow and stick it to Poppy's forehead then remove the wrapping paper. It's a Princess Box. The carvings make me smile as I notice each one: hyacinths, weka, a coffee cup, books, and a basketball.

I lift the lid to find two envelopes. Donald Jenkins II isn't on either. For a moment I thought Gran had left me another property. I open the first envelope to find the official stationary of King Hamish Charles Wellesley I.

Despite the officialness of the heading the words themselves are handwritten.

> *Let it be known that on this day, September 24, 2025, Abigail Rosiah Morgan, because of her service to the kingdom of Northargyle, for her love and care and protection of its people, the honorary title of Dame has been awarded her. She is hereafter to be known as Dame Abigail Rosiah Morgan. Her grandmother, Laurel Rose Campbell, as a citizen of Northargyle, has posthumously been awarded the title Lady for her sacrifice and love for Princess Rosiah Catherine Brisbane.*
> *King Hamish Charles Wellesley I*

"There's more," Aunt Vi says. "Check the secret compartment."

"Not so secret now," Philip says with a smirk.

I press the front and the back. The drawer opens, revealing Abigail

Rosiah embroidered in the fabric and a pink sticky note. Two words in Aunt Vi's scrawl instruct me to Go Outside!

Aunt Vi holds out her hand, tugs me up, and almost pushes me to the French doors. My family converges behind me. But once I'm outside, Aunt Vi shuts the door and motions for me to turn around.

The yard is empty. Peaceful. No crowd waiting to yell surprise. No DJ. No burgers. No table of trophies. No baby book. The lights strung up flicker to life. It's the perfect scene for something.

"What am I supposed to find?" I call.

"Me."

I twirl to find Colter. Then I'm in his arms. The hug is tight and fierce, his embrace wrapping around me like it's the only thing that makes sense in the world right now. I bury my face in his chest, his heartbeat thudding against my cheek, strong and steady.

"You're here! You're here!" I squeal with unrestrained glee. "Happy birthday to me!"

"Your aunt tried to find a box big enough," he teases, his hand smoothing over my back, grounding me.

I squeeze him tighter, reluctant to let go, wishing this moment could stretch on forever. "Best gift ever. Although, I think your father gave me a title."

"Dame Abigail suits you." Colter chuckles. "Father was so impressed by your dedication and care with the Royal Northargyle Museum. And that I didn't run away and marry you against his wishes."

After a moment, he frees himself from my arms to pull an envelope from his pocket. On the outside, written in Queen Seneca's steady hand, is For Colter's Bride.

I quirk an eyebrow as I open the letter.

> *To the daughter of my heart,*
> *From the day Colter was born, I began to pray not just for him, but for you as well. As I write this, your story has yet to begin or is in the first few chapters. Being a woman is hard, full of not only the expectations others place on us, but the expectations we place on ourselves. We hide insecurities deep in the corners of our hearts. We feel unseen, forgotten, unloved, overlooked. I want you to know that I do not expect you to be anyone other than yourself—who He created you to be. I celebrate the creativity of my Creator and thank Him for the intricate, unique ways He crafted you. You are now a princess*

of Northargyle who will one day bear the title queen. But no matter the title you possess, I pray that you are a daughter of the true King. I pray you found that security in knowing Who knows you and loves you at an early age, just as I pray my son will give his life to the King of Kings.

I have loved Colter from his first moments of life. I may not have understood exactly how deep that would be, but God chose me to be his mother and for Colter to be my son. Your marriage will be the same. You may feel love at the beginning, but you can know deeper, stronger, more beautiful love as you grow together.

I've prayed for Colter to be a man of God. As his mother, I've shed many tears and have pleaded with the Lord on his behalf. I will continue to do so and pray you will join me in the battle as you become his wife. Prayer changes what every day looks like. I pray that you and Colter will both love the Lord more than anything else in the world. Because when we love Him more than anything, everything else flows from there. Keeping God at the center of your marriage is the secret to lasting success.

You are a gift to our family. I love you already, not based on any criteria other than the fact that God loves you and chose you to be the wife of the son He chose for me to raise. I don't expect perfection from you, because there is only One who is perfect, and He's the one who will create the marriage He has for you. Please give me grace for my failures as well, because it's hard being a mom, and I will make mistakes.

Remember that love is a choice and make it daily. You may be royalty, but don't forget to laugh together and sneak away to enjoy God's creation whenever you can.

I love you,
Seneca
Faith. Service. Leadership. Romans 12.

"Oh my goodness," I say on a half sob. "Your mother prayed for me." My eyes widen. "Did your father read this?"

"Yes, and he instructed me to hand deliver it along with his blessing."

I gasp. "Does this mean what I think it means?" I barely can speak from happiness.

"Get on your knee!" The door is open behind me, and my family is chanting, led by Aunt Vi and the young voice of my nieces and Molly. Although Lily's sounds like "get on your theee."

Colter laughs as he gets on one knee. He reaches for my left hand and takes off Gran's ring. Instead of asking me to marry him, he slides it onto my right hand, back to where it was when we first met.

"I know that ring means a lot to you, but—" He takes a small box out of his coat pocket and opens it to reveal a ring I recognize from the painting in the museum.

"That was your mother's," I say in awe.

"With the blessing of my father and my mother," he peeks around me with a grin, "and your parents, even though I didn't have a chance to ask them beforehand."

"Yes!" my parents as well as everyone else yells.

"Abigail Rosiah Morgan, will you marry me?"

"Yes," I say, laughing.

"Kiss her!" The chanting begins, and Colter and I willingly comply.

Well, we kiss, but not for long. Children are present, not to mention my entire family. The brothers whoop and whistle until Colter pulls away and gives me a look, his delight as unmeasurable as mine.

I lift my hand and yell, "Team Wellesley!"

At the behest of the royal family of Northargyle,
your presence has been requested for the grand
opening of the Royal Northargyle Museum.

Join us for an evening of opulence and discovery
as we unveil the treasure, stories, and traditions that
have shaped our beloved kingdom.

Enjoy live music, exquisite hors d'oeuvres, and a tour
led by our expert curators. Don't miss this exclusive
opportunity to immerse yourself in the
history of Northargyle.

16 April 2026
Northargyle Palace - The Brisbane Wing

Formal Attire Required

16 April 2026

Queen Seneca's letter sits beside my vanity in a gilded frame. I read through it again as I tie off the end of my fishtail braid. Rereading her words has become part of my routine, my anchor before the big moments.

Tonight is a very big moment.

A quick knock on my dressing room door sounds before a piece of paper slides underneath and toward me on the wooden floor. I glare at it. There's no consideration for a princess in a ball gown. While gorgeous and designed by my sister-in-law, this gown is not conducive to toe touches. And in the event of a squat, I'm not sure if I'd be able to stand again let alone find the paper amid the layers of fabric.

"A little help, please," I say to Zoe.

She laughs as she picks up the note, handing it to me. I unfold the piece of notebook paper to find a placard. Well, an attempt at one.

Princess Abigail Rosiah Morgan Wellesley
Princess. Former Dame. Indiana Abbie. Placard writer.
Museum curator. Muse. Storyteller. Author. Closet poet.
Great kisser.
Married to the handsomest man in the world—
a literal prince. Also a great kisser.

Colter knocks three times on the door: *I love you.*

I allow him entrance, my lungs forgetting to work as they always do when he's in full court attire. Though they often don't work when he's in jeans and a polo, or even the personalized photo pajama pants my sisters-in-law gave me at my bridal shower. No matter what he wears, he is my dashing prince. My husband. My best friend.

"Lovely choice of dress." He touches my bare shoulder. Lovely is such a tame word. This dress is radiant. *Purple flowers seem to burst from the navy gown like a fireworks display. The cut is simple yet elegant with a V-neck and long skirt that flows from the perfectly fitted sleeveless bodice. It honors the rich history of the island.*

"It was either this or my Team Wellesley shirt."

"You can wear that later." He presses his lips to mine.

My arms go around his waist. We probably would have stood there all day if Zoe hadn't cleared her throat. I'm not even sure if that was the first attempt. Probably not. I have zero regrets.

Colter groans, resting his forehead against mine. "Alas, our public awaits us." He tugs the end of my braid. "Where's your crown?"

"I was about to help her," Zoe says before I can remind my dear husband that I don't have one yet.

When Zoe lifts the lid of the wooden box in her hands, I gasp.

Rosiah's crown.

"That's supposed to be on display in the museum," I say.

"It will be on display in the museum. On my lovely wife." Colter removes the crown from the blue velvet cushion. He gently rests it on my head, lingering.

Zoe practically elbows him out of the way to add pins, so it will stay, arranging pieces of hair to hang on either side of my face. When she steps back, she nods like she's finished painting a masterpiece.

"Are you ready, Princess Abbie?" Colter says.

"Always."

We make our way down the once-forbidden hallway to the Brisbane Wing. People congregate outside on the terrace, waiting for our appearance. I scan the crowd as Colter and I take our places beside King Hamish and Eliana and Bradley. Yes, the king, so gracious in giving his consent for Colter to marry me, also allowed Eliana and Bradley to wed.

Aunt Vi offers a little wave, her hand in Bishop's. His kids surround them. My parents, as well as all the brothers and Rachel and Stefi. Angie Thorne, Prudence Ellery, Mary Campbell, Roy Currie along with so many people who have supported me as I took on the official role as a royal of Northargyle three months ago.

King Hamish steps up to the podium. "Welcome to the opening of the Royal Northargyle Museum. My beloved wife, Queen Seneca, my Cadence, had a passion for truth. It was her dream to open a museum on Northargyle to celebrate and share our great history. Today, her dream becomes reality as we open the doors of the Brisbane Wing and invite you in."

Colter squeezes my hand.

God, I never thought I'd be here. I never thought I'd be the one giving speeches. I smile thinking of the goodness of God and the threads of my story that led me here, that have now been woven into the Northargyle tapestry.

"My son, Crown Prince Colter, and his bride have been instrumental in organizing and coordinating the opening of this museum. Princess Abigail's love and care and passion have been an inspiration to so many. I am forever grateful that God brought her to our island and to our family."

King Hamish holds his hand out to me. I take it, joining him at the podium.

Drawing courage from all my friends and family, I say, "Let me tell you a story."

Acknowledgments

> ## 1 SAMUEL 12:24
> Only fear the Lord and serve Him in truth with all your heart; for consider what great things He has done for you.

When I pitched the idea for the Royally Austen series, I fully expected someone else to write it. But then WhiteCrown, in a very Colter to Abigail way, said, "Why not you?" I've been a fangirl of Jane Austen ever since I read *Pride and Prejudice*. Austen's novels have been my inspiration for witty banter, unforgettable characters, friendship, love, and stories you think about long after you've put them down. Writing a modern reimagining of Jane Austen's works was a dream I never thought I'd have the opportunity to pursue. But then God! His goodness is truly overwhelming. I'm so thankful my identity (title) rests in Him. I am a child of God!

So many people have played a role in my life in and outside of this story. Naming you all would fill a hundred pages! (I owe you all hugs and cookies.) Thanks for your friendship, listening to me talk about fictional characters like they're real, fangirling over Austen, coffee dates, shenanigans, allowing me to sit in my booth for hours and write, and to those of you who opened your homes for writing escapes.

Team Loons: Like a steady compass guiding me through uncharted waters, you're my biggest cheerleaders, encouragers, prayer warriors, and motivational speakers. I couldn't survive this writing journey without you all. (Happy Birthday, Rachel! Your wisdom and heart overflows in every scene where your namesake character makes an appearance. I'm so proud of you for answering God's call on your life and writing your story.)

Stephanie Cardel: The best agent in the world! Thank you for choosing me, for speaking truth into my life, and for loving my characters and stories as much as I do. Here's to many more projects together!

Team WhiteCrown: David & Roseanna White—It's been such a

blessing to be part of the WhiteFire family as an editor and now as an author. Roseanna, I can't stop looking at the cover! Marisa—I'll never forget the "I'd like to seriously pursue your idea" email. Thanks for the opportunity to write what I'm passionate about. Kim Peterson—Thank you for your eagle editing eye and heartfelt comments.

Hannah Currie: I love our story! Getting to chat with you is the highlight of my day. Thanks for understanding my quirks, seeing the heart of my stories, culling all the nonsense, and for lending your Australian expertise to Abigail and Colter's story. (I still think mozzies is the cutest word.) Looking forward to the day we get to meet in person.

TEAM BESTIES: Juliana—Thanks for always being there, for escaping with me for writing weekends and to Ireland, and for being a medical questions expert. Laurel—Thanks for "not putting me down" when you learned I was a pastor's daughter. Your friendship and expertise have made a huge impact on my life. Thanks for taking every random question seriously. Your answers are the best! Sarah—I'll always be thankful for our epic road trip where we went from acquaintances to besties. God knew I needed you.

Abbie Crank: Thanks for your encouragement, friendship, and being my title's muse. (*Northanger Abbey* still autocorrects to *Northanger Abbie* every time!) I'm proud of you for sticking with your writing dreams. Can't wait to read your next book!

Natasha: You've pushed me to be the best writer I can be, refilling my bucket to overflowing.

Alyssa Grizenko: Your ability to transform "Stick figures with Janelle" into masterpieces is truly an amazing gift. Thanks for bringing my characters to life. I'll meet you on the front porch at Camp Lamoka!

TEAM ODD DUCKS: So many of you have been with me since the beginning. You've supported, prayed, cried, laughed, and edited all the crazy worlds I've lived in. Vie Herlocker—You'll forever be my favorite Aunt Vi. LaJoie—Thanks for sticking with me through this long journey. Your friendship is such a blessing. Love ya much!

TEAM HOWARD: Woohoohoo! Thanks for your never-ending support, love, and for introducing me to stories and sports. Megan—Thanks for pouring your wisdom into my life and writing. Aunt Von—So many wonderful and silly memories came to mind as I plotted the relationship between Abigail and Aunt Vi. I love being your niece.

TEAM PASTOR'S DAUGHTER: Praying you feel loved and a little less alone today. I'm here if you ever want to share your story.

TEAM LEONARD: My book is published!! This is what I was up to when my office door was shut. Thanks for filling my life with love, silliness, fodder, adventures, and loud noises. I love you all so much.

TEAM READERS: Thank you for traveling with Abigail and Colter. I pray you've had just as much fun reading their story as I had in writing it. Go forth and live boldly!

www.ingramcontent.com/pod-product-compliance
Ingram Content Group UK Ltd.
Pitfield, Milton Keynes, MK11 3LW, UK
UKHW021629110325
456071UK00009B/62